Madness Through the Looking Glass

THE LOOKING GLASS SERIES
BOOK TWO

JONI SAUER-FOLGER

OLIVERHEBERBOOKS

Cover art by Dar Albert at Wicked Smart Designs

Map Design by Diane Kreider

Published by Oliver-Heber Books

0 9 8 7 6 5 4 3 2 1

Acknowledgments

First and foremost, a shout out to my agent extraordinaire, GDC Christine Witthohn. You are always there when we need you. Love and smooches. And as always, thanks to my CP, Liz Lipperman for her friendship, encouragement, and red pen. You're the best, my friend.

Special thanks to my long-time buddy, Natalie Bellissimo for challenging me, supporting me (no matter what I write), and for correcting my grammar and punctuation. I'm so grateful for your friendship.

To Melissa Jenck, my fantasy barometer, and Val 'Valine' Braun, the greatest beta reader ever (even though you don't normally read fantasy), I am once again, indebted.

Love you all for hanging with me for the 'Wysterian' saga.

Now, on to the next chapter ...

Map

Prologue

Wysteria, Realm of Artemysia
Present day

Tisharu, faerie Queen of Wysteria's Twilight Court stood tall and vigilant with a squad of twelve of her most skilled and trusted warriors, silently scanning the region around them. Willow Glen Wood, a lovely forested area on the northern end of the Eastern Glade was a pleasurable spot during daylight hours, but at dusk and at this late hour on a cool spring evening was now blanketed in undulating fog and mystery.

Wysteria's eastern border was just over a mile away, with the tip of the dangerous Eastern Barrens beyond. A desolate place, indeed, but was nothing compared to the Wastelands to its north.

Few with any sense—or love of life, for that matter—dared venture across the border into either place. To do so was quite simply madness, especially so after sundown. Tisharu's great uncle had been killed there centuries ago during the Great War with the kingdom of Roseland, the other half of the Artemysian realm.

The terrain was harsh and inhospitable year-round, unspeakably hot half the year, frozen tundra the rest. All things that went bump in the night—Buggars: shape-shifting goblins, murderous Redcaps with their thirst for blood and mayhem, ogres, desert trolls, and a

1

great host of other unspeakable nasties—flourished within those forsaken boundaries. And most came out to hunt under cover of darkness.

Tisharu had travelled extensively through various portals to numerous different realms, but had traversed the eastern border into the Barrens only a handful of times in her long, long life. However, though it may become necessary in the near future, it was not something she was anxious to do again anytime soon.

She'd reigned over Wysteria's Twilight Court for more than a century, though she had not a line on her face to mar her beauty, nor a touch of gray in her long, fiery red hair. She'd led her legions into battle on many occasions, fought beside them without fear. She was a seasoned, formidable warrior in her own right, but she could admit, if only to herself, that just to be this close to the Barrens at twilight was a bit unsettling. Dangers from it or the Northern Wasteland rarely crossed into Wysteria as Artemysia's security wards were once again strong and protected their borders, but Tisharu could sense the disquiet in the warriors at her back all the same.

She took a deep breath and let it out slowly to calm herself. This meeting was probably not the smartest move, and their contact was late. The thought of a trap was never far from her mind. And yet ...

It had been several months since Aramond, Roseland's Red King, had once again brought the prospect of war to their doorstep. Aramond and his armies had come close to decimating Wysteria in his quest for retribution over the death of Renata, the Red Queen. And though Renata's hatred and madness had been her own downfall, Aramond had blamed the Red Queen's younger sister Beatrice, Wysteria's White Queen, for the loss. It was a thirst for vengeance that had festered within him for a very long time.

Tisharu took another deep breath of moist, cool air.

Centuries ago, in the midst of the Great War, a child named Alice had followed a faerie through a portal from another dimension on a lark. She'd been given the Scepter of Fire by the Blessed Oracles, which she'd then used to put an end to the heinous conflict. Oracles be blessed, they'd been lucky with the recent battle as well. This time around, the descendant of that very child had come from the New York realm to save them once again, annihilating Aramond's armies with the same Scepter of Fire and bringing peace to Artemysia at last. But it had been a long, bitter fight … and a very close outcome.

Most in both kingdoms had come to accept that the Red King had perished with the bulk of his armies in those terrible last moments. But in scouring the destruction and aftermath, the remains of ash and torn, ruined bodies, evidence of Aramond himself had never been found. Though the Scepter of Fire's wrath left little but cinders behind, there were many like Tisharu who were skeptical of Aramond's demise.

Spies from Tisharu's court and others had been searching since the battle, keeping a vigilant eye, running down tantalizing rumors and hushed whispers, yet never finding a solid lead. It was frustrating and a bit like chasing the elusive vapor which surrounded them now. This meeting was just another in the long pursuit for answers that, at times, seemed futile.

Over the past months, the White Queen had done her best to reunite the two kingdoms, to calm the realm. However, doubts, fears, and bitter feelings still roiled beneath the collective surface. One thing was certain—it would take more time to heal old wounds.

"How long do you plan to wait, milady?" Raef, her most trusted lieutenant asked quietly, breaking Tisharu out of her dark thoughts. "It has been close to an hour, and the men are tense."

Tisharu spared the fae warrior a bland look. "Then perhaps they need to stiffen their spines. If waiting for a clandestine meeting has them tense, maybe a bit of training in the virtues of patience is required."

"The waiting is not the problem, my queen." Raef chuckled and shot her a hasty grin but sobered just as quickly. "I will say, this doesn't feel right to me, either. And I sense that you feel it too— particularly being so close to what lies beyond the eastern border this near to nightfall."

Turning, Tisharu scanned the misty forest again and nodded. "I concur, Lieutenant. But we'll tarry here just a bit long—"

She felt it then—the quickening of air around them, the sense of something moving in the ether, something close. The informant at last? Or something more dire? Before she could decide, the very air shimmered, and Old Minerva, the Witch of the Eastern Glade materialized before them in a swirl of silver smoke.

Diminutive in stature, Minerva was an ancient being, though how old, no one actually knew or dared ask. However, she was the most powerful sorceress in all of Artemysia, and the old hag had a mercurial nature that was unpredictable at best. Tisharu took a small step back before she could check herself.

"Well, well," the old woman said with a cluck of her tongue. "What do we have here? The Queen of the Twilight Court and her merry men? You're a long way from home, Tisharu. What brings you to Willow Glen Wood?"

Knowing better than to show fear, Tisharu lifted her chin and smirked. "I suppose I could ask you the same thing, old one."

Minerva cackled, her gray eyes glittering like silvery jewels in the gathering gloom. "Ah, but my Eastern Glade is to the south, just the other side of this Wood. Conversely, the Twilight Court is located on the far side of the mountains to the west. So, I will ask you again—what brings you here? And at dusk, no less?" The old sorceress made a rude noise when Tisharu didn't respond. "Chasing smoke and mirrors, I'll wager."

"Oh, please. You don't believe we're free of Aramond, that he perished with his armies, any more than I do," Tisharu retorted with narrowed eyes. "Don't make out as if you haven't been scouring your runes daily for any sign of his return."

"There may be some veracity to that." The old sorceress tilted her head and gave a sly smile. "His stench does linger, does it not?"

"So, I'll wager that you know exactly why I'm here."

"That I do, young queen."

"The Eastern Barrens are the most logical place for him to hide."

"That may be so, but coming here tonight was exceedingly foolish." Old Minerva sobered and took a step closer, a dangerous glint in her eye. "The Red King is most certainly not dead, that I feel in my bones. Rest assured, faerie, the runes may not have shown me Aramond's fate—just yet—but I've seen enough to know that your meeting here tonight was ill-advised. You should have consulted me before you travelled to these woods."

Tisharu glanced around uncertainly and slipped a hand to the hilt of the sword at her belt. The men behind her followed suit. "So, a trap?"

"Your informant is late, yes? What do you think?" The old woman shrugged and made a show of slowly perusing Tisharu and her men. "I would advise you all to leave before it's too late. However, ..." Minerva's arm suddenly shot out, and she literally snatched an incoming arrow out of the air. "I fear that it already is."

"It's a trap!" Tisharu shouted at her men as the old sorceress began to spin in place, her powerful magicks shooting out in all directions. "Fade! Fade now!"

Rogue fae accompanied by a smattering of dwarves began pouring from the surrounding tree line as Tisharu's squad began to vanish, fading into the ether. She saw three or four fall as they tried to return fire, but there was nothing she could do for them. They were heavily outnumbered and to engage—though her soul screamed to do so—would be folly.

Raef appeared at her side and grabbed her arm. "We have to go, my queen! *Now!*"

"Yes, yes. Fade, lieutenant. I'm right beside you."

Together they vanished into the night but not before Tisharu felt the sting of the arrow.

One

Mid-July in New York City was shaping up to be a record breaker with its steamy heat and cloying humidity. And at five-forty in the afternoon, it hadn't gotten much better out on the street when Alyssa Montague was blasted with a rush of warm, sticky air as her best friend and cohort came barreling through the gallery door.

"Sweet *Jesus*, it's nasty out there," Isabella Christensen complained, echoing Alyssa's thoughts and rolling her bright, green eyes for emphasis. "And mercifully cool in here, I might add, for which the mop on the top of my head thanks you and the Montague Art Gallery."

"You're more than welcome, my friend." Alyssa chuckled, because Isabella's naturally curly, fiery red hair was indeed beginning to frizz. "Man, do you believe this weather, Izzy? It was stifling in here at the first of the week. So, I finally had Lenore turn up the air conditioning when it got just shy of unbearable." Alyssa laughed again. "We have had a ton of business since then, but I think that's only because people are trying to get in out of the heat."

"Well, who can blame them?" Isabella shook her head, a sour look on her face.

"Not me, that's for sure. We've at least got some lookie-loos out of the deal, though."

Isabella twisted her unruly mane into a knot at the top of her head and stabbed a pin into the mess to hold it. "You know how I love the city, but this weather makes me want to weep. Maybe an escape for a few weeks is in order to the 'wonderland' of Wysteria where it's lovely this time of year. You know, just until the temps here become more reasonable."

The thought of that other realm, an enchanted land straight out of a child's fantasy—quite literally—made Alyssa's smile grow. The Kingdom of Wysteria was a place filled with magick and wonder that few knew existed. That she and Isabella knew about it at all, had been there and seen it with their own eyes, was completely by accident and only because Alyssa was the direct descendant of the original Alice—the child upon whom a certain Mr. Carroll had based his story. No one had been more surprised than Alyssa to find that little Alice's fantastic story had its basis in truth. Unfortunately, along with the magick and wonder, Wysteria, which shared the Artemysian realm with its twin kingdom of Roseland, also held great dangers, some of which Alyssa had faced first hand.

Shaking off the dark thoughts that threatened, Alyssa gave her friend a side-long glance. "So, why don't you have Chancellor Winchester whisk you away to Wysteria for a few days? I'm sure Valian would be more than happy to accommodate you."

At the mention of the gorgeous Elven warrior who Isabella had been seeing since their return from Wysteria in January, her friend's eyes sparkled briefly. "Ha! Don't I wish. Unfortunately, Party Poppers is jam-packed with bookings right now, and I just don't have the time. It is summer after all, and that's when literally everyone who's anyone plans their events and soirées. I'm telling you, we had so many bookings the week of the fourth that I think I slept only a handful of hours that entire week."

Alyssa nodded. "But that's a good thing, right? I mean, after you handled my New Year's bash, the article about it in Roth Business

News really jazzed things up for your company. I would think you'd be over the moon with all that business."

"Oh, I am. Don't get me wrong. Poppers is doing very well, but the flip-side is that it seems like I don't have time for anything else these days."

"Hmm, let me tell you what a dear friend said to me several months ago." Alyssa pretended to think back. "Let me see ... it went something like '*You're the boss, idiot. And one of the perks of being the boss is that you get to hire people to work in your establishment so that you can go off and enjoy yourself*.' Yes, I think that's pretty close."

Isabella made a rude noise. "Don't be a smart-ass, Aly. That was different."

"Oh, really? And how is that?"

"Well, you don't have to be present in the gallery twenty-four-seven for it to function properly. Lenore and Candy are very sharp and well versed in all manner of artwork you display and sell."

"That's true. But there's more to running this gallery than—"

Isabella steamed right over her. "Conversely, planning and executing a fabulous event takes time and effort, and there are a lot of moving parts. While I may have an amazing staff, I haven't gotten to the stage where I can just hand off implementation of an event to anyone in particular yet."

Alyssa's mouth dropped open. "Seriously, Izzy? You're talking about apples and oranges here. This gallery is a very different operation than Party Poppers, with diverse needs and challenges. You have no idea what it's taken for me to get it to the level we've achieved. And it's not just about a warm body to answer questions, or sales and manning the counter, for that matter. It's the consignment deals, inventory, advertisement and publicity for shows, all of which is on me."

"Okay, okay. Take a breath." Isabella threw up her hands in surrender. "Look, I didn't mean to say that you don't have a lot on your plate, too. It's just that ... oh, I don't know. It must be the heat. I guess I'm just feeling sorry for myself for no good reason." She sighed and scrubbed her hands over her face. "Anyway, Valian has been so preoccupied with his official Chancellor duties that even

9

when I've had the time to actually go through the portal with him to Artemysia, I've been lucky to see him at all once we're there."

Alyssa clucked her tongue and gave Isabella a sad look. "Such are the perils of a chancellor's girlfriend."

"Yeah, bite me." Isabella said before suddenly grinning. "But at least Gryphon and I have become fast friends. I'm telling you, the queen's royal chamber elf has a wicked sense of humor, which I simply adore. There aren't many in the White Palace willing to give him grief, I can tell you. Valian included."

Laughing out loud, Alyssa threw an arm around her friend's shoulder. "Yes, I've been witness to Gryphon's lethal wit, not to mention his sharp tongue. Yet, he is the sweetest little guy once you get to know him. Anyway, I'm just glad that you and I have finally found time for dinner. And speaking of elves, where is Valian? I thought he was having dinner with us?"

"Oh, he is. He was just in the middle of some edits for his new book and wanted to get to a stopping point." She glanced at her wristwatch. "He'll meet us at the restaurant in half an hour or so."

"Oooh, so his new fantasy is in the editing stage? Sweet!" In addition to being Chancellor in that other realm, Valian Winchester was also a celebrated fantasy author in their world as well. He'd been living in New York for a little over five decades and had quite a fan base. Alyssa counted herself among them. "What's this new book about? Any hints?"

Isabella gave her a pointed look. "You know he would skin me alive if I told you that. Valian's very protective of his work."

Alyssa grinned. "In any case, I so can't wait to read it."

"Yeah, well, I can't wait to dig into a huge plate of gnocchi, so chop-chop, girlfriend. Let's go, already. I'm starving."

"Yep. Right behind you. Just let me grab my purse and tell Lenore that I'm leaving."

ALBERTO'S, ISABELLA'S FAVORITE RESTAURANT, WAS already bustling when they arrived for their reservation at just shy of six-thirty. After being seated, they'd decided to wait until Valian got there to order their entrees and had each just ordered a glass of wine when a thought popped into Alyssa's head.

"Oh, hey, guess who I ran into at the first of the week," she said, crunching into one of Alberto's tasty bread sticks.

Isabella narrowed her eyes. "You know how I hate guessing games."

When Alyssa just continued to smile at her, Isabella finally caved. "Okay, I'll bite. Who'd you run into?"

"None other than your favorite little buddy, Bradley Scarborough."

"Brad—gak!" Isabella made a gagging gesture. "I mean, don't even! I thought you'd finally gotten rid of him after the whole New Year's Eve fiasco. Did you run screaming from your loser ex-boyfriend before he could clap eyes on you?"

Alyssa shook her head. "Didn't need to. Valian's Elven mind-meld, or whatever he did took care of the problem. Believe it or not, Brad was actually quite pleasant."

"Well, I don't believe it." Isabella swirled the end of her own bread stick in the small bowl of seasoned olive oil on the table. "So, he didn't remember your heinous breakup?"

"Nope. He seemed to think that our breakup was a mutual decision. Which I'm fine with, by the way."

The conversation paused as the waiter came back with their wine, but the moment he was gone, Isabella leaned in. "And what about your New Year's Eve bash? Did he remember crashing it with that evil faerie Kasandra Delacourt or spending the entire evening as her mindless boy toy?"

"I got the impression that he was a little hazy on memories of that night and *really* didn't want to talk about it."

"That man was such a tool before. I really hope that Valian left something terribly embarrassing in his memories to torment him." Isabella fluttered her eyelashes innocently. "Is that wrong?"

Alyssa laughed out loud. "I'm just happy that Valian handled that hot mess. He's a treasure. So, how are things going with you and the Elven hunk? Seems like ages since I've seen him."

"Fine."

Alyssa studied Isabella over the rim of her wine glass, the way she looked everywhere but directly at her. She took a sip of the excellent Merlot. "Just ... fine? That's it?"

"Mmm-hmm, nothing much to report."

"You know, there was a time not so long ago that you would have regaled me with every single detail of what you two had been up to every minute of the day, whether I wanted to hear about it or not. Now it's 'nothing to report'?"

"Yeah, well, we've both been busy, that's all. So, no, nothing much to talk about."

Isabella sounded almost sullen. It was very unlike her friend, especially when it came to the gorgeous Valian Winchester.

Setting her wine glass down, Alyssa leaned in and spoke in a low voice. "Okay, spill it. And I mean right now ... before he gets here."

Isabella glanced over with a guilty look. "Spill what?"

"Whatever it is that's pin balling around inside that head of yours. Something's up. Not only can I feel it, it's written all over your face. You've been unusually quiet since we left the gallery. And you don't want to talk about Valian, whom you normally can't quit yammering about, so what's going on, Izzy?"

Isabella stared defiantly at her for a moment or two, and then finally sighed. Taking a gulp of her own wine, she took a deep breath and let it out slowly.

Concern for her friend had Alyssa reaching over and laying a hand over Isabella's. "Izzy? What's wrong? Talk to me. What's going on?"

Isabella shook her head. "That's just it. I don't *know* what's going on. But there is something wrong. Valian has been going back and forth between here and Wysteria more than usual lately."

"Well, he is Chancellor, Isabella, and he has duties there. What did you expect?"

"Duh, Aly, I know that, and trust me, I understand duty. But I'm telling you that this has been ... different. He used to take me with him frequently, but lately he always has a reason for me not to go."

Alyssa smiled and tried a different approach. "Come on, Izzy. You said it yourself, this is the busy season for Party Poppers. Have you even *had* an event-free weekend in the last month or two? It could be that he's just trying to be considerate of your work schedule."

"Maybe. But it's not just on weekends. And he's been very careful with what he says around me, careful with the phone calls he gets. It's like ..." Isabella looked thoughtful for a moment. "You had dinner with Gray last week, didn't you? Did he say anything about something happening in Wysteria? Maybe having to do with security? Did he talk about anything of concern?"

The mention of Graydon Hartford, Wysteria's Crown Prince, had Alyssa leaning back. "I did meet Gray for dinner on Wednesday night. And no, he didn't allude to anything out of the ordinary. But then, our relationship has been ... a bit strained over the last couple of months, so I doubt he'd tell me anything of significance."

"You mean, strained since you went back to Wysteria looking for Niall?"

Niall. The devastatingly handsome High Lord of Roseland's Twilight Court. A dangerous and powerful faerie with a mercurial personality and the fierce warrior who'd saved her life on several occasions when she'd been lost in the wilds of the hostile kingdom. Of course, he had been the one to get her imprisoned there at one point by turning her over to the Red King, so there was that. But Niall had come through for her in the end when it counted the most. And he'd understood her in a way no one else had.

Still, Isabella's insinuation was closer to the truth than Alyssa would've liked, and she bristled at the comment. "I didn't exactly go looking for Niall, Izzy. And from what I could tell, he wasn't even in Artemysia at the time."

"I know, I know. But I wouldn't judge you if you had. I mean, he did come looking for *you* two months after we came home. Showing up at the gallery out of the blue all glamoured so you wouldn't recognize him, and then revealing himself just before disappearing into the night. Very mysterious ... and annoying." Isabella gestured with her wine glass. "The High Lord of the Twilight Court is a big fae tease, if you ask me."

"Don't be so dramatic." Alyssa sighed. "Besides, I just needed to see him, to thank him for his help, that's all. I had wanted to talk to him before we came home in January, but he ignored my request."

"Mmm. I remember. So, you wanted to thank him, even though he was part of the reason you needed help in the first place?"

"That's not fair. He did some questionable things, yes, but he did deliver the Scepter of Fire to the White Palace, which turned the tide with the battle. Anyway, Gray did say that they were still searching for any sign of the Red King. I guess there are those in Artemysia of the mind that Aramond didn't perish when ..."

"When you used the Scepter to destroy his armies and end the conflict?"

Alyssa took another sip of wine and cleared her throat. "Yes."

That was a memory of her time in Artemysia that still haunted her—that she'd been the one to wield the powerful artifact to put an end to the fighting. Of course, she'd had no choice. The Trinity of Oracles had created the Scepter to avert war between Roseland and Wysteria over a century ago, and Alyssa's ancestor had been the one to use it then. Her family had been entrusted with its safe-keeping for generations, but its meaning and purpose had been lost somewhere along the way.

Alyssa was the great-granddaughter of the great-granddaughter of the original Alice. And as with the Trinity of Oracles—the mystical number of three governed. So, like her ancestor before her, by design, she'd been the only one capable of channeling the power of the Scepter.

Shaking off the disturbing memories, Alyssa took a breath. "If what Gray said is true and Aramond is still alive, maybe that's why Valian has been spending more time in Wysteria lately. Perhaps he's coordinating the search. It could explain his secrecy, right?"

"Possibly." Isabella frowned. "But this is very alarming. I mean, I remember that they didn't find his body, but that only stands to reason when the Scepter's wrath left nothing but ash behind." She pointed at Alyssa with what was left of her bread stick. "But that doesn't explain why Valian wouldn't tell me that they suspected Aramond was still alive—or you, for that matter. Geez, Aly, you have the Scepter. If the Red King is still alive and kicking, you could be at risk. Aramond would love nothing more than to get his hands on that artifact."

Alyssa shook her head. "But I'm the only one that can power

it, Izzy. It's how the Oracles designed it. Every third generation, remember? The mystical number of three? Besides, it's safe and well hidden, believe me. The Witch of the Eastern Glade made sure of that. And only Valian and I know where it is or how to get at it."

"Right. Old Minerva's spell." Isabella nodded. "But what's to say that Aramond's supporters wouldn't try to abduct you and make you retrieve it and use it for them?"

"For the love of *God*, Izzy! Thanks for putting *that* in my head."

"For putting what in your head?" Valian Winchester asked with a smile as he leaned down and gave Isabella a peck on the cheek.

They'd been so involved in their conversation that they hadn't noticed him arrive, and Alyssa studied the tall, Elven warrior as he pulled out a chair and sat down. She marveled at the differences between the glamour he wore to disguise his heritage when in New York and what she knew him to truly look like beneath the subterfuge.

Here, his normally long, silvery hair was disguised in a shorter blond style, and his pointed Elven ears were nowhere to be seen. But if you knew what to look for, the smooth, tan skin of his face held an almost ethereal quality, and the crystalline blue of his eyes seemed a bit otherworldly. Either way, Valian Winchester was an attractive specimen, though she agreed with Isabella. She found that she preferred him without the glamour.

"Isabella, what terrible things have you been putting into Alyssa's head now?" he asked with a chuckle as he signaled the waiter.

"Why do you always assume the worst?" Isabella asked, giving Alyssa a meaningful look. "Aly was just saying that she ran into Brad 'the tool' Scarborough earlier this week. I simply asked if she thought they may get back together."

"*Izzy!* Gross." Alyssa rolled her eyes.

Valian frowned. "Did he make that suggestion, Alyssa? I thought I'd taken care of that."

Alyssa glared at Isabella before turning with a smile. "No, Valian. Whatever you did was perfect. Brad was pleasant but not overly so. And it was a brief encounter all the same. Izzy's just being evil, that's all."

"So, did you get through your edits?" Isabella asked, deftly changing the subject.

"Partially. I still have quite a ways to go, but I'm at a stopping point for now."

The waiter brought Valian his own glass of wine and then took their orders, and the conversation moved on to safer topics with Alyssa trying to pry details of his new novel out of him. But once their food was delivered, Isabella once again put Alyssa on the spot.

"Valian, Alyssa tells me that Gray said you're still looking for signs of Aramond, that there are concerns he's still alive. Is that true?"

Valian's fork halted a few inches from his mouth, and his look became shuttered. "Did he now?"

Alyssa took a breath and plunged in. "Yes. He mentioned it at dinner on Wednesday."

"Is that why you've been going back to Wysteria so often lately?" Isabella asked. "Why wouldn't you tell me that?"

Valian sighed and put down his fork. "Alright, yes, we've been investigating the possibility, but there's no indication of that as yet. I didn't want to worry you over something that there's no evidence to support. However, that's not the only reason I've been going home so often. I do have other duties that need my attention."

"But what if—"

"You and Alyssa are perfectly safe here in this realm, Isabella, as is the Scepter. And I mean to keep it that way. So, there's no need for concern, okay?"

"I guess."

Alyssa had questions of her own, but before she could voice them, Valian's cell phone rang.

Glancing at the readout, he frowned. "You'll have to excuse me, ladies. I need to take this. I'll be right back."

As he left the table, Alyssa turned to Isabella. "Did he seem a bit defensive to you? And reluctant to talk about it?"

"Ya think?" Isabella huffed out a breath. "That's what I've been dealing with for the last month or so."

"He sure didn't seem to like the fact that Gray had spilled the beans, either."

"No, he didn't. What do you think that means?"

Before Alyssa could answer, Valian returned looking none too pleased.

"I'm sorry, ladies, but I'm going to have to leave. Duty calls."

"What? Why?" Isabella asked with a worried look. "Has something happened?"

He paused briefly, but Alyssa thought his hesitation was telling, and the smile on his face didn't quite reach his eyes.

"Nothing for you to worry about, love. It seems a chancellor's work is never quite done." He leaned down and dropped a kiss on her forehead. "I've put dinner on my account, so you two enjoy the rest of your evening. I'll see you tomorrow, okay?"

"Okay," Isabella replied with a sigh, but he was already gone. She waited only a few beats before turning to Alyssa. "Now do you believe me?"

"Yes. I think you may be right. There's definitely something fishy going on."

"So, what do you want to do about it?"

Alyssa narrowed her eyes and gave her friend a thoughtful look. "I want to finish my excellent meal, and then consider our options."

"And by options you mean?"

"Doing some investigating of our own."

Two

F lanked by two fae soldiers, Valian entered the White Palace later in the evening and crossed the Great Hall at a brisk clip. His cousin, Field Marshal Alexi Tovin, was just coming down the grand staircase on the far side of the hall as Valian arrived and met him halfway.

"Val," Alexi said by way of greeting. "Glad you're here. Sorry to interrupt your dinner with Isabella and Alyssa, but I knew you'd want to know about the ambush."

"Where is she?" Valian asked in a strained voice.

"Upstairs in the hospital wing." Alexi blew out a breath. "It doesn't look good, cousin. Tisharu was barely conscious by the time Raef brought her in a few hours ago. Looks like some kind of toxin. It may be something similar to the fae poison that nearly killed Gray several months back, but this time the healers are having a hard time isolating it." He shook his head. "It's all too coincidental for my liking. To my mind, it's just another indication that even if we find conclusive evidence that the Red King is truly dead, what may be left of his following is alive and well. I seriously doubt these sporadic attacks we've been chasing all over the realm are mere happenstance or civil unrest."

"Agreed. As you know, I'm not much for coincidence, either." Valian ran a hand over his face. "What the hell happened, Alexi?"

The Field Marshal shook his head again. "Not entirely certain yet. We're still sifting through the details and the few witness statements available. Evidently, Tisharu was following a tip and had set up a meet with an informant. Raef said that she was looking to get information she'd hoped would lead to a possible location for Aramond. The meeting was set for dusk in Willow Glen Wood."

"Interesting. Close to the eastern border ... and the Barrens. Who were they meeting?"

"Unknown. And if Tisharu knew the informant's identity, she held it close to the vest because Raef had no idea, either. Anyway, he said the informant was almost an hour late, and they were just about to abort the whole deal when Old Minerva showed up. A few minutes later, all hell broke loose."

Valian frowned. "Old Minerva? What was the Witch of the Eastern Glade doing there? She's been reluctant to get involved with our search for confirmation of Aramond's death and has made it clear in the past that she's had no interest in the discord between our two kingdoms."

"That's true, but she definitely had no love for the Red King and despite her initial refusal, she did fight with us in the final conflict. The Eastern Glade is just south of Willow Glen Wood, and she likes to patrol her area, so maybe she was there to find out what Tisharu was up to so far from the Twilight Court. Then again, you know how contrary Old Minerva can be. Maybe she was just there to poke at Tisharu and ruffle some feathers."

Valian raised an eyebrow. "If she was present for the ambush, what did she have to say about it?"

Alexi made a face. "Yeah, about that. I would've asked her but she's missing."

"Define 'missing', Field Marshal."

"Just what I said, and there's no need to take that tone," Alexi answered in a tight voice. "Believe me, we've followed every available lead and have been on top of this latest attack from the get-go."

Valian sighed and gave a curt nod. "My apologies, cousin. It has been an eventful few weeks."

"That it has," Alexi replied with a sober face. "In answer to your question, Queen Beatrice sent Minerva a message, but got no response, and her hut in the Eastern Glade was dark. We did a thorough search of the area but came up empty. Raef said the last time he saw her was just before he and Tisharu faded from the Wood, but from what I can tell, she hasn't been seen since then."

"I see."

There had been a number of attacks over the last couple of months but never in the same area and not to this scale. So far, they'd gotten no closer in getting to the bottom of the assaults. But this one was much more pointed, more than a simple 'hit and run'. If the Queen of the Twilight Court had been set to meet with someone for information, then this latest ambush was well planned and executed with purpose.

"Look, Val, I've had patrols out there from the minute Raef brought Tisharu to the palace and we learned of the ambush. Like I said, we thoroughly searched Willow Glen Wood and the surrounding area. With the exception of a host of spent arrows and a few dead Twilight Court warriors, we found absolutely nothing to give us any further leads to follow."

Valian shot his cousin a lethal look. "Then we go back and take another pass. Put together a small squad. Choose competent warriors that you trust without question."

"Valian, it's dark out there."

"I'm aware of that, Alexi. I do have eyes in my head. But we can at least search the sorceress's hut for additional clues."

Alexi stared at him open-mouthed and looked slightly stricken. "You want to search *inside* Minerva's cabin? Do you think that's the wisest course? And by that I mean *are you fucking insane*? By the Oracles, Val, Minerva is the most powerful witch in the Artemysian realm. You know that. She's probably got that hut boobie-trapped with all sorts of hideous spells. She won't be pleased—and that's putting it mildly—if she comes back to find that we've ransacked her home."

"Scared of Old Minerva, are you?"

Alexi threw his hands in the air. "Hell, yes! The thought of her wrath terrifies the shit out of me. And I'm not afraid to admit it."

"Well, buck up, cousin," Valian said as he turned and started for the stairs. "Maybe she's returned home by now and a search won't be necessary."

"But—"

Stopping in his tracks, Valian spun around and gave his cousin a hard stare. "If you've a better idea to offer, I'm listening, Alexi." When his cousin had no response, Valian continued. "No? Because I'll not sit on my hands until morning, you get me? I'll meet you back here as soon as I've seen Tisharu for myself. Find Gray and be ready to leave in twenty minutes." With that, he turned and took the steps of the grand staircase two at a time on his way to the medical wing.

THE HOSPITAL ROOM WAS QUIET WHEN VALIAN ENTERED. Too quiet. As he approached the bed where his former lover lay pale and motionless, he took in her ashen face, the bandaged right shoulder, and was filled with conflicting emotions.

A beautiful, multifaceted female with a biting wit that constantly challenged, Tisharu had always been a bit of a paradox to him. She could be a ruthless, formidable warrior, yet she was fair-minded and compassionate with those she ruled. She could be loving and incredibly giving, or equally obstinate and hard by contrast. While he and the faerie queen shared a complicated past, he felt a swell of grief— and another less tangible emotion that he was uninclined to examine at the moment—at seeing her in her current state.

Their time together had been passionate and tempestuous, yet though they'd gone their separate ways a very long time ago, he realized that she still held a special piece of his heart. They hadn't seen each other face to face in over a decade until the conflict several months ago, but he now found himself willing her to open her emerald eyes, to look at him, if only for a moment.

"Oh. Chancellor Winchester." The Elven healer's voice snapped Valian out of his thoughts as he entered the room. "I didn't know you were here."

"I've only just arrived. I came to check on Tisharu before I head out again. What's the status of her condition, healer?"

The tall, gangly elf glanced over at the unconscious faerie queen. "She's been in and out of consciousness for the last hour and a half. We've been able to bring down her raging fever and stabilize her for now, but that has been the extent of our progress."

"Field Marshal Tovin tells me the poison may be similar to the toxin that nearly killed the prince several months back."

The healer nodded sagely. "And the Field Marshal would be correct, though there are significant differences. For example, we've been unable to identify the toxin's base properties as yet, but I will say that your faerie queen was exceedingly lucky."

Your faerie queen ... Valian felt that phase like a prick to the heart but concentrated on the last part of the healer's comment instead. "Lucky? Please explain how her condition can be called lucky."

"Well, it is my understanding that the offending arrow struck her as they attempted to fade, which is the singular thing that more than likely saved her life."

Valian closed his eyes briefly in an effort to reign in his frustration and hold onto his patience. "And how, exactly, would fading have saved her life?"

The healer blinked several times before responding, as if the answer to the question was perfectly obvious. "Um ... because, of course, the arrow only grazed her upper arm as opposed to embedding itself in her shoulder, which would have introduced much more of the poison directly into her system. I have serious doubts that she would have lived long enough for her to be brought to the palace, had that been the case."

"I see." Valian took a moment to digest the information. Had Tisharu stood her ground and fought, they would've probably retrieved her lifeless body from the Wood. But why wouldn't she have stayed to fight? He'd never known her to run from conflict of any kind. Were they seriously outnumbered? Serendipity? It was a sobering thought. "And what is your prognosis for her condition? You said you've been able to bring down the fever."

"Yes. And that's a good first step. She has a strong constitution, and from previous dealings with her, an iron will." The healer gave a brief smile before sobering. "But make no mistake, though she's stable for the moment, her situation is grave. Prince Graydon wanted to use his powers to attempt a healing, but without knowing what unseen properties the toxin contains, Queen Beatrice wouldn't allow it. And I concurred. I'm afraid if we don't find an antidote within the next twenty-four to thirty-six hours ... well, I can't make any promises that she'll survive. I'm sorry."

Valian stared at the healer for a moment, thoughts swirling in his head. Then he nodded. "Understood. Then don't let me keep you. You obviously have some important work to do. And I don't think I need to tell you what would be at stake should the Queen of Wysteria's Twilight Court not survive this ordeal."

The healer blanched and wrung his hands. "Uh ... no. I, uh ... no, I understand. We'll work around the clock, Chancellor. You have my word," he stammered, then fled from the room.

Valian turned back to Tisharu. Going to her side, he took her hand in his. She'd called him *Mo chroí*, 'my heart' the last time they'd spoken, even though it had been decades since their split. And she had always been his 'bright love'. "Don't worry, *A ghrá geal*, all will be well. But you must stay strong. Be the warrior that I know you to be."

Leaning down, he tenderly placed a kiss on her forehead, before turning and striding from the room without a backward glance.

Gray, Alexi, and a squad of ten armed Elven warriors in full field gear were awaiting him when he returned to the Great Hall.

The prince greeted him with an outstretched hand and a look of concern. "What's the news? Any change in her condition?"

Valian shook his head. "They've brought her fever down but have yet to isolate the toxin's base properties. If they don't find an antidote soon, the healer's not confident that she'll survive." Valian met the prince's dark brown eyes. "He told me what you wanted to do. You realize that trying to heal her yourself would have been a dangerously foolish move, and could have exposed you to the poison as well."

"Perhaps, but I was willing to try," Gray replied with a rueful smile. "She's strong, Val. And the healers are very good at what they do. We both know I wouldn't be here if that weren't true. So, I wouldn't count Tisharu out just yet. With or without my questionable healing skills."

Valian tried to smile back but couldn't quite get there. "It's just ... it's hard to see her like that. So pale and weak, when ..."

"When she's normally so formidable?" Alexi finished for him. When Valian's gaze snapped to his, Alexi grinned. "Just a bit of levity, cousin. I dare say Tisharu will be back to her *formidable* self before you know it."

Clearing his throat, Valian did finally achieve a smile. "In any case, I know you and your men have already done a thorough search of the area. But I want a look inside the witch's hut with my own eyes."

Alexi shrugged. "Hey, a fresh set of eyes never hurts. Though I'm not all that jazzed with the thought of going inside Minerva's cabin, or for being that close to the eastern border after dark, for that matter."

"I know you're afraid of what horrors may lay in wait within the witch's cabin, but are you scared of the dark, as well, Field Marshal? Or is it being a tick away from the Eastern Barrens that worries you?" Valian teased.

Alexi laughed. "Yeah, you can kiss my ass, cousin, because it's pretty much a combination of the three. Then again, hopefully the old sorceress has finally returned and we can get some answers. The possible consequences of invading her privacy would be one worry off my mind."

"I have to say, I'm with Alexi on that," Gray said, as he turned and led the way out of the Great Hall. "So, let's get this over and done as quickly as possible."

The Eastern Glade was located several miles northeast of the White Palace, but in a blink, the group faded to the short path leading to Old Minerva's cabin. Gray came from a magickal heritage and had considerable skills, yet he'd been lax in their usage and had never actually learned to fade properly, for which Valian and Alexi gave him perpetual grief. So, with Valian on one side and Alexi on the other, they'd whisked him along with them and all made it without incident.

The path to the cabin was brightly lit with magickal stones on both sides, which they all thought was a good sign, but when they got to the little hut back in the trees, it was dark and eerily silent.

"What the hell?" Alexi complained. "Why would the path be lit up when she's not even here?"

Gray chuckled. "It's an earth spell, Alexi. Probably a permanent one, so her path is always lit after dark, whether she's here or not."

"That it is, Your Highness," a melodic, female voice came out of the darkness. "It's meant to light her way home. 'Twas a gift from someone who loves her very much."

The Elven warriors pulled their swords and swiftly surrounded the prince, but Gray raised a hand and waved them back. "Áine? Is that you?" he asked in a stunned voice.

Out of the darkness through the trees to their right came a tall, slender woman with long, braided auburn hair and pale gray eyes that seemed to sparkle in the moonlight.

"It is, yes."

The last time any of them had seen Áine Ó Mordha she was a gangly, slip of a girl, and Valian studied the way she carried herself now as she came toward them. It seemed the awkward girl they'd all once known had grown into quite the confident beauty. Áine was a Halfling: half faerie, half human, and more importantly, Old Minerva's goddaughter.

"The last time we saw you we were in Ireland accompanying the queen to your grandmother's memorial service," Alexi said. "You've ... grown up since then."

"Time waits for no one, Alexi," she replied with a soft chuckle.

"It's been too long," Gray said, pulling her in for a quick hug. "You're looking well."

"As are you, Graydon."

"Are you still living in Ireland?"

"Mmm, yes," she answered as she turned and gave Valian the once-over, putting her hand over her heart as if to swoon. "And by the Oracles, the great Valian Winchester, as I live and breathe."

Valian smiled and stepped forward. He bent to place a gentlemanly kiss on the back of her hand. "Gray's right. It's been too long, Spindly."

She laughed out loud at that. "Nobody's called me Spindly in too many years to count."

"And one has only to look to see why."

"Oooh, smooth, very smooth. I've read all your books, you know. You always did have a delightful sense of fantasy. But then, given your heritage, how could you not, right?" She looked between the three of them. "It is lovely to see you all after so long."

"But what are you doing here, Áine? And so late at night?" Gray asked.

Áine's pale gray eyes sparkled in the moonlight like diamonds, giving them a wraithlike quality. "I suppose I could ask you the same thing," she replied quietly. "This is my godmother's cabin. I could be just visiting. In any case, I have every reason to be here. But you?" She glanced around for emphasis. "I see that you've brought a handful of armed Elven soldiers with you." She turned and gave Gray a pointed look with a raised eyebrow. "Now, why would that be?"

"I think you know exactly why we're here," Valian said. "And I think you're here for the same reason ... to find out what's happened to the Witch of the Eastern Glade."

"Is that true, Áine?" Gray asked. "Is that why you've come back?"

Áine hesitated briefly before finally nodding. "I spoke with her earlier through the fire line. I caught her at the cabin, so it must have been just before she went out. I could tell she was troubled, that there was something weighing on her mind. When I asked her about it, she told me that there had been ... unrest in the realm over the last couple of months, and that her runes had showed her something disturbing."

"Disturbing? In what way?" Valian asked.

Áine shook her head. "She wouldn't say, even when I pressed her on the subject. She said she was going out to 'intercede'. I asked her to wait for me, told her I could come a bit later but she wouldn't hear of it. Said it was too dangerous for me right now." She made a face. "As if. Anyway, when I got off work, I tried to contact her, and have been trying almost constantly since but haven't gotten an answer, not even through our mind bond. I was starting to worry, given our previous conversation, so I came through one of the eastern portals to see what was up."

"One of the eastern portals?" Alexi chuckled. "Brave little Halfling."

When Áine only smiled, Gray gave her a concerned look. "Alexi brings up a good point. Using an eastern portal probably isn't the safest route right now, Áine. I'm sorry to tell you but there was an ambush earlier not far from here in Willow Glen Wood. That may have been what Minerva saw in the runes. The Queen of the Twilight Court and her men were attacked, and Minerva was there just before the attack but is now missing. We came here tonight looking for clues to her whereabouts."

"Wait— What?" Áine cried. "Tisharu was ambushed? Is she alright?"

Gray sighed and glanced at Valian.

"She was struck with a poisoned arrow, Áine," Valian answered. "Her condition is critical, and the healers are having a hard time pinning down the toxin used. If they don't find an antidote within the next day or two, she may not survive."

A hard look came into the Halfling's silvery eyes. "Well, screw that! I was a chemistry major at university. And being half fae, have studied fae potions extensively, as well as learned much about magick and remedies at my godmother's side. Maybe I can help to find an antidote."

"We would be grateful for any help you could give," Gray said.

"I'd be happy to assist. Tisharu has always been good to me." Áine held up a finger. "But first, I want a look inside my godmother's cabin. There may be a clue as to where she's gone."

Alexi laughed out loud. "That's what we were here to do, though given Minerva's proclivity for spells and magicks, I thought it was a dicey proposition to try to enter her hut without permission."

Áine smiled ruefully. "And there you would've been spot on, Field Marshal. Unless you have permission to enter, you would be taking your life in your hands, I can assure you. My godmother is very keen on security. She ain't the most powerful sorceress in all of Artemysia for nothing, my friend."

"Can you get us in?" Gray asked.

A mischievous look crossed the Halfling's face. "It just so happens that I have permission."

A slow smile spread across the prince's face. "Then what are we waiting for?"

"Not a thing. Stay behind me, and don't do anything until I tell you it's safe. Oh, and your soldiers will have to wait outside."

"No problem," Alexi replied, and instructed the Elven warriors to stand guard around the cabin.

"Okay. Then right this way, gentlemen."

Three

The group waited in the small yard in front of Minerva's cabin as Áine began the tedious process of clearing the way for them to pass through the security wards the old sorceress had put into place around her home. Though he didn't voice his concerns out loud, like Alexi, Gray was apprehensive about entering the witch's hut when she wasn't there, even with Áine along to smooth the path. Hell, being here when Minerva *was* at home wasn't all that appealing. Come to think of it, of the many times he'd been here in the past, he couldn't remember ever stepping foot inside the dwelling. And there was probably good reason for that.

He watched Áine place her hands on each side of the door frame and begin to murmur an incantation that he couldn't quite hear or understand. But soon the door and entire threshold began to glow an eerie, florescent blue, almost as if electrified. Slowly, the security spell around the entrance began to fade, and finally winked out completely.

Áine turned and smiled over her shoulder. "That's a wrap, gentlemen. All clear."

"Are you sure?" Alexi asked in a skeptical tone.

The Halfling's smile morphed into a mischievous grin. "What's the matter, Field Marshal, don't you trust me?"

"Yeah, don't push it, Halfling. Like I said, this wasn't my idea in the first place," he answered, giving the entrance a wary look. "And it's not so much that I don't trust you, Áine. It's more that I don't relish the thought of being turned into a lizard or rat or some such heinous thing if you've screwed it up."

Áine tilted her head and gave him a sad look. "Oh, Alexi, you're just as adorable as I remembered. But let me ease your mind. Transformation security spells are such a thing of the past. No, sweetie, today's spells are all about incineration."

Alexi narrowed his eyes at her. "Ha-ha. Very funny." After a beat, he slid a nervous look to Gray and whispered, "She's just messin' with me, right?"

Gray shrugged and worked to keep a straight face.

Lifting the latch and swinging the door inward, the Halfling smiled sweetly. "Come on, 'fraidy-cat, if you dare. Just don't touch anything in here. Are we clear?"

"Crystal."

With that, she turned and entered the hut.

Though he and Valian had a good laugh over Alexi's unnerved facial expression, Gray held onto his own misgivings. But he took a deep breath, and mounting the porch steps, led the way for the others.

At the first tentative step through the doorway, he was immediately struck by the sheer size of the interior. Inside, the cabin was much larger than it appeared from the outside. Three, maybe four times over, were he to venture a guess. The old witch had obviously used some kind of expansion spell. But for all of the cabin's artificially created space, Gray was surprised by the cozy, comfortable feel of it. Sure, there were obvious trappings of the mystic scattered throughout, but it was certainly not what he'd expected by any stretch of imagination.

"You look confounded, Gray. Not what you expected?" Áine echoed his thoughts, as if reading his mind.

"No. Not what I anticipated at all." Shaking his head, he gave her an amused look. "Though, to be honest, I'm not really sure what I thought to find."

"Perhaps the stereotypical lair of a practicing witch? *'Eye of newt and toe of frog, wool of bat and tongue of dog ...*" she recited, quoting Shakespeare with wide eyes and a spooky tone.

"Perhaps," he answered honestly, and then laughed out loud. "Minerva is quite the enigma, isn't she?"

"Yes, Godmother is that in spades. But she does like her creature comforts." She laughed along with him, a warm, throaty sound that vibrated along his senses.

But when she fisted her hands on her hips and muttered, "*Seriously?*" under her breath, Gray followed her gaze to see Alexi reaching out to flip through an old, tattered book on a side table.

"*Alexi!*"

The Field Marshal snatched his hand back as if he'd been burned, hiding the offending appendage behind his back. "What?"

"What part of 'don't touch anything' did you not understand?" she asked with a pointed look.

"I ... uh ..."

"That means, you can look, Field Marshal, but unless you intend to live dangerously, no touching."

"Right. No touching. Roger, that. Sorry," he babbled in response, the guilty look on his face almost comical.

Áine rolled her eyes and the corners of her lips twitched but she kept a straight face. When she was obviously satisfied that Alexi was sufficiently cowed by her scolding, she gestured for Gray to follow her toward the back of the cabin. "Come on, then. The eye of newt and other such things are back here in Godmother's casting room. I want to have a look at her runes. Maybe I can coax some information from them about what she's been up to."

The earthy scent of herbs—and something more pungent that Gray couldn't readily identify—wafted over him as he entered the chamber at the back of the cabin. As Áine went to the small desk near the window and began studying Minerva's runes for clues, he took in the space around him.

Scarred and chunky, a large wood-hewn work table occupied the center of the room, with the small desk and a plethora of shelves and book cases stationed around the perimeter. The shelves contained all manner of odd instruments and utensils, rows of neatly labeled glass jars filled with various dried herbs and oils, as well as a few containing items that he didn't want to look at too closely. Drying aromatic plant clippings, apparently to be used at a later date, were suspended from hooks in bunches from a ceiling beam over the center table.

The bookcases were filled to capacity. And where a handful of the tomes housed there seemed almost brand new, the bulk of the collection looked as old as time itself, their spines cracked and fraying around the edges.

Curious, Gray stepped over to study their titles, and in spite of Áine's admonishment not to touch, ran his fingers over a few of the ancient spines. Most of the volumes dealt with magick in some form —spells and potions, ingredients, history. No real surprise there, considering that Old Minerva was revered as the most powerful sorceress in Artemysia. He was amused to find an old copy of a child's tale based on his realm of birth residing there among the rest. The magickal tale of Alice and her wonderland.

Gray himself came from a magickal family, or so he'd been told since childhood. Yet it had always baffled him as to just whom he'd inherited his magickal talents from. As his abilities had grown, he'd begun to wonder about that with increasing frequency. He definitely had some impressive powers to prove an enchanted heritage, powers he was embarrassed to admit that he'd been quite careless with until recently. But how and where had he received those gifts?

His mother, the White Queen had reigned over Wysteria since the Queen Mother had split the realm into the two kingdoms of Wysteria and Roseland, giving Wysteria to his mother and Roseland to his bat-shit-crazy Aunt Renata, the Red Queen. But neither sister had magick, nor did the Queen Mother, as far as he knew. And he'd been quite young when his father had been killed in one of the many skirmishes between the two kingdoms. Gray still had only vague memories of the man, but knew there had been no magick in him, either.

So, where did his own gifts come from? That question had been plaguing him off and on in recent years but had only intensified since the ugly battle with Aramond several months ago had ended. Oh, he'd queried his mother on the subject many times, but the only response she'd ever given was that he'd inherited his magick from his father's side of the family. So, did magick, like other inherited traits, skip a generation occasionally?

Gray had never gotten satisfactory answers to his many questions, and over the last few months he'd become more and more interested in his powers and how magick worked. How it was connected to the elements—to earth, water, fire, the very air they breathed. He'd found that magick touched something vital deep inside him, and it had begun to fascinate him in a way nothing ever had.

Heaving a sigh, Gray turned to survey the rest of the room. The work table held several ancient-looking burners with stands to match and an array of beakers and small pots, most blackened from centuries of use. One burner stood alone in the center of the table. Atop its stand was a large, glass beaker filled with an iridescent, bubble-gum pink liquid. For some reason, Gray felt compelled to get closer.

As he leaned over the beaker, the rainbow-like quality of the liquid contained there began to swirl with intensity, as if alive with color and energy. Its spicy, pleasing scent filled his nostrils and engulfed him in a cloud of such startling fragrance that it nearly took his breath. Spontaneously, his head filled with soft light, and a strange euphoria overtook him. It all happened so quickly that his knees buckled as the room began to spin.

"Gray!" Áine cried as he stumbled backward.

He reached for the table to steady himself, but missed it by a good foot.

Catching hold of his arm before he fell, Áine guided him to the dusty, over-stuffed chair in the corner and eased him down onto the seat as he shook his head to try to clear the dizziness. Unfortunately, that action only intensified the spinning of the room and the sensation of drifting.

"What is *wrong* with you?" Áine muttered. "Perhaps I should've said 'don't touch or *smell* anything', you big dufus."

"I ... wow ... I feel so weird." Indeed, his own voice sounded strange to his ears, oddly reverberating inside his head. "What is that stuff?"

"It's Faerie Bomb, idiot, made from the essence of Aquaro root."

"Faerie Bomb?" Gray asked, marveling that his lips had gone tingly and slightly numb. "Mmm ... Aquaro root ..." He racked his brain, sure that he should know what Faerie Bomb was and the significance of Aquaro root but couldn't quite get a handle on either. Leaning back in the chair, he closed his eyes and watched the faerie lights sparkle behind his lids. "Faerie Bomb smells really good—like field flowers on a warm summer's day."

"You could smell its fragrance?"

Gray opened his eyes to slits and looked up, mesmerized by the halo of colors swirling around her. "Of course, I could smell it."

Áine frowned. "That's ... interesting. And like the frost pixies say, curiouser and curiouser."

"What's so interesting about it? The fragrance is so strong. Can't you smell it?"

"I can, yes, but purposely avoid it when I'm here in the cabin. And I never deliberately breathe it in." She tilted her head and stared thoughtfully at him. "Godmother makes the potion for a few of the fae courts, but I've never known a human to be able to even detect its scent. And it shouldn't have affected you at all, let alone made you high as a kite."

"I'm not high," he scoffed with a sloppy grin. He pointed at her, and would've said more, but was distracted by the trails of light flowing from his own fingers as he made circles in the air. It was amazing and really quite beautiful.

"Not high. Right." Áine shook her head and laughed out loud. "Says the hallucinating man in the easy chair."

"Who's hallucinating?" Valian asked as he and Alexi entered the room.

Áine turned as they approached, then gestured to Gray. "Your prince, it seems."

"Guys, check this out," Gray said, as Valian watched him swirl his fingers in the air. "Isn't that cool?"

"Isn't what cool?" Valian asked with a frown, then turned to Áine. "What the hell's wrong with him?"

"Nothing's wrong with me," Gray insisted. "I'm fine."

The Halfling shook her head again. "He took a whiff of one of the beakers on the table."

Alexi fisted his hands on his hips. "Are you kidding me, Áine? You tear me a new one for almost touching a stupid book, but let him huff whatever potion Minerva's got just lying around?"

Áine folded her arms across her chest like armor. "I didn't *let* him do anything, Alexi. I turned my back for a moment. I thought when I said not to touch anything, that not *sniffing* an unknown liquid would be a given."

"You don't need to talk about me like I'm not here, you know. I said I'm fine." Gray said in a distracted tone, then presumably went back to watching the colors trailing from his fingertips that only he could see.

"Oh, yeah," Alexi said with a smirk. "You look fine, buddy. Just juiced up on some potion-y shit, is all."

"I'm telling you, I'm not high." At the look on Áine's face, Gray relented with another goofy grin. "Well, maybe just a little high."

"Holy Mother, Áine." Valian glanced heavenward, and then leveled a concerned look at her. "What did he sniff? And is it dangerous?"

"It's not necessarily dangerous but ..."

Valian narrowed his eyes when she didn't finish her thought. "But what?"

"Well, it's an interesting turn of events, that."

Valian worked to hang onto his patience and pinched the bridge of his nose. "Would you just tell me, already? We're talking about the Crown Prince here. Do we need to be looking for an antidote for him as well as Tisharu?"

"Oh, cool your jets, Chancellor. It's not poison, and the effects will wear off on their own in time." The Halfling gave him a pointed look that spoke volumes. "He got a whiff of Faerie Bomb."

Valian went perfectly still when he realized what the Halfling was implying. "I see."

"Just a whiff of Faerie Bomb did this to him?" Alexi leaned down and waved his fingers in front of Gray's face, to which the prince laughed out loud. "Yep, he's toast."

"It's made from Aquaro root, Alexi," Gray supplied happily. "Old Minerva makes it for the fae courts."

"Yes, thank you, Gray," Valian replied with a touch of sarcasm that he knew was lost on his prince. "We're all aware of how it's made. As, apparently, so are you."

"But that can't be right," Alexi said, confusion written all over his face. "Gray's human. Faerie Bomb shouldn't have affected him in the least."

"Exactly, Field Marshal. That would be the interesting part," Áine murmured, and tilting her head, again gave Valian a contemplative look. "And why do you suppose that is, Chancellor?"

"That's something I'd rather not discuss here and now." Or ever, Valian thought, but was careful not to show his concern. It was a turn of events that he definitely could not have predicted, but that was for later. "In the meantime, we should get him back to the palace," he replied in a tone that brooked no discussion. Turning to Gray he held out his hand. "Come on, my impaired friend. Let's get you home."

"Okey-dokey." Gray gave Valian a lazy grin. "I think home sounds fantastic. Let's go."

And though the prince had never once in his life faded on his own, he disappeared before their eyes.

"Well, shit," Valian spat and scrubbed his face with his hands. That was unexpected as well, and now that it had begun, would get out of hand very quickly. He'd have to apprise the queen immediately.

"What ... the ... *hell*?" Alexi gave Valian a shocked look. "When did Gray learn to fade?"

"He hasn't, to my knowledge," Valian replied in a cautious tone. "Hopefully, his sense of direction isn't as impaired as he is, and he's gotten back to the palace safe and sound for his first go at it."

Alexi shook his head. "But setting aside the fact that he's never faded on his own, like, *ever*, how by the Holy Trinity did he fade from *inside* Minerva's cabin? I thought her security wards prevented fading in or out. After all, she's the one that put the fading wards in place around the White Palace."

"That would normally be true, but I disabled them so we could enter, remember?" Áine replied. "It's just a slivered opening, but enough to fade through."

"A sliver, huh?" Alexi rolled his eyes. "Well, hopefully he didn't wreck himself on his first attempt."

"Let's go make sure," Valian said. "God forbid the queen sees him in his condition before we can explain."

"You two go ahead," Áine replied. "I need a bit longer with Godmother's runes. I'll be there as soon as I'm done and can secure the cabin again."

"Yeah, well make it snappy, Áine. We still need your expertise with an antidote for Tisharu, and time is running out," Valian reminded her just before he and Alexi faded from Minerva's hut to the palace courtyard.

When they entered the Great Hall moments later, Gryphon, the queen's chamber elf was just coming out of the Grand Salon at the far end carrying an empty tray.

"Ah, gentlemen, there you are. Considering the condition of the wandering prince, I figured it wouldn't be long before you came looking for him. Your presence is requested in the Grand Salon." For an elf standing just over three feet tall, he gave them a surprisingly elegant bow. "However, I would gird your loins, were I you," he suggested with a cackle, before continuing on his way.

"Little turd," Alexi said under his breath as they headed toward the Grand Salon.

"Don't let him hear you say that." Valian replied. "He is the queen's favorite, after all. And you never know what he'll put in your food or drink as retribution."

"For the love of ... thanks for putting *that* in my head."

"My pleasure." Valian chuckled as they entered the Grand Salon together, but his laughter died abruptly and the jovial mood evaporated at the scene before them. It was worse than Valian had feared. The prince had indeed made it back unscathed, which was a blessing, but he was not alone. Her Majesty, Queen Beatrice Myriam Elizabeth Hartford, the White Queen of Wysteria—and now all of Artemysia —sat glowering at them from her settee, a sleepy but merry-looking Gray lounging by her side.

"Ah, Chancellor, Field Marshal, do come in," she murmured in a wintery tone, her brittle smile frozen in place.

She was obviously furious, but Valian knew the worst was yet to come. "Majesty," he greeted her with a respectful bow.

"Good evening, Majesty," Alexi echoed, uncertainly and followed suit.

"Since midnight has come and gone hours ago, Field Marshal, I believe good morning would be the more appropriate salutation, but no matter. Take a seat." Though the frigid smile never left her face, the queen's short command was issued in an abrupt tone.

Resigned to what was about to unfold, Valian led the way and sat down on the opposing settee, Alexi tentatively perching beside him.

"I have questions, gentlemen," Beatrice began. "Graydon tells me you've all been at Minerva's hut this past evening."

"That's correct, Majesty." Alexi bobbed his head like a marionette.

"It must have been a very entertaining visit. Which one of you would like to explain your prince's condition to me?"

Valian cleared his throat. "I would be glad to explain the events leading up to our return, Majesty. However, may I request a private audience to do so?" No need to involve Alexi in what was to come.

The queen narrowed her eyes at him. "And what would be the need for such a request, Chancellor?"

Valian stared back at his queen with unflinching regard. "I fear the topic discussed and ensuing conversation will be sensitive in nature and one you'll prefer to have alone."

Beatrice stared back at him for a long moment, and Valian could sense Alexi's eyes on him, his confusion, but he ignored his cousin and continued to hold the queen's gaze. He knew by the gradual change in her icy demeanor, the resignation that came into her eyes, the instant understanding of what was to come dawned.

She looked back and forth between him and Alexi, and then gave her son now sleeping beside her a tender look, before turning back to Valian with a small sigh. "As you wish, Chancellor. Field Marshal, please take Graydon to his chambers and see that he's not disturbed."

Alexi rose slowly and gave another deep bow. "Of course, Majesty."

Crossing to where Gray slumped on the settee, Alexi took his arm, and after a quick *what-the-fuck* look for Valian, they faded from the room.

And silence descended.

Finally, the queen spoke in a strong, unwavering voice. "It is finally coming to light then?"

"I'm sorry, Majesty, but yes," Valian replied with a nod. "I believe with the events of this evening, it's unavoidable."

"Tell me how this happened."

Valian took a deep breath and told her what he knew. "It was unavoidable as it happened so quickly. It was something that couldn't have been predicted."

Beatrice waved away the sympathy in his voice. "If there is fault, it is mine to bear. This outcome was inevitable, Chancellor. I should have told Gray the truth long ago, but the more time passed, the easier it became to procrastinate, to tell myself that it didn't matter, that there were more important issues at hand."

Valian gave her a half smile. "Well, to be fair, that was certainly true. We have only just dug out of a war that could very well have destroyed the kingdom."

The queen returned his smile. "That is certainly gracious of you to say, considering how you've felt on this subject. But I have lived in denial for too long and now must face the music. I will sit Gray down and tell him all."

"If I may, Majesty. I would not wait to tell him. I know he's been ... questioning where his magick comes from for some months now. After tonight, when he surfaces and his head clears, he will only have more questions. He deserves the answers and the sooner the better."

"You're right, of course. However, with this business of Tisharu's poisoning, and the spontaneous attacks escalating, that must be dealt with first." She put up a hand when he frowned. "But you have my word that I will speak with him within the next day or two."

With a nod, Valian stood and started for the door before Beatrice spoke again.

"And Valian?"

Valian turned at the door. "Yes, Majesty?"

"Thank you."

Frowning, he blinked at her. "For what, Majesty?"

"I know how you've felt about this topic from the beginning, yet you've been true and loyal. Thank you for watching over my son all these years ... and for keeping my secrets."

Valian bowed low. "It has been and continues to be my honor to serve, Majesty. And as for secrets? They were never mine to tell. Good night, my queen."

With that, he left her alone with her thoughts.

Four

It was well past the wee hours when Áine finally arrived at the palace. To her surprise—and despite the fact that the sun was just beginning to peek over the horizon—Valian met her in the Great Hall.

"I was beginning to worry about you, Spindly," he said with a tired smile as he approached. "Especially with these random attacks that have been popping up all over the realm."

"Sorry to worry you. It took me longer than I thought. I hate to think I've added to your burden, but I'm fine, as you can see." She tilted her head and made a show of studying him. "You, however, look exhausted, Chancellor. You should get some rest."

"Yes, well, sleep is something that's evaded me of late. Did you get any answers out of Minerva's runes in regards to her whereabouts?"

Áine nodded. "Some. That's why I'm late. It wasn't easy, but it was as I'd thought. She'd definitely seen the ambush in advance and tried to intercede. Though it's still unclear, from what I could tell it looks like she'd intended to follow the culprits to wherever they were going after the attack. And I think she was tracking someone named Yulis and seemed determined to pinpoint his location."

"That makes some sense. Yulis was the Red King's sorcerer," Valian replied. "During the battle earlier this year, he was the one who found a way to disengage the fade barrier Minerva had put in place around the palace. And she was not happy about that, as you might imagine."

Áine laughed. "No, she would see that as an affront, not only to her reputation, but to her pride."

"We'd originally thought that Yulis had been eliminated along with Aramond and the bulk of the Red army when Alyssa used the Scepter of Fire to end the conflict."

"Unfortunately, from what I gathered from the runes, that doesn't seem to be the case."

Valian blew out a breath. "Then we've been right to search for clues regarding Aramond's fate. If Yulis did indeed survive the battle, chances are good that the Red King is still alive as well. And these recent attacks are more than likely his doing."

Áine frowned. "Which means that the safety of the scepter, as well as the descendant, could very well be in jeopardy." At the surprised look on the Chancellor's face, she laughed. "What? Residing in Ireland, my home may well be in the human realm, but being half fae, I do keep abreast of what happens here."

Valian raised an eyebrow. "Being half fae, you have a home here as well."

Áine swallowed hard and had to look away from the compassion on the Chancellor's face. Growing up, her time in this realm had been a very mixed bag. "Yes, well, that's kind of you to say."

"Kindness has nothing to do with it, Áine." Valian reached out and took her hand. "It is simply the truth." He cleared his throat. "And on that subject, I've never had a chance to tell you how sorry I was to hear of your father's death."

"Sorry? Really?" Áine steeled herself against the old dreadful memories that never seemed to vanish completely, though she longed to rid herself of them.

"I know it was a long time ago, and you were still a child, but it had to be hard."

She tilted her head and watched him for a moment. She had no doubt that Valian meant well, that at his core was empathy for a fatherless Halfling, but it still rankled. She disengaged her hand from his. "Hard? Which part? That he died? How he died? Or perhaps, *why* he died?"

Valian sighed. "Arien's death was unfortunate."

"Unfortunate for whom, Valian?"

"Áine, none of what happened was your fault. You know that, right?"

Áine gave him a steady look. "Not my fault, no. I was a mere child, as you said. But he did die because of me, wouldn't you agree?"

"Áine, Niall would never have—"

She shook her head, cutting him off. "You misunderstand, Valian. Niall may have been the instrument of Arien's death, but I harbor no ill will toward him. Indeed, he was my avenging angel."

Valian looked torn for an instant. "Still, Arien was your father, Áine," he replied softly. "Losing family, no matter how distant, has to take a toll."

"Family?" She laughed out loud before she could check herself, a harsh sound to her own ears. "Oh, Valian. That's where you're so terribly wrong. He may have participated in my conception, but he was never a father by any stretch of the imagination. And as you well know, the last thing he wanted was for me to be a part of his *family*."

Valian frowned. "But I was under the impression that you enjoyed your time at the Twilight Court. You said that Tisharu was always good to you."

Áine's smile was bittersweet. "Oh, she was—incredibly so. It's my belief that she didn't want to consider that one of her own court could be such a shit to his own offspring, so she tried to smooth my path in every way she could when I visited." She shrugged. "But Tisharu had to rule that court as well and didn't have the time required to protect a Halfling child from a scheming asshole of a father."

Taking a deep breath, Áine tried to reign in her anger. She hadn't meant to let it get out of hand, but it so often did when this particular subject arose. "Anyway, I did enjoy my time spent there—for the most part. But the only reason I spent any time at the Twilight Court at all was at my mother's insistence. She wanted me to know that part of my heritage. And of course, without Arien I wouldn't have the many fae gifts that I possess. However, we both know that I was just some random Halfling to him, an inconvenience at best. My very existence was something he wanted no part of and refused to take any responsibility for."

"I'm sorry for that, Áine. Arien was a fool."

The pity on the Chancellor's face was almost her undoing and the old anger threatened again. She'd worked so hard to get past her feelings of loathing for the faerie that had sired her.

"A fool?" She shook her head and gave him a look of disappointment. "No, Chancellor, he was something much more dangerous than that. You know, at night before the lights go out? Human children ask their parents to check under their beds for monsters, to search their closets for malevolent beasties. Arien's kind? That's what they're terrified of. He was evil to the core, Valian. Make no mistake. I have not mourned Arien ... ever. And if you think less of me for that, I'm sorry for it."

"I could never think poorly of you, Áine, for any reason," Valian murmured. "Children should be protected from evil, not subjected to it."

"Anyway, I will be forever grateful to Niall, because were it not for him, in that dreadful moment I have no doubt that my *father* would have killed me. My only regret is the rift Niall's actions caused in saving me—a rift that has lasted for so long between him and his twin."

Valian smiled at that. "Yes, well I do believe that frozen tundra has begun to thaw just a bit. I know for a fact that he and Tisharu have been on speaking terms again over the last six months. So I wouldn't concern myself overmuch with that."

"Really? Oh, that is good to hear. I know the situation has been a source of great pain for them both."

"Again, they're family. And then there's the whole 'twin' thing on top of it. So, it may have taken a decade and a half, give or take, but they are finding their way back to that core concept."

Áine gave him a calculating look. "Speaking of family, are we going to talk about the huge elephant in the room?"

Valian's eyebrows rose, and he looked perplexed. "What do you mean?"

"Oh, don't give me that wide-eyed, innocent Elven stare. You know exactly what I'm talking about, Chancellor. Are you going to explain what we witnessed at my godmother's cabin just hours ago? The prince isn't completely human, is he?"

"Áine—"

"It's been widely known for ... well, *forever*, that Gray possessed magick—that he came from a magickal family. Which I've always thought odd, considering that there's no magick on Queen Beatrice's side of his lineage, nor is there magick on his father's side, at least not that I've ever heard of. Of course, I don't live in this realm, but after tonight's events, it's clear that somehow Gray has fae blood in him." She pointed a finger at him. "Don't bother to deny it. It's the only explanation for his reaction to Faerie Bomb. Only those with fae blood can even detect its scent, let alone be affected by it in any way."

The Chancellor was silent for so long that Áine began to wonder if he would answer at all. But when he finally looked up at her, there was resignation in his eyes along with a touch of sadness.

"No. You're correct, Áine. Gray isn't completely human. He obviously has fae blood running through his veins. But beyond that, I can't tell you more, as it isn't my story to tell. However, the truth will come out soon enough, and I would ask that you not speak of what you saw, what you've deduced, to anyone until that time."

Áine stared at him for a few moments, chaotic thoughts swirling in her head. The Crown Prince a Halfling? Interesting ... very interesting. But how? And why keep it a secret for decades? Then another thought dawned. "Dear God, he doesn't know, does he?"

"No, which is why you can't speak of it. The queen intends to have that discussion with Gray as soon as he recovers. Until then, you can't say anything."

Putting her unasked questions aside for the time being, she nodded. "As you wish. I have no desire to complicate royal affairs, nor is it any of my business. However, considering the severity of his reaction, I'd say this was his first encounter with the potion, so his recovery will take longer than normal. I wouldn't be surprised if he was out for a good twenty-four hours. Regardless, he will have questions when he wakes, so I do hope the queen is armed with appropriate answers."

"That would be my hope as well."

After a moment, Áine laughed out loud. Really, she couldn't help herself. "The Crown Prince of Artemysia is a Halfling like me. Now that is a kick in the pants, isn't it? I mean, what are the odds, right?" Her eyes went wide as another thought crossed her mind. "Does my godmother know?"

"*Áine*," Valian said in a warning tone.

"Of course she does." Putting up a hand, she tried to contain her mirth ... quite unsuccessfully. "Don't worry, Chancellor. I promise to keep this delicious information to myself. You have my word."

Valian closed his eyes briefly and shook his head. "You are incorrigible, you know that? Now, can we please get back to the problem at hand?"

"Which is?" At the narrowing of his eyes, Áine laughed again. "Oh, right. Curing Tisharu. Yes, by all means. Lead on, Chancellor. Let's get this party started."

As they crossed the Great Hall and climbed the staircase together, Áine filed away the tidbits of information and intriguing revelations that she'd gathered since arriving in the realm. That was for later and required more thought. Right now, she needed to clear her mind and focus on the task at hand. Tisharu's dire situation needed her undivided attention.

But as she and Valian ascended toward the hospital wing, that attention was drawn to the opulence of the palace. It was everywhere she looked. In the artwork and tapestries hanging on the walls, the thick, ornate carpets covering amazing stonework, the heirlooms and statuary. And it was all a bit overwhelming. She'd only been to the White Palace a time or two in her lifetime, and then she'd never been past the Great Hall.

By the time they reached the hospital wing, Áine's wonder was overflowing, but it all evaporated like a fine mist the moment they entered Tisharu's room. Crossing to the bed, Áine studied the Queen of Wysteria's Twilight Court. Tisharu was pale as freshly fallen snow and still as the marble statuary in the Great Hall, so still that Áine could barely detect the faerie queen's breathing.

Placing one hand on the queen's forehead and the other on her chest, Áine closed her eyes.

"What are you doing, Áine?" Valian asked. "You can't try to heal her. You could compromise yourself."

But she shook her head and shushed him. "I'm not trying to heal her. I'm not stupid." Cracking an eye at him, she conveyed her irritation. "I'm assessing her situation. Expert in fae poisons here, remember?"

"Here, what do you think you're doing?" a stern voice asked from behind her.

She turned to find an Elven healer glowering at her from the doorway.

Valian put out a hand. "It's alright, healer. This is Áine Ó Mordha. She's Old Minerva's goddaughter and an expert in fae poisons. She's here to help."

The healer continued to glare at her. "With all due respect, Chancellor, I don't know what Miss Ó Mordha can do that we haven't already tried. The queen's situation is dire, and we've exhausted all known options without much change in her condition."

"Well, that's exactly why I'm here, isn't it? Because you *are* out of options, and Tisharu's death would be unacceptable." Áine stared down the healer. "Now, if you don't mind, I need to concentrate, so button it, both of you," she muttered and went back to her appraisal.

Letting her mind roam, she assessed the point of entry, the path the poison had taken, and any damage it had caused so far. She did a thorough evaluation, and when she was done, she turned to Valian and nodded.

"Áine?" he asked. "What have you found?"

"Okay. Your healer is correct. Her situation is bad, but not as bad as I'd feared. I have seen worse cases of fae poisonings ... though not many."

Valian frowned. "That's not very encouraging. Can you fix this or not?"

Áine gave him a sympathetic look. "I'm sorry, Valian. I wish I could give you a straight out yes, but it's not that simple." Turning to the healer, she gave a slight nod. "You've done the most important thing, and that's bringing down her temperature and staying on top of it. Because if I'm right about what I've sensed here, that's the driving component of this poison, how it kills the victim. They simply burn up from the inside out."

The healer's mouth dropped open. "You mean to say that you know what kind of poison this is ... by just scanning the queen with your senses? That's ... quite astonishing."

Áine shrugged. "It's a gift and a curse, healer. Anyway, though I don't know the exact poison used, I have an idea of how it works. I do believe this is something similar to a heinous demon poison from Europe in the Middle Ages. It was called Dragon's Breath, hence, the burning up aspect. The name says it all. At least, it has similar properties."

"Well, can you make an antidote?" the healer asked in an anxious tone. "I'm afraid the queen is running out of time, and we've made little headway in isolating the poison's base properties."

Áine rubbed her burning eyes. She'd been up for almost twenty-four hours straight and was beginning to feel fatigued but muscled it back. "Yeah, well, that was the problem with Dragon's Breath, or so I've read. It was a mixture of three or more demon poisons in very specific measurement. So, coming up with an antidote was nearly impossible, because if you were off at all in your quantities, you were just as likely to kill the victim you were trying to save. Dicey ... very dicey."

Valian gave her a stony look. "Are you saying that's what we're dealing with here?"

Áine shook her head. "You weren't listening, Chancellor. I said that it has similar properties, but this is a fae compound and has fae origins. That's where the two are radically different. Instead of layering demon poisons together to make a super-poison, whoever concocted this fae toxin augmented it with a few layers of magick instead."

She made a face. "Godmother could fix this with her eyes closed, but since she's MIA, I'll have to do. It may take me some time, but I think I can find a cure. I'll just have to work backward and undo the layers one by one. Then it will be a simple task of administering the correct antidote for the poison itself."

"Very well. Then I suppose I'll just have to trust you, Áine." Valian let out a breath and his shoulders visibly relaxed.

Áine's heart went out to him. "I'll let you know the moment I have something. I promise. I won't let her die, Valian."

The Chancellor glanced down at the pale faerie queen. And the range of emotions that flickered across his previously stony visage in that brief instant told Áine all she needed to know regarding the depth of his feelings toward the faerie queen.

Then the moment passed and he gave a brief nod. "I'll leave you to it, then. As the healer said, we're running out of time." With that, he turned on his heel and left the room without a backward glance.

Áine watched him go and wondered if he even realized how deeply he still cared for Tisharu ...and how terrified he was of losing her.

"What do you need?" the healer asked, bringing her back to the moment.

"For starters, I'll need some basic herbs for healing, protection, and purification. So, rosemary, sage, mugwort—"

"Comfrey and cinnamon, as well," the healer jumped in. "Obviously."

Áine narrowed her eyes. "Hmm, obviously. Also, angelica and herb-of-grace. That should do quite nicely for the magickal base. We need to clean up these messy magickal layers first. There'll be at least three, possibly four layers to get her clear. I assume you took blood? I'll need to see her work-up."

"Of course. I have the reports in the lab."

"Excellent. I'll want to get the antidote prepared before we begin work on the magicks. With time so short, we need to be ready to give it to her the minute we break down the last magickal layer."

"Agreed." The healer gestured to the door at his back. "It's right through here. Follow me."

And we're off, Áine thought with a glance back at the faerie queen. *I just hope, for Tisharu's sake, I can pull this off.*

Five

"Are you sure about this?" Isabella asked Alyssa as they headed along the sketchy path toward the older section of Central Park. "This area of the park isn't very safe."

Alyssa sighed. "It's broad daylight, Izzy."

"Are you kidding me?" Isabella rolled her eyes. "Plenty of people have been mugged or worse in this park during daylight hours, and you know it. It happens all the time. I'd rather not become part of that statistic, thank you very much."

"Oh, relax, would you? Nothing's going to happen to us. Besides, we're almost to the portal."

"And that's another thing. You know that I've never gone through a portal on my own. I'm not even sure I can. Valian's always taken me. And you've only done it once by yourself, and even then, that evil faerie bitch Kasandra Delacourt—may her soul rot in Hell —opened the portal for you. Don't you think there's some kind of access code or something that we need? Maybe some kind of spell that opens it? And how do you know exactly where it is, anyway?"

Alyssa heaved another sigh.

When Valian had received the phone call at dinner Friday night calling him back to Artemysia, the Wysterian Chancellor assured them there was no big emergency, that it was just routine business. But though Valian had a stellar poker face, Alyssa had seen his hesitation and knew in her gut there was more to it than he was willing to say. He'd told Isabella he'd be returning the following morning and would give her a call when he got back to his loft. But when there'd been no word on Saturday and then not a peep on Sunday, they'd decided to make the trip to the Artemysian realm to find out what he was hiding.

And Alyssa was certain now that something was afoot. Just as she could tell by Isabella's prevaricating that her friend was having some serious second thoughts about what they'd decided to do about it.

"Izzy, we've been all through this. We've both gone through the portal several times, have seen it with our own eyes."

Alyssa adjusted the strap of the small supply pack on her back. She'd made Isabella bring one, too. There was no way they were going through any portal again as unprepared as she'd been that first time on New Year's Eve when she'd wandered around for days in the same party clothes and a broken high heel shoe.

"Look, I don't think it has anything to do with codes or spells. I don't even think you need to have fae or elven blood. I'm pretty sure you just have to know what to look for. In any case, if we can't get through, then it's no harm, no foul. At that point, we'll just go home and wait for Valian to call."

"And you're sure you know what to look for?" Isabella asked in a skeptical tone.

"Actually, yes, I'm quite certain." Alyssa smiled and pointed toward a grove of trees about twenty yards to their left and the swirling vortex of the old, mostly forgotten portal. "Look. It's right there."

"I don't get it." Isabella shook her head. "How is it that no one's seen this before? I mean, it's been right here for literally eons, right?"

Alyssa stared at the whirlpool of color and light, could feel its pull even from this distance. "I don't know. It's probably glamoured or something. Or maybe you just need to have been shown, and once you've seen it, you can't un-see it. Come on. Let's get this show on the road."

Alyssa started toward the portal, but turned back when she realized that Isabella wasn't with her. Her friend was still rooted to the same spot, staring at the portal with a wary look on her face.

"Isabella?

"Do we really need to do this, Aly? Maybe going home and waiting for Valian to call is the better plan," Isabella said in a small voice.

Alyssa walked back to her friend and took her hand, finding it ice cold. "Izzy, don't you want to know what's going on? Why Valian has been so secretive, what he's hiding?"

"Well, sure—"

"And what if you were right? What if Aramond isn't dead, and he's just biding his time to come for me and the scepter?"

"I know. That's a scary prospect, but—"

"Valian said he didn't want to worry you about unsubstantiated rumors, but he was obviously hiding something. Don't you want to know what that is, if the royals know more than they're saying?"

"Of course, but ..."

"But what?"

"I don't know if I can go through that thing alone." Isabella swallowed hard and gestured to the portal. "Don't laugh, but to be honest, every time I've gone through with Valian, I've held on tight to him and closed my eyes," she whispered.

Alyssa struggled to keep a straight face. After all, this was Isabella Christensen. Isabella, who'd fearlessly come looking for her when she'd been lost in another realm, who'd taken the knowledge of faeries and elves and magick—and 'wonderland', for that matter —in stride. She'd faced a very real war in which they could've both easily been killed, and yet was afraid of going through the portal alone. It would be comical were it not for the terror on Isabella's face.

Alyssa gave her friend's hand a squeeze. "If you're afraid of going through alone, then we'll go through together. And if you don't want to go at all, that's fine, too. I don't mind going by myself. But, Izzy, I am going."

Isabella's eyes widened. "You're not scared? Like, after everything you went through that first time?"

Alyssa laughed out loud. "Don't be an idiot. Of course I'm scared. Well, more like apprehensive at this point. But I guess *because* of everything I went through that first time and everything that happened ... well, after ... I sort of know what to expect. So, it doesn't scare me as much."

Isabella glanced at the portal and then back at Alyssa. She took a steadying breath and let it out slowly before finally nodding. "Alright, then. We go together."

"Are you sure?"

Isabella snorted. "What are you, stupid? I'm not sure at all! But what I am sure of is that I'm not half as scared to go through the portal with you as I am to go home through this damn park alone. So, let's go before I change my mind."

At that, they joined hands and walked the few yards to where the portal swirled with its color and light.

Just as they were about to step into the maelstrom, Isabella tugged Alyssa back a few steps. "Wait!"

"*Izzy!*" Alyssa huffed out a breath. "What is it now?"

"I just had a disturbing thought. How do you know where we'll come out on the other side?"

Alyssa frowned. "What do you mean?"

"Aly, this portal obviously connects with multiple others in the Artemysian realm. I mean, it has to, right? Kasandra sent you through this very portal, and you ended up in Roseland." Isabella paused and gave her a knowing smirk. "Of course, that *is* where you met the High Lord of Roseland's Twilight Court, so maybe that wasn't as bad as Kasandra had intended it to be."

"Izzy, what's Niall got to do with anything? Do you have a point?"

"He doesn't have anything to do with it, other than the fact that you're smitten with him, and I like to poke at you."

"I am not smit—"

"Whatever," Isabella said, cutting her off her denial. "My *point* is this, dummy. Valian and I have used this entrance several times as well. The first time, when we came looking for you, we arrived in an ancient tunnel under the White Palace. Each time since then, it was a portal just a mile or so from the White Palace's northern gates."

"So?"

Isabella threw her hands in the air. "Don't you get it? If you can land in different places or different portals on the other side, how do you know where we'll come out now?"

Alyssa hadn't really thought about it like that. But now that Isabella had raised the question, she realized that it was a valid concern. The handful of times she'd gone back to Wysteria with Gray, they'd used this portal as well ... and arrived on the *south* side of the palace grounds.

"Well?" Isabella prompted, waiting for her answer.

"Okay, I see your point. So, maybe we just have to *think* about where we want to end up."

"You're joking, right? Like a mind portal?" Isabella laughed out loud. "Really? That's what? Your best *guess* at how it works?"

"Maybe." Alyssa sighed and ran a hand through her hair. "Look, Izzy, this isn't about science, it's about magick. And no, I don't know for certain, but it makes as much sense as anything else, doesn't it?"

"So, what you're saying is that we just have to think real hard about where we want to end up?" Isabella asked in a skeptical tone. "Doubtful, party of one here, but I'll play along. Say that's true. What happens if we're thinking about two different portals when we step through?"

"Then we just have to make sure we're thinking about the same exit location. And we hold on tight to each other to make sure we don't get separated."

"Do you at least have a compass or something ... in case?" When Alyssa didn't answer right away, Isabella threw her hands in the air again. "Seriously? You made me put together this stupid supply pack, but you didn't think to put in basic tools?"

Alyssa frowned. "Did you bring a compass?"

"Of course I did. Hello?" Isabella poked herself in the chest. "Ex-outdoor scout, remember?"

"Well ... good job. If we get lost, you can be in charge of figuring out which direction we need to take to find our way back, okay?"

"And how is that going to help you if we get separated?" Isabella stared at her for a few moments and then waved away the question. "You know what, never mind. I would just like to go on the record as saying that this is not the best scheme we've ever hatched. And if we end up in some God-forsaken Artemysian wasteland, I will say I told you so."

"So noted. Now are we going or not?" Alyssa took Isabella's hand again and grinned as they stepped up to the portal's threshold. "And Izzy? I won't let go, so you can close your eyes if you want to."

Isabella narrowed those eyes and hissed. "Yeah, and again, you can bite me, Montague."

Laughing out loud, Alyssa turned, and they stepped into the spiraling whirlpool of color and light together.

Alyssa had only been through this portal a handful of times since that initial trip on New Year's Eve—and never on her own, as Isabella had been quick to point out. Kasandra Delacourt had used faerie magick that night to enchant her, sending her into a wonderland alone and completely unprepared.

Each time she'd gone through on subsequent trips she'd found traveling by portal exhilarating and a bit disorienting. But there was definitely something different this time around. She felt the change from the moment she and Isabella stepped into the swirling portal. The vortex seemed somehow more turbulent and chaotic than her previous trips. She had a brief thought that perhaps Isabella might have been right after all, and there was some code or spell that they were missing. But she didn't really start to panic until she heard Isabella shout 'something's wrong' and then felt her grip sliding. She watched in horror as her friend disappeared into the colorful maelstrom leaving her to drift on her own.

Moments later, the frenzied feel of the portal seemed to calm a bit. And as she stepped out into a forested region, she felt the gateway close at her back. Immediately doing a three-sixty, Alyssa slowly scanned the area. She took a few deep breaths to try to quiet her galloping heartbeat, but it didn't help that there was nothing noteworthy or familiar about where she'd landed.

And Isabella was nowhere to be seen.

"Izzy?" she shouted. "Isabella, where are you?" She called over and over but each time, received no answer. "Well, crap, Izzy. Where did you end up? And where the hell am I?"

Of course, this was just what Isabella had warned her about, and she was the one with the damn compass. "Okay, you can't do anything about that right now, so calm down and think, Alyssa," she muttered to herself.

Looking around again, she noticed a well-worn path off to her right. She crossed the short distance and stepped into the middle of it. If she'd thought that looking both ways would give her an idea of which route to take, she was sorely mistaken. That was absolutely no help, as the scenery was the same in both directions. So, she could flip a coin, do an 'eenie-meenie-minie-moe' deal, or just start walking one way or the other. She figured she was bound to find someone eventually who could point her in the direction of the White Palace.

Following her gut, she turned to her left and began to walk. She wasn't sure which forest this was, but it was serene and lovely with beams of sunlight piercing the tree canopy here and there, the sound of birds chirping and insects buzzing, and the sweet smell of earth and foliage. It could've been any forest in her home realm, and it didn't take long to become engrossed in the sights and scents of the scenery, which made her trek much more pleasant.

She'd been walking for nearly thirty minutes or so when she began to hear male voices shouting from the direction she'd just come. Since she was a bit wary, she stopped to listen. Should she stay where she was and wait for them to overtake her or continue on and pick up her pace? She needed help in finding her way to the palace, that was certain, but she'd hoped to come across a village of friendly people, not run into who knows what in an isolated area. And of course, the last time she'd been on her own in this realm and asked a stranger for help she'd ended up in a dungeon for days.

The voices were getting closer by the second, so they were moving at a good clip. She might not outrun them even if she picked up her speed. And she had no idea how far it was to any kind of village or town. Making a split decision, she stepped off the dirt track and slipped behind a huge tree. Crouching down, she peered around it through the bushes at the pathway ten yards or so away. In that moment, she was glad the clothing she'd chosen to wear for the trip to Wysteria was in earth tones and not bright colors. At least she had a chance at concealment. She didn't know who was coming her way, but as she'd learned the hard way, it was better to be safe now than sorry later.

Minutes ticked by, and just when she'd begun to wonder if she'd imagined the whole thing, what looked like three fae or elven soldiers came into view. As they grew nearer, she could see that they were indeed fae warriors. And though she couldn't tell what court they belonged to, they were dressed in field gear with burgundy breast and shin plates. They also carried lethal-looking swords, and it was obvious from her vantage point that the way they were scouring the bushes on either side of the path, they were looking for something or someone.

Adding to her concern, the three warriors stopped on the path directly across from her hiding spot. She literally held her breath as one of the soldiers turned her way and seemed to look directly at her through the foliage. Her pulse rate began to climb as a slow smile spread across his face. The next thing she knew, someone suddenly grabbed her by the arm, and she squealed in surprise and fear as she was unceremoniously hauled out from behind the tree.

"Well, well. What do we have here?" a fourth fae warrior asked, as he leered down at her. "Are you what came through our region's portal?"

As he began to drag her toward the path and the three other soldiers, Alyssa looked him over. He was huge with hard muscles bulging everywhere and was at least a foot taller than she was. How she hadn't heard him coming through the brush, she couldn't fathom. But then it dawned on her. He'd faded in behind her. They'd known where she was hiding all along.

"Look, my name is Alyssa Montague, and I just arrived through the portal from the New York realm," she said, as she struggled in his vise-like grip. "I got separated from my traveling companion, and now I'm a little lost. We were on our way to the White Palace."

"Were you now?" he asked in a skeptical tone as he deposited her on the path. "Then you're going in the wrong direction, for one thing. And for another, the White Palace is in Wysteria. You, Alyssa Montague, are in Roseland."

"But-but, that can't be. We were going to the White Palace," Alyssa stammered. "Is this Roseland Wood then?"

The warriors all chuckled at that.

"Oh-ho! You've landed far north of Roseland Wood," the big soldier replied. "This is Roseland's northern territory."

Alyssa ran a hand through her hair in frustration. How had she gotten so far off track? More importantly, how did she now find her way back? And where the hell was Izzy? "Okay. This is all pretty inconvenient. So, can you get me to the White Palace or at least point me in the right direction? I'm sure Prince Graydon would be very grateful."

"Would he indeed?" the lead warrior asked, narrowing his eyes at her.

"Y-yes. He would. He may even compensate you for your time. Listen, it's really important that I get there."

The warrior stroked his long red beard and studied her for a moment. Finally, he shook his head. "I'm afraid we're on our way back to court and can't escort you to the palace, but I know someone who may be willing to accommodate you. That is, if you come with us now, because time is short."

It was Alyssa's turn to narrow her eyes. "Come with you to your court? I'm not sure that would be a good idea."

The warrior grinned. "Good idea or not, I'm afraid that I'm going to have to insist."

Before she could object, he took hold of her arm again and faded. In the next instant, they arrived in a long corridor, and Alyssa struggled to free herself from the warrior's grip as he hauled her toward a set of massive wooden doors at the other end of the hallway. She couldn't help remembering that first time she'd arrived in Roseland and how it had ended.

"Hey! Let go of me, you big lummox. I didn't agree to be kidnapped."

The warrior laughed, shoving open the doors and dragging her into the huge chamber beyond. "My Lord, look what we ran across on our way back to court," he said. "I thought perhaps you'd be interested in our find."

Alyssa looked toward the dais at the far end of the chamber and her mouth dropped open as Niall, High Lord of Roseland's Twilight Court turned and gave her a very familiar wicked grin.

"Darling Alyssa, have you come looking for me ... yet again?"

Six

Alyssa was speechless for all of about three seconds before venting her outrage. With a growl, she jerked her arm out of the warrior's grasp and stalked toward the High Lord.

"You!" she snarled, pointing an accusatory finger at him. "Why am I not surprised to find you here?"

"Well, if you've come looking for me, darling Alyssa, why *would* you be surprised to find me in my own court?" Niall grinned at her and gave her a genteel bow. "But it is ever so lovely to see you again."

"Oh please. Don't try to charm me. And don't change the subject, Niall."

The High Lord spread his arms wide and gave her an innocent look. "I'm afraid I'm not entirely confident of what the subject is, my cherub, but had I known you were looking for me in advance, I certainly would've met you at the portal myself."

Alyssa growled again before taking a calming breath and holding up a finger. "Okay, let me be clear, I most definitely did *not* come looking for you. And, oh my God! The size of your ego really is astounding."

The High Lord laughed out loud at that, a deep baritone sound that seemed to echo around the great room, and it poured over her like a warm summer breeze. Strolling down the steps of the dais toward her, he addressed the warrior at the door. "Go and confirm that all is ready for our departure, Kassair. I have a feeling this may take more than a few minutes but be ready to leave within the hour."

Kassair gave a short bow. "As you wish, my Lord."

Shaking her head, Alyssa held tight to her annoyance and hooked a thumb over her shoulder at the warrior as he retreated. "Like I told your henchman there," she began, waiting until Kassair had closed the massive doors behind him and she was again alone with Niall before continuing. "Isabella and I were on our way to the White Palace. I don't understand how I ended up here, but I repeat—I was *not* looking for you."

She hadn't set eyes on the High Lord since he'd suddenly appeared in her gallery a little over three months ago, and she'd requested an audience with him twice since the war. He'd ignored her both times. She steeled herself against the almost seductive look in his eyes now and the effect it had on her composure.

"First of all, Kassair isn't a 'henchman'. He's my top general in charge of the Twilight Court's small yet fierce army of warriors." Niall tilted his head and smiled sweetly, which only served to exasperate her more thoroughly. "And second, I do find it quite odd that if your intended destination was the White Palace, you would come through the northern portal. You may not have been actively looking for me, as you say, but you must have at least been thinking of me."

"Ah-ha!" She jabbed a finger at him again. "I was right. I told Izzy that's how it worked." Immediately recognizing her error, she cleared her throat and quickly backtracked. "Not that I was thinking about you, though, because I absolutely wasn't. Izzy may have mentioned your name just before we entered the portal, but I-I don't really recall."

He came toward her then, slowly, like a predator stalking its prey, and his eyes danced with mischief. In conjunction, her pulse picked up speed, and to her further annoyance, she took two or three involuntary steps backward before she could stop herself.

"You don't really recall?" he asked in a honeyed tone. "Then why are you so angry, darling Alyssa?"

"I-I'm not angry ... I'm just ... frustrated, that's all," she stammered. "I didn't expect to ... see you."

"Alright." Niall reached out and tenderly tucked a wayward

strand of hair behind her ear. "Then tell me why you're really here, descendant of Alice," he murmured. "And where is your auburn-haired friend now?"

"I've already told you," she insisted, slapping his hand away. "Isabella and I were on our way to the White Palace, and we somehow got separated in the portal, so I don't know where she is, do I? And I'm very worried that she's all by herself somewhere in the realm."

She stepped away from him then and began to wander around the room to put some distance between them, and more importantly, to get a handle on her emotions. She supposed—if she was truly honest with herself—that she was a bit angry with him.

She'd been stunned when she'd learned that as the descendant of the original Alice, she was the only one who could power the Scepter of Fire. But she'd been horrified to find out what was expected of her, that she alone would have to wield a weapon of destruction to end a conflict, and that without her, a kingdom might fall.

Niall had been the only one to really *get* her, to understand her fears and inner conflict throughout that crucial time during the battle. He'd never coddled her or tried to bully her into accepting her fate, yet he'd instinctively known what she was capable of and how to help her move forward on her own terms. Then, when she'd wanted —no *needed*—to thank him for his understanding and support, he'd shunned her.

She could almost feel his eyes on her now as she ran a finger along a side table and fussed with the fresh flowers in an ornate vase while gathering her thoughts. Knowing that he was probably fully prepared to wait her out, she finally gave in and voiced the question that had haunted her for the last seven months. "Why didn't you come to see me before Isabella and I went back to New York after I wielded the ... when the battle was over? The queen sent a request on my behalf."

When he didn't reply, she turned and found him watching her with a guarded look.

"And that first time I came back to this realm after your visit to the gallery you refused to give me an audience. Why? I only wanted to thank you for ... well, everything."

"For everything?" he asked quietly with raised eyebrows.

She rolled her eyes. "Okay, obviously not everything. You did take me to the Red Palace when you knew I was looking for Prince Graydon. And because of you, I spent several days in Aramond's dungeon waiting to have my head removed from my shoulders." Folding her arms, she gave him a mutinous look. "But on the other hand, if it hadn't been for you, I don't know if I could've found the strength to wield the scepter. So no, not all of it, but undoubtedly enough. After everything we went through, why would you just ignore me that way?"

He gave her a sympathetic look, and his voice was full of sorrow when he spoke. "When the battle was over, there were heavy casualties in several of the courts. Though my Twilight Court had its share, we were luckier than most. However, every loss, no matter how small, is felt by the whole and grieved. I'm sorry if you felt I ignored you, but I did have my hands full in those days after the battle had ended."

His explanation was like a dousing of cold water and made her feel petty and small. She'd felt sorry for herself because he hadn't come to say goodbye to her, yet all the while he'd been dealing with death. "I-I'm sorry, Niall. I had no idea." But in the next instant she narrowed her eyes as another thought dawned. "But that doesn't quite explain why you completely snubbed me when I came back three months ago and sent another request, does it?"

He seemed to shake off his sorrow fairly quickly and the wicked smile she associated with him emerged. "Hmm. Let me see. As I recall, when you returned it wasn't to see me, now was it? You came back as a visitor to the White Palace, and in the escort of the Crown Prince, I might add. Or do I have that wrong?"

"Seriously?" Alyssa stared at him wide-eyed. "Are you telling me that you ignored me because you got your feelings hurt that I came back here with Gray? Because that's just childish, even for you."

Niall laughed again. "Of course not. I'm merely clarifying the circumstances."

"Oh my *God!* Tell me you're not jealous of Gray."

The High Lord's playful demeanor vanished in the blink of an eye to be replaced with righteous indignation. "Absolutely not. What a foolish thing to say, *even for you*."

"Ha, ha, you're so funny." She took a few steps away from him, and then turned back. "Then why, Niall? Were you trying to hurt me?"

"Hurt you? Not at all." He came to her then and looked down at her as if he could see all the private feelings bubbling up inside her. His gaze dipped briefly to her lips before returning to meet her eyes. "Did it never occur to you," he murmured, "that I wasn't looking for your thanks?"

Alyssa opened and closed her mouth twice before swallowing back her surprise and confusion, as her heart pounded in her chest and wild thoughts swirled in her head. Did his answer mean that he wanted nothing from her? Or that he'd wanted something more ... something entirely different. "Then why come to the gallery out of the blue like that and glamoured so that I wouldn't recognize you?"

"Perhaps I only wished to see for myself that you were well." He smiled then, and the twinkle was back in his eyes. "And of course, to return the lovely party frock that you'd left at Kaleb's cabin."

His eyes went wide, and his deep laughter again filled the chamber when she reared back and punched him in the chest before she could check herself. "Oooh, that really gets me." She shook her stinging hand and glowered at him. "Just when I maybe start to like you again, you say or do something that makes me completely insane. Why do you do that?"

He made no attempt at containing his mirth. "I do so adore the way your eyes sparkle when you're annoyed, darling Alyssa. Now, come." Taking her arm, he led her to a sitting area just to the right of the dais. "Tell me what's so important that you'd risk coming to the realm at this time. I'm actually quite surprised that Valian allowed it."

Alyssa frowned as she sank down onto the settee. "What do you mean 'at this time'? And why would Valian bar me from coming to Wysteria?"

"Because it's not safe right now, of course, especially not for you." Niall looked perplexed. "Surely the Chancellor explained recent happenings to you."

"No. He's actually been pretty tight-lipped lately. It's one of the reasons that Isabella and I decided to come and find out what he wasn't telling us." She paused and studied the High Lord's face. "And why is it especially not safe for me? I mean, I know there's still an ongoing search for confirmation regarding Aramond's demise, but Valian said that there was no evidence he'd survived the scepter's destruction. He said Isabella and I were perfectly safe in New York."

Niall frowned. "While that may or may not be true, I still had Kassair and a small team of my warriors keep an eye on you in your home realm."

Alyssa's jaw dropped. "You did *what*? So, it wasn't a coincidence that they intercepted me that way. They'd followed me from New York." She shook her head. "But why would you do that? Valian is in New York most of the time and charged with my safety, as well as the scepter's security."

"Mmm, yes. But then, he's been in this realm more often than not over the last couple of months, hasn't he?" The High Lord's gaze hardened. "Did the Chancellor happen to mention the attacks?"

It was Alyssa's turn to frown. "Attacks? What attacks?"

"For the love of the Oracles." Leaning back, Niall crossed his arms and suddenly looked like the dangerous fae warrior he was. "I think the Chancellor and I need to have a little chat," he murmured in a quiet yet steely tone.

"Niall?" Alyssa put a hand on his arm. "What are you talking about? What attacks?"

The High Lord blew out a resigned breath. "There have been sporadic yet ongoing ... incidents around the realm, both in Wysteria and Roseland, for the last four months or so. At first, they were more of a nuisance than anything and seemed purely random—thefts and vandalism mostly. But then they began to escalate."

"Oh no! If that's the case, Isabella is alone out there and could be in terrible danger."

"Yes, depending on which portal she came through. The realm is not stable right now, and with this last pointed assault on my twin and her men, it is obvious these attacks aren't random at all, and definitely much more dangerous than originally thought."

Alyssa gasped. "Oh, my gosh! Tisharu was attacked? When? Where? Is she alright?"

"She and her men were to meet an informant three nights ago in Willow Glen Wood just north of the Eastern Glade and very near the border between Wysteria and the hazards of the Eastern Barrens. Supposedly, this spy had proof that the Red King was still alive and information regarding his alleged location, but he or she was a no show and clearly part of the ambush. The Witch of the Eastern Glade arrived just before the attack took place to warn Tisharu, but my twin was injured as she and her men faded."

"But Minerva got there in time, and they're okay, right?" Alyssa's disquiet ramped up a notch when he didn't answer, and for the first time since her arrival, she could see the worry in his eyes. "Right?"

Niall reached out and took her hand. "Several of her men were killed and my twin was grazed with a poisoned arrow as they faded. She's been gravely ill and in the hospital wing at the White Palace where she's been fighting for her life."

"No, no, no! Then what are you doing here, Niall? We should go to the palace immediately."

He again reached out and smoothed the hair back from her face. "I've been at her side off and on to monitor her condition. I was preparing to return when Kassair arrived with you in tow. But do you see now why you aren't safe in this realm?" He frowned again. "Although, I'm not certain that you'd be any safer in the New York realm with Valian here."

Alyssa nodded. "You mean because Valian and I are the only two who know where the scepter is or how to access it?"

Niall's look was grim. "That's a fear, yes, and the fact that you are the only one who can power the weapon is even more of a concern. If my men could track you here, you could be just as vulnerable in the New York realm, so perhaps it was best that you've come."

"But does anyone know for sure that these attacks are Aramond's doing? Could it just be a handful of his followers acting out?"

"We can't be certain yet that this is Aramond's work but we can't discount it, either. Regardless of who is behind these attacks, your safety is paramount. Should someone get to you, they would have the power of the scepter at their command."

Alyssa made a face. "Yes. Isabella put that horrible notion into my head just Friday night at dinner. It hasn't been far from my mind since."

"Your friend seems very wise."

"I suppose, but I think she mostly has an evil thought process."

Niall chuckled. "Nevertheless, like my twin, I am skeptical that the Red King died in the battle all those months ago. In fact, I'm convinced that we've not seen the last of Aramond."

Alyssa shook her head again. "But if the power of the scepter left nothing but ash behind, how can you be sure Aramond survived?"

The High Lord shrugged. "Simply *because* not a trace has been found—not his armor nor his weaponry, both of which were engraved with his insignia. But more importantly, his signet ring has yet to be found. The scepter destroys organic matter, but these items should have been left in the ash." Niall's brows drew together. "And then there's the fact that during the last hour of the battle, neither Aramond nor his most trusted sorcerer, Yulis, had been seen. The Red King may be mad as the Hatter, but he's also as dangerous as a starved mountain troll, and I for one learned long ago never to underestimate him. Unfortunately, I fear the worst may be to come. That, descendant of Alice, is why it is imperative that you are protected at all times, whether here or in the New York realm."

A chill went down Alyssa's spine at Niall's comments. She'd seen firsthand how crazy and dangerous the Red King could be. If he had survived the scepter's wrath, then they could all be in deep trouble. Especially her. But why wouldn't Valian tell her or Isabella what was really happening? It made no sense to keep them in the dark when their safety was at stake.

"And what about Tisharu?" she asked, mostly to give herself something else to worry about rather than imminent danger. "You said that you'd been monitoring her condition. Is there nothing the healers can do?"

Niall nodded. "They are getting closer now that Old Minerva's goddaughter has arrived. Áine Ó Mordha lives in your world—the realm of Ireland. She's a Halfling and well versed in fae poisons and a variety of toxins."

Alyssa tilted her head in confusion. "A Halfling? What does that mean?"

"It means she's half fae and half human. Her sire was a worthless shite of a faerie from my twin's court."

"Was?" Alyssa watched him closely, but his look became shuttered and unreadable.

"Mmm, yes. He's been dead for many years, may the Oracle's curse his black and poisoned soul. But that's a story for another time."

"I see. But since this Áine arrived, they've been making progress? Tisharu's going to recover?"

"It's too soon to tell, but the Halfling has finally isolated the base components of the poison, so she's hopeful that she can concoct an antidote soon. My twin's time is running out."

Alyssa stood then and held out her hand. "Then we should go. You need to see if there's been progress, and I need to find Izzy. I also have some very pointed questions for Chancellor Winchester."

Niall rose and took her hand, and the wicked smile was back. "As do I, love. As do I."

Seven

When the mad swirling of the portal's vortex dissipated at her back, Isabella took a quick inventory of her surroundings. Other than a trail heading in three different directions, nothing looked even remotely familiar. She had no idea whether she just hadn't paid that much attention on previous trips or she'd come through at an entirely different location this time around.

Bending at the waist, she did some deep breathing in an effort to calm the pounding of her heart and push back her rising panic. This was just the damn outcome she'd feared the most, but she would *not* freak out. When she got hold of herself after a few minutes, said panic was slowly replaced by a brewing anger at Alyssa. Though she could admit to a portion of the blame—she had, after all, agreed to this stupid scheme—it still annoyed her that Alyssa hadn't heeded her warnings.

"Aly?" she yelled a couple of times, knowing full well there would be no answer. They'd gotten separated in the portal and who knew where her friend had ended up. At least she'd come prepared with a compass. Alyssa, on the other hand, was on her own in this realm ... yet again.

"This is New Year's Eve all over again. And did I not just outline this particular scenario a brief five friggin' minutes ago?" she asked to no one in particular, and then continued to mutter under her breath. "For the love of God, I hate being right all the time. Why nobody ever listens to me, I'll never know."

Taking off her pack, she rummaged around inside until she found her compass, then did a slow circle until it pointed south. If she'd come out of the portal to the north of the palace gate as she'd done with Valian on several occasions, walking due south should easily get her to the intended destination. Then Gray or Valian could send out a search party for Alyssa. Of course, she was going on the assumption that this *was* the portal they'd used several times. If she was wrong, she could be walking for a very long time or worse, end up in the opposite direction of the palace.

It was a crap shoot and a huge 'if', but what other choice did she have?

"We are so going to have words when I see you again, Alyssa Montague. I can tell you that," she mumbled. Throwing on her pack, she checked the compass again and then set off on the well-worn path to the south.

It didn't take but twenty minutes of walking at a steady clip and continuously checking her compass direction for Isabella to realize that the path she was on was veering a bit farther west than she thought it should. When she came out of the tree line into a lovely meadow and felt the warm sunshine on her face, she made a course correction, angling across the field. She found a path on the other side that seemed to cut eastward through a wooded area. Hoping for the best, she took a hard left on the path and headed into the shadows of the forest.

The earthy scent of vegetation was strong and sweet here, evoking memories of childhood vacations in the Catskills and camping trips into the wilds of the Pacific Northwest with her family. The track was well-traveled, and she took that as a good sign but kept a close eye on her compass—and for any potential dangers. With Valian being so secretive of late, she had no idea what she might run across. And since nothing had looked familiar from the moment she'd stepped out of the portal, she was becoming more and more concerned that perhaps she'd taken the wrong path after all.

Stopping for a moment, she slipped off her pack and pulled out a bottle of water. Twisting it open, she'd just taken a long drink when a sing-song voice had her choking on it and just about jumping out of her skin.

"Well, well, well. What *do* we have here?"

The voice sounded close by, but frantically looking around, she saw no one.

"Who's there? Show yourself."

When deep baritone laughter was her only answer, she felt panic begin to rise again. "I'm not kidding. Show yourself. I have a weapon, and I know how to use it."

"*Reeaally?*" Further up on the path a pair of golden eyes appeared and seemed to hover in mid-air. "And exactly what do you plan to do with that bottle of water?" the voice continued. "Hmm? Perhaps melt me like a wicked witch? I must warn you, Isabella Christensen, unlike most felines, I quite enjoy watersports."

Isabella's jaw dropped, and she wiped her mouth with the back of her hand. "Halifax? Is that you?"

As the Cheshire Wood cat began to materialize, Isabella caught a glimpse of his leopard persona before he morphed into a dark-skinned man dressed all in black.

"In the flesh ... at the moment, that is," he replied, giving her a deep bow.

Getting past her fright, Isabella fisted her hands on her hips and scowled at him. "You are so not funny. What are you trying to do, give me a stroke?"

"Dear me. Did I frighten you?" The cat leveled an unrepentant grin at her. "That was, of course, never my intent."

"Yeah, right. What are you doing lurking around here, anyway?"

His grin broadened. "Why, where else would I be? You are in my Wood, after all."

"This is Cheshire Wood?" Isabella grinned back at him. "So, I am going in the right direction." She pumped her fist in the air. "Yes! Take *that*, outdoor scouts!"

"Mmm." Halifax tapped his lips with a finger and then waggled it in the air. "Well, I suppose that would depend on your intended destination, now, wouldn't it?"

"Look, Alyssa and I were heading to the White Palace, but we got separated in the portal. I'm really worried about her and thought that if I could get to the palace, Valian or Gray could send out a search party."

The cat frowned. "If she didn't come through the portal with you, and you don't know where she came out, wouldn't that be a bit like looking for a thimble in a hay field?"

Isabella gave him a confused look. "What?"

"I'm sorry, do I have that wrong? Isn't that one of your sayings ... when you're looking for something difficult to find?"

Isabella rolled her eyes. "Do you mean 'a needle in a haystack'?"

"Thimble, needle ... whatever. I knew it had something to do with sewing and hay. No offense, but I must tell you that I find you humans with your axioms quite the curious bunch. My point is this, the descendant will be difficult to locate if you don't know through which portal she emerged. There are close to a hundred gateway locations between our two kingdoms, you know."

"Now, how in the world would I have known that? And are you telling me that you don't have some way of checking portal activity?"

"Shocking, isn't it?" Halifax replied in a dry tone, smiling serenely.

"For the love of God, what the hell kind of security system is that?"

"Obviously, a terrible one. Seems anyone can come and go as they please." The cat raised an eyebrow and gave her a pointed look. "Just no way to monitor the comings and goings of riff-raff."

"Yeah, you're hilarious."

He pursed his lips and looked thoughtful for a moment. "Speaking of security, I'm quite surprised that the Chancellor allowed you and the descendant to come into this realm unaccompanied—especially with recent events."

When Isabella hesitated, she saw understanding dawn on his face before he spoke again. "Ahh ... I see. He doesn't know you're here, does he?" Halifax clucked his tongue.

"Yeah, well, I don't need Valian's permission. He's not the boss of me."

"Be that as it may, coming to Artemysia at this time without a proper escort was very foolish of you both."

Throwing her hands in the air, she growled with frustration. "Why? And what do you mean by 'with recent events' and 'at this time'? You make coming to this realm sound dangerous."

"Mmm, that could be because it *is* dangerous, especially for the descendant, I would think."

"Would you stop talking in circles and tell me what on earth has been happening here? Does it have something to do with the Red King?"

Halifax tilted his head and gave her a curious look. "Has the Chancellor not told you about the attacks?"

"No! Attacks? What attacks? He's been incredibly secretive lately and hasn't told me anything. That's why Alyssa and I decided to come and see for ourselves, because it was obvious he was hiding something. Then we got separated in the portal. So, what are you talking about? Spill it, cat."

Halifax heaved a sigh, as if greatly put upon. "There have been sporadic attacks all over the realm in the last few months. They seemed like random occurrences at first, so the general thought was it was just a bit of leftover unrest from the battle with the Red King's armies."

"And then?"

"And *then* ... the assaults began to increase in frequency and became more intense. They started popping up all over—without a clear pattern—in both kingdoms."

Isabella nodded. "Gray told Aly they were searching for signs of the Red King, and that they were afraid that maybe Aramond didn't die when Alyssa used the scepter to end the battle."

The cat's expression became shuttered. "There has been talk of that, yes, and some are convinced that he survived and has gone into hiding, that maybe these attacks are his doing."

"So, what do you think?"

He smiled then but Isabella didn't think he was at all amused. "My thoughts are my own, but do you see now why coming here unescorted was a terribly foolish scheme?"

"Well, it's really Valian's fault that we came at all, isn't it?"

"I beg your pardon? And how would your imprudent actions be the Chancellor's fault?"

"Don't be obtuse, Halifax. If Valian would've just told us what was going on, trusted us enough to put us on guard, we wouldn't have come at all. But, oh no, he had to protect us by keeping useful information to himself. And now Aly is lost again somewhere in this realm and has no idea the danger she's in."

"Mmm, fair point." The cat made a face. "Elves. A questionable bunch, at best."

"Right now you'd get no argument from me on that score. So, if you'll just *escort* me to the palace, Valian and I will be having this very conversation in person. He's got some explaining to do."

Halifax heaved another sigh of displeasure. "I suppose I could assist you just this once, as that exchange is something I would rather enjoy watching. However, I do have other things to do that are—" He whirled around so quickly that for a moment he was almost a blur.

"Halifax? What is it?"

"It seems that we're about to have company." The cat lifted his head and scented the air several times before finally relaxing his stance and wrinkling his nose in distaste. "Smells like elves." He took another sniff. "Ah, yes. I do believe it's the Field Marshal and some of his merry men."

"Seriously? How can you tell?"

He gave her a bored look. "Please. I'm a cat, remember? Heightened senses and all that?"

"Oh, right."

After a moment or two, Alexi and five Elven warriors came into view on the trail. The look of surprise on the Field Marshal's face as they approached gave Isabella a small jolt of satisfaction.

"Isabella?" he exclaimed. "What are you doing here?"

She slapped her hands on her hips and scowled at him. "We were about to head to the palace so that I could give Chancellor Winchester a piece of my mind. That's what."

"Look, Isabella, this isn't a good time." Alexi shook his head. "You shouldn't have come. It's not safe for you here."

"So I've just heard." She jerked a thumb toward Halifax. "Though why I had to hear that little tidbit from this one after we'd already come through the portal is the part that infuriates me the most."

Alexi glared at Halifax.

"Don't look at me," the cat responded with a cheesy smile. "She dragged it out of me."

"I'll bet." Alexi turned back to Isabella. "Isabella, it's not that we were keeping information from you but—wait, did you say 'we'? Who came with you? Please tell me Alyssa hasn't come as well."

"Of course she has, idiot." Isabella threw her arms wide. "It was her idea. Valian has been so tight-lipped about what was going on over here that we decided to come and find out for ourselves."

"Oh, by the Oracles. Of all the hair-brained ideas—"

Isabella gasped. "Don't you dare make this out to be our fault, Alexi Tovin! If Valian had just been honest with us when we asked, we never would've come."

Alexi put up a hand. "Okay, okay, settle down. I didn't mean to imply otherwise. It's just that things have been a little chaotic here. Anyway, we'll sort this out at the palace. Where is Alyssa now?"

"How should I know?" Isabella shouted at him. "We got separated in the portal, dummy. And now Halifax tells me that there's no way to track her."

"For the love of ... this is not good. Not good at all."

"Ya think?"

Alexi ran a hand over his face. "With the latest attack on Tisharu and her men, with her fighting for her life, now the descendant is MIA in the realm somewhere? Valian will have a full-on conniption."

"Wait, what?" Isabella frowned. "Tisharu was attacked? When? How? And what do you mean she's fighting for her life?"

Alexi's mouth dropped open, and he turned to glare at Halifax again. "Are you kidding me? You told her about the attacks but not about Tisharu? What is *wrong* with you?"

Halifax made a show of examining his fingernails. "Mmm, yes, that little tidbit wasn't mine to share."

"Right. Like that's ever stopped you before. You really are a turd, you know that?" Alexi shook his head.

Halifax shrugged. "It's not my fault if the Chancellor chooses to keep secrets about an old flame from his ... present girlfriend."

"That's enough." Alexi responded menacingly. "It had nothing to do with that, and you know it."

"Yes," Isabella said, stepping in between the two men. "That really *is* enough." She punched Alexi in the chest and then pointed a finger in his face. "You're gonna tell me everything this minute or we're going to go a few rounds right here and now."

Alexi blew out a breath and took her hand in his. "Isabella," he said quietly. "Valian should be the one to explain it all to you."

"Oh, yeah, and he's done such a bang-up job of it so far, hasn't he? I've asked him several times what was going on, even questioned him point blank Friday night at dinner. Do you know what he told me? Nothing, Alexi. He told me *nothing*. Even when Aly told him Gray had expressed concerns that Aramond didn't die in the battle, Valian said there was no evidence that was true and not to worry about it."

"Darlin', there isn't any evidence," Alexi insisted. "So far, it's all just speculation. That's what Tisharu was doing when her party was ambushed ... looking for confirmation one way or another."

"And that's how she was injured? In the ambush?"

Alexi nodded. "She was struck by a poisoned arrow as they faded."

"Oh, my God. Just like Gray ..."

"I'm afraid so. The healers are working on finding a cure even as we speak. But you should wait and get the full story from Val."

Isabella shook her head. "I am *done* being lied to. Just done."

A pained look crossed Alexi's face. "Isabella, come on, Val would never lie to you."

Isabella gave him a sad look. "He may not have out and out lied about what was happening here or Tisharu's situation, but omission is just as bad, Alexi. It's actually worse in this case, because he put both Alyssa and me at risk by not telling us about the danger."

Halifax smirked. "She does have a point."

Alexi turned his head slowly and pinned the cat with a steely look. "I don't want to hear another word out of you. Not one more word."

The cat cleared his throat and took a step back. "As you wish, Field Marshal." With that, he disappeared in a blink.

Alexi turned back to Isabella. "I'm sorry you and Alyssa were kept in the dark. And maybe you should have been told, but I'm sure Val had the best intentions."

"Maybe. But you know the old proverb about good intentions? Pathway to hell, my friend."

Alexi shook his head. "Come on. Let's go to the palace so you can talk this out with Val. And we'll see about locating Alyssa. Okay?"

Isabella took a steadying breath and nodded as he took her by the arm.

And then they faded.

Eight

Gray came around gradually, peeling back his sticky eyelids and wincing at the offending daylight pouring through his bedroom window. He felt like he'd been hit with a bag full of bricks—more than once—and his head began to pound in earnest as he gingerly sat up and swung his legs off the bed. Pausing to get his breath from that little bit of exertion and putting a shaky hand to his head, he waited for a bout of dizziness to subside before looking around the room and contemplating his next move.

For the love of the Holy Trinity, what the hell had happened to him? He tried to think back but found his memories to be a jumbled kaleidoscope of images and sound. There didn't seem to be a cohesive order to any of it, though he could clearly remember going to Minerva's ... and finding Áine there. He could also vaguely recall waiting for her to disable the security the old witch had installed so they could enter her cabin, but from there on his memory got very hazy. Did something happen to him after they went inside? He couldn't seem to dredge up much after entering the cabin and definitely didn't remember coming back to the palace—or when and how that may have occurred, for that matter. Had this inexplicable something happened to the entire group or had he been the only one affected?

JONI SAUER-FOLGER

He needed to find Valian and Alexi and get some answers, but first things, first.

"Like getting some relief for this throbbing headache," he mumbled, and then winced again at the sound of his own words when they seemed to reverberate between his ears. To that end, he was working up to seeing if his wobbly legs would hold his weight when the bedroom door opened, and Gryphon entered the room carrying a tray.

"Ah, I see that you're finally awake, my prince," the house elf said in an overly cheerful voice, the sound of which careened around inside Gray's skull like a jagged blade.

Rubbing his forehead with trembling fingers, he scowled. "Lower you voice, elf. I'm right here. There's no need to shout."

Gryphon gave him a sympathetic look. "I'm sorry, my lord. I take it you're not feeling well then?"

Gray glared at the elf. "And *I* would take that question a bit more seriously if you didn't have aspirin and a pitcher of water on that tray you're carrying." He made a come-on motion with his fingers. "Bring it."

"I also brought you a bowl of piping-hot porridge to soothe your stomach in case you're feeling queasy as well," Gryphon replied as he set the tray on the side table and filled a glass with water.

Gray's scowl deepened as he took the glass and the pain reliever Gryphon offered. "I'm not, so thanks but I'll pass on the gruel. I don't think I could eat anything right now, anyway, and definitely not that."

"As you wish, but it's here if you change your mind, though I wouldn't wait too long. We wouldn't want to let it get cold and congeal."

"Mmm, what an appetizing thought. Thanks for putting that visual in my head. Just what in the name of the Oracles happened to me last night?" Gray stopped with the aspirin halfway to his mouth. "Wait—it *was* last night, right?"

"Hmm ... yes, about that."

"Gryphon? Is it not Saturday? How long have I been out?"

The royal chamber elf clasped his hands behind his back and

smiled. "It's just shy of eleven o'clock on Sunday morning, sire. You've been 'out', as you say, for quite some time."

"What the ... *Sunday morning!* How can that be? Are you telling me that we came back to the palace Friday night, and I've been asleep since then?"

"To be accurate, you and the rest of the party arrived back at the palace long after midnight, so technically you've only been asleep since early Saturday morning."

"Yeah, and you're *technically* hilarious." Gray made a face. "Just tell me that everyone got back safe and sound."

"Yes, sire. Everyone is intact and accounted for."

"Okay, at least there's that." Gray took a deep breath and blew it out slowly before washing down the aspirin. He gulped down the rest of the water in one breath and shook his head. "I don't get it. This feels like the worst hangover I've ever had ... in my entire life ... but I don't even remember drinking anything. And if I've been out that long, what the hell happened to me?"

Gryphon's face remained impassive. "I'm sure I don't know, my lord."

"Oh, please." Gray rolled his eyes. "Come on, Gryphon. You know everything that goes on around here. And the fact that you knew when we got back and brought me just what I needed now tells quite a different story, so spill it."

"I do apologize, sire, but I'm going to have to decline your request, as it's really not my place," the elf replied with a sniff. "I'm afraid you'll need to speak with the queen if you want answers to your questions."

"Oh, my sweet—" Gray felt the blood drain from his face and his mouth dropped open. "Are you telling me that my mother was awake when we got back and knows what happened?"

"Mmm, yes, I'm afraid so." Gryphon smirked and turned to leave. "Though I will say, she was not pleased. But I'm certain she can answer all of your questions," he replied over his shoulder before turning back at the door and wrinkling his nose. "In the meantime, I would suggest cleaning up a bit before you speak with her."

With that parting shot, the elf left the room, closing the bedroom door quietly behind him as he did so.

"Well, shit." Gray poured himself another glass of water and guzzled it down as quickly as the first. "This ought to be a whole bunch of fun," he muttered as he headed toward the bathroom to take the elf's advice.

But even with a hot shower and fresh clothes, he still wasn't feeling quite himself, so it took him longer than usual to 'clean up'. A little over an hour later, he left his room in search of Valian or Alexi. He figured his best option was to find out from them exactly what had transpired and what kind of apologies he would need to make before facing his mother.

However, finding his friends and dodging the queen turned out to be a different kind of challenge. After speaking with several of the guards, it seemed that Alexi had left the palace for parts unknown with a handful of Elven warriors about the time that Gray himself was just regaining consciousness. So it was anyone's guess where they'd gone or what time they might be coming back. To make matters worse, no one Gray spoke with claimed to know the where-abouts of the Chancellor or if he was even still in the realm.

After wandering around the palace for close to an hour and trying to avoid any place his mother might be in attendance, it finally dawned on him to check the hospital wing for Valian. And there he found the Chancellor, in Tisharu's room with Áine.

The Halfling looked up when Gray came into the room and smiled. "Hey, Gray. You're finally awake. And I can't say you look any worse for wear. How are you feeling?"

"Shaky at best, but about a thousand percent better than I felt an hour ago." Gray glanced at Tisharu, looking so still and pale, and gestured. "How's she doing? Any change?"

Áine shook her head. "Not so much yet, but we have come up with a serum to keep her internal temperature a bit more stable. I've also isolated all but one of the poison's elements, so I'm hopeful. I'm working as fast as I can, Gray, but I'm just not sure how much time we have left. Tisharu's chances are diminishing literally by the hour."

"Well, I have faith in you, Spindly. I know you'll figure it out, and she'll recover from this in record time."

"Yeah, thanks for the confidence, but no pressure, right?"

Gray smiled at that, and then turned to study Valian for a

moment. His friend looked like he hadn't slept much, either. And he probably hadn't, knowing Valian. "So, what the hell happened Friday night? For some reason, I seemed to be missing an entire day."

The Chancellor looked up with a shuttered look. "What do you mean? We went to Minerva's cabin looking for answers, remember?"

"Gee, how informative. I do remember that part, smart ass, but what else? Did we crash some raging party afterward? Why is it that I wake up a day and a half later feeling like I've guzzled down a keg of Elvin whiskey all by myself?"

"What exactly do you remember about Friday night?" Áine asked in an odd tone, and there was amusement sparkling in the pale gray of her eyes.

"Not much." Gray scratched his jaw. "I recall you disabling Minerva's security ... and going into the cabin. But then it's all a bit of a blur—a kind of a warm, hazy blur. Does that make any sense?"

"Actually, more than you know." Áine giggled, and Gray watched Valian nudge her, but she ignored him and continued. "So, how about when you and I went into Godmother's casting room? Does that ring any bells for you?"

"Áine," Valian murmured in a warning tone.

"The casting room?" Gray asked with a frown. "No, I—wait, yes. Now that you mention it, I remember ... the scent of earth and herbs ... and something else, something spicy."

"Yes. There are quite a few spicy *scents* in the casting room, that's for sure," Áine replied with another snicker. "Some of them *very* spicy."

Valian sighed and shook his head. "Áine, for God's sake. Stop."

The Halfling gave him an innocent look. "What? I'm just trying to help Graydon find his way through the fog."

"If you'll recall, we talked about this. I mean it. Stop."

"Okay, okay. Take a breath, wouldja?"

"Alright, you two. What's going on?" Gray finally asked. "What am I missing that you both obviously seem to know? And why do I feel like I drank myself into oblivion two nights ago and woke up today with the worst hangover in history?"

Valian put up a hand before a still chuckling Áine could respond. "The truth is that you basically stuck your nose somewhere it shouldn't have been when you were in Minerva's casting room. Áine warned us all not to touch anything, but evidently you ... inadvertently sniffed one of her potions."

"I did *what*?" For a second time in the space of two hours, Gray felt the blood drain from his face. "What in the name of the Oracles did I sniff? And do I need some kind of antidote?"

"Look, Gray, it's not dangerous," Áine assured him, and then put her hand over her heart. "It's really not ... I swear. So, no, you don't need an antidote. I promise you, the effects wear off much like alcohol or any other recreational drug once your body metabolizes it."

"I don't know of any type of alcohol or drug that takes two friggin' days to metabolize, Áine." Gray blew out a breath. "So, why doesn't that make me feel any better? Just tell me what the hell this mysterious potion was."

Before either Valian or Áine could answer his question, an alarm on the monitor next to Tisharu's bed began to blare, and Gray followed as they both hurried to the faerie queen's side.

"Oh, no, no, no, no. Her temperature is spiking again," Áine said in a worried tone, her jovial attitude evaporating. "I'm so close to finding an antidote, but it's imperative that we keep her fever under control."

"Áine, do something," Valian shouted, his eyes wide, a look of terror flooding his features.

Gray couldn't remember a time when he'd seen his friend panic this way. As far as he'd ever witnessed, Valian didn't seem to fear anything. He was always a rock and the voice of reason—in just about any situation. But Tisharu's condition was something his friend had no control over, and Gray's heart went out to him.

"Shouting at me is not going to help, Valian. Go and get the damned healer, and be quick about it. Tell him to bring me another vial of my base serum." When Valian seemed frozen to the spot, she gave him a shake. "*Now!*"

"No. You stay, Val. I'll go," Gray said over his shoulder as he hurried into the adjacent lab. He found the healer quickly, and within moments they rushed back with the serum.

"Is that going to stabilize her again?" Gray asked as he watched

Áine administer the dosage into the IV tubing from the bag hanging next to the bed.

Áine sighed and handed the emptied syringe to the healer. "Hopefully it will do the trick ... for now. Unfortunately, we've had to administer it more and more frequently, which is not a good sign."

"And that means what exactly?"

Valian cleared his throat. "It means that the serum is becoming less effective. It means we're running out of time, Gray."

"Also, that was the last of the serum on hand," the healer added. "But I'm working on another batch right now. If should be ready in thirty minutes or so." With a meaningful look at Áine, he headed back to his lab.

Áine checked the monitor and then placed one palm on Tisharu's forehead and the other on her chest. Closing her eyes, she took a deep breath, her eyes moving rapidly back and forth beneath the lids. After a moment, she opened her eyes and nodded. "Good. It's working pretty fast. Her temp is already starting to come down. I need to go check on my last lab analysis. If the results are what I'm hoping they'll be, we'll have the last piece of the puzzle and we can finish the antidote."

"What can I do?" Valian asked, glancing down at the again peaceful-looking faerie queen.

Áine reached out and took his hand. "You can sit right here and talk to her. Let her hear your voice, Valian. It'll help as much as anything right now."

Valian stared at her a moment and then looked to Gray. "I'm sorry. I know you have questions about—"

"Don't even worry about it. My questions aren't that important and can wait. We can talk later." Gray turned and started out but Valian's quiet voice stopped him at the door.

"Gray. You need to speak with the queen. She'll have the answers you're looking for, the answers I can't give you."

With that, Gray nodded and left the room in search of his mother.

And the search didn't take long. He found her in the first place he checked, in the salon sitting next to the window where she looked to be lost in thought. He'd just about decided to leave her to those thoughts when she glanced up and smiled.

"Ah. There you are," she said. "I was just thinking about you and wondering if you were up yet."

"Since I apparently went to sleep early Saturday morning and it's now after the noon hour on Sunday, I should hope that I'm up."

She tilted her head and gave him the once-over. "How are you feeling? You had quite an ordeal the other night, from what I could tell."

"Yeah." Gray sighed and crossed to her. "About that ... I'm sorry, Mother. I didn't mean to worry you."

"You have nothing to apologize for, my love."

Gray sat down next to her on the settee. "I don't really even know what happened. Valian said I took a whiff of something in Minerva's casting room that affected me poorly, but I have no idea what that was and no recollection of doing it. I don't even remember coming back to the palace."

"Graydon ..." The queen paused and seemed to be gathering her thoughts. "I feel the need to apologize, because what happened to you the other night is actually my fault."

After a moment of surprise, Gray burst into laughter and poured himself a cup of tea from the pot on the coffee table. "Don't be ridiculous, Mother. I was careless when I should have known better. How in the world is my idiocy your fault? You weren't even there."

When he glanced up and saw the crestfallen look on the queen's face, his laughter died in his throat. "Mother? What is it?"

"This is not a laughing matter, Graydon. I'm afraid that I'm very serious."

Gray frowned as an unsettling feeling began to take hold. He deliberately set down the cup he'd just poured and took her hand in his. "Yes. I can see that," he said slowly. "But I don't understand. I'm fine. Really. Áine says the effects of whatever it was I inhaled will wear off, and in fact, they already are. I'm feeling almost normal again." He searched her face. "But there's something else troubling you, isn't there? I can see it in your eyes."

"I've failed you, my son," Beatrice replied softly, and then sighed. "I only hope you'll try to understand once I've explained."

His unease deepened, but he gave her hand a squeeze. "Mother, that's just not true. You could never fail me. Where is this notion coming from?"

"Graydon, please, let me finish. This is a conversation that we should have had years ago, but I've been weak. And because of my weakness, the events of the other night—or something similar—were inevitable. I've failed you by leaving you unprepared for that moment." She looked down briefly at their entwined fingers. "Valian was correct in that matter. I can see that now," she murmured.

"Val? What does he have to do with this?"

"Nothing ... directly." She looked up with a sad smile. "With the exception that I should have listened to his counsel on the issue all those years ago."

Gray shook his head. "All those years ago? Mother, you're talking in riddles. And what did you mean I was unprepared? Unprepared for what? Me being careless? That's completely on me, not on you."

The queen pulled her hand from his grasp and patted his knee. "That's very generous of you to say, sweetheart, but if you'd have understood your heritage more thoroughly, these recent events may have never occurred. So, I'm going to do my best to explain it to you now. I can only hope that when I've finished you can find forgiveness in your heart for all involved."

"Alright," Gray replied carefully. "But I seriously doubt that there'll be anything to forgive."

The queen took a deep breath and let it out slowly. "Graydon, you know that I loved your father with all of my heart, don't you?"

"Of course."

"Sir Edward William Clariage Drake took my breath away from the moment I set eyes on him, and he was the kindest, most loving man that I've ever known. But his life was not easy as a queen's consort. He stood by my side through thick and thin, gave up everything for me, yet endured much and asked for so little in return."

Gray gave her a smile. "He loved you just as much as you loved him. He would've done anything for you."

Beatrice nodded. "Yes, and did on numerous occasions. That's why when he asked for the one very specific thing he wanted most of all, I could not deny him."

"What was that?"

"He wanted—"

The knock at the door and Gryphon clearing his throat interrupted the queen in mid-sentence. "Gryphon, this is not a good time," she admonished. "The prince and I are in the middle of a very important discussion."

The royal chamber elf gave a deep bow. "I humbly apologize, Majesty, but the Field Marshal has just returned to the palace and is insisting that he speak with the prince."

"Tell Alexi it will have to wait, Gryphon." Gray snapped in annoyance.

"Unfortunately, he was adamant, my lord. You see, he's returned to the palace with Miss Christensen in tow."

Gray frowned. "Isabella? What's she doing here?"

"That is unclear. The Field Marshal found her in Cheshire Wood as she was on her way to the palace. It appears that she and Miss Montague came through the portal together earlier today."

"The descendant came with her?" the queen asked in concern. "That's not good news. It's not safe for her in this realm with the recent attacks."

Gryphon nodded. "Yes, Majesty. That is Field Marshal Tovin's concern as well, especially since it seems that the two got separated in the portal ... and Miss Montague is now missing."

Nine

The High Lord watched Alyssa retrieve her backpack from the table where Kassair had left it when he'd thrust her into the court's great room. As Niall finished donning his armored breastplate, he smiled when she hugged the bag close to her chest, as if somehow gaining comfort from it.

"Tell me, darling Alyssa, what precious items have you brought with you on your journey to this realm?" he asked, nodding to her bag.

"What?" She looked confused for a moment, and then seemed to realize what he was implying as she looked everywhere but at him. "There's nothing precious in here, Niall. I just ... well, the last time I came through the portal alone I had nothing but the clothes on my back—"

"And a broken shoe," he finished for her.

She made a face at him. "Don't remind me. Anyway, I had no food or water and nothing to defend myself with, so I didn't want to repeat that mistake this time in case Isabella and I got separated."

"Which, of course, you did." He bent to fasten his scabbard and sword in place before turning back with a curious gaze. "So, you brought rations to sustain you ... just in case. Admirable plan. What else did you bring of use? Did you bring a weapon for your defense?"

Her face pinkened. "A weapon?"

"Yes. Something to defend yourself. What did you bring?"

"I-I'm not going to tell you."

Niall raised an eyebrow. "You're not going to tell me? And why not? After all we've been through, do you still have so little trust in me?"

Alyssa's mouth dropped open. "Don't be an idiot. Of course, I trust you."

"Then why won't you tell me what weapon you have in your bag?"

"Because you'll make fun of me, that's why." She crossed her arms over her bag and looked away.

Niall frowned. "Now who's being the idiot? Why would I make fun of you for bringing a weapon with you for your defense? It was the smart thing to do."

Alyssa sighed. "Alright, I'll show you. But don't you dare laugh at me."

Putting a hand over his heart, he replied in a serious tone. "You have my word."

After opening the bag and rummaging around inside for a moment, she finally pulled out an object and handed it to him. His lips twitched with his struggle to keep his word and not laugh out loud as he stared down at the small folding knife she'd placed in his hand.

"You promised not to laugh," she reminded him, jabbing a finger in his direction.

"And I'm not," he managed to choke out. "But ... help me to understand why you've brought a child's knife for defense? This would do little good in that respect."

"I know that, you big jerk." She snatched the knife out of his hand and glowered at him. "This is exactly why I didn't want to tell you. With the exception of kitchen utensils, it's all I could think of, and it's a Swiss Army knife. It has other uses. See?" She began pulling different utensils out of numerous slots from the knife's housing. "It has scissors, a cork screw, a fingernail file, and a small hack saw in addition to the knife blade."

Niall rubbed his chin and gave her a thoughtful look. "Mmm, very versatile, indeed, and all quite useful in different situations."

She narrowed her eyes. "But? Go ahead. Say it."

"Say what, my sweet?"

"You may not be laughing out loud, but I can see it in your eyes. You think it's pitiful," she replied in a miffed tone. "That I'm pitiful."

Reaching out, Niall slipped a wayward strand of hair behind her ear and then cupped her chin, raising her gaze to his. "Don't be absurd. You are the descendant. I watched you save this world by wielding the most powerful weapon the realm has ever known. Pitiful is not a word I would ever use to describe you."

"Yeah, well, that was different. It was life and death, and anyway, it was the scepter's power, not mine."

"Perhaps that is partially true. But no one else could've powered the scepter, only you. And that's a fact." He grinned down at her. "And don't forget, I've also watched you go toe-to-toe with a ravenous mountain troll, remember?"

She scoffed at that too, and rolled her eyes. "Again, a life and death situation. So, duh. And besides, you stepped in and saved me just when he was about to eat me, so you can't really count that, now can you?"

Niall chuckled softly. "That, darling Alyssa, is not the point." He tilted his head and studied her for a moment. "Let me ask you this. Were you afraid to come through the portal alone this time?"

Her eyes went wide. "Well, sure I was afraid. Why wouldn't I be? Considering my first experience when Kassandra sent me through on New Year's Eve, I'd be stupid not to be scared."

Niall nodded. "Exactly. On that occasion, you had no choice in the matter, yet you learned from that event. You packed a bag with essentials and came anyway just to find answers to your questions. Now, what else have you brought with you?"

She hesitated but after a moment began to pull items from the bag's interior and lay them on a side table. "I brought a few power bars and a bottle of water, you know, just in case I got hungry or thirsty. There's the knife, of course, and a sweatshirt with a hood, a small first aid kit, a pack of tissues—"

"And what is this?" he interrupted her inventory, picking up the small object she'd laid next to the first aid kit. "I recognize this material from your gallery. Its blown glass like the art piece I purchased."

The egg-shaped bit of polished glass was a riot of color in golds and russets and about the size of a small skipping stone. Turning it over in the palm of his hand, Niall smiled at the word engraved on the other side. "Faith," he murmured.

She took it from him and rubbed the etching with a fingertip. "It's just a charm for luck. It serves to remind me that no matter what situation I find myself in, I need to hold onto my faith, because I think people are inherently good."

"You have a noble and steadfast heart, Alyssa Montague, and this is a fine talisman, indeed. I believe you are stronger and braver than you know."

"Well, I don't feel strong or brave." Alyssa blew out a breath and shook her head. "I wish I had a few ounces of your confidence."

He gave her a wink. "I think I have something that may help a bit in that area."

Crossing to a cabinet along the wall, Niall opened it and retrieved a small, jeweled box. From its depths, he found the amulet he was looking for. Returning to her, he held up the necklace with its heart-shaped charm for her to see.

"Oh, Niall," she whispered. "It's beautiful." She stared at the charm in wonder, but after a moment, frowned, her confusion evident. "Look, please don't get me wrong. I do love jewelry and all, but how is this going to help me with my confidence? Other than making me look ever so stylish, that is," she finished with a wriggle of her eyebrows.

"It's more than jewelry, pet. This amulet is quite old and has magickal properties. It's called a searching stone. With it, I can locate you wherever you are. So, if you're ever in peril, you need never worry. I will come."

"So, it's what? Like some kind of a homing beacon?"

Niall laughed out loud. "In a sense, yes. With it, I will always know when you need me."

"Oooh, pretty *and* useful. I like it!"

Enclosing the charm between their palms, Niall closed his eyes briefly and infused the jewel with her essence entwined with his own. When he'd finished, the red stone was warm and radiant between their palms, and he slipped the necklace over her head where the amulet came to rest just above her heart.

Alyssa lifted it and studied the jewel. "Thank you, Niall."

"My pleasure, darling Alyssa." But when she looked up at him, he could see the question in her eyes. "What is it?" he asked. "You have something you wish to ask me?"

"Um ... yes. I was just wondering ... well ... how long have you had someone watching me in my realm?"

"Why do you ask?"

She paused for a moment. "I-I don't know. Just curious, I guess."

"Then what does it matter?"

"It's just that ... Was it since you visited the gallery at the end of March?"

Niall stared at her, asking himself for the thousandth time what it was about this human that affected him so, made him want to protect and cherish her above all else. They were from different worlds and had nothing in common. She was the descendant of the original Alice, of course, and the savior of his realm, but his feelings for her went far beyond that—had from the moment they'd met. It was a constant source of bewilderment for him, and the reason he'd gone to her gallery in the New York realm that day, in spite of his better judgement. Though he'd been getting daily reports about her welfare from the instant she'd left his realm in the days after the battle, he'd wanted to see for himself that she was safe. Strangely, he'd missed her face, her wit, her strength.

"Niall?"

Alyssa's voice snapped him out of his musings, but before he could answer her question, the doors to the chamber burst open and Kassair rushed in, saving him from embarrassing himself—for a faerie can never lie.

"Ah, Kassair, perfect timing. Is all ready for our departure?"

"I'm sorry, my lord, but we need to delay for a time. We've got a critical situation."

Niall turned with a hard look. "Explain, General."

Kassair cleared his throat and sent a meaningful glance to Alyssa. "I, uh ..."

"Do not concern yourself with her, Kassair. Just spit it out. What's this dire circumstance which requires our delay?"

"Very well." The warrior gave a concise nod. "There's been another random attack. Ten minutes ago, during the shift change at the outer wall, two of the sentries on duty were found dead and another is missing."

"I see. Do we know if the wall was breached?" Niall asked as he briskly pulled on his gauntlets. With the descendant in court, his instincts were screaming that perhaps this wasn't random at all but deliberate. Nonetheless, they couldn't afford to take chances with Alyssa's safety.

"It doesn't seem so, but that has yet to be determined. I have warriors scouring the perimeter as we speak."

"Good man. But I want that missing warrior found, Kassair. And get two of your most dedicated to post outside this chamber. No one in or out." Niall spared a look at Alyssa. "The descendant must be protected at all cost."

"Consider it done, High Lord."

As the general left the chamber, Niall turned and gave Alyssa a stern look. "You will stay in this chamber until my return. Do you understand?"

"Yes, but—"

"No buts. You'll be safe here, and I won't be long. If all is clear, we'll leave for the White Palace the moment I get back, so pack up your belongings and be ready."

"Alright." Alyssa nodded, but pulled him back when he turned to leave. "Please be careful, Niall."

He smiled then and leaned down to place a kiss on her forehead. "Worried about me, darling Alyssa?"

"You bet I am. If something happens to you, what good is this amulet? Who's going to save me when I'm in peril?" She slipped the necklace beneath her blouse, concealing it there, and grinned at him in a show of bravado. However, he could clearly see the concern in her eyes.

"Well, your worry is wasted, as I'll be fine. Think no more of it. I won't let anything or anyone hurt you. Not in my court."

With that, Niall left the chamber, making certain the guards were indeed posted outside the entrance before heading out to the court-yard to be briefed on the progress of the search. To that end, he was informed that no breach of the outer wall had been found, which gave him some relief. Unfortunately, the missing warrior was still unaccounted for, and *that* was of great concern to Niall.

"Who is this missing soldier, General?" he asked Kassair. "And do we know if he's simply a victim or perhaps somehow nefariously involved in this mess?"

"I had the same questions." Kassair shook his head. "Unfortunately, it's hard to tell. Since I didn't know him well, I did some checking, spoke to his lieutenant. Seems he's had a few scrapes in the past but nothing too serious. He's come up in the ranks, though not far … and not well. He mostly keeps to himself, has no close friends among the other warriors in his division." The general paused. "You know, I hate to think it of one of our own, but what if …"

"You echo my own thoughts, old friend." Niall glanced around the courtyard. The possibility of his domain being penetrated was unsettling, especially with the recent attacks … and in broad daylight. Was it a coincidence that this had happened while the descendant was here? He didn't think so. That meant that someone knew Alyssa was within the Twilight Court's walls. Turning back to Kassair, he came to a decision. "Make certain the court is secure and then gather your finest and most trusted warriors. We leave for the White Palace in fifteen minutes. I want the descendant inside those palace walls within the hour."

"By your will, my lord. We will collect you directly."

Niall watched Kassair hurry away before heading back to the Great Hall. There he found Alyssa pacing back and forth.

"Finally!" she wailed when he entered the chamber. "I was beginning to worry that something had actually happened to you."

Niall chuckled. "Ah, darling Alyssa. I was gone for less than thirty minutes. You let your imagination run away with you."

She stopped and stared at him. "Oh. Well, it felt much longer than that."

"It seems as if you've worked yourself up into a frenzy for nothing. You were perfectly safe the entire time."

"So, what happened out there?"

Niall put up a hand. "All is well. No intruders were found."

Alyssa put a hand to her chest where the amulet lay beneath her blouse. "But those warriors were killed."

"Yes, but that occurred outside the perimeter wall. There is no evidence of any intruders gaining access to the interior courtyard."

"And the missing warrior?"

"Not yet located."

Alyssa began to pace again. "But what happened to him, Niall? Is this because of me? I mean, it can't be a coincidence, right?"

Niall took her arm to stop her pacing. Turning her to face him, he gave her a direct look. "The missing warrior may have been a victim, but we can't be certain that he wasn't involved, either. And I don't believe in coincidences. So, yes, I think someone may have realized that you were here or perhaps were tipped off to your location. However, regardless of how it happened, this is not your fault."

"But if I'd have just stayed in New York, maybe this wouldn't have happened at all. Your men would still be alive."

"We don't know that. If you'd have stayed in New York, they could have very well found you alone there with Valian absent and unable to protect you or the scepter. As I said, I don't believe in coincidences. Everything happens for a reason."

At that moment, Kassair entered the chamber. "All is ready, my lord. We leave on your command."

"We're leaving now?" Alyssa asked with a frightened look.

Niall nodded. "Grab your things."

"Are you sure it's safe to travel?"

"Alyssa, right now there's nowhere in this entire realm that's safe for travel. But don't worry, you'll be protected the entire way."

"What if we get attacked?" The fear in her eyes as she reached out a trembling hand to him was nearly his undoing. "If it's not safe, why can't we just stay here?" she pleaded.

He cleared his throat. "Well, we could, but if Isabella is at the palace, then they already know you're missing, perhaps even have sent out search parties. Don't you want to let them know you are well?"

Alyssa looked back and forth between him and Kassair. "You could send someone to tell them I'm here, right?"

"That's true, but what if your friend didn't make it to the palace? The Chancellor would have no way of knowing that she's missing unless we go and tell him."

"God, I hadn't even thought of that," Alyssa admitted in a shocked voice. "What kind of friend am I?"

"Don't be foolish. With recent events, your distraction is understandable. There is, however, another issue to consider regarding your safety. The missing warrior has not been located, which leads me to believe he may have been involved in the attack. And I don't think that it's mere happenstance it occurred upon your arrival."

Niall sighed and pulled her into his arms, speaking quietly at her ear. "I will breathe much easier when you are safely inside the walls of the White Palace. I need to make certain this court is secure, and I can't do what needs to be done with you here. Do you understand?"

She leaned back and looked into his eyes for a long moment before slowly nodding. "Alright. But can we at least fade there? Or maybe we could use the old portal under the palace. Izzy told me that's how she and Valian got there during the conflict when the areas around most of the other portals were so unsafe. They didn't have to travel by foot out in the open."

He shook his head. "We can only get within a mile or so of the palace. The Witch of the Eastern Glade restored the fade restrictions just after the battle. The old portal was closed for security at that time as well. We can fade to Tarkington Forest just this side of the restriction zone, but we'll have to walk from there. I'm sorry."

She slowly shook her head. "No, it's not your fault. Like you said, things happen for a reason."

"I can send a scout to the palace to inform them of our imminent arrival," Kassair spoke up. "At least they'll know to expect us."

"Good thinking, Kassair." As the general went to take care of the matter, Niall smiled down at Alyssa. "You see? We'll take every precaution."

Reaching up, she gently caressed his cheek. "I do trust you, you know. I'm sure you'll do whatever it takes to get us there in one piece."

Niall turned his head and placed a kiss in the palm of her hand. "Then let's go. It will be dark in a few hours, and I want you there safe and sound before nightfall."

Picking up Alyssa's backpack from the table where she'd left it, Niall handed it to her, and they left the chamber, joining up with Kassair and the security team in the Great Hall. In a burst of starlight, they were standing just inside the tree line at the north end of Tarkington Forest within moments.

"You see?" Niall said again with a grin. "It's a lovely afternoon, and just up ahead, at the end of this path is Larkspur Meadow. Do you remember?"

As she nodded, Alyssa's soft laughter lightened his heart. "This is the same way we came when we traveled from Kaleb Pilliar's cabin, when you finally took me to the *correct* palace in January before the battle began in earnest."

"It is." Niall smiled. He had fond memories of that time before the war. The wood sprite had given them refuge so that Alyssa could recover her strength after being set upon by the mountain troll. It was also the first time that she'd actually let down her guard with him.

"And on the other side of the meadow, just a stone's throw from the palace gates, is Cheshire Wood," Alyssa continued. "I wonder if Halifax is home."

Niall frowned. "Now, why would you want to ruin a lovely walk with mention of that infernal Cheshire cat?"

Alyssa giggled. "Halifax isn't so bad."

"Ha! I lump him in the same category as the Hatter. Idiotic and bothersome, the both of them."

"Oh, come on now. Duncan Maddux may be quirky and a bit mad, but he's an adorable little guy. And he did offer to transport me from Kaleb's to the palace that day."

"*Transport?*" Niall couldn't believe his ears. "In that rickety wooden wagon of his? Ridiculous. Why, you wouldn't have gotten half a mile in that pathetic thing, and you know it. And it would've jarred the teeth out of your pretty little head, to boot."

When Alyssa laughed out loud, he realized too late that she was having fun at his expense, and he gave her a bland look. "Yes, I see. You are very funny, indeed."

"Had you going for a minute, didn't I?"

He couldn't help the grin that crossed his face, but his reply was lost when the first warrior fell.

The ambush happened quickly, before they'd even made it out of Tarkington Forest, with rogue fae fading in all around them. Niall cursed himself for dropping his guard even for a moment and shoved Alyssa behind him.

"Incoming! Take cover!" he bellowed to his warriors as arrows and the sound of clashing swords began to fill the air.

He and Kassair, fighting back-to-back, worked to keep the descendant protected between them surrounded by an outer perimeter of warriors, but it was a difficult task with the enemy seeming to come at them from all directions. He thrusted and parried to keep from being sliced open by one of three fae deter-mined to do just that, and he'd just side-stepped a blade when he heard a sound that had his blood running cold.

Alyssa was screaming his name.

He quickly dispatched the three aggressors before him and turned seconds later to find that their missing warrior had faded inside their circle beside Alyssa, who was trying to wrest her arm from his grasp. Before Niall or Kassair could take another step, the man grinned and disappeared ... taking Alyssa with him.

"*Noooo!*" he roared in righteous anger before cutting down three more rogue fae in quick succession in his fury.

This was the plan all along, he realized, as the enemy began to rapidly fade from the forest. When silence descended, the only sounds left were the moans of the injured and the rustle of leaves in the light breeze.

It had obviously been a trap—the dead warriors at the Twilight Court's wall, the inciting incident—to get the descendant outside the court ramparts. In his arrogance, he'd played right into their hands. And now Alyssa was gone. He might as well have handed her over himself.

"My lord, what do you want to do?" Kassair asked.

Niall turned to his general with a look of steely resolve. "Have your lieutenant coordinate efforts to get the dead and injured back to court. Then round up a small and lethal team. We go first to the White Palace ... and then to retrieve the descendant."

"Yes, Sir!" Kassair replied and went to find his lieutenant.

"They can run, but not nearly fast enough to save themselves from me," Niall murmured before following.

Ten

"Isabella?" Gray greeted her with surprise and concern as he entered the Great Hall. "What in the world are you doing here? This isn't a good time for a visit."

"Oh, I'm sorry," she said with a touch of sarcasm. "Have we come at a bad time?"

"Uh, it's been a bit chaotic, yes," he answered slowly. "And you know you're always welcome in this realm, but it's really not safe for you right now."

Isabella felt the keen urge to thump the prince, but resisted the impulse—barely—and instead, crossed her arms and glowered at him. "Well, duh! Now *that's* some pertinent information that would have been pretty handy to know before we stepped foot through the damned portal. But then again, were we any safer in New York?"

"Of course, you were." Gray frowned. "You're infinitely safer in that realm under Valian's care."

She tilted her head and studied him for a moment. "It's interesting that you should mention his 'care', considering that he's been here more than there over the last couple of months and has been consistently making up various excuses why I can't come with him."

Gray reached out to her, but when she only stared at him, he dropped his hand. "Isabella, Valian isn't the only one keeping an eye you and Alyssa in the New York realm. Trust me, you are watched over at all times, even when Val's here in Artemysia."

"Really? Then why are you so surprised to see me here? If we were being 'watched over' so thoroughly in New York, then how is it that you didn't know we'd come? Seems like whoever you've had doing the watching isn't handling their job very well, now are they? So, if that's supposed to make me feel safer, I gotta tell you, it doesn't inspire much confidence, Your Highness."

"Isabella—"

"You're absolutely correct, child," Queen Beatrice interrupted, putting a hand on Gray's arm. "I don't know what happened with your security detail in the New York realm, but it will be dealt with severely. Your safety and that of the descendant are of the utmost importance." She paused and glanced at the prince before continuing. "As for the rest, it was all done at my command."

"Mother—" Gray began, but the queen cut him off with a brisk shake of her head.

"Though it was done to protect you, Isabella, I'll admit that keeping you in the dark about recent events here was a mistake. However, what's done is done, and recriminations at this juncture are a waste of time. Where is the descendant now? Gryphon said you left the New York realm together but that you got separated."

Isabella took a calming breath and looked back and forth between Gray and the queen before answering. "To be honest, I don't know, Majesty. We were holding hands when we entered the portal in Central Park. And then ... Well, it was just so different from every other time that I've gone through with Valian, somehow more turbulent, and I guess we lost our grip on each other. The next thing I knew, I was stepping out of the portal in this realm ... alone."

"Turbulent, you say?" The queen looked concerned. "That is very disconcerting."

"Yes, Majesty," Alexi spoke up. "With the recent barrage of attacks popping up around the kingdom, and depending on which portal she came through ..." He shot a meaningful glance at Gray. "We need to find her as soon as possible. Isabella, do you have any idea where she might have been thinking about when you went into the old park portal?"

"For the love of ..." Isabella threw her arms wide. "How on earth would I know that?"

Alexi rolled his eyes. "Come on, Isabella, think. What were you talking about before stepping into the portal? Is it possible Alyssa may have been thinking about a different location?"

Isabella's mouth dropped open. "Oh ... my ... God! Are you seriously telling me that's how the portals really do work—that you just have to *think* about where you want to go? Because that was Aly's theory, but I thought it was a pretty ridiculous notion at the time."

Alexi pressed his fingertips to his eyes for a moment before taking a breath and nodding. "Yes, Isabella. That's exactly how they work."

Isabella stared at him for a second or two. "Okay, but what about when that evil faerie-wench Kasandra sent Aly through on New Year's Eve? Aly had never been here, had no idea this place even existed, so how would she know to think about where she was going?" When Alexi continued to stare at her with a frustrated look, she nodded. "See what I mean? Ridiculous."

"Isabella, you said it yourself. Kasandra Delacourt was a *faerie*. Once she'd put the enchantment spell on Alyssa, all she had to do was put the vision in her head and send her through."

"Oh." Isabella frowned. "Well, I still think the whole setup is a preposterous way to work things. So many things can go wrong, and did, for that matter."

"Yes, thank you for your clever insights. We'll take that under advisement the next time we decide to design another portal system," Alexi said, dryly.

"Look, you don't have to be so snippy about it. I'm just saying."

"By all that's holy, would you forget about the damn portal system for a minute and think? This is important."

Isabella punched him in the shoulder before she could stop herself. "Do you think I don't know that, Alexi? My friend is lost somewhere in this realm. Again, I might add. And from what you've said, it's just as dangerous here as the last time around. So, yes, I get how important this is."

Alexi sighed and took her hand, holding it to his chest. "Okay, okay. I'm sorry. Truly, I am. But I really do need you to focus now.

Did you talk about any other portals or areas in the realm before you went into the vortex?"

"No! I told you ... well, wait a minute. We did talk about Niall briefly. Would that count?"

"Niall?" Gray frowned and stepped forward. "What about Niall?"

Alyssa had said that her relationship with Gray had cooled after she'd come looking for the High Lord earlier in the year, so Isabella swallowed and chose her words carefully. "Oh, you know. Just about how she'd wanted to thank him for his help during the conflict but he'd refused to see her every time she'd asked for an audience. And then about him coming to the gallery back in March. That sort of thing." She looked back and forth between Gray and Alexi. "Wait, you don't think that would be enough to make a difference in ..."

Alexi ran a hand over his face. "Unfortunately, if Alyssa was thinking about Niall when she stepped into the portal, it could have made all the difference. It also may have been the reason that the vortex was so turbulent. You were concentrating on two different locations. If Alyssa was thinking about the High Lord, she may have been sent to the portal closest to his court."

Isabella's heart sank. She'd been the one to bring up Niall in their conversation before they'd entered the portal, teasing her friend about her infatuation. Was Alyssa still thinking about him when they'd stepped into the swirling vortex? "Um ... if that's the case ... then it may be my fault that Aly's missing."

"Why would it be your fault, Isabella?" Gray asked.

Dicey, very dicey.

"Well, see, I was worried about how Aly could be so sure we'd come out at the correct location, so we were speculating on how the portals work and discussing that first time for her with Kasandra. And ... well, I was the one to bring up Niall in the conversation."

And that's all I really want to say about that, thank you very much.

"Anyway, my point is, if that made the difference in where Aly came through, can't you just send someone to the Twilight Court to see if she's there? That's the only other thing we talked about before stepping into the damn thing."

"Alright, good, then at least we have a place to start," Alexi said, giving the hand he still held against his chest a squeeze. "Don't worry, darlin'. We'll find her. I promise."

Looking up into his ice-blue eyes, so full of confidence, she felt a pull of emotions she hadn't felt since the first time they'd met.

Inappropriate, Isabella. Very inappropriate.

She cleared her throat and tried to concentrate on Alyssa. "But what if—"

"Isabella?" A voice from the main stairway landing interrupted her thought, and they all turned to find Valian hurrying toward them. "What's happened? Are you alright? Why are you here?"

Alexi dropped her hand like a hot potato and stepped back. "Hey, Val. Look who we found in Cheshire Wood. Isabella's here."

The Chancellor sent him a sardonic look. "Yes, Alexi. Thank you. I can see that, as I do have eyes in my head, don't I?"

"Right ... right." Alexi sent an apologetic look to Isabella before stuffing his hands in his pockets and looking away.

"My question was '*why* is she here'?" Valian repeated as he crossed to her. "For which I'd appreciate an answer."

"And I'd appreciate you not talking about me like I'm not standing right in front of you," Isabella replied with a mutinous glare.

"Isabella." Valian reached for her, but she crossed her arms and continued to scowl at him.

"Uh ... Gray, we should probably ... you know ... discuss those security matters," Alexi stammered, awkwardly.

"Yes. Good thinking," the prince replied in a sober tone, sparing Valian a hasty glance. "We'll just be in the war room when you're done here, Val. We can fill you in when you're ready."

With that, they both headed down the hallway like their backsides were on fire.

Cowards.

Isabella looked at Queen Beatrice, who was obviously amused by the exchange. The queen gave her a discreet smile and a quick wink before turning to follow them.

And then she was alone with Valian.

"Isabella. Why have you come?" He smiled down at her and

reached out to take her hand. "And why do I feel as if you're angry with me?"

"Seriously?" She shook her head and slapped his hand away. "You have no clue why I would be angry?"

"What have I done now?"

"Oooh, don't you dare make this sound like I'm being unreasonable."

The Chancellor smiled patiently, like a father indulging an overwrought child, which only served to inflame her sense of outrage.

"Tell me what's wrong. I'm just trying to understand, love."

"Well, I guess since you're obviously having a hard time getting there on your own, why don't we start with how secretive you've been over the last few months, figuratively patting me on the head like I'm some kind of mental deficient."

"Isabella, come on, now. That's not true."

"It most definitely is true," she insisted. "Then let's add the fact that you told me before you left Friday night there was nothing to worry about and you'd be back to New York on Saturday. 'Just routine business, love'," she said, mimicking him. "Then when you didn't show up by Sunday and hadn't even bothered to send word that you'd be detained, I was terrified that something had happened to you."

"I'm fine, as you can see. We've had a few skirmishes here. That's all. As I've said, nothing for you to worry about. I'm sorry that I failed to let you know I'd been held up, but you needn't have come to check on me."

"Stop it! Stop lying to me and just be honest for a change."

"Isabella, what are you talking about? I've never lied to you."

"A few skirmishes? Nothing to worry about? Those may not be lies in the strictest sense of the word, Valian, but don't you think omissions are just as deceitful? I've been asking you for the last three or four weeks what's been happening over here and all I've gotten were platitudes and evasions. Hell, you used to bring me with you when you came back to Artemysia, but for a while now it's been one excuse after another why I can't accompany you."

When he reached for her again and she took a step back, his look became shuttered. "Alright, I'll admit that there have been some issues here that have needed my attention, so I thought it best that you stayed in New York."

"Issues? *Issues?*" Isabella shook her head. "Geez, even now that I'm here you can't quite bring yourself to tell me what's been happening, can you? Like the random attacks that aren't so random? Like the fact that your former lover is lying in a hospital bed right now somewhere in this very palace fighting for her life because of one of those attacks?"

He had the good grace to look surprised and mildly uncomfortable then. "How did you ..."

"How did I find out about the attacks? Or how did I find out about Tisharu?" She frowned at him and then ran a hand through her hair. "Look, I found out about the attacks from Halifax and about what had happened to Tisharu from Alexi."

"Alexi?"

"Yeah, well don't worry about it. I'm sure he wouldn't have said anything, but he thought Halifax had already told me, so it really wasn't his fault."

"Isabella, it's not—"

"Not what? Not what I think? Is that what you were going to say? Because, to be honest, I seriously don't know what to think, Valian, since you didn't have the decency to tell me. Not about the attacks or how it could very well affect our safety—and certainly not about Tisharu." She shook her head and gave him a sorrowful look. "What? Did you think I'd be upset that you rushed back here when you heard of her assault or that you were worried about her? That's what the phone call Friday night at dinner was about, wasn't it? The reason you left so abruptly?"

He sighed and then nodded. "I was just so stunned when Alexi told me on the phone that she was close to death. I guess I wasn't thinking very clearly at that point, and I didn't want to worry you, didn't know how to tell you in that moment."

"I would've never questioned your motives had you just been honest with me. But you weren't. You hid it from me like some guilty little secret, which only serves to make me wonder what else you're hiding from me."

"Isabella, it's not like that. It's really not."

111

"Are you so sure?" she asked, looking into his eyes for an answer that didn't come. "Look, don't get me wrong. I get it. You have a long history with her, and she and I may have gotten off to a rocky start the one time we met, but I would never wish something like this on her." She put up a hand when he started to speak. "And I would expect nothing less of you, because I know that she still holds a piece of your heart. How could she not?"

"To be truthful, I don't really know what I'm feeling right now." He took her hand then, and his tender smile nearly broke her heart. "But you know that I would never intentionally hurt you, right?"

Putting her free hand to his cheek, she did her best to smile back. "I do. It's not who you are. But matters of the heart are fickle and sometimes it's not up to us, you know? I just need you to promise me that when you figure it out, you'll be upfront with me. Deal?"

He pulled her in and kissed her forehead. "Deal," he murmured.

"So, how is she doing?" she asked against his chest. "Is she going to be okay?"

Leaning back, he shook his head. "I don't know. Áine, Minerva's goddaughter, is doing all she can, but we're running out of time, and she still hasn't isolated the last component of the poison."

"Well, then I'll keep Tisharu in my prayers. She's a kick-ass warrior, right? I have a feeling she'll come through with flying colors."

When she stepped away from him to remove her backpack, she saw him eyeing the bag. "What?"

"Is that little backpack all you brought with you from New York? How long did you intend to stay? Fifteen minutes?"

Isabella rolled her eyes. "Very funny. Aly made sure we both had food and water and stuff for the trip because she had nothing with her that first time Kasandra sent her here. She didn't want to be stuck without provisions if something went wrong, which, again, it did. But I was the only one with a compass, thanks to my outdoor scout days, so I found my way."

Valian froze. "Wait. Please tell me that Alyssa didn't come with you."

"Of course, she did, dummy. It was her idea. We knew you were hiding something and wanted answers."

"What did you mean 'if something went wrong, which, again, it did'? What went wrong?"

Isabella sighed. "I guess I got so focused on my annoyance with you that I forgot to tell you that Aly is missing. We got separated in the portal."

"*What?* We have to find her immediately. It's not safe for either of you here, but definitely not for her."

"Well, no kidding," Isabella shouted at him, her irritation starting to rise once more. "Again, if you'd have just been honest with us about that we might not have come in the first place."

"Calm down, both of you," Alexi said as he and Gray came down the hall. "We're on it. I'm sending a scouting party to Niall's Twilight Court. We think that may be where she ended up."

Valian scowled. "And why would that be, Field Marshal?"

"Because she and Isabella were talking about him before they went into the vortex," Gray answered. "If she was still thinking about him when they stepped over the threshold ..."

"Then that's more than likely where she ended up," Valian finished.

"Gray and I thought we'd go with them," Alexi said. "Alyssa will probably want to see a familiar face or two."

"Good idea."

"There is one other thing that needs to be addressed, gentlemen," Queen Beatrice announced as she approached.

"What is that, Majesty?" Valian asked.

"The scepter, Chancellor, it needs to be recovered. We cannot take the chance that, under duress, the descendant is compelled to collect it."

"True," Gray agreed. "However, I think it's safer in the New York realm than here, Mother. Perhaps Valian could just move it to another secure location there. Alyssa can't be force to retrieve it if she doesn't know where it is."

Before they could get much further in the discussion, the massive vestibule doors opened and several Elven warriors entered, escorting Niall and his men into the Great Hall.

"High Lord." Gray called. "Thank the Oracles! We were just on our way to your court."

Isabella ran to him. "Did you find Aly? Is she with you?"

The High Lord's countenance seemed etched in stone. "She was."

"What do you mean 'was'?" Valian asked, his concern evident. "Where is she now?"

Niall gave Valian an angry look. "We were on our way here but were ambushed in Tarkington Forest. The descendant was taken during the attack."

"Oh, no!" Isabella cried. "Was it the Red King?"

"It is my belief that they were working for him, yes." He turned back to Valian. "It'll be dark in a couple of hours. We must go after her before it's too late and we lose the trail completely."

The queen stepped forward. "Field Marshal, send word to the Winter Court. Ask Finvar to assist in the rescue. As the High Lord says, time is of the essence. Meanwhile, the issue of the scepter needs to be addressed before anything else happens. Chancellor, you will see to it."

Valian nodded. "Yes, Majesty. I'll handle it."

"And I'll go with him," Gray added. "We'll see Isabella home as well."

"You most certainly will not," Isabella replied with a shake of her head. "I'm staying right here."

"Isabella—" Valian began.

"Don't even go there, Chancellor," she interrupted him. "I'm staying, and that's final."

While she and Valian stared at each other in uncomfortable silence, Alexi cleared his throat. "Alrighty, then. If that's settled, let's move like we have a purpose, people."

Eleven

$\mathcal{A}$lyssa was still fighting against the rogue warrior who had whisked her away as they materialized—along with a small group of fae soldiers—in a meadow near a beautiful wooded area.

"Let go of me, you idiot!" she yelled. "Where do you think you're taking me?"

The accompanying soldiers all chuckled when the faerie obliged Alyssa's shouted request so suddenly that her momentum had her stumbling backward and ending up on her butt in the soft grass.

She ignored them and narrowed her eyes at the lead faerie. "You're the missing warrior they were looking for at the Twilight Court, aren't you?"

"Very good, Alice," he replied with a chuckle.

"My name's not Alice."

The faerie smirked. "You may go by any name you wish, but I've been charged with retrieving you by any means necessary, and paid well to do it."

"Let me guess. You're not actually part of the Twilight Court, right?"

For a moment she thought he wasn't going to answer, but then he shrugged. "Infiltrating their ranks wasn't difficult."

"So, you were the one who killed those men at the perimeter wall. Was the ambush in Tarkington Forest the plan all along?"

"You ask too many questions."

"Yeah, well, you're going to be so sorry for this when Niall finds me," she muttered as she glared up at him.

"Do you think so?" he asked with a grin. "He'll have to find you first, won't he? In any case, I think it will be you who's sorry when we arrive at our intended destination."

"And just where would that be? On whose orders have you kidnapped me? Who's paying you?"

The warrior laughed out loud at that. "And here I thought you were such a clever girl. Why, the Red King, of course."

Alyssa's breath came out in a *whoosh*, and she literally felt the blood drain from her face. "Aramond?" she whispered. "So, it's true. He's alive."

"Oh, I'll say. Alive and ... um ... perhaps not well at the moment, but planning his triumphant return to power in the feared Eastern Barrens, nevertheless."

"The B-Barrens? Dear God in Heaven."

"Indeed." He pointed to the east at the tall towers in the near distance. "The Barrens lay just to the other side of those ward towers. Unfortunately, we'll have to cross the border on foot, as the wards prevent fading in or out and protect the kingdom's borders from all manner of evils that live and thrive in the Barrens."

"Niall was certain Aramond was still alive. He said they'd been looking but hadn't located him. This is why. He's been in the Barrens all along."

"Mmm, yes, he's been well hidden, though the Eastern Barrens wouldn't be my choice for a hideout. He's none too happy about it, either—nor with you, pet. You've made a right mess of things, for him as well as yourself."

"You can't do this. He's delusional and dangerous to all life in this realm, you have to know that. If you turn me over to him, he'll ..."

The warrior squatted down in front of her. "He'll what? Kill you?" He shook his head. "Don't worry, Alice. He won't kill you ... at least not straight away. Not until he gets what he wants."

"I don't care what he wants. And my name is not *Alice*," she shouted in his face. "How many times do I have to tell you people that?"

"Ah, right. You're the descendant of that irksome little pipsqueak who caused such havoc all those years ago. Then you recently instigated some of your own by using the Scepter of Fire to murder thousands of my countrymen."

"Murder thou—I *murdered* no one. And I didn't have a choice. I had to use the scepter to stop Aramond's invasion before *he* could murder thousands of innocent people in his insane quest for power and vengeance."

"Lies." The warrior's face became a mask of hatred. "The Red King was simply attempting to take back what was his after Queen Renata died. That White-bitch-of-a-Queen Beatrice should never have been given half this realm in the first place. The king wants nothing more than to reunite the kingdoms in peace under his rule."

Alyssa gaped at him. "You seriously can't believe that. Aramond meant to use the scepter to wipe out everyone in Wysteria. He as much as told me so during my incarceration. He planned to decimate the entire kingdom. He didn't care that innocent people would have died, and he certainly had no thought of instilling peace in this realm."

He shrugged again. "The king gave the White Queen a chance to comply, but she refused. The decimation of Wysteria and those innocents would have been on her head." He shoved a finger in her face. "You murdered my brothers that day on her behalf, and those of us left behind barely escaped with our lives. So, if you're looking for a sympathetic ear, you'll find none here. Were it up to me, descendant of Alice," he sneered, "I would gladly gut you now and dispose of your lifeless, rotting body in a deserted pit and be done with you. So, you're lucky I've been paid well to deliver you alive."

Alyssa shrunk away from the wild look in the faerie's eyes. "You're as bat-shit crazy as Aramond," she whispered.

He grabbed her by the arm and jerked her to her feet. "I would try to remember that, were I you. May I also suggest that you keep your lying gob shut the rest of the journey, lest I decide to do as I please with you ... orders or not. Do you follow?"

Pressing her lips together and putting her free hand to her chest, she nodded. Taking comfort in the feel of the amulet beneath her blouse, she could only hope that Niall would find her quickly, because she couldn't imagine what horrors awaited her in the Eastern Barrens, if her previous dealings with the Red King were any example.

"A very wise choice." The faerie studied her for a moment and seemed content with her cowed response, but his next words shot a harbinger of dread through her like a poisoned arrow from an archer's long bow. "I'd also think twice about trying to escape once we cross into the Barrens. You'd make a satisfying meal for many of its inhabitants, and I don't know that I'd be obliged to intervene."

With that final barb, he dropped her arm and dismissed her altogether. Scanning the area, he made a circle in the air with a finger. "Let's move out."

By Alyssa's calculations, they walked for forty-five minutes or so to get to the eastern border. With each step closer to the boundary, her anxiety increased tenfold until she was in near panic mode by the time they'd reached the soaring pinnacles of the wards. Why they hadn't just faded up to the barrier and walked across, she couldn't fathom, but she had a feeling the faerie—in making her walk—was intent on inspiring the hopelessness and terror she was now experiencing. She swore to herself that she wouldn't show her fear, so she swallowed hard and worked to bury her panic.

"Well, here we are, pet. Beyond this point, the Barrens await."

She kept her face emotionless as she turned to him. "You know, you don't frighten me, faerie."

"No?" He grinned and leaned down to look into her eyes. "I think I do," he murmured. "For your eyes tell a different tale."

She shoved him back and smirked. "I tangled with a mountain troll during my escape from the Red Palace all those months ago and lived to talk about it. Like I said, you don't scare me."

Though she'd implied that she'd fought the troll on her own, leaving out the part where Niall had saved her, she enjoyed watching the grin fade from the warrior's face.

"You? Fought a mountain troll?" He narrowed his eyes at her and disbelief was heavy in his tone. "And where would this impressive and monumental event have taken place?"

"We were attacked at the base of the mountains just as we crossed into the northwestern end of Rosewood Forest. Poor thing was sent scurrying back up the mountain like his life depended on it." She smiled sweetly. "Which it did, I might add."

The faerie snorted. "We?"

"Yes. Me and a pixie friend of mine. We made quite a team." Where there was skepticism on his face, she could tell he wasn't quite certain what to make of her story.

"I see." He straightened to his full height then and smiled back at her. "Well then, since you're brave enough to fight a mountain troll, I suppose the Barrens won't hold much worry for you, right?" He turned to lead them across the border but just as quickly stopped and slapped a hand to his forehead. "Now, where are my manners?" Turning back to her, he gave her a slight bow and swept his arm toward the Barrens. "Please. Ladies first."

He was obviously calling her bluff, and when she made no move, he raised his eyebrows. "No?"

Alyssa tilted her head and made a show of studying him. "Now, why in the world would you trust me to lead? In the first place, I have no idea where we're going. And in the second place, even if I did, would you expect me to take you where you wish to go?" She leaned in close and continued in a loud whisper that the others could surely hear. "Doesn't seem like a very sound plan to me and really does call into question your judgment ... and in front of your men, no less."

She felt her spirits rise when the amused look disappeared from his face.

"I was, of course, joking. I'll be taking point. But I'd stay close and keep an eye on the terrain if I were you. It would be such a shame for you to fall and hurt yourself. Predators in this region can smell even the slightest injury for miles." He smirked at her before turning and setting off across the border.

Rolling her eyes at his receding back and silently cursing him, Alyssa swallowed back her fear and followed him into the Barrens with the other warriors bringing up the rear. But once they'd cleared the tree line, she did as he'd suggested and scoped out the terrain. Better safe, than sorry, she thought.

And what a desolate landscape it was. Uneven and rugged, it seemed to consist of nothing but hardened clay and scrub brush for the first mile. Massive rock cliffs and steep mesas rose skyward in the distance and looked as unforgiving as any alien environment she'd ever seen. Boulders the size of small cars framed the path they were taking as it began to wind and climb in elevation, and Alyssa was grateful for the sturdy hiking boots she'd worn when she and Isabella had left New York. However, what worried her most was that the sun was now riding low in the sky and would be setting within three or four hours.

"So, why is it that we're walking instead of fading to wherever we're going?" she asked, forgetting for the moment that he'd told her to keep her mouth shut for the rest of the journey. "Is this more punishment? Or does the fade restriction extend into the Barrens as well?"

The warrior stopped and looked heavenward for a moment before frowning at her over his shoulder. "Why do you ask? In a hurry to meet your demise, are you?"

She gave what she hoped was a carefree shrug and glanced around at the harsh locale. "My feet hurt, and I'm tired of walking."

"For the love of the Oracles." Scrubbing his hands over his face, he shook his head. "Fading in and around the Barrens isn't a good idea. As you can see, the terrain here is quite dangerous and unstable, as are the inhabitants who make this forsaken place their home. You wouldn't want to materialize into the middle of a bugger's den or too near an ogre's lair, now, would you? Not to mention how unfortunate it would be to emerge from a fade and find yourself within the proximity of a Red Cap just waiting to slaughter you with his pick axe so he can soak his cap with your blood." He grinned at her and scratched his jaw. "But then, I suppose since you've tussled with a mountain troll, those kinds of dangers wouldn't worry you much."

It was obvious that his intention was to terrorize her with his imagery, but Violet, the pixie who'd helped her escape from the Red Palace, had told her all about some of the dangers he was talking about. She was determined not to let him get to her, so she repeated back what Violet had told her.

"Ogres are slow-witted and can be outmaneuvered, and buggers can be bargained with or bribed. Red Caps or dunters are a nasty bunch, true, but rare these days, from what I hear. In any case, have it your way. You've made your point." Feigning disinterest, Alyssa yawned. "So, how much farther is it to this hideout of Aramond's? The sun is starting to set and it's going to be dark soon. With the dangers this place presents, I can't imagine it would be healthy to be traipsing around after dark."

The warrior's surprise at her recitation was evident, and he threw back his head and roared with laughter. "No, no. You're quite right. That would be very foolish of us, indeed, but we haven't got far to go now. We'll be there within the hour. And then the evils of the Barrens will be the least of your worries."

"Fine. Whatever. At least hold up a minute so I can get a drink of water." She removed her backpack, but he was on her before she could even open the flap.

Snatching the pack away from her, he rummaged around inside, pulling out a bottle of water.

Folding her arms, Alyssa glared at him. "Satisfied? Did you think I had some weapon to spring on you or something? Don't you think I would've sprung it by now?"

He literally hurled the bag back at her, bottle and all. "Make it quick then. I'm out of patience with your incessant whining."

Setting the pack on the ground, she made a show of opening the bottle and taking a good long drink. When the warrior briefly looked away, she felt around inside the bag as inconspicuously as possible until her fingers found what she was looking for. Then she dropped the object she'd taken from the pack at her feet.

"Come on, come on. What's taking so long?" he growled as he swung back her way.

"Okay, okay. I'm done. Geez, take a pill and chill out," she said as she replaced the bottle in her bag and stood.

He stepped right into her bubble then and sneered, "Do not anger me. We are close to our destination, but do not make the mistake to think I won't *tenderize* you a bit before we get there. Are we clear?"

When she just glared up at him, he turned on his heel and continued on. She reluctantly followed but not before sticking out her tongue at his receding back. It was a childish gesture, but it made her feel better, if only for the moment. She could only hope that if Niall came looking for her, he would find the bread crumb she'd left and recognize it for what it was.

Thirty minutes later, the group entered a chasm between two buttes separated by a deep river. A rickety-looking rope suspension bridge spanned the gap and hung far too low over the water for Alyssa's comfort. It wasn't that she was afraid of falling in or that she couldn't swim, but her mind balked at whatever terrors might live beneath the inky waters.

As if reading her thoughts, the warrior turned and narrowed his eyes at her, giving warning. "Mind you, have a care as we cross this bridge. Kelpies are known to inhabit this river. Though a dangerous exercise, we succeeded in capturing one from this very stretch of water not a month ago."

"What is a kelpie? And why is it a dangerous exercise to catch one?"

"Kelpies are shape-shifting spirits that, in their natural form, appear as magnificent water horses. They are quite striking to look upon, and their siren song can be hypnotic and irresistible. They've been known to seduce mortals and immortals alike, whisking their prey down into the depths where they feast upon them."

Alyssa made a disgusted face. "Thank you. What a lovely story," she said with a heaping of sarcasm. "So, how did you manage to capture this kelpie of yours and for what purpose?"

"Kelpies are very strong and are capable of carrying heavy loads. They usually wear a magickal silver necklace or halter that once removed, can give one command over the creature. If you come across a kelpie without tack, as with the one we acquired, the creature can be captured by use of a halter emblazoned with a cross ... if you can get close enough without notice, that is."

The faerie paused and gave a loud whistle. On what looked like some sort of an animal trail that wove its way along the cliff on the other side of the river, a number of armed guards stepped out of several recessed openings in the rock face.

"Anyway, we will have to put the kelpie down once we're done with it, as they have many powers. Like flight, conjuring storms, and granting wishes ... or conversely, cursing those who treat them poorly."

Alyssa nodded sagely. "Mmm, yes, it would be a terrible shame for you to be cursed."

The warrior laughed out loud and signaled to the soldiers on the other side of the river. "Right this way, descendant of Alice. The king awaits your arrival."

Stealing herself and swallowing back her fear, Alyssa followed him as they began to cross the wide expanse of water. The rope bridge groaned and creaked with the weight of the group, and she couldn't help searching the dark, still water for movement as they crossed the low point where the waterline was only three or four feet beneath the bridge.

Breathing a sigh of relief when they made it to the other side without incident, she catalogued the surrounding area as they ascended the trail. She would need to keep her wits about her. As much as she'd like to, she couldn't count on a rescue anytime soon. In the meantime, she may have to save herself or as least find her own way out of this immediate mess until Niall could come for her.

At a certain point on the trail, they entered one of the dark openings in the rock face. Inside, faerie lights lit the way along the shadowy passageway, and it took a moment for her vision to adjust. She stumbled and nearly jumped out of her skin when the warrior behind her clamped a hand onto her shoulder, propelling her forward.

The tunnel meandered along as they moved deeper into the bowels of the mesa before opening up onto a large circular room of sorts where another ten warriors stood guard. Like the center of a spoked wheel, a number of other passages led off into the darkness in different directions, and the lead faerie took her arm, steering her into the center right passageway. After more twists and turns, this tunnel opened up into yet another, more cavernous chamber where additional fae soldiers gathered around the perimeter in groups.

And there at the far end of the chamber, lounging on a crude throne made of rough stone ... was the Red King.

As they advanced toward the dais, Alyssa's pulse began to race faster with each step, and the closer they got to him, she was increasingly stunned by his disheveled appearance. His once pristine royal cloak was now dirty and torn, his hair and beard scraggly and unkempt. But it was the fevered gleam in his eyes that struck terror into her heart. If he'd been riding the crazy train when they'd last met, it was obvious from where she stood now that he'd reached his destination.

"Ah, Alice," he called in a jovial tone as they approached. "I've been waiting for you, little girl. We have unfinished business, you and I, don't you think?"

WELL, THIS WAS A DISTURBING DEVELOPMENT, MINERVA, the Witch of the Eastern Glade thought as she watched the warrior drag Alyssa Montague into the Red King's makeshift throne room. Though trying to hide her feelings, the child looked terrified. As well she should be, for Aramond had definitely slipped across the threshold into insanity during his months of concealment in the Barrens.

Minerva's runes had indicated that Aramond was alive and in hiding, but they'd been scant on details. When she'd followed the hunting party after their attack on Tisharu and her men, she had no idea where they were going. It had been nightfall once they'd crossed into the Barrens, and she'd glamoured herself as a non-descript warrior to blend in with the group. She was certain the hunting party would lead her to Aramond, and by association, Yulis, the king's sorcerer. She and Yulis had unfinished business, as well. Business she'd intended to conclude once she'd found him.

But the presence of the descendant confounded Minerva's original plan. As Witch of the Eastern Glade, she was the most powerful sorceress in the realm, so had no fear for her own safety. But with the descendant here she would need a new plan to get them both out of the Barrens unscathed.

But how or what that plan would be, Minerva had no idea just yet. She would need some time to think. And she was afraid time was a commodity they had very little of.

Twelve

～～

Niall, along with Alexi, Finvar, the High Lord of the Winter Court, and a small group of both fae and elven warriors made quick work of fading to the border between Wysteria and the dreaded Barrens at the far side of the Eastern Glade. Finvar had been reluctant to bring his warriors and cross into the dangerous Eastern Barrens to search for Alyssa with so little to go on. But once Niall had shown him the tracking amulet—the other half of which he'd given to Alyssa before the attack—and the strong signal it was producing, Finvar reluctantly agreed.

Of their search party, only Niall and Finvar had spent any time in the Barrens long ago during the Great War. Having seen the horrors that inhabited the ghastly place with their own eyes, both were well aware of its peril, which made Niall even more grateful that Finvar would step up in this way. However, even with the tracking signal, neither was excited about where they were going or had confidence in what they would find.

"How's that signal holding up, Niall?" Finvar asked as they crossed through the security wards into the treacherous territory beyond. The High Lord's bushy white eyebrows drew together over his ice-blue eyes. "We have precious little daylight left, and I for one do not relish the idea of spending much time in the Barrens after darkness falls."

"Nor do I, Fin," Niall replied, keeping a close eye on the amulet and their surroundings. "We both know its terrors quite well. I've made a point of steering clear of this monstrous place in the years since the Great War and have only ventured this way when absolutely necessary. Nothing good resides here. But though the amulet's signal is not as strong as it was when we left the White Palace, it's still clear to follow. Looks to be pointing maybe fifteen miles or so to the southeast."

"Man, that's a bit farther than I'd hoped," Alexi put in.

Niall nodded. "Unfortunately, they've had about an hour and a half head start on us."

Giving the sun's location a quick measure, Alexi shook his head. "Without the option to fade, it'll be dangerously close if not dark by the time we clock fifteen miles on foot, even at a good clip. We should've brought horses."

"Yes, well, too late for that now." Niall slid his glance to the Field Marshal. "Fading into the Barrens would indeed be perilous. Therefore, we need to find and retrieve the descendant, and then fade *out* as soon as possible. I refuse to leave Alyssa to the fates and allow the trail to go cold simply because it's inconvenient or hazardous."

"Okay, that's not what I meant, and you know it. Look, Niall, I want to find Alyssa and get her back to the palace as much as you do, and I get that you feel like her being taken was your fault, but it wasn't. You couldn't have known about an ambush."

Niall stopped and turned to Alexi with a stony look. His anger at the situation seeped out along with his words. "While it's true I feel that I should have seen the attack coming, been more prepared, the only one I blame for Alyssa's kidnapping and this colossal mess we're now facing is your cousin."

"Valian?" Alexi's mouth dropped open. "For the love of the Oracles, Niall, you can't seriously blame Val for this."

"Can't I?"

"Hell, no! I mean, why would you? For what reason?"

"*What reason?*" Niall clenched his jaw as he worked to tamp down his fury. "Since my rationale is a bit vague for you, let's start with a question, shall we? Is Valian Winchester still Chancellor of this realm?"

"Well, yes. You know that he is, but—"

"And was he not responsible for the descendant's safety, as well as the security of the Scepter of Fire?"

Alexi sighed. "Of course, but the scepter is being retrieved even as we speak, and Val wasn't even present when Alyssa was taken."

"True. But had he taken the precautions in the New York realm beforehand and made clear to the descendant and her friend what was happening here, they would never have come to this realm in the first place. Though the more I ponder the subject, the more doubtful I become that the two would have been much safer there with Valian here so much of the time."

"Come on. You don't know that. And besides, just because Valian was here doesn't mean that Alyssa and Isabella weren't being carefully watched over and protected in New York."

Niall looked out across the desolate landscape and thought about Alyssa being held here somewhere, of what she may have to endure before all was said and done ... and he had to swallow back another wave of anger.

"Is that so?" he asked in a dangerously quiet tone. "Then kindly explain to *me* exactly how is it that they traveled from the New York realm through the old portal in the great park without anyone being the wiser?"

The Field Marshal had the good grace to look uncomfortable before clearing his throat. "That matter is being addressed."

"Mmm, being addressed ... Yes, so very good to know, Alexi. Then I guess it was one of my better notions to have sent a few of my own men into the New York realm to keep an eye on them as well, wouldn't you say?"

"Wait, you did what?"

"Had it not been for Kassair and his men, Alyssa may never have made it to the Twilight Court, and the Oracles only know what would have happened to her then. She may well have been taken before we even learned that she was in this realm."

Alexi blew out a breath. "Okay. Okay. I get your point, and you're right. Sending your men was fortunate, I'll give you that. But you can't blame everything on Valian. Look, I know you two have had your issues in the past—and the thing with Tisharu ended poorly—but most of that is ancient history, right?"

He put up a hand at the granite look Niall sent him, and then went on in a quiet tone. "Come on, Niall, I know you and Val used to be good friends. I mean, you fought together in the Great War, for crying out loud. He would never do anything to harm Alyssa, or put either of them at risk. Surely you know that."

"Valian and I used to be ... comrades once upon a time, that is true. And we've had our *issues*, as you put it. This is also true." Niall contemplated the situation for a moment and then sighed, scanning the horizon once more. "You know, there are many things that perhaps I would pardon, that I might overlook for friendship's sake." He turned then and skewered the Field Marshal with another steely gaze. "But hear me now, Alexi. Should any harm come to Alyssa Montague over this episode, should we be unable to rescue her without cost, I'm afraid that it may be outside of my capacity to forgive. And there will be consequences for that, I assure you."

Without another word, Niall turned away and pushed on, leaving the rest of the party to follow in uneasy silence.

They continued to follow the amulet's signal and within the first hour Alexi's elven trackers also picked up signs of recent travel. But after following those signs for a couple more miles, the hard clay terrain became increasingly rocky and the path harder to follow. Another hour still, and their route began to narrow and climb toward the tall mesas and immense rock outcroppings. A handful of fae scouts were sent ahead in the direction indicated by the amulet's earlier signal in hopes of recovering the scent.

But as the afternoon began to decline, Niall kept a concerned eye on the sun. It seemed to sink closer and closer to the horizon at an ever-increasing pace. They were running out of daylight quickly with maybe two hours until sunset and another five or six miles to go to reach the spot the amulet had originally indicated. He knew if they didn't find a tangible clue of Alyssa's whereabouts soon, they would be forced to turn back.

And *that* he would not do until the last possible moment.

However, adding to Niall's apprehension, the amulet's signal began to falter. As they entered a ravine with high cliff walls to either side, the signal became intermittent at best within a matter of minutes.

Finvar frowned. "As much as I hate to say it, Niall, if the amulet is no longer viable, continuing on would be unwise. I think we should turn back as soon as our fae trackers return."

Niall silently weighed their options. Finvar was correct. It would be folly to continue on without a beacon to guide them. Another concern plaguing him was that they'd been lucky so far, had traveled well into the depths of the Barrens but had yet to run across any of its dreaded inhabitants. Having spent more time than he liked in this terrible place, Niall knew that would not last. They would need to be all the more vigilant from here on, especially the closer to nightfall they got.

Unfortunately, as if only thinking about the perils of this region conjured it, a thundering roar came from the cliffs somewhere to their left. They all drew swords and went on alert, forming a protective circle and scanning their surroundings for possible attack.

"Alrighty then," Alexi murmured into the following silence, and Niall could clearly read the sudden concern in the Field Marshal's eyes. "So, what do you think that belongs to? Desert trolls maybe?"

Niall shook his head. "Desert trolls make their dens in high caves, true enough. But they normally only come out to hunt after sunset in the cool of the evening." He narrowed his eyes as an answering roar came from a plateau to their right. "They're also solitary creatures. They don't hunt together and don't play well with others."

"Uh-huh. So, perhaps highland ogres?"

"Doubtful. While ogres have been known to hunt in pairs, they don't roar quite like that. Theirs is more of a bellow, and besides, that sounded much larger."

"*Larger* than a highland ogre? Seriously?"

"I'm thinking Wolvataurs," Finvar added quietly, his eyes never leaving the cliffs above.

Niall could almost feel the apprehension pouring from the High Lord. He nodded. "Yes. Unfortunately, I concur."

"Uh, wait. What?" Alexi asked. "I thought Wolvataurs were some kind of myth, a vicious man-wolf hybrid. Just an image my father used to scare us kids into behaving when we were young."

"Regrettably, they're quite real," Niall replied. "They look like an enormous wolf but walk upright similar to a man and average between six to twelve feet tall. They have razor-sharp claws on hands and feet, and can also leap close to six feet into the air from a standing position. They are rather formidable."

"Well, that's terrifying to learn," Alexi muttered.

"Don't forget the powerful jaws and enormous teeth, Niall," Finvar added. "During the Great War my unit was attacked by a small pack of them. I watched one literally bite off the head of a six-foot warrior with ease not twenty-five yards from where I stood."

Alexi put up a finger. "No-no ... that's not *any* kind of detail I need to hear right now, thank you very much. For fuck sake, Fin. What is *wrong* with you?"

Finvar shrugged. "Not to worry, boy-o. Like Red Caps, Wolvataurs are fairly rare these days. I've only seen them here in the Barrens and in the Wasteland to the north, and that was many, many years ago. And I may be wrong. This may not involve that species at all."

Alexi shook his head, and even given the situation, Niall struggled not to laugh at the look on his face. "Just stop talking, would you? You're not making me feel any better."

When yet another terrifying growl filled the air, Niall perused the cliffs on both sides. "Sound can travel for miles in these canyons, so they could be quite a ways from here or just around the next bend. It's difficult to say, but we need to get out of this ravine, none-theless."

"What about the scouts?" Alexi asked. "We just can't leave them."

"No, and we won't. But we definitely need to move to higher ground up ahead and see if we can get a better vantage point. Hope-fully they'll be back with more to go on soon, and we can find Alyssa and get the hell out of the Barrens."

"And while we're at it, avoiding any entanglements with possible Wolvataurs would be great," Alexi replied with a grin.

"Agreed. We have a clear shot, so let's fade up to the plateau there on the right and get a better view of the area." Niall pointed to a nearby mesa. "And everyone stay vigilant. We have no way of knowing exactly where those roars came from or how close whatever made them may be."

Quickly and carefully, the entire group faded, and each made it to the mesa's plateau safely. From there, Niall again scanned the horizon. In the distance, he could just make out movement, and was pleased to recognize the fae scouts fading from one clear spot to another on their way back to the group's location. When they got close enough, they spotted the plateau where the rest of the group now stood, and they faded up to meet them.

"Did you find anything of consequence?" Finvar asked one of the scouts. "Anything that might indicate where the descendant has been taken?"

"Aye, my Lord." The faerie nodded. "We picked up the trail again a few miles out and followed it several more to a chasm between two buttes separated by a river. There was a rope bridge spanning the water, so we concealed ourselves and watched and waited. They are well hidden, but there were fae warriors guarding what looked to be openings along the cliff face on the other side of the river."

"Good work," Finvar said with a nod. "Did you catch sight of the descendant?"

"No, but there is something else." He turned to Niall with a hesitant look. "We almost missed it because it blended so well with the rocky clay surface of the trail. Do you recognize this, High Lord?" The warrior dropped the item he'd found into Niall's outstretched hand.

"What is it, Niall?" Finvar asked.

Just when he'd begun to lose confidence that they would find any clues to Alyssa's location, he looked down at the object the scout had brought, and a sliver of hope began to take hold. Turning to Finvar, a smile broke out on his face as he stared down at the small egg-shaped bit of polished glass in his palm. The russet and gold swirls woven throughout glinted in the waning light as the sun began its slide over the horizon. Turning the piece of blown glass over, he read aloud the word etched there. "Faith."

Finvar frowned. "I beg your pardon?"

Holding up the object for all to read, Niall murmured, "Smart girl, our Alyssa Montague."

"So, this belongs to Alyssa?" Alexi asked. "You're sure?"

Niall nodded. "Yes, Alexi. I held this very bit of polished glass in my hand earlier this afternoon. She brought it with her from New York for luck. And it seems, she's found a way to leave it for us to find—which is lucky, indeed."

"Okay, then," the Field Marshal said with a nod. "So, what's the next move? The sun's just gone down, so whatever we're gonna do, we need to do it now."

Niall looked around at the anxious faces staring back at him. His instinct, of course, was to go after Alyssa. Every fiber of his being railed against leaving her in this heinous place for one more minute, but he'd be no good to her alone, and he couldn't ask the others to risk their lives by following him into jeopardy. He wouldn't think twice about putting himself into harm's way here in the Barrens, but he would never place others there as well.

Turning back to Finvar's scout, Niall placed a hand on the faerie's shoulder. "I do not wish to place you in danger, but are you willing and up to taking me to this spot? Do you know the way back well enough to fade with me there?"

The scout nodded immediately. "I do, High Lord, yes. I'll take you there. Absolutely."

"Niall, you can't be serious," Alexi blurted. "It's going to be dark very soon. And fading from down in that ravine to the top of this mesa is one thing, but anything more than that is insane in the Barrens, and you know it."

Finvar ran a hand over his snow-white beard and frowned. "I tend to agree with the Field Marshal, old friend. This is not an advisable plan."

"I just want to see the area with my own eyes. Nothing more. In and out quickly. I want to be clear on the location so that when we return, I will know exactly where we're going and can fade in small bursts to save travel time."

Looking back and forth between Niall and the scout, Finvar took his time, but finally nodded. "Alright. But if you both go, I go as well."

"This is crazy," Alexi muttered. "But I suppose I'll need to go with you idiots, if only to say 'I told you so' when shit goes sideways."

Niall shook his head. "You two don't need to come with us. You can wait here or head back to the border. We won't be long, that I can promise you. I don't want to be here after darkness falls and don't intend to spend a minute more than needed to accomplish this task."

Alexi grimaced. "Then we better get going, because I want to be back across the border by nightfall. You get me?" Giving his elven trackers a nod, he gave them their orders to return to the palace.

Finvar turned to the other warriors. "You all head back to your respective courts. We'll return before dark." Then he swung back to Niall. "Let's go before I change my mind."

"Then the Oracles protect us," Niall murmured.

"Oracles protect us!" each responded.

And with that, the group all faded from the plateau in different directions.

Thirteen

Áine couldn't help but smile as she extended her arms into the air to stretch the kinks out of her lower back after the long and stressful hours she'd been working. She'd finally broken through and found the last piece of the poison puzzle she'd been missing—and in the nick of time. The last twelve hours or so had been quite tense when Tisharu's temperature had spiked again, and the serum Áine had concocted to keep the faerie queen's fever under control had become less and less effective.

Just when she'd started to think that her efforts were a losing battle, the last round of tests had ultimately made all the difference. Unfortunately, with Tisharu's condition in such a critical state, they'd had no time for a trial run or probability assessments of any kind. And over the healer's vehement objections, Áine had crossed her fingers and toes and administered a full dose on the spot. When the antidote had begun to work almost immediately, then and only then had she finally allowed herself to breathe a cautious sigh of relief.

So far, Tisharu hadn't regained consciousness, and she wasn't completely out of the woods, but after that first hour her fever had broken and within another two her bloodwork had already shown a marked improvement. Though it may take a few weeks, Áine was now certain the faerie queen would ultimately make a complete and full recovery.

After checking Tisharu's vitals one last time, Áine had been prepared to leave her in the healer's care and search out Valian when a rusty voice stopped her in her tracks as she headed for the door.

"Hello?"

Spinning toward the voice, Áine hurried to the bed where Tisharu lay pallid and weak but with eyes wide open.

"Oh, my gosh! Tisharu. You're awake. I didn't expect you to regain consciousness for perhaps another twenty-four hours."

The faerie queen reached out a trembling hand, and Áine took it immediately, giving it a squeeze. "You gave us quite a scare, dear Queen."

"Áine Ó Mordha, is that you, child? You're all grown up," Tisharu murmured weakly with a half-smile.

Filled with a surge of joy, Áine laughed out loud. "It's true. I am indeed."

"But what brings you to my Twilight Court, sweet girl?" Tisharu asked, and then struggled to clear her throat. "I've not seen your face in too many years to count."

Áine patted the hand she held. "We're not at court, Tisharu. You've been gravely ill and are in the medical ward at the White Palace."

Tisharu's brows drew together, and Áine could almost see the wheels turning in her head as the faerie queen sought to puzzle out what had happened to her. She also saw the moment when Tisharu put it all together.

"Ah ...the ambush," she finally whispered.

Áine nodded and pulled a chair up close to the bed. "Yes. The arrow you were grazed with was poisoned with a terrifying concoction. We had a very difficult time finding the right formula for an antidote and only just broke through in the early hours this morning."

"We?" The queen gave her a shrewd look. "So, I guess I should be glad that your years of training had its uses."

At Áine's astonished look, Tisharu smiled. "Don't look so surprised, child. I have checked in on you periodically over the years

... just to make certain you were well." She cleared her throat again. "I should like some water, please. My throat is very dry."

"Of course!" Áine poured a half cup from the pitcher on the bedside table. "Here, let me help you."

Assisting the queen to raise her head, Áine watched as Tisharu fairly guzzled the entire contents. Laying back into the pillows, she closed her eyes and took a deep breath before letting it out slowly. "I feel as if I've been at war, though I don't recall feeling this drained after the last battle with the Red King. I ache all over."

"In a way, you have been at war. At least your body has been battling the worst poison I think I've ever seen. That is, outside of a textbook or spell book. How much of it do you remember?"

"Of the ambush, you mean?" At Áine's nod, she sighed. "It's all still a bit hazy, but I do recall the attack and the pain in my arm as Raef and I faded from Willow Glen Wood. I remember not thinking much of it at first. I've had worse injuries too numerous to count in battle, but I soon realized that this was much different."

Tisharu motioned for more water, and Áine complied. She took a few sips and then laid back, the task leaving her again weak and breathless. After a few moments, she continued. "The last thing I clearly remember was stepping out into the Grand Hall at court and feeling like the whole of it was turning on a spit ... and then falling in what felt like slow motion. Raef's voice was echoing in my ears as he kept calling my name. Then darkness."

"Do you remember seeing my godmother? Raef told Valian that she was there."

"Ach! She was—the unpleasant, old crone." Tisharu closed her eyes briefly and a smile touched her lips. "I think she'd seen the attack in her runes and came to warn us, but you know how she likes to prevaricate and verbally poke around a bit with a sharp stick. By the time she got to the cursed point, the ambush was upon us." When she opened her eyes, Áine saw grief and anger arise. "We'd had many such assignations with informants in recent months and had gotten complacent. *I'd* gotten complacent. We were outnumbered and unprepared. I yelled for my fae warriors to fade but some were cut down before they could do so."

"I'm so sorry for your loss, Tisharu." Áine took the queen's hand again and asked the question on her mind, though dreading the possible answer. "And Godmother? What of her?"

"Do not look so worried, young one. Minerva was spinning up a lightning maelstrom in the center of the glen—swatting the rogue warriors down like insignificant flies—when Raef and I faded." Respect and admiration colored the queen's word, and her eyes sparkled with it. "I must say, she was quite magnificent ... for an old hag."

"So, you don't know her fate?"

Tisharu frowned. "Have you not spoken with her?"

Áine shook her head, and she couldn't help the tears that filled her eyes. "She hasn't been seen since that night. I went to her cabin and searched her runes. You're correct in thinking that she saw the ambush and came to warn you, but the rest was quite vague. I think she meant to follow the rogue warriors into the Barrens, and she was fixated on locating Yulis. I'm so very worried for her."

"Well, don't be." The queen squeezed Áine's hand and gave her quite a fierce look for someone just coming out of a poison-induced coma. "Do not forget of whom you speak. Old Minerva is the most feared and powerful sorceress this realm has ever known. Her magicks have no equal." Tisharu gave an exhausted sigh then and closed her eyes again. "If she followed them into the Barrens, I almost feel sorry for them all—including Yulis—as well as any other creatures in her path. Old hag ..."

Áine laughed out loud at that and swiped at her eyes, feeling the weight of her concern lighten just a bit. Checking the queen's vital signs, Áine nodded with satisfaction. "Are you hungry? I could get you some broth, something light to sooth your stomach?"

Tisharu cracked an eye in her direction. "What kind of broth?"

Áine chuckled. "Oh, just something tasty to warm you and fill the void, fortify your depleted system. After that, you should rest again. You've been through quite an ordeal."

"Well, well. What is this?" Gray asked as he entered the ward followed by Valian and Isabella. "The Queen of the Twilight Court awake after giving us all a scare?" He turned to Valian. "I told you she was virtually indestructible."

"Yes. You are most amusing, young prince," Tisharu groused as the three came closer. But Áine noted that her eyes sought out Valian as she continued. "As Queen of the Twilight Court, I am, for the most part, indestructible."

Gray chuckled. "How are you feeling?"

Tisharu gave the prince a bland look. "As you've had your own experience with a similar poison, I suspect you know exactly how I'm feeling at the moment."

"Hmm, yes, I probably do. Like you've been waging a battle with unseen adversaries for weeks? Exhausted? Sore all over? That about it?"

"See? I knew you would understand. However, I am also fortunate to have competent, caring friends and loved ones to come to my aid in my time of need."

"That you do, Tisharu," Gray agreed, then turned to Áine with a smile. "And we were *very* fortunate to have Áine show up when she did. Looks like she turned the tide."

"Ha! By the skin of my teeth, but I'll take it," she replied and then gestured to Valian. "Are you two just back from New York?"

"We got back a while ago, but wanted to stop in and give Queen Beatrice an update," Valian replied.

Gray nodded. "I'm sure mother will be up shortly. She's a bit worried. Fin, Alexi, and Niall were supposed to be back from the Barrens before dark, hopefully with Alyssa in tow, but they have yet to arrive. She's awaiting their return in the Grand Salon, afraid something's gone wrong."

"Wait, they're not back yet?" Áine frowned. "That's disturbing."

"Mmm, yes," Valian murmured. "Going into the Barrens during daylight hours is dicey enough, but I've been there after dark. It's something to be avoided at all costs."

"Yeah. I would imagine so. I haven't been there myself, and I'm just fine with that," Áine said with a shiver. "I've heard the horror stories of the horrible things that live there, which is why I've been so worried about Godmother. Hopefully, the group will return soon unharmed."

"That is my prayer as well, and I include Minerva in that hope,"

Gray said, then chuckled. "Since she is the most powerful sorcerous in the realm, I'm thinking she can hold her own with just about anything she might come across in the Barrens."

Áine nodded and glanced at Tisharu. "Yes, I've heard that sentiment recently."

As the healer on duty came into the room, she motioned him over. "Would you ring for Gryphon and have him bring up some broth for Queen Tisharu."

The healer swung toward the queen with a surprised look. "Oh my! She's awake. Yes, of course. I'll do it right away."

"Thanks." She watched him hurry away and then caught Gray smirking at her. "What?" she asked.

"Oh, nothing. Just admiring how you've taken charge of the ward."

Rolling her eyes, Áine waved a hand in the air. "Yeah, yeah. Trust me, I have no problem turning it all back over to them now that Tisharu's on her way to recovery."

The faerie queen spoke up then in response. "Well, I for one would feel much better about it if you would hold onto that control for just a bit longer."

"I'm with you on that, Tisharu." Gray laughed.

Áine nodded. "Don't worry. I'll hang out until you're up and about. I want to make sure you're completely out of the woods where this poison is concerned."

"Amen," Valian spoke up quietly.

Áine watched a range of emotions flood his countenance, watched his face as Tisharu reached out a hand to him. He turned to Isabella briefly—who nodded and ran a hand over his shoulder—before crossing and taking the seat Áine had vacated.

"*Mo chroí*," Tisharu murmured as he took her hand. "I had a dream that I heard you speaking softly to me, telling me to be a warrior, but I couldn't find my way to you. Very silly, isn't it?"

"Not at all, as I did say those words to you. It's a relief to hear your voice, see you awake and clear-eyed, *A ghrá geal*. You had us all terribly worried."

Being a halfling, one of Áine's fae gifts was reading emotions in others. She wasn't even sure Valian realized the true depth of his feelings where Tisharu was concerned, but you didn't need a gift to read them. They were clearly on display for all to see. However, what she found more interesting was not Valian's emotions, which Áine had long suspected, but Isabella's.

Humans were the easiest to read, and Isabella was no exception. Yet in scanning the woman, what Áine found was surprising. There was the anticipated bit of jealousy for Tisharu but it was a very shallow layer. Deeper were the feelings of envy, of longing. When Isabella glanced over and their eyes met, Áine could also feel the woman's regret ... and a profound sadness. Still, what was absent in her emotional aura was also of interest. Oh, Isabella cared deeply for Valian—that was plain to see and feel. But what Áine found quite unexpected was the understanding that went along with those other emotions, for what she now realized she would never have with Valian Winchester, and Áine's heart went out to her.

However, before Áine could ponder the revelation further, there was a commotion in the hallway and the tardy Barrens search party stumbled into the room. If Áine was relieved to see them, her relief was short-lived as it was obvious there had been trouble, and they were all worse for wear because of it.

Finvar was covered in lacerations, blood, and grime, and he was supporting Alexi who was limping badly. Alexi's shirt was also covered in silver elven blood from his left shoulder to his waistband, and with each step, he winced in pain. But what had Áine truly concerned was Niall being half-carried by two of his fae warriors. He too was covered in blood, and his color was not good. Neither was his disposition from what she could tell.

"Ouch! For the love of the Oracles, Fin, take it easy," Alexi cried as Finvar aimed them toward a chair across the aisle from Tisharu's bed.

"Alexi!" Isabella cried and ran to help. "Oh, my gosh, are you alright? What happened?"

"Yes, Alexi. What did you do?" Áine asked.

"*Me?*" Alexi gaped at her as Isabella and Finvar eased him down into the chair. "Why the hell would you think this is *my* fault?" He jabbed a finger across the aisle at Niall, as the warriors carefully helped the High Lord to the bed next to his twin's. "This fiasco was all *his* doing not mine."

"I will remind you that *he* saved your life, you ungrateful squidge," Niall muttered.

Alexi flashed the High Lord a grin. "That's true. Then again, since it was your lame idea in the first place, you were obligated not to get me killed."

As one of the healers helped the Field Marshal remove his armor, Áine studied what she could see of his wounds. "These are pretty deep lacerations along your shoulder, Alexi. What made them?"

Alexi sighed and watched her cut his pant leg open to check out the deep gash on his right calf. "We ran into a pack of Wolvataurs."

"What?" Gray exclaimed with a stunned look. "Seriously? I thought they were a myth."

"I *know*, right?"

"What's a Wolvataur?" Áine asked.

"You really don't want to know."

Valian came over to join the conversation. "So, what exactly happened?"

Alexi turned to him as the healer worked on his shoulder. "The fae scouts located what they thought was a rogue base where Alyssa had possibly been taken. But it was getting close to dark, and I tried to tell the Knave of Hearts over there that it was a bad idea, but he just had to see the rogue stronghold with his own eyes. 'In and out, Alexi. Just a quick look, and then we'll be out of the Barrens before dark'," he mimicked.

"We needed to know where we're going at first light, and you didn't have to come along, so quit your yammering and bellyaching. You're making me nauseous," Niall said, just before his eyes rolled back in his head, and he passed out cold on the bed.

Áine rushed over just as another two elven healers came running. "Help me get this armor off of him. He's lost a lot of blood." They did as she asked and what was revealed gave her pause. Something very sharp and lethal had penetrated his armor, slicing deep claw marks into his flesh along his ribs and upper torso.

"Though he has lost quite a bit of blood, his vital signs are decent," one of the healers said as he started an IV and administered a fae sleeping potion. "Looks like there's something buried in the one of these wounds. We'll need to clean them all thoroughly and close them up, then check for any further infection. It would be best if you could clear the ward and get the others to leave us to it."

"Of course." It was Áine's turn to nod and back away. She was an expert in poisons, but not a surgeon. She most certainly didn't want to get into their way. Turning to Tisharu, she patted the queen's shoulder. "Don't worry, Tisharu. The healers will take good care of Niall."

The faerie queen shook her head. "My twin may be bullheaded and tend to make rash decisions from time to time, but he is strong. I'm certain the healers will give him the best of care."

Áine nodded. "We're going to clear the ward so they can do their work and you can rest once you've had your broth. I'll check in on you later."

As she turned to go, Queen Beatrice entered the ward with a surprised smile as she saw that the search party had returned. Áine thought it interesting that the queen sought out Finvar first.

"Well, here you are," she began as she started toward the High Lord. "I've been anxiously awaiting your return in the salon." But her smile faded quickly, to be replaced by alarm when she realized the High Lord was covered in blood. "Finvar? What's happened? Was there another attack?"

The High Lord took a step toward her then paused when he realized that they had the attention of the others in the room. "Uh ... no, Milady. At least, not the kind of attack that you fear. We were set upon by Wolvataurs before we could leave the Barrens."

"Wolvataurs! But there hasn't been a sighting in years. I thought them all but extinct."

"Evidently they're thriving in the Barrens," Alexi muttered under his breath, and then yelped as the healer addressing his shoulder injury worked to close the worst of the wounds. "Could you maybe be a bit more careful, healer? Or here's a thought. Perhaps you could numb the area up before you go poking around in it."

"Are you alright, Field Marshal?" Queen Beatrice asked, distress evident in her voice. "That shoulder looks painful, and I see that your leg is injured as well."

"They both smart some, Majesty. I'm not gonna lie, but I'll be fine. Both injuries probably look worse than they are. My concern right now is for Niall." He nodded to the bed where the other two healers were working on the High Lord. "He saved my life but took the full brunt of the assault. He's pretty messed up."

"Oh, dear. Well, our elven healers are the best in the realm. I will send up a prayer to the Oracles that he is recovered soon."

"Yes," Gray agreed. "To have him brought in here in such bad shape just when his twin has only just regained consciousness is unacceptable, so we will all pray that he heals quickly."

As if just remembering Tisharu, Queen Beatrice sought her out. "Oh, it is such good news in the midst of all this chaos that you are on the mend, Queen Tisharu. You gave us quite a scare. I have no doubt that both you and Lord Niall will be up and about in no time."

"And to that point," Áine put in before they could get off track again. "I think we should all clear out of the ward and let the healers do their job unencumbered."

"Yes. You're quite right, Áine," Queen Beatrice agreed. She turned to Finvar and spoke quietly. "This could have been much worse. I think it's time that we address a certain matter before it's too late," she murmured for his ears alone.

However, Áine was close enough to catch the gist of it.

Well, here's another curious batch of emotions, she thought as her attempt to scan the queen's aura met with some resistance. There was the obvious relief that Finvar and Alexi were both relatively unharmed, and worry that Niall was more seriously injured, but when the queen glanced at her own son, Áine found the emotions harder to read and mingled with anxiety ... and a touch of fear. Now what was up with that? And why was Queen Beatrice so hard to read? As she was human, it should have been easier.

"You all heard Áine. We need to clear the ward." Turning to Gray, the queen cleared her throat. "Graydon, sweetheart, we need to finish our earlier conversation, and while the healers work, this might be a good time to do that."

Gray looked surprised but nodded. "Of course. Alexi can brief

Val on what they found in the Barrens and then give me the rundown later."

The queen turned to Finvar. "I'd like you to be present as well."

Finvar looked a bit distressed but agreed. "If that is what you wish."

As she followed the group out of the ward, Áine smiled. To quote certain frost pixie twins, again, *curiouser and curiouser*, she thought to herself.

Fourteen

Gray could feel the tension rise as he followed his mother and Finvar down to the Grand Salon on the main floor of the palace. As they entered the room, the queen sat down and gestured for him to do the same. Finvar, however, crossed to the mullioned window—just about as far as he could get from the conversation—and looked like he wanted to be anywhere else but in this room.

Taking a seat on the settee directly across from his mother, Gray looked back and forth between the two and scratched his head. "Okay, what's going on here, Mother?"

With a quick look toward the window where Finvar stood with his back to them, the queen gave him a distracted smile. "I don't know what you mean, sweetheart. I felt we needed to finish our conversation from this morning, that's all. As I've said, it's a discussion we should've had years ago, and we were interrupted this morning before I could get to the heart of the matter."

"Uh-huh." Gray nodded in Finvar's direction. "Fin wasn't part of our conversation this morning, so why exactly is he here now? No offense, Fin."

The High Lord mumbled a 'None taken' without turning from the window.

Queen Beatrice cleared her throat. "Finvar has been ... a part of what I'm about to tell you from the beginning. He should've been here this morning when we started this discussion."

"Alright," Gray answered slowly. Looking back and forth between the two again, he shook his head. "Look, I'm sorry, but I gotta say, I don't have a real good feeling about finishing this 'discussion'. We were talking about my father this morning. You said there was something he'd wanted that you couldn't deny him, and that you hoped for forgiveness, which didn't make a lot of sense then. Now you look like somebody's just died, and you're trying real hard to find a gentle way to tell me. And Fin over there looks like he wants to sink into a hole in the floor and then pull it in after him. Maybe you should just get to that heart of the matter you were talking about."

Beatrice nodded, but still looked distressed. "You're right, of course. It's just that this is a very sensitive situation, Graydon." She looked as if she was going to say something else, but instead sighed and said, "Sweetheart, you know that I would never do anything to hurt you, don't you? That I only have your well-being in mind—always."

"Yeah, now you're starting to worry me, Mother. Just say it already. Please."

The queen put up a hand. "Yes. Alright. As I said, your father wanted something that I desperately needed to give him."

"And Fin helped you attain this something? Is that it?"

There was a slightly distraught sound from Finvar, though he still didn't turn from the window.

"You could say that." Beatrice sighed again. "Graydon, Edward couldn't have children."

Gray didn't know what he'd expected her to tell him, but it was definitely not this. He stared at her for a long moment thinking he must have misunderstood her—yet knowing he hadn't. "I beg your pardon?"

"Darling, you are my great joy, and I love you more than life itself, but when we found out about Edward's ... condition, I tried to make it clear that I loved *him* and that having children didn't matter to me. But he was devastated by the news."

Gray was so stunned by her pronouncement that he couldn't

speak. When he finally remembered to breathe, it was around the lead weight that had suddenly lodged in his chest. "So, you're saying that Edward Drake was not my father."

The queen drew herself up and sent him a stern yet somehow compassionate look. "Sir Edward William Clariage Drake loved you with every fiber of his being and was your father in every way that mattered ... save one."

"Biologically."

"It's true. Edward was not your biological father, which is why you have magick when he did not. You are actually a combination of two very powerful lineages."

It suddenly became stunningly clear why Finvar was in the room and a part of this conversation. He glanced at the High Lord's rigid stance at the window and then back at his mother. "So, let me get this straight. You and Finvar ... hooked up one night for the greater good? And everyone was okay with that?"

Beatrice gasped. "For the love of the Oracles, Graydon! We did nothing of the kind!" She looked as if he'd struck her, and although Finvar kept his back to them, a strangled sound, barely audible, escaped his lips. Glancing in that direction, the queen directed her next terse command to the High Lord. "Finvar, come away from the damned window and join this discussion like an adult, please."

With a deep breath, the High Lord finally turned and did as she asked. Red-faced, he crossed to the settee and took a place next to the queen.

"We did not *hook up*, as you say," the queen continued in a mortified tone. "It was all done with magicks. Minerva handled that, and yes, Edward agreed it was the best way forward. He was incredibly grateful to Finvar for agreeing as well. And to insinuate that it was some sort of sordid affair is insulting to all involved."

Gray felt numb. Everything he knew about his life suddenly seemed in question, but one thing she'd said caught his attention. "Wait. You said two very powerful lineages. There's Finvar's ancestry, obviously, but if both you and Edward Drake were human, what other lineage are you talking about? And why don't I have any of Finvar's features, for that matter?"

Beatrice nodded, and he watched her place a hand over Finvar's.

"I know you've been wondering where your magick comes from for some time now, and it's true that Edward had no magick. And being half human, my magick is very limited so I choose not to use it at all. But the other half of my ancestry is reason that I will live for a very, very long time."

Gray frowned. "Wait— You're not human?"

"I'm *half* human and half Ellurian, which is a very old race of royal Immortals who are closely—"

"Related to an ancient Elven line," Gray finished for her. "Yes, I know who the Ellurian royals were."

"My father was Ellurian."

Gray nodded. It was all starting to make a weird, convoluted kind of sense. "That's the reason elves play such a large part in the kingdom and that they make up the bulk of our military forces."

"Yes. When my mother married Seanchán, he was ruler over several northern Elven conclaves. He was very powerful and a great warrior, and also, as most Ellurians are, an Immortal. But he contracted an unknown and highly unusual plague during a visit to the Wastelands, and even though he was immortal, it ravaged him. In the end, neither the healers nor his immortality could save him. Of course, that was long before my mother split the realm into the two kingdoms. Anyway, since I'm only half Ellurian, I'm not actually immortal, but I will live for centuries ... as will you. You take after that side of the family."

Gray got up and began to pace. It seemed that he'd been deceived all of his life, had important truths hidden from him, yet others obviously knew and were sworn to secrecy. He stopped and pinned his mother with an angry glare. "So, who else knew about this? Valian? Alexi? Your advisors?"

His mother looked pained but met his gaze boldly. "Very few know about your true heritage. Valian was told when Edward was killed in the Great War. He was vehemently against keeping it from you, but I insisted. He was also charged with keeping a close eye on you until I was ready to tell you everything."

"Which, of course, has taken almost a century it seems," he accused bitterly.

The queen got up and came to him then, reaching out a hand.

"You were grieving so for your father, my darling. I thought it best to give you time to find a place for your grief before explaining it all to you."

Gray glared at her. "My da— Edward Drake died in the Great War. I can certainly understand wanting to protect me, to give me a few years to grieve for the only father I'd known, but it's been *decades!*" he hissed at her.

The queen visibly winced. "I know, and I'm so sorry. As I've said, I was weak. I kept putting it off, and the longer I put it off, the harder it became until I finally told myself that it didn't matter. You had your memories of Edward and that was enough."

"But it isn't enough, and it does matter. For the first decade you could say you were protecting me, but after that, you were just making it easy on yourself."

"Now, see here, Graydon. Don't speak to your mother that way," Finvar spoke up.

But Gray pointed a finger at him and shook his head. "Huh-uh. You don't get to chime in on this."

Beatrice cleared her throat and stretched out her hand again. "Graydon, I can only say that I'm sorry. I realize now how unfair this has been to you. I only hope that at some point, you can find it in your heart to forgive my weakness."

His mother stood there with misery written all over her face, yet he couldn't seem to get past his anger and feelings of betrayal. Gray stared at her outstretched hand but made no move to take it. "Who else knows? Alexi?"

The queen shook her head. "No. Alexi doesn't know, nor does anyone else outside of this room other than Valian and Old Minerva."

He glanced over at Finvar. "My magick comes from my fae side?"

"Aye," Finvar replied. "A good portion does. However, being a quarter Ellurian, there is no way of knowing how much of that old power you actually have within you. But you have the normal magicks of my people in abundance. Of that I'm certain. Healing, mending, fading. Yet you are special, Graydon. You have more powerful magicks than I've seen in decades. You've inherited powers from the ancients in my bloodline going back centuries."

Gray frowned. "Okay, healing and mending, I'll go with that, but until Friday night—or should I say early Saturday morning—I'd never been able to fade. Why is that? And you have the power to conjure winter storms, ice and snow. I can't do that either."

"Yet." Finvar grinned for the first time. "You haven't been able to do that yet. However, from what I'm told, you faded right back here to the palace from Minerva's cabin that night on your own. You've not used the abilities you have in any substantial form, and as I said, there are powers within you that haven't even been tapped." The High Lord nodded. "You may not be able to conjure winter storms —again, yet—but you have something else that I've witnessed—an ancient magick from another time and much more lethal."

"What are you talking about?"

Finvar stroked his snowy-white beard as a thoughtful look appeared in his eyes. "You have what is known by my people as the Blood Storm. It's a very rare ancient power. In fact, other than you, I've not seen it used by anyone in close to two centuries."

Blood Storm

Gray's mind flashed back to New Year's when he and Alexi had been attacked by rogue fae warriors on the edge of Tarkington Forest as they transported the Scepter of Fire from the New York realm. He remembered seeing Alexi struck down and bellowing, '*Noooo*', feeling a force burst out of him from somewhere deep inside, and watching every rogue warrior explode into a fine red mist for thirty yards in all directions before he himself had passed out.

Finvar nodded again. "Aye. I see you know what I'm talking about. I watched you use the Blood Storm to save me during the battle with Aramond's armies. And that's just one of the abilities you will find over time."

"Graydon. Please—"

The queen reached out to him again, and Gray watched her dark brown eyes, so like his own, fill with tears. But he found he wasn't quite ready to forgive and forget. "No." Shaking his head, he turned toward the door. "I can't talk to you now. I need to think about this."

With that he hurried from the room without a backward glance and headed for the one place he always went to think—the ramparts.

. . .

GRAY HAD BEEN ON THE BATTLEMENT FOR SOME TIME when he heard her. He could smell the warm, earthy scent of her long before Áine hopped up onto the rampart wall beside him.

"Thought I might find you up here," she said by way of a greeting.

Curious, he glanced over at her. "Hmm. Am I that predictable, then?"

She laughed and shook her head. "I saw you heading for the third level like it was on fire." She looked down at the courtyard lights far below and then out at Cheshire Wood in the distance marked in the darkness by its twinkling faerie lights. Taking a deep breath, she let it out slowly and smiled. "Just smell that night air, Gray. Man, if I lived in the palace, I'd be up here all the time—especially at night."

"I know what you mean. This is where I usually come to think—day or night. But yes, after dark is my favorite time as well."

She smiled at him. "Had some important thinking to do, did you?"

He barked out a laugh devoid of humor. "You might say that."

"Yeah, I couldn't read exactly what you were feeling when I saw you—which would normally be weird because humans are the easiest to read—but I figured they'd finally told you about your fae blood. Hence, the difficulty in reading you."

Gray gaped at her. "For fuck sake! You knew, too? Did *everyone* know but me?"

"Oh, for the love of God. Take a breath and don't be stupid. Halfling here, remember? I've watched enough fae tripping on Faerie Bomb to snap to it when I saw your reaction at Godmother's cabin. Anyway, kinda hard to miss, particularly with the stunned look on Valian's normally stoic face when I explained your condition to him."

"Yeah. Valian. My good friend who's evidently known that Edward Drake wasn't my biological father and about my true lineage for five or six *decades* and has never said a damned word."

Áine gave an exaggerated gasp. "That dirty rat *bastard!* You'd think he was Chancellor and supposed to be loyal to the *queen*, like, until death or something? I mean, what a worthless *tool*."

Gray frowned. "Very funny."

She gave him a sideways glance and tilted her head. "Oh, right, but he *is* Chancellor, so he's *supposed* to be loyal to the queen, right?"

"Certainly, but—"

"Then it wasn't his truth to tell, was it? In the end, it was down to Queen Beatrice."

"Yes, but—"

"And you know that Valian loves you like a brother, so would you have him choose between you and his duty? Betray his queen and tell you a secret that wasn't his to tell? Do you think Valian enjoyed keeping that information from you? Do you think he was secretly chuckling to himself all these years?"

"No, of course not. That's ridiculous." He made a face. "My mother said he argued against keeping it from me from the start."

"Well, there you go. So, blaming Valian is ludicrous and a waste of time." She put up a finger before he could comment. "Now, should the queen have explained everything to you long before this? Perhaps. But neither of us knows what demons she's wrestled with over the decades or the circumstances that had her keeping your ancestry to herself. She'd lost her love in a war, had a kingdom to rule, and a young son to consider. Maybe she had to keep going any way possible. Maybe she was just doing the best she could."

"Come on, Áine, that's not fair and definitely not that simple. She kept this from me for almost a century."

"Yeah, well, life isn't always fair, is it? Trust me, I know all about that. I learned about my biological ... sire—I would never call him a father—when I was eight years old. He was, as it turned out, a malicious asshole who wanted no part of a Halfling, sire or not. And had it not been for Niall's intervention, he would've killed me. So no, life isn't fair. And it's never simple, Gray. Never."

Gray took a breath and stared out into the darkness. He'd forgotten about Arien and the devastation he'd caused before Niall had ended the faerie. "I'm sorry, Áine," he murmured at length. "Arien was a piece of work, for sure. No child should be subjected to that kind of treatment, especially from a parent."

Áine sighed. "Yeah, well, in a perfect world, right?"

He blew out a breath. "It's just that everyone knew, Áine. All this time. Everyone knew but me."

"And who's everyone, your Pitifulness?"

"I beg your pardon?"

She ignored him and plowed right on. "I didn't know until last night. So, who's everyone? Does Alexi know?"

"No. Not that I'm aware."

"Then it's only Queen Beatrice, Valian, and Finvar?"

"And Old Minerva. She handled the ... well, it was evidently done with magicks."

"Oooh, Godmother really does *rock* it, doesn't she?" Áine laughed out loud at the uncomfortable look on his face.

"Hey, wait a minute. I never said anything about Finvar."

"Yeah, I guessed about that part." Áine chuckled and shook her head. "Look, I get it. It's important information that may have somehow made a difference in your life. Then again, who knows? It may not have changed anything. But Gray, getting all twisted up about the 'what ifs' is just another waste of time. That ship has sailed. It's what you do with that information now that matters most."

"I suppose."

Áine waved a hand in the night air. "It doesn't matter who your biological father is or isn't. The point is that you've been given this incredible gift. You've just been told that you've been graced with not one but two remarkable men who have loved you, fathers who would each go to the ends of the world for you. And though one may be gone, the other is still here, has been here all along." She turned and grinned at him. "Besides, look at it this way. You're now doubly blessed. You're not only prince of the realm, but as Finvar's son, you are now heir apparent to Wysteria's Winter Court."

Gray laughed out loud and felt some of his tension drain away. "Good point. Although that's not all of it."

Áine frowned. "What do you mean?"

Looking out across the darkened landscape, Gray blew out a breath. "Well, it seems that in addition to being half fae, I'm only a quarter human."

"I beg your pardon?"

He turned and gave her a dry smile. "Turns out, my mother is half Ellurian."

"Holy shit!" Áine gaped at him. "Queen Beatrice is half Ellurian? Are you kidding me? Gray, that's huge!"

"Wait, you know who the Ellurians were?" he asked, unable to keep the shock from his voice. "Because I knew but in a vague sort of way. The Ellurians existed so long ago."

She stared at him for a moment. "Don't be stupid. Of course, I know who they were. I've studied most of the races from this realm going back several centuries. To be honest, I'm kind of stunned that you seem to know so little about them."

"Geez, Áine, don't hold back."

"Well, Gray, come on, these are your ancestors."

"Sure, but I didn't know that until tonight, did I?"

Áine gave him a sad look. "But this is your homeland. Didn't you study its history in school?" When he just stared at her, she sighed and put up a hand. "Never mind. Look, the Ellurians were amazing —real badasses. They were one of the most powerful of the ancient Immortals of this realm." She gave him a considering look. "You know, since it took a while for your fae traits to begin to come to the surface, it will be interesting to see what Ellurian abilities are running through those veins of yours and when they will eventually pop up." She wiggled her eyebrows for emphasis.

Gray laughed out loud. "Yeah, well, I'm okay with waiting on that." He shook his head and gave her a sidelong glance. "So, how'd you get to be so smart? All that book-learnin' in Europe?"

She punched him in the shoulder and then giggled. "No. I'll have you know that I was born this way. And of course, my Godmother is the most powerful sorceress in the entire realm. Remember?"

"Oh, yeah, right."

Slipping her arm through his, she leaned her head on his shoulder. "So ... what are you going to do, your Pitifulness?"

Gray chuckled, enjoying the evening and her company. "I guess I'm gonna go get a good night's sleep and then sit down and make amends with my mother and my biological father."

"Moving forward. Excellent choice." He felt her nod her head against his shoulder, but after a moment, she asked another difficult question. "So, on another important issue, what are you going to do about the descendant?"

Gray shook his head again. "That's a hard question to answer definitively. There are so many variables involved."

"But you're going after her, right?"

"Oh, absolutely. But time is a factor, so it will have to be soon. At first light, we're going to have to come up with a plan."

"Finvar looked like he escaped serious injury during the attack in the Barrens, but what about Alexi and Niall?"

"I think Alexi's injuries looked worse than they are, but regardless, he should heal fairly quickly. Niall is another story. Though he's high fae and should have some incredible healing abilities as well, his wounds seemed pretty severe."

Áine looked up at him in surprise. "You're not seriously considering going without him, though, right?"

"We might have to, depending on what the healers say."

Her eyebrows shot up. "Have you lost your mind? Gray, he's already nearly frantic about Alyssa being taken, but if you go without him? Well, that could be lethal."

Gray blew out a breath. "Trust me, I'm aware. And those kinds of tensions in the realm we do not need. Unfortunately, we may have no choice. The longer we wait, the less chance we have of getting her back unharmed. We don't know who's taken Alyssa or what their plans may be, but we can't wait any longer than a day or two to go after her." He shook his head again. "It's a rock and a hard place situation, Áine. If we do go after her without Niall, he'll go ballistic that we went without him. On the other hand, if we don't go after her and wait for him, when he regains consciousness, he'll come unglued that we didn't try to rescue her. Can't win."

Áine sighed. "I guess you have a point. I suppose we'll just have to hope and pray that the healers and his fae physiology can get him on his feet quickly." She gave him a mischievous smile. "In the meantime, I have an idea to help protect you all from any more of those heinous poison arrows that took down Tisharu."

"Oh yeah? Do tell."

"After finding the antidote, I put together a potion using the same properties. It'll work similarly to a vaccine and should protect you against this particular poison."

Gray grinned at her. "Nice. Sort of like the potion that Minerva gave us when we went into battle with Aramond's forces after I was infected with a similar toxin."

"Well, similar. Unfortunately, it may not give you much in the way of enhanced power or strength, but it will protect you from the poison. I just have to make up another batch to cover as many as possible."

"Well, you might want to get on it. Like I said, we need to move quickly with this rescue operation."

Laughing out loud, Áine shook her head. "But no pressure, right?"

"None whatsoever." Gray took her hand and brought it to his lips. "Come on, Halfling. I'll walk you down. Looks like we're both gonna need a good night's sleep."

Fifteen

Between the dank, airless cell and the raised hard rock slab—
the only furnishing, such as it was in the tiny area—Alyssa
struggled to get some semblance of rest in this latest respite
given to her, however brief it might turn out to be. It was undoubtedly Aramond's intention to not only starve her physically but
mentally as well. She was exhausted from his unrelenting interrogations, threats, and insane rantings. So far, he hadn't mentioned
removing her head as he had the last time they'd met, but she was
certain that would come sooner or later should she continue to
refuse his demands.

One saving grace was that she still had her little backpack, and
she adjusted it under her head in an effort to find even the slightest
bit of comfort in this terrible prison cell. She had no idea why they'd
let her keep the bag, but after thoroughly searching it upon her
arrival, it had been given back to her. Of course, she'd made sure to
slip her little army knife into her pant pocket before they'd reached
the mesa, and amazingly, they'd never even searched her person. So,
she still had that small tool should she need it.

She hadn't eaten in what felt like days. Of course, as with the
dungeon of the Red Palace, being held in a stone cell with no
windows deep inside the caves of a mesa, she could only guess at how
much time had passed. She'd rationed the three trail bars from her

pack for as long as she could, but once they were gone—and even with the rumbling of her stomach—she'd refused to eat even a bite of the nasty gruel that had been left on the floor of her cell from time to time.

However, of even more concern to her was that she was also beginning to feel the effects of dehydration to go along with her lack of food and sleep deprivation. The water bottle from her pack was empty and had been for a while now, and she was starting to struggle with dry mouth and confusion during the torturous sessions with the Red King. And the tension headache she was now living with served to sap her energy even further. She'd been offered a goblet of some kind of liquid on two separate occasions, but though she was aware that she could die of dehydration long before starvation, she'd refused those as well, not knowing what Aramond's sorcerer, Yulis may have added to whatever the goblets contained.

Up to this point, Aramond's main goal had been to learn the location of the Scepter of Fire. To that end he'd tried a myriad of schemes over the numerous interrogation sessions she'd gone through since being brought to the hideout. He'd alternately berated, cajoled, and pleaded. He'd even had a go at bribery and the promise of riches to extract the information from her, but she'd steadily refused to give in or even discuss it. She knew that once he had the scepter, it was only a matter of time before he'd try to force her to use it against Queen Beatrice and the people of Wysteria, and that was something for which she would die before doing.

When none of his whining or pathetic ideas had done the trick, Aramond had turned to Yulis to compel her to tell him what he wanted to know, and the sorcerer had cast several spells and grueling incantations to that end. Alyssa was just as dumbfounded as they were to find that, though painful and harsh, none of Yulis' efforts had accomplished the end they'd anticipated. She didn't know how she'd been able to resist his powerful magick this far, but she was grateful for it.

In truth, she really couldn't tell Aramond where the scepter was located—no matter how he tried to coerce her to do so—because once word of her kidnapping had reached the palace, it had more than likely been moved. Since she was the only one who could wield the weapon, that specific security protocol had been put into place from the moment it had been returned with her to the New York realm in case of just this kind of situation.

However, her refusal to discuss the scepter or its whereabouts had only served to inflame the Red King's anger. If it was possible to make matters worse, Aramond had changed his strategy during this last agonizing session, and his new tactic struck much deeper than any he'd tried before. He was now threatening to harm her family. She had no idea if he actually knew where to find them—or how to get to them for that matter—but she'd continued her refusals and had hidden her absolute terror of his threat until, in a fit, he'd finally had her thrown back into her stone cell.

Adding to her fears, Alyssa now worried that the searching amulet Niall had given her might no longer be working, or possibly functioning so poorly inside the mesa as to be of no help at all. She seriously didn't know how much longer she could hold out under these conditions. If Niall didn't come for her soon or she didn't find a way out of this mess on her own, she was afraid her condition and the entire situation was going to deteriorate further—or worse, Aramond might actually lop off her head like he had promised to do previously. He was definitely crazy and blood-thirsty enough to do it.

On top of everything else she was dealing with, there were also those fae that Alyssa was certain were being paid or compensated to provoke her in the brief rest periods that she'd been allowed. They seemed to find all manner of ways to keep her from sleeping and to antagonize her, adding to her exhaustion. On the heels of that thought, Alyssa felt something like a pebble ping off of the arm she'd thrown over her face. She tried to ignore it but soon there was another ... and then another.

"*Alice* ..." the accompanying voice said in a sing-song fashion. "Come on, Alice, come play."

"For the thousandth time, my name is *not* Alice, and I'm not going to take the bait," she muttered, and with a sigh, rolled over on the hard rock slab turning her back to the perpetrator. "So, you might as well move on."

She immediately felt another pebble bounce off of her shoulder, but after a moment she heard a different voice grumble, "I told you she wouldn't bother with you."

"Yeah, yeah. No fun at all. Come on. Let's take a break out in the fresh air. It's stuffy in here. We'll come back for her as soon as the Red King has had his dinner and is ready for her again."

"Yeah, nothing better to do, I guess."

After their footsteps died away, silence reigned for a few moments, and Alyssa thought she may finally be left alone, but it was not to be.

"So ... you're the descendant of the little Alice of legend?" a voice called softly.

With another heavy sigh, Alyssa turned over and glanced toward the hallway, but there was nobody in sight. Was she now beginning to imagine voices to go along with her confusion and fatigue? "Who's there? Who said that?"

"Over here," the voice said from somewhere to the left of her cell.

Curious, Alyssa rolled off of the slab and went to the cell bars. Looking up the hallway in the direction of the voice, she found a handsome man looking back at her from behind the bars of a similar cell.

"It's true, then," he said. "The Red King has imprisoned the Angel of Artemysia."

Alyssa blinked at him. "I beg your pardon?"

"That's what some call you, you know. Like the legend of your ancestor before you, you saved the realm from Aramond's tyranny. Unfortunately, he escaped retribution and brought his tyranny here to the Barrens instead."

She wondered what the man had done to be imprisoned as she had been. He didn't look fae, but upon closer inspection, she realized he was wearing a necklace—or harness—emblazoned with a cross. "Oh, dear God, you're the kelpie they caught, aren't you?"

The man looked surprised. "How could you know that?"

She nodded to the yoke around his neck. "The harness with the cross. They used it to capture you and then control you, right?"

He nodded and then leaned his forehead against the bars of his cell, his dark eyes full of anguish. "I was dozing in the morning sun on the banks of the river where I live when they ambushed me. I tried to fight back, and I did some damage, but one of them got the harness around my neck before I could get away."

"That must have been truly frightening."

He shrugged. "They've used me for a pack mule for weeks. Some of my captors aren't too bad, but most treat me poorly or try to humiliate me at every turn."

"How awful for you. What's your name?"

"My name?" he asked in a distrustful tone.

Alyssa nodded. "Yes, your name. You do have one, right?"

The kelpie narrowed his eyes. "Don't be daft. Of course I have a name," he snapped.

"Look, you don't need to get touchy about it." She narrowed her eyes back at him when he didn't answer her question. "Well, what is it, then?"

"Why do you want to know?"

"Have you forgotten it?"

"Again, don't be daft. Who forgets their own name?" He pursed his lips and studied her for a moment. "It's just that your kind never asks or doesn't seem to care. Most just want what they can get from us, but other than that, we're usually just thought of as lowly creatures to be used rather than the powerful, intelligent beings we are."

"I'm not 'most', am I? Well? Are you going to tell me your name or should I just refer to you as 'what's your name'?"

The kelpie made a face and shook back his thick mane of jet-black hair but finally relented. "Cianán. My name is Cianán."

"Well, it's nice to meet you, Cianán." She tilted her head and gave him a thoughtful look. "So, can't you just remove the harness yourself while you're in human form?"

The man shook his head. "No. *I* can't remove it, no matter what form I take. Someone else has to do it, which of course will never happen. These fae know that once it's removed, I will exact my revenge upon them. No matter how superior they act, they are afraid of me without the halter's constraints."

Alyssa recalled then the conversation she'd had with her abductor about kelpies and their various powers. Many could fly, conjure storms, grant wishes or even curse individuals who'd wronged them. She also remembered the warrior saying they would have to 'put this kelpie down' when they were done with him. She shook her head and felt an incredible sorrow for what had been done to him. "I'm so sorry, Cianán. I would remove it if I could."

The kelpie frowned at her. "You would? Why?"

"*Why*? Because I believe that no one, no living creature has the right to imprison or enslave another. That's why. It's just wrong. But it looks like you and I are in much the same boat for the time being."

He stared at her for a long moment but then finally nodded. "Very true. And we'll likely meet the same fate, descendant of Alice."

"My name is Alyssa."

"Well, *Alyssa*, even if you give the Red King whatever it is that he wants, he will kill you in the end just as they will kill me."

Alyssa nodded. "I know, and since I can't give Aramond what he wants, my only other alternative is to escape from this place before that happens."

Cianán snorted. "And how, pray tell, are you going to do that?"

"I don't know yet, but I have friends who will be coming for me. I'm just afraid that they won't get here in time." She gave him another thoughtful look. "So, if I could find a way out and could free you as well, would you help me get to the border?"

Cianán looked dumbfounded. "Are you saying that you would save me, too?"

"Of course, I would. No man left behind. That's my motto ... well, I think it's more of a military thing, but I'm adopting it," she said with a smile.

"And you would trust a kelpie? That seems ... unwise. If you knew the myths and legends, you may have a change of heart."

Alyssa sobered and leaned her cheek against the bars of her own cell. "If you gave me your word, I would trust you, yes."

"You are definitely not like any human that I've ever met," Cianán replied with a shake of his head.

"So, is it a deal? I save you, and you get me to the border safely?"

The kelpie laughed out loud. It was a rich, warm sound that poured over Alyssa and had her smiling back at him. "Alright," he said reluctantly. "If by some miracle you find a way to free us both, I will get you to the border safely."

"Do you swear it?"

Cianán nodded. "You have my word, Alyssa, descendant of Alice."

"Great. Now, all we have to do is figure out how to get out of these cells, elude the guards, and escape from the caves. Easy-peasy."

With a wry grin, Cianán shook his head again but immediately sobered and looked toward the end of the hallway.

"What is it, Cianán?"

"Someone is coming," he whispered. "You should go back and lie down. It would not bode well for either of us if we were to be seen conversing."

"Good point."

She hurried back to her stone slab and once again lay down with her back to the cell bars. If Aramond's flunkies were coming back for her, she would have to go through another round of interrogations or worse without sleep, but she was suddenly feeling more energized than she had in what felt like days. She now had an ally of sorts, and if they could find a way out, maybe they both would make it through this horrible experience and live to fight another day.

It wasn't long before the sound of a door opening and footsteps could be heard coming toward the cells.

"*A-lice.* We're *ba-a-ack*," a voice said. "It's time to go."

Looking over her shoulder, Alyssa found two fae warriors at her cell door and another smaller warrior off to one side.

"I told you. My name's not Alice. Go away and leave me alone."

Both fae looked surprised, but before either could respond, the smaller warrior waved a hand in their direction and seemed to freeze them in their tracks ... literally. It was as if they were suddenly in some kind of suspended animation. One even had his mouth open as if about to reprimand her for her impertinence.

"What ... the ...?"

The small warrior came over to stand next to them. "Rouse yourself, descendant," he hissed in a raspy voice.

"What is this?" Alyssa asked in disbelief as she swung her feet to the stone floor and got up. "More torment? Some kind of dark magick?"

The faerie narrowed his eyes but didn't answer her question. "We have much to discuss and little time to do it."

Taking a few tentative steps toward the cell door, Alyssa gave the warrior a cynical look. "Yeah? Who are you? And what could we possibly have to discuss?"

"I am ... an ally of sorts."

"An *ally*?" She laughed out loud. "Yeah, right. Why in the world would I trust you? You're a fae warrior, part of Aramond's insane plans."

"No. I am not." There was a steel conviction in the warrior's words, but then he smirked and made a show of checking out the cell bars. "But regardless of who I am, it doesn't look to me as if you have much of a choice but to accept my help."

"And why would a fae warrior want to help me? This could just be another ploy to get me to tell Aramond what he wants to hear. You could be Yulis in disguise for all I know."

"Do not insult me, girl." The warrior's gray eyes glinted with fire, but then he let out a sigh and the glamour he wore melted away along with it. In the warrior's place stood a diminutive old woman in blood-red robes, her long, silver hair wild about her shoulders and a crafty look in her eyes. "Does this ease your curiosity?"

Alyssa blinked in surprise and took another step closer. "Who *are* you?" she asked again.

The old woman tilted her head and gave her a toothy grin. "Though we've not met face to face, I feel certain that you have heard of me, descendant of Alice."

Alyssa gasped as the answer flashed through her mind in that instant. "Oh, my gosh! You're ... you're Minerva, the Witch of the Eastern Glade."

The sorceress cackled, spreading her arms wide and giving a brief nod of her head.

"But what are you doing here?"

"I could ask the same of you."

"We were attacked as Niall was escorting me to the White Palace. I was abducted and brought here. Have you come to rescue me?"

"Ha! I was here long before you arrived, girl." Minerva frowned and shook her head. "There is quite another reason for my presence, and I was not pleased to find you here, that I can tell you."

"Aramond is planning another war and is intending to use me to wield the scepter again, only this time to destroy Wysteria and regain Roseland."

"What the Red King intends and what is actually within his capability are two entirely different things."

Alyssa shook her head. "But I've heard the stories about you. You're the most powerful sorceress in Artemysia. You could probably stop him and save the realm all by yourself if you wanted to."

Minerva dismissed the notion with a wave of her hand. "Yes, yes, the stories you speak of are quite true, but I have no interest in the squabbles between humans and the factions that follow them."

"How can you say that? Surely it would affect the entire realm, you included."

"Perhaps. However, I fear nothing from Aramond ... the imbecile. Besides, his forces were much diminished with the last skirmish. The White Queen and her army, aided by the fae courts, can certainly handle the fool and anything he attempts with ease."

"Maybe so, but there will still be loss of life. Innocent life. Doesn't that bother you?"

The sorceress just shrugged. "There is loss of life in any struggle, child. It is the circle."

"Okay. If you won't intervene, then you could at least help me to escape. I don't know how long I've been here, but I haven't eaten for some time, and now I'm out of water as well. I don't dare eat or drink anything that they give me for fear of what may be added to it."

"You've been imprisoned here for just over two days."

Alyssa felt her spirits take a nose dive. "Is that all it's been? It feels much longer than that."

Pulling an ornate bottle from the folds of her robes, the sorceress held it out to her.

"What's this?" Alyssa asked as she reached through the cell bars to take it.

"You are wise to consume nothing you're given in this heinous place. This elixir will keep you strong and hydrated and will give you sustenance to carry you through."

Alyssa looked down at the bottle and frowned. "Look, don't get me wrong. This is great and very much appreciated, but Aramond has had me tortured. Has even had Yulis use his spells on me. I don't know how I've resisted up to this point, but I don't think I can hold out for much longer. And an elixir, no matter how amazing, isn't going to shield me from more of the same, is it?"

"You don't know how you've *resisted*?" Minerva asked with incredulity. "Don't be thick, girl. *I'm* the reason you've been able to resist. You would never have survived Yulis' dark incantations were it not for me countering his magick."

Alyssa blinked in surprise. "Oh … well … okay, then. I guess that makes more sense. But if you can counter his magick, can't you just get me out of here?"

"I'm only here to take my revenge on Yulis, and there is no room or time in my plan to escort you back to Wysteria."

In her desperation, Alyssa came closer and grabbed the cell bars between them. "Oh, but you wouldn't have to take me back to Wysteria. I have an ally in the next cell over who has agreed to take me to the border if I can get us both out of this mesa. I know you could at least do that, right?"

The old sorceress narrowed her eyes and then glanced toward the cell where Cianán was being held. "An ally, you say? Here?"

"Yes. His name is Cianán, and he's given his word to see me safely there."

Minerva looked skeptical, but strolled over to his cell. "Come into the light, Cianán. Let's have a look."

When he stepped into view, Minerva stared at him a moment and then threw back her head and laugh heartily. Looking back at Alyssa, she shook her head. "Surely you cannot be serious. This one is a kelpie, girl."

"Yes. I'm aware of that. He's been enslaved, which is monstrous, and I've made him a deal. I get us out of here, and he gets me to the border in one piece. At that point, I remove the harness and set him free."

"Oh, for the love of the Oracles! You can't take the word of a kelpie. He would just as soon take you to his home in the river and devour you there as look at you, let alone take you to safety."

Alyssa glared at the old woman. "Well, if you won't help me, I have no other choice, do I? Because it's only a matter of time before

Aramond starts talking about lopping off my head again. And I'll tell you this, I refuse to die in this place at the hands of that mad man."

She held her breath as the sorceress studied her in a stoic manner, and then looked back at Cianán before addressing him. "Do you know who I am, kelpie?"

Cianán nodded slowly. "You are the ancient one of Artemysia, the one with unknown beginnings ... the one with unimaginable power like no other in this realm."

This answer seemed to satisfy Minerva but she was obviously not convinced quite yet. "Hmm. You've agreed to these terms, have you? You've given your word to the descendant to deliver her safely?"

The kelpie nodded once. "I have, Old One."

"Very well," Minerva began in a quiet and dangerous tone. "Then know this, kelpie. The descendant's safety is the most important charge of your pitiful life. I will allow this against my better judgment, but should you fail to keep your word, should any harm come to her, *I* will come for *you*. I will destroy not only you but your entire family as well ... without mercy. There is no place you will be able to hide from the Witch of the Eastern Glade. Do you understand me?"

"I do."

"And knowing that, you are still willing to proceed with this ridiculous scheme?"

"I am."

With a skeptical look and another shake of her head, the sorceress walked back to Alyssa's cell. "Prepare yourself, descendant, for you will have to endure another round with the mad king before we can proceed with this foolish arrangement."

"Wait— What?" Alyssa blurted in disbelief. "Why can't we go now? Can't you just wave your hand and beam us out of here or something? I can't go through another round with those two. I can't!"

Fire flashed again in the old woman's eyes, and she took a step closer to the cell. "You can and will! If you plan to actually escape this place, then we must wait for the cover of darkness, which won't begin for another hour or so. The very minute you're found to be missing, Aramond will send warriors after you. In daylight, you wouldn't get far before being apprehended." Taking a calming breath, Minerva took her place behind the other two suspended warriors and prepared to replace her glamour disguise. "Get through this last round and then be prepared. I will come for you both just before dawn."

"Dawn? You want to wait until *dawn*?" Alyssa gaped at the old woman. "Why can't we go the minute its dark?"

Minerva shook her head. "Use your head, girl. We must get you to a reasonable distance under the cover of darkness, but to travel for a prolonged period in the Barrens after nightfall is to court death. All manner of beasties come out to hunt after the sun sets."

"The Ancient One is correct, Alyssa," Cianán called softly. "It will be safer for us if we go just before sunrise."

"Survive this last session with Aramond, and I will come for you before dawn." With that last command, the witch then waved a hand, and the frozen warriors came to life. They both blinked and looked around as if confused about what had taken place.

With a quick glance in Minerva's direction, Alyssa turned to the warriors. "Well, are we going or not. I can just as easily go back and take a nap if you're going to putz around," she told them as a distraction.

The more antagonistic of the two cleared his throat and jerked open the cell door. "If you're in such a hurry, then let's go. Though were I you, I wouldn't be so anxious to meet your demise."

Alyssa left the cell then, and as they passed Minerva, she gave the glamoured sorceress one last look. She would have to place her trust in the witch and hope that for this last time she could withstand whatever Aramond and Yulis had in store for her. But she would be counting the minutes until she and Cianán could be out of this place and on their way to Wysteria.

Sixteen

~~~

It was getting late, and the trek to the Barrens at dawn would come all too soon. But thinking to detour toward the medical wing, Valian told himself that he was just going to do a quick check on Tisharu before turning in, if only to set his mind at ease and make certain that her health was continuing to improve. He'd 'checked on her' at least once a day for the last two days since she'd regained consciousness on Sunday evening, and he told himself this, knowing in his heart that merely checking on her wasn't quite the extent of it. In fact, there was much more to it than that.

He now found himself in an uneasy spot, torn between what he felt for Isabella—whom he did care for—and the faerie queen who'd stolen his heart decades before. He'd been a fool back then—young (well, younger) and arrogant, with a wild streak that he couldn't or wouldn't rein in. And he was just now realizing the magnitude of what he'd walked away from when he'd turned his back on Tisharu all those years ago. And what it had cost them both.

Their years-long affair had not ended well. Again, his doing. She'd wanted more from him at the time than he was capable or willing to give. What he still felt for her was something he'd refused to confront for over a decade, and it had taken her near death to finally make him see it for what it really was—he was still in love with the Queen of the Twilight Court. Always had been.

Unfortunately, he had no idea what to do about it. On one hand, he had no desire to hurt Isabella, but if he did nothing, he feared it would eventually destroy their relationship entirely. And that would be tragic. On the other hand, because of his stupidity and denial, he had badly hurt Tisharu, and they'd lost so much time because of it. It was a difficult situation all around.

Just as he started up the grand staircase from the Great Hall, Isabella appeared on the landing above him directly in his path, as if he'd conjured her out of his thoughts.

"Oh, there you are," she said. "Were you heading up?"

"I was. I just had one stop to make first."

She met him on the staircase and stopped a step above him, putting them close to eye-to-eye level. "Tisharu?"

"Isabella—"

She shook her head and put a finger to his lips. "No, Valian, it's fine. I'm glad she's out of danger and healing quickly. That's actually something we need to talk about."

"Is that why you were coming down? Were you looking for me?"

She shook her head. "No ... well, yes, I intended to find you eventually. I was actually heading out to the courtyard gardens to get some air and do some thinking."

"About?"

She smiled at him. "I think you know. Remember our deal? We need to revisit that conversation. And this time I think we both know how it will end."

Valian sighed and nodded. "I don't want to lose you, Isabella Christensen."

She reached out and took his hand. "You won't lose me, no matter the outcome. You are dear to my heart, Valian Winchester, and always will be. But you deserve to be happy."

He leaned down and pressed a kiss to her forehead. "We both deserve happiness, love. And you are dear to me, as well. Meet me in my chambers? I won't be long."

"Of course. Take your time."

He watched her go and felt sadness well up inside him. She was an extraordinary woman, and if they went their separate ways, he would miss her daily presence immensely. Turning, he put it all out of his mind for the time being and headed up to the third level.

As he entered the medical wing and crossed the dimly lit room, he realized that Tisharu was still awake, sitting up in her bed, and watching him as he approached.

After his recent revelations, he stopped at the foot of her bed and suddenly felt like an inexperienced youth, uncertain of himself or how to proceed. "You're awake," was all he could think to say.

"I've spent enough time sleeping over the last week or so, wouldn't you say?" She lifted the book she'd been reading and waved it in the air. "Though it's late, I thought to lull myself with a few poetic pages." She smiled then and held out a hand to him, and he felt some of his uncertainty fade away.

Crossing to her, he sat down in the chair next to the bed and took her hand, bringing it to his lips before he could stop himself. "You're feeling better then? Your color is back."

She squeezed the hand he still held. "I am much recovered, Valian, and ready to be out of this bed. I look forward to tomorrow morning with greedy anticipation, I can tell you."

"Tomorrow morning? What do you mean?"

With a tilt of her head, she gave him a confused look. "Why, heading into the Barrens to retrieve the descendant and hunt down that bastard Aramond, of course."

Valian frowned. "Tisharu, you don't seriously think to go with us."

She pulled her hand from his grip and gave him a stony look. "Why wouldn't I be serious? Surely you knew that the Field Marshal had asked for my Twilight Court's assistance."

"Yes, but—"

"Raef brought my battle armor to me earlier today, and he and my warriors will arrive just before dawn, as we leave at first light." She gave him a pointed look and spoke sternly. "I am their queen, Valian. I will lead them."

"For the love of the Oracles, that's just crazy," he blurted before he could temper his words. "I just came close—*we* just came close to losing you only days ago."

"And your point would be?" she asked in a quiet and dangerous tone.

Running a hand over his face, Valian knew he needed to tread carefully. Any assertion of weakness would not be taken well. Tisharu was a proud and fearless warrior in her own right, but he was worried that she wasn't up to all-out war quite yet. And he was fairly certain that something close to an all-out war was just hours away in the Barrens.

Taking her hand again, he pressed a kiss to her palm and then brought it to his chest. "My point," he began in a gentle manner, "is that I never want to go through that kind of terror again. Ever."

Her facial expression softened then, and she reached out and ran the back of her free hand over his cheek. "*Mo chroí.* I am healed. So, you have no need to worry. We fae have much the same physiology as elves. You know that. We heal very quickly."

He looked away for a moment. "I'm aware of that. It's just ..."

When he was at a loss as to how to explain, her throaty laughter had him looking back and into her beautiful green eyes.

"You and I are warriors, Valian. We wield our weapons with confidence and ease but often find it difficult to articulate our inner-most feelings. Is that not so?"

He gave her a rueful smile. "Yet I don't seem to recall you having a problem in that area when we were together."

"Of course not. Everyone knows that the female of any species matures emotionally long before you hard-headed males do. It's one of the abilities that make us superior."

Valian thought about his recent conversation with Isabella and laughed out loud. "Point taken." After a moment his grin faded. "I have missed you, *Mo ghrá*. And I am sorry for any pain I may have caused you ... before."

"Valian, there's no need—"

"No, Tisharu. Let me finish, please, because there has always been a need. You deserved better than what I gave you." He paused, needing to find the words, the right words to convey what he was feeling, had felt in his heart for some time. Entwining his fingers with hers, he stared down at their joined hands and began to explain as best he could. "I was cocky back then and unwilling to commit to anything that even smacked of permanence. I enjoyed being with you, I did. I was obsessed with your every facet. Your intelligence, your battle prowess, your beauty, your confidence. Yet I think part of me became resentful over time that, without my realizing it, you had somehow reached inside me and taken my heart for your own. When you pressed for more ..."

"You weren't ready, my love. And I was ... too grasping."

He looked up at her as a lone tear spilled over and trickled down her cheek.

It was nearly his undoing.

Valian shook his head and reached out to wipe the tear away. "No. Our messy ending isn't on you. It was my doing entirely. You wanted what we had—what I had treated so thoughtlessly—to blossom and grow. I was insensitive and thick-headed. But please know that it was never my intention to hurt you and knowing that I did has weighed on my heart like a stone over the years."

She also looked down at their entwined fingers and sighed. "It is true. I was wounded at the time. I wanted so much for us." She raised her eyes to his. "But over those same years, I've come to understand that you weren't ready, and that you didn't mean to cause me pain."

"No, never. I adored you." He brought her palm to his lips again and murmured against it, "I adore you still."

She searched his face, looking for the truth of his words. "Tell me," she whispered.

He boldly met her gaze then and spoke the words that he'd always felt but had never said aloud. "*Is tú mo ghrá*, Tisharu. I've loved you for an eternity." He cleared his throat, and before he lost his nerve, forged ahead. "You loved me once, too. Do you remember? Do you think that you can find it in your heart to forgive me? To ... perhaps ... love me again?"

He'd bared his soul and confessed to her what he'd been unable to admit to himself for over a decade, which was no easy feat for him. He'd given her the perfect weapon with which to strike at him and cut deep but held his breath for her answer just the same.

Finally, the smile that spread across her face became a grin, and then she laughed out loud. "How I have waited to hear those words from you. But no, I cannot love you again, *mo chroí*. Because I love you still, indeed have never ceased to love you."

The rush of joy that flowed through him at her response robbed him of speech for a moment. She still loved him? After all this time? How could that be?

"Truly?" he asked with surprise.

"Yes. Truly," she replied and then hesitated. "But what of your human? Are you not committed to her?"

Valian shook his head. "Don't get me wrong, I do care for Isabella and don't wish to cause her pain, but I'm not *in love* with her. And to be honest, I don't believe she's actually in love with me, either. It's an uncomfortable conversation that we will have before the night's end."

She gave him a sympathetic look. "What will you say?"

"I'll be truthful with her with as much compassion and care as I can muster. I think it's possible that she and I can come to an agreement that will satisfy us both and preserve our friendship without damage."

"You have a kind heart, my love. You will find the right words. I know you will."

"For the love of the Oracles, will you two quit your yammering and be done with your overdue reconciliation, already?" a voice muttered from the next bed over. "I don't think that I can bear to listen to much more of your foolishness."

They both turned to find Niall awake and glaring at them.

"Oh, goodie." Valian grinned at Tisharu and waggled his eyebrows. "It lives."

"Yes, yes, you're so very amusing, you elven buffoon."

Valian chuckled and shook his head. "It seems you're a bit out of sorts this evening, High Lord. Did you wake feeling poorly?"

"OH, SHUT UP, WOULD YOU?" IF FACT, NIALL'S HEAD WAS pounding, and surfacing from sleep to hear his twin being wooed by Valian Winchester only served to add to his foul mood. "I'm just a bit groggy, that's all."

"Mmm, yes, that would be the fae sleeping potion the healers gave you after you passed out Sunday night."

Niall turned and skewered Valian with a hostile look. "What are you saying? That I was drugged?"

"Well, yeah. Don't be an idiot," Valian replied. "Considering the critical state you were in when your warriors carried you through the door, you should be thankful that putting you under for a couple days was all it took."

"My warriors did not carry me into this wing," Niall insisted.

"Maybe not literally, pal, but you sure required some heavy assistance—as I said—right before you passed out cold from the loss of blood. It was everything the healers could to do to staunch the gush from your wounds before there was none left in your veins at all." Valian shook his head. "Then, of course, there was the process of stitching you up and hoping you would survive the ordeal. They gave you the fae sleeping draught so that you wouldn't wake up and destroy the measures they'd put in place to save your miserable life. So, do us a favor and quit your bitching."

As Niall opened his mouth to respond, Valian's earlier words sank in. "Wait. Did you say that I've been out for two *days*?"

Valian nodded. "Yes. The search party got back on Sunday night. It's Tuesday evening."

Rearing up too fast, Niall put a hand to his head as the room briefly spun. "Tell me that you've sent another group to retrieve the descendant, that she's safe and sound somewhere in this palace."

"We leave at first light."

"You've left her there for *two days*?" he roared, and his head paid the price. "What is *wrong* with you people? Do you not know the peril she's in? It may be too late already."

"Oh yes, and you would have been just fine with us going without you, right?" Valian yelled back at him. "You're pissed that we didn't go, but if we had, you would've been just as pissed about that. We were damned either way. So, we decided to prepare instead of going off half-cocked like fools and maybe getting out asses kicked—as you did, I might add—as well as placing Alyssa in a more dire position." Valian blew out a breath and met Niall's angry gaze. "Look, we've gathered a small army.

Wysterian and Roseland guards, forces from a handful of the fae courts, as well as a couple of dwarf clans. We'd planned to head out at first light with or without you. As you said, we couldn't afford to wait any longer."

Tisharu cleared her throat and turned to Niall. "Brother, you know this is the only way. I, for one, don't relish a war in the Barrens. Once was enough for me. But if Aramond has the descendant and has barricaded himself in that vile place, we have no choice but to take the fight to him before he can act. And that requires more than a search party. We need an army."

"I don't know what you were thinking hanging around past dark in the Barrens with just a handful of men, anyway. You put them at risk and should've known better, Niall," Valian stated, earning him a pointed look from Tisharu. "Well, he should have. We've fought side-by-side in the Barrens on several occasions, he and I. He knows the dangers quite well." He turned back to Niall. "You're lucky no one was killed, though you were a close thing. That Wolvataur tore through your battle armor like it was tissue paper. It could have killed you, and then where would Alyssa be?"

Niall glared at Valian, but the truth of his words stung. He had acted foolishly. His promise to Alyssa to come for her no matter the circumstance had outweighed his better judgment. Still, he focused his anger, instead, on Valian. "Well, we wouldn't have had to go into the Barrens at all were it not for you."

Valian looked toward the ceiling and sighed. "Ah, yes. Alexi told me that you blame me for everything. But you're working under at least one false assumption, old friend."

"Really?" Niall gave him a skeptical look. "And what would that be?"

"Well, first of all, you assume that I blithely left Alyssa and Isabella alone in New York without protection, but that's not the case. I had several elven lookouts keeping watch round the clock." Valian gave him a questioning look. "Did you really think that I was unaware that your warriors were in my city? I was informed the moment they arrived, just as I was briefed on your visit to Alyssa's gallery soon after."

Niall frowned. "You knew? But the Field Marshal said nothing of this."

Valian raised an eyebrow. "Yes, well, I tell Alexi what he needs to know to do his job in this realm. The New York realm is my turf. And all he needed to know about Alyssa's safety was that I had it under control." Valian tilted his head and shrugged. "Why do you think I was unconcerned about traveling between the realms so often, leaving the two women unattended? I knew they were under the watchful eyes of not only my warriors but yours as well."

"I see." Niall thought for a moment. He should have known that Valian would leave nothing to chance where both the descendant and the scepter were concerned. But that didn't answer his next the question. "While that does ease my mind to some degree regarding the descendant's safety in the New York realm, it doesn't answer the question about how Alyssa and her friend slipped through the old park portal, with your lookouts being none the wiser."

"That was unfortunate timing." Valian had the good grace to look embarrassed. "It seems that there was an issue with several fae warriors from Roseland's Evening Court showing up in Soho where they had no business to be. Since Mabry's court fought alongside Aramond's troops during the battle earlier this year, and knowing Kassair and several of your men had an eye on Alyssa, my scouts went to check it out. As it happens, Alyssa and Isabella chose that particular time to make their trek."

That explanation made sense to Niall, but he was not yet ready to let the Chancellor off the hook. "Yes, but had you been honest with the two women and told them what was happening here, they probably wouldn't have come to this realm in the first place, and we wouldn't be in this mess, now would we?"

"I will give you that, Niall." Valian sighed. "The decision was made to keep the information from them both against my objections. The queen thought it best not to worry Alyssa, but you make a good point. Had we explained the situation to them, maybe they wouldn't have come." He shook his head and grinned. "And I will say that I did underestimate their curiosity and ... tenacity. Neither Alyssa nor Isabella had ever traveled through the portals on their own, and I just assumed they wouldn't think to try it. That was bad judgment on my part."

"Either way, what's done is done," Tisharu said. "The time for recrimination is past. From here on, we need to work together. Going into the Barrens without a solid plan is never a good idea."

Niall nodded. "Agreed, sister."

Valian gave him a sharp look. "Tell me the truth, old friend. Are you well enough for the task?" He put up a hand when Niall would've given him an angry response. "Because if you're not, you will only be a liability to our effort and to Alyssa, and you put yourself at risk, as well. There is no shame in it, so I ask again, are you well enough?"

Before Niall could answer, another voice offered another possibility. "That might not matter," Áine said from the lab doorway. "I think I have something that will greatly boost your advantage."

"And what would that be, young Áine?" Niall asked.

She crossed to the foot of Niall's bed and smiled. "Well, I'd been working on a concoction to protect you all from the poison that almost killed Tisharu. You know, just in case those poisoned arrows were used again in the Barrens tomorrow. Anyway, I had an idea, so went back to Godmother's cabin and studied the recipe and adjoining spell for the enhancement potion she'd made for the last battle."

"Yeah, I got in on that action," Valian said. "I have to say, that potion was amazing. I've never felt so strong, so fast, so ... powerful."

Áine nodded. "It also had a protection element, though it was geared toward the fae poison that nearly took Gray's life."

"Yes. It worked like an invisible shield against the poison quite well. I have first-hand knowledge of that part of it."

"Well, I thought, what if I combined the two?" She grinned and held up a vial.

"You've come up with an enhancement potion that will protect us against both poisons?" Tisharu asked. "That would be quite the benefit, indeed, especially going into the Barrens."

"It will definitely safeguard you from either poison. I've made certain of that." Áine blew out a breath. "However, I don't know how far it will go with the enhancement element. It should definitely give you a boost in stamina, and probably some increase in the powers you already possess, but that's the part I'm not a hundred percent sure about. I doubt it will be as good as Godmother's potion."

Valian crossed to her and put a hand on her shoulder. "If it does what you say it will, it will be a huge advantage for us. I'm impressed, Spindly. And I know Minerva will be so proud of you when she returns."

"Will it help with healing?" Niall asked. He glanced at Valian in defiance. "I'm not quite up to full strength yet, but I'm going tomorrow morning, nonetheless."

Áine shook her head. "No. You shouldn't take this until you're ready to head out at dawn. But I also have something for both you and Tisharu that should give you a good night's sleep and have you battle-ready by the morning. I'll go fetch it now." She turned to Valian. "FYI, I've made quite a bit of the potion, so I'll let you decide who gets a shot of it."

"Thanks, Áine."

Niall watched her go with a half-smile on his face. "Our little Halfling has turned into quite the chemist."

"And quite the healer," Tisharu added.

Valian took her hand, and Niall watched the flood of emotion in his twin's face. He smiled to himself. It had been too long since he'd seen such joy in her.

"I'll go now and let you two get some rest," Valian said to Tisharu.

"You should get some as well, *mo chroí*," she responded. "The morning will require cool heads and strong bodies, as well as a sound battle plan."

"I intend to, but there is that uncomfortable conversation to be had. I want to clear the air and come to an accord with Isabella before we leave at dawn. Sleep well, the both of you." He shot a brief glance to Niall. "Tomorrow should definitely be ... interesting."

Niall watched him go and shook his head. Turning to his twin, he grinned. "He took long enough."

"True." Tisharu smiled back at him. "But he was well worth the wait, my brother."

Seventeen

〜

Alexi was annoyed that he was getting back to the palace later than he'd originally planned. The two competing dwarf clans from the southern quadrant had worked his very last nerve with their bitching and moaning about who'd get the better position in line once the assembled troops headed into the Barrens. By the Oracles, he'd been completely out of patience and wanted to slap both leaders cross-eyed by the time it was all said and done.

He really should be shutting it down to get a good night's sleep, but he was now behind schedule and still had several tasks to finish up before they left for the Barrens at the butt-crack of dawn. There would also be a meeting with leadership in the war room to nail down the final details. That gathering would take place an hour before sunrise and would be here before he knew it.

He wasn't a morning person as a rule, preferring the evening hours. It was the time that he felt most alive. But one couldn't pick and choose when it came to military actions. There would be numerous guards, squads, and battalions to organize before heading across the border into the hostile territory, so he'd just have to suck it up.

Added to his plate was his secret fear that just before sun-up all the nasties would still be out and prowling, which was a daunting thing to even contemplate. He was praying to the Trinity not to run into any more Wolvataurs tomorrow morning—or in his lifetime, for that matter. The one encounter was definitely enough to last him an eternity, thank you very much. But there were so many other monstrosities that lived and hunted in the Barrens besides Wolvataurs—horrifying things, the stuff of nightmares—that it was hard to narrow down the worst of the lot. And they all came out to play at night.

Alexi didn't scare easily, and he had no qualms about being the first one to wade into a battle, but no, he really didn't want to think on that whole part of the coming adventure too hard lest he go mad with the ghastly possibilities.

Preoccupied as he was, he entered the outer courtyard and was heading toward the main palace entrance when movement in the gardens to his left caught his attention. With all the chaos the realm had been living with over the last few months, he put a hand on the hilt of his battle knife and detoured toward the movement. It would be damn hard for someone with malicious intent to breach the outer palace walls undetected, but then, stranger things had happened. During the battle earlier in the year, the security shield had been breached and rogue fae were fading right into the damn palace in the height of the conflict. He wasn't ashamed to admit that he was still fairly gun-shy about it and didn't want to get caught with his pants down around his ankles by being careless.

He relaxed some when in the dim twinkle of the faerie lights that lit the gardens in the evenings, he realized it was Isabella who had caught his eye, sitting alone on a bench amongst the greenery and night-blooming flowers. Pausing for a moment, he watched her, struck by how unhappy and alone she seemed.

Finally, he crossed to her. "Isabella?" he called softly, not wanting to startle her.

She looked up at him and smiled, and some of the unhappiness fled her features. "Good evening, Alexi."

"What are you doing out here all by yourself?"

"Mmm, just doing some thinking, that's all. I needed some alone time and a bit of space."

Alexi sat down next to her on the bench and blew out a breath. He was running out of steam pretty fast but he couldn't stand the melancholy that seemed to envelop her. "You look troubled. Are you worried about tomorrow? Because we're going to bring Alyssa home safe and sound. I promise you that."

She smiled again. "That's part of what's on my mind, yes, but I know you'll do everything you can to make that happen. I trust you and Gray and Valian."

"Well, you don't need to worry about us, either, you know. Val and Fin, Niall and Tisharu, they all fought in the Barrens during the Great War and know what they're doing out there. Plus, we're going in with a small army, so there'll be less chance of an ambush. More eyes on the ground, so to speak. We'll be fine."

"Yes. I'm sure you will."

"But that's not it, is it?" Alexi tilted his head and studied her. "Our trek into the Barrens isn't what has you so unhappy. So, if it's not tomorrow's festivities that are bothering you, then what is it?" When she looked away and didn't respond, he took a guess. "Isabella? Is it Val?"

She looked over at him then, and the shadows in her eyes in the soft fae light made him want to beat his cousin's ass. "Where is he now? With Tisharu I'd wager?"

Isabella shook her head. "It's really okay, Alexi. He was on his way up earlier and we met on the stairs. We're going to have a chat about our 'deal' in a while."

"Deal? What deal?"

"We made a deal when I arrived." She gave him a wry look. "Do you remember when you and I first got to the palace, and I was so mad at being kept in the dark about what was happening here in Wysteria? And I was crazy-worried about Aly being missing again?"

"Yeah." Alexi chuckled softly and shook his head. "Gray and I got out of the line of fire as fast as we could. I have to say, you are one scary lady when you're angry and crazy-worried."

Isabella laughed along with him. "Yes, I am. And don't you forget it, mister."

"No, ma'am."

"Anyway, I gave Valian a piece of my mind, told him that I didn't appreciate being kept in the dark … and that I'd found out about what had happened to Tisharu." She sighed. "He said that it wasn't what I thought, but I think we both knew better even then, because he also said he wasn't really sure what he was feeling toward the situation, toward her. So, we made a deal. I made him promise that the minute he figured it out he would be up front with it and tell me."

"Isabella, you know that Val cares for you, right?"

She nodded and the sorrow she radiated just about killed him. "I know that, Alexi. But ... is that enough, do you think?"

He frowned. "Isabella, I can't answer that for you. I guess that depends on your expectations."

She sighed again. "But would it be enough for you?"

He looked directly into her bright green eyes and gave her an honest answer, the only answer he had. "No. Not even."

"Exactly. And here's the thing. He's not in love with me. He's in love with Tisharu, has been for over a decade."

"Isabella—"

She put a hand on his arm. "No, Alexi, he's just been living in denial, that's all. But I think he's finally figured it out. It took her nearly dying, but there it is. Sometimes that's just how it goes, and I really am okay with it because I care about him, too. I just want him to be happy."

He cleared his throat and looked into her eyes again. "I'm so sorry, Isabella."

"Are you?" she asked in a whisper, and he caught the scent of her perfume as she leaned toward him.

Looking down at her hand on his arm, he tried to quell the sudden craving that rose up inside him, thought about how inappropriate his feelings were in the moment. One part of his brain screamed '*No! I'm not sorry at all!*' but yeah, *very* inappropriate. So instead, he stammered like a fool. "I ... uh—"

Isabella laughed out loud and squeezed his arm. "Oh, my gosh, if you could see your face right now. You look so guilty, like you just betrayed your best friend. It really is alright, Alexi. My heart is still intact. No need to tiptoe around your thoughts."

"I just think that you deserve better than that. You deserve to be happy as well," he replied slowly.

"And that's not really an answer, is it?" She grinned at him then, and he swallowed hard. "But in any case, you're quite right. I do deserve to be happy. I guess it's fortunate then that—though I do love Valian in my own way—I'm not *in* love with him, either."

Alexi's mouth dropped open before he could catch himself. "I beg your pardon? You're not?"

"I never have been, Alexi. Look, over the last few months we've had a really good time and grown very close. And I'd be lying if I said there weren't times when I wondered if that's where the relationship was headed, but to be honest, I think if you don't feel it inside like, *bam!*, or if you have to work it over too hard, it's just not meant to be, you know?"

She shook her head and patted his arm. "Don't get me wrong, I'll always have a soft spot in my heart for Valian Winchester, which makes me a bit melancholy, yes, that this part of our relationship is changing. But I think I came to the conclusion weeks ago that he and I are much better friends than lovers."

He was so confused by her convoluted logic that he was at a loss as to how to respond. "Well ... I see," was all he could think to say.

She chuckled again and, leaning over, kissed his cheek. "But thanks for the concern. You are just the cutest thing ever ... contrary to what I thought when I first met you."

That comment struck a nerve, and he frowned. "What the hell is that supposed to mean?"

"Now, don't get all twisted up. I just had a very different impression of you when we first met, that's all."

"Oh, really? And what was that?"

"Well, if you must know, I thought you were just a little too cocky for your own good."

"*Me?* Please." He folded his arms over his chest and snorted. "And you were hoity-toity and condescending."

"Arrogant and full of yourself."

"Ha!" He grinned. "I think you mean professional and charming."

She grinned back. "I do not. More like cheeky and annoying."

He shook a finger at her. "Come on now, admit it. You thought I was adorable, funny, and downright irresistible. And the only reason you went with Val on New Year's Eve was because you were afraid of how attracted you were to me."

There was a brief pause before she caught him completely off guard when she whispered, "Maybe."

They stared at each other for several moments as time spun out and their grins slowly began to fade. Alexi was suddenly very aware of the warmth of her touch on his arm ... the way she licked her lips.

Again, very inappropriate, pal. She and Val haven't made any concrete decisions yet, he thought.

He opened his mouth to say something, anything, but before he could get there, Isabella suddenly stood up.

"I shouldn't hold you up," she said in an uncertain tone. "I know you must still have things to do before morning."

He stood as well and watched her nervously work her bottom lip. "Yep."

"I really should go up."

"Probably." He moved in closer before he could think better of it, directly into her path of flight. Reaching out, he slipped a hand around her waist and gave her a gentle tug toward him. "That would undoubtedly be safer for us both."

"Alexi," she murmured in a breathless voice.

She put a hand to his chest, but whether to push him away or pull him to her, neither of them knew, but he'd started this and was now determined to at least have a taste of her once and for all.

Oh, yes. Yes, he was.

When she made no move in either direction, a wicked smile eased across his face. "Funny, I never figured you for a chicken, Christensen?"

Narrowing her eyes and grabbing a fist-full of his shirt, she pulled him in, her lips a breath away from his. "Never, and I mean *never* call me chicken, Tovin."

He crushed his lips to hers almost before his name was out of her mouth and felt that connection like an explosion in his system. Something clicked inside him, and he hauled her up against his chest, plundered as he'd wanted to do since that first meeting so long ago— and appropriate behavior be damned.

He felt the heat rise between them as she wrapped herself around him, as her fingers dove into his hair and her tongue danced with his. Underneath that cool veneer, white-hot passion simmered, just as he'd always suspected. She smelled like fragrant meadow wildflowers and tasted like heaven, and in that moment a part of him realized that one kiss was never going to be enough.

No, not even.

Now may not be the time or the place, but soon, oh yes, very soon. Easing back, he took her by the shoulders and set her from him, noting with some satisfaction that she was just as breathless as he was ... and looked just a smidgen stunned.

She cleared her throat. "Well, that was highly inappropriate."

"Uh-huh."

A seductive grin spread across her face. "But highly satisfying."

"I'll say."

"On that note, I guess I'll say goodnight before we take this any further and get into highly inappropriate trouble."

She took a step back and turned to go, but he found that he was not quite ready to let her. Snagging her wrist, he spun her back into his arms. "I think just another quick taste, don't you?" he asked, his voice sounding thick even to his own ears. "Just to be certain that it was as satisfying as we both thought."

Sliding his fingers up and into that glorious riot of red hair, he took her lips again, and felt the zing of desire at the hum of pleasure she uttered as she melted against him.

Oh, yeah, he thought. *No question there.*

When he raised his head a few moments later, she smiled and this time took a quick step back out of his reach. He was a little dismayed that it was more of a struggle to get himself under control than he'd liked as he watched her lick her lips, as those lips curved into a very sexy smile.

Narrowing her eyes, she tilted her head and studied him. "This development is going to require some proper thought."

"I don't suppose thought had much to do with what just happened here."

He grinned and took as step toward her.

She took a step back.

"No, and that's my point. I think we may need to take a closer look. So, do us both a favor and be safe out there tomorrow, Alexi Tovin. Come back in one piece, do you hear?"

"Uh-huh. That's the plan, darlin'," he replied with his heart pounding in his ears. He stood rooted to the spot as she turned and walked away, not trusting himself to move until she was out of sight lest he charge after her like an idiot with only one thing on his mind.

Blowing out a breath he hadn't known he'd been holding, he shook his head. Isabella Christensen. Who would've thought? Oh, he could admit—at least to himself—that he'd been attracted to her the minute he'd set eyes on her on New Year's Eve, even with her aloof demeanor and condescending attitude—even when she'd taken up with his cousin that same night. But he'd let it go. After all, she'd seemed to make that choice without much hesitation. It wasn't the first time that he and Valian had been attracted to the same woman, or at least the same type of woman.

However, it had become apparent to him in the last ten minutes that there was something more between him and Isabella than simple attraction, and that she'd felt it too. The extent of that something wasn't yet clear, but he was damn sure gonna figure it out—and soon. What was crystal for him was that now that he'd had a taste, he was gonna require a more ... in-depth encounter very soon.

Oh yes, *very* soon.

With another wicked smile playing about his lips and a few interesting scenarios running on a loop in his mind, he finally headed into the palace. He still had those things to do before sunrise, and with thoughts of Isabella and the kiss they'd shared adding to the mix in his head, he was pretty sure sleep would be elusive tonight anyway.

ISABELLA WAS MORTIFIED THAT HER HANDS WERE STILL trembling ever so slightly as she climbed the grand staircase on her way to Valian's chambers on the third floor. Geez, Alexi Tovin? Really? Who would've thought he would be the one to fire up her engines in quite that way? But fire her up, he had. Good Lord, that first kiss had been so hot that she'd very nearly jumped him and wrestled him to the ground.

Of course, he had been correct when he'd teased her about being afraid of her attraction to him. She'd had a feeling from the moment they'd set eyes on each other that he'd present a dangerous entanglement for her. She just hadn't realized exactly what kind or the extent of that danger until now. This was definitely more than simple attraction. How had she not seen it before?

And what the hell did she tell Valian now? *No, no, it's really fine that you want to be with Tisharu because I just had a make-out session with your cousin, and boy was it hot!* God! Did she actually need to tell him what had happened? Or did she just let it go? If he and Tisharu had decided to get back together, did it really matter?

She was still grappling with the issue as she entered Valian's suite. She could hear voices as she neared the living room and realized that he wasn't alone. Rounding the corner, she stopped short when she found him and Gray clasping hands and doing a kind of half man-hug.

"No, no, we're good, brother," Gray was saying. "I just wanted to clear the air and let you know that I understand now the position my mother put you in."

"I appreciate that, Gray," Valian replied. "I just wish this situation could've been resolved much sooner, and in a better way for everyone. I hate that you found out in this way."

"It is what it is, and I'm getting used to the idea," Gray said with a chuckle. "I talked it out with the queen and Finvar last night, apologized for my earlier nasty response. We're not completely through it, but we've come to an accord. It will take some time to digest it all."

"And all three of you will be better for it, I'm sure."

In that moment, both men realized Isabella was standing awkwardly at the doorway, and she felt like she was intruding on something intensely personal. "I'm sorry. I didn't mean to interrupt," she stammered. "I can come back later."

"No. Don't be silly. You're not interrupting, Isabella," Gray assured her. "We're done here. I was just leaving."

"Please. Don't let me chase you off, Gray."

The prince laughed. "You're not. This was just a quick stop to clear up a few things. Believe me, I'd rather hang out with you two for a while, but I still have a couple of other things to finish before heading to bed. You didn't happen to see Alexi, did you?"

"Alexi?" she squeaked, and was dismayed that just uttering his name had her pulse rate climbing again.

"Yeah. He went to the southern quadrant to meet with the dwarf clans who'll be joining us in the morning. He should've been back by now. Did you happen to see him?"

"See him?" *Why yes, I not only saw him, I had him in a lip-lock down in the courtyard garden just a few minutes ago! Dear God, I have to get a grip,* she thought.

"Isabella? Are you alright?" Valian asked with a frown.

"Me?" Her smile was overly-bright and she knew it, but couldn't seem to help herself. "Of course. I'm fine." She quickly turned to Gray and nodded. "Alexi was downstairs earlier, but I don't know where he is now."

"No worries. I'll find him. You two have a good evening. I'll see you just before dawn in the war room, Val."

She watched him go and could almost feel Valian's curious gaze on her. Turning to him, she decided on distraction. "What was that about?"

He picked up his wineglass from the coffee table and took a sip, eyeing her over the rim. "Gray has just recently found out about his true heritage, and he and the queen quarreled about it. It was something that had been kept from him, and he was angry."

"I can understand that. I guess I'd be angry if my heritage had been kept from me."

Valian nodded. "He also found out that I've known about it for decades and was angry with me as well for not telling him."

"Though it sounded like he's forgiven you."

"Gray's realized that the secret wasn't mine to tell, that waiting to tell him was Queen Beatrice's decision. I voiced my opposition to it at the time, but ultimately it was her choice. Regardless, the cat's out of the bag now. So, yes, we're fine."

"And Gray's true heritage? Is he no longer heir to the realm?"

"Oh, yes. Queen Beatrice is his mother, so he will always be prince and heir to the throne. But Sir Edward was not his biological father."

"I see. And can I ask who his father is?"

Valian looked down and swirled the wine in his glass before

answering. "It's been a closely held secret since Sir Edward was killed in the Great War, and it's still not readily known except to a few. It will be made public at some point but you understand that it needs to be Gray's decision how and when that will happen."

"Of course." Isabella nodded. "Really. Who am I going to blab to? I live in the New York realm, remember?"

"I'm aware." Valian smiled and then sighed. "Lord Finvar is Gray's biological father, Isabella."

She stared at him with her mouth open. "As in the High Lord of the Winter Court? That Finvar?"

"Is there another Finvar that you know of?"

Isabella made a face. "Don't be a smart-ass. I mean, wow, that's just fantastic. Does that mean that Gray is not only prince of the realm and heir to the Artemysian throne, but heir to the Winter Court as well?"

"Mmm, yes, I do believe that would be the case."

"So, he's half human and half fae. Amazing."

Valian crossed to the bar to pour her a glass of wine. "Actually, he's half fae, a quarter human, and a quarter Ellurian."

Taking the glass he offered, she frowned. "What the hell is Ellurian?"

Valian took her arm and guided her back toward the sofa. "The Ellurians were an old Immortal race that was very closely related to an ancient Elven line."

Isabella laughed out loud. "Are you kidding me? So, half fae, a quarter human, and a quarter ancient Immortal slash Elven? I gotta say, most families in my realm have secrets, but you people take the prize."

She turned to him then and her humor fled. It was time to get down to business, their business. Her nerves were suddenly back, which would've been amusing if it wasn't so pathetic. If they would've had this discussion just an hour ago, prior to her encounter with Alexi, it would've been no big deal. But now? It added a brand-new layer of complication to the situation. She'd just made out with his cousin.

"So ..." she finally uttered, not knowing exactly how to begin.

"So."

"How is Tisharu? Did you two talk?"

Valian nodded. "Yes. She's actually doing quite well, although I'm not convinced that she's battle ready. Still, she insists that she's going into the Barrens with the assembled troops in the morning. I tried to talk her out of it, but she's very stubborn."

"And still totally in love with you." It popped out of her mouth before she could stop it.

His eyes widened briefly in surprise. "How did you ...?"

"How did I know?" Isabella rolled her eyes. "The question is how did you not know? I saw it the first time she and I met." She shook her head. "Oh, she covers her feelings well, but underneath that rude, indifferent exterior was a yearning when she looked at you, and then a sadness and hurt when you pulled away from her to stand with me. It was only a flash but it was there. Then later, when you told me what was between you was ancient history, I thought you'd moved on. But in reality, not so much."

"I guess I'd been in denial about my feelings for her for so long that I'd blocked it from my mind, didn't really even consider it."

She nodded. "And it can take something as dire as near death to make us see what's been there all along."

"I've hurt her, Isabella. I apologized to her tonight for my behavior back then. I ended our relationship badly, and then stayed as far from her as I could get for over a decade so as not to even think about her. But think about her, I did. More often than I cared to admit, even to myself."

"Yes. I'd say the New York realm was about as far as you could get, but then distance wasn't the issue, was it, Valian? Distance doesn't matter to the heart." Isabella took a couple healthy swigs of her wine. "So, you talked about it, then? About how you both feel?"

"We did." Valian sighed and crossed to the windows overlooking the outer courtyard. "It's not easy for either of us, talking about our feelings." After a moment, he turned back to her, and there was sadness in his eyes. "Isabella—

She put up a hand before he could apologize to her—as she was certain he was about to do—and crossed to him. "It's okay. I think we both knew this day was coming. You've loved her for a very long time."

"I never meant to hurt you or to deceive you in any way."

"I know that." He was feeling guilty. She could plainly see it in his eyes and felt her own guilt rear its ugly head. So, she began to pace. "I'll be fine. Seriously, don't worry about me."

"But I do," he insisted as he followed her. "I may be in love with Tisharu, but I do care for you."

She took another gulp of her wine. "And I care for you, too, but I'm not in love with you, so it's all good."

"Isabella, I want you to know that nothing has happened between me and Tisharu. I wanted to talk to you before she and I made any further plans."

Oh, for the love of God!

"I kissed Alexi!" she blurted before she could stop herself, and then pressed her fingers to her lips as if to hold back any more incriminating admissions.

Valian had his wineglass halfway to his lips but stopped and stared at her. "I beg your pardon?"

"I said, I kissed Alexi."

Slowly, he lowered his glass and narrowed his eyes. "I see. And when did this kiss take place?"

She licked her lips and rubbed a sweaty palm on her jeans. "About an hour ago in the courtyard garden. And actually, it was two kisses."

"And who instigated these two kisses? Alexi?" When she didn't answer him, he nodded. "That's what I thought."

She slapped a hand on her hip and felt annoyance flare, though she really wasn't sure why. This time she was the one in the wrong, not him, and her guilt demanded that she point it out. "It doesn't really matter who started it. He gave me a choice, and I dove right in. And if we hadn't been in the palace courtyard where anyone could see us, it may not have stopped with a couple of kisses. Look, to be honest, I've been attracted to Alexi since I first met him on New Year's Eve."

At that admission, Valian burst into laughter. "Yes, love. I know."

"You what?"

"Isabella, I think everyone in the room that night who witnessed the exchange when you two met probably knew."

She blinked at him several times. "But we only said a handful of sentences to each other. How could you have known from that?"

He came to her then and smiled down at her. "Sometimes it doesn't take much."

Taking her wineglass, he set it on the coffee table with his own and pulled her into his arms, then kissed the top of her head. "We are a pair, aren't we?"

She looked up at him and grinned, feeling as if a weight had been plucked from her shoulders. "Yes. I guess we are." After a moment, she asked another question that had been circling in her head for days. "Valian, when this thing tomorrow is done, when Aly is safe and you've taken care of this uprising, will you come back to New York? Or will you remain here?"

"I don't know yet, love. Alyssa will still need security, whether the scepter goes back to the New York realm or not. What that will look like will be the queen's decision."

"But if Queen Beatrice asks you to stay, you will?"

"Yes, Isabella. I am still Chancellor. I serve the queen."

She nodded. "But can I come and visit if you move back here for good?"

Valian chuckled. "Of course. Isabella, once the realm is safe again, you are always welcome to visit this world."

"We may no longer be together as a couple, but we're going to be the best of friends, right?"

"Indeed, love. And we always will be."

"Good deal. So why don't we turn in and get some sleep, friend? You're gonna have quite the big day tomorrow."

Eighteen

⤜∽⤛

By the time Alyssa was escorted into the cavernous chamber where the Red King awaited, her heart was already hammering in her chest. Minerva had said that she would need to get through one more round with Aramond before they could execute their plan of escape, but Alyssa wasn't certain the sorceress realized how crazy Aramond had grown. He'd become incredibly volatile, so mentally unstable that she didn't really know what to expect from him now and had no idea how to prepare herself.

At the end of her last session with the king, he'd been so angry and frustrated with the fact that none of their tactics had worked, that she'd been convinced her time was running out. However, now she found him lounging on his throne of stone with a contented look on his face as if he hadn't a care in the world and they'd not been through all of this before. As always, his sorcerer Yulis was at his side, an evil smile gracing his sharp features. The scene worried her more than any of Aramond's screaming and cursing binges could have and only served to remind her of how dire her circumstances had become. She didn't know what they had planned for her, but there was no doubt in her mind that it wouldn't be good.

She thought she could sense Minerva's presence somewhere in

the group behind her, and in an effort to comfort herself with that knowledge, glanced over her shoulder in hope of confirmation. But the glamoured witch was nowhere to be seen, and Alyssa could only pray that old sorceress was still close at hand and ready to counter any spells that Yulis would undoubtedly cast.

"Ah, here's our little Alice now," Aramond called in a booming, jovial voice.

Alyssa rolled her eyes. She'd ceased to correct him about her identity. It had become an incredible waste of energy and had absolutely no effect. She didn't know if he was so far gone mentally that he couldn't remember that she wasn't the Alice he'd known, or if he continued to call her by her ancestor's name to simply get under her skin.

As she was pondering these oddities, the fae warrior behind her put a hand on her shoulder and gave her a rough shove forward. Unprepared, she stumbled and almost went to her knees before regaining her balance. He grinned as she turned and glared at him.

"Touch me again and I swear you'll draw back a bloody nub," she hissed. It was an empty threat, which they all knew, but at the surprised look on his face, she felt better for it.

Aramond chuckled then and gently reprimanded the warrior. "Now, now, let's not be overly zealous and damage the goods, Captain. I may need her in one piece if she continues to refuse my requests and I decide to trade her to the Wysterian government." Turning to Alyssa, he narrowed his eyes. "On the other hand, she's been so uncooperative and ill-mannered that I may just lop off her head and be done with her. So, what say you, little girl? Are you ready to tell me what I wish to hear?"

"As I've said on occasions too numerous to count, I can't tell you what I don't know. I can't make it any clearer than I already have."

"Yet you *are* the only one who can wield the scepter, is that not correct?"

"Yes, but—"

"And you've already admitted to having the scepter in your possession in the New York realm?"

"Of course, but—"

"Then tell me where it is and perhaps I'll spare your life ... after you use it to do my bidding, that is."

"You're not *listening!*" Alyssa pressed her fingers to her eyes in her frustration and felt like pulling out her hair. "As I've told you over and over again, I did have the scepter. Unfortunately for you, the minute your fae scumbags abducted me, it would have been retrieved and moved to an undisclosed location that I know nothing about to prevent this specific scenario. That was the security protocol put into place before I even took it home with me. So, it will do no good for me to tell you where it *was*, because I can guarantee it's no longer there."

Aramond leaned forward and contemplated her for a moment. "I must say, you are something of a puzzlement to me, Alice. I just don't understand why you would continue to resist and put yourself through all this misery." He gave her a sad look. "And for what, I ask you? Some sort of misplaced loyalty to that odious White Queen and her incompetent whelp? Trust me when I say they do not feel the same for you."

Alyssa sighed and pinched the bridge of her nose. "Look, it has nothing to do with loyalty, although Queen Beatrice and Prince Graydon have always been good to me." She shook her head in disbelief. "Seriously, you can't really be this obtuse, can you? I mean, I don't know how else to make you understand that the scepter is out of your reach—and mine, for that matter. You can do whatever you like to me but I can't change that fact. No matter how many times we have this conversation, I still can't tell you where it is because I *don't know,* you simple-minded idiot!"

The Red King started to rise at her slur, his face mottling with red splotches in his mounting anger. But before he could blow his top, Yulis put a restraining hand on his arm and spoke quietly to him. "My Lord, we talked about this, remember?" The sorcerer glanced at Alyssa with obvious disdain. "Do not let this ... sad little *human* dissuade you from finding the truth. Let me assist you. I'm certain I can get to the answers you are searching for this time around."

At Yulis' smug look, Aramond nodded and slowly settled back

onto his makeshift throne. Taking in a ragged breath, he wagged his finger at her with a tight grin. "Oh, dear girl. That was a very good try, I'll give you that. You almost had me, but you can't bait me into anger as you've done in the past." His grin was over-bright and his dark brown eyes turned almost obsidian and shimmered with his madness. "But Yulis is right. Because you insist on doing this the hard—and painful—way, he's going to assist me in getting to that truth, since you refuse to comply and obviously cannot be trusted."

With that, the king gestured to Yulis to proceed, and Alyssa steeled herself as the sorcerer stepped off of the stone platform and came toward her.

In her dread over what was to come, she took an involuntary step backward before she could stop herself, but in doing so, collided with the solid bulk of the fae warrior standing behind her.

And felt her panic begin to rise.

"You know I'm the only one who can wield the scepter," she told the sorcerer as he neared. "If you hurt me, it'll be useless to you. You'll never be able to use it, even if you do manage to get your grubby hands on it."

Yulis shook his head and his eyes glittered dangerously. "Oh, I'm not going to damage you too badly. However, by the time I'm finished, you'll be begging to tell the king anything he wishes to know, pleading with him to do whatever he asks of you. And I'll have seen all your secrets by then as well. Now, do hold still, and I suggest you prepare yourself, as this is going to hurt quite a lot. That, I can guarantee." He gestured to the warrior behind her. "Hold her."

"No!" she screamed as the warrior took hold of her arms and held her in place. She tried to twist and turn in his vise-like grip but to no avail. He was a foot taller and much too strong and muscular.

Yulis grinned down at her. "A word of advice, my dear. The more you resist, the more painful this will be. However, I have no preference one way or the other. Your choice."

"I hope you burn in Hell, you evil bastard."

Chuckling at her terror, Yulis placed a hand on either side of her head and closed his eyes. The pressure inside her head began to build almost immediately as he sought to break into her innermost thoughts. It was intense and nearly unbearable, and Alyssa could almost visualize his greasy thoughts probing at her mind, demanding entrance. The pain that quickly followed was raw and excruciating, and felt as if Yulis was cracking her skull wide open. She gasped as it weakened her knees and robbed her of breath.

Stop it! Get out of my head, she thought frantically.

"Oh, I've only just begun. You can't resist me for long," Yulis murmured aloud as he increased his effort.

The next agonizing wave was razor-sharp and ripped a guttural scream from her with its force. Squeezing her eyes shut against the burning light that exploded inside her head, she heard someone sob and realized that it was her as tears leaked down her face.

"Ah, now we're getting somewhere," Yulis murmured. "Is this where your hidden secrets lie? This little corner of your mind? Show me all."

Then she heard another voice, a much different voice inside her head. *Hold*, it said. *Do not waiver. Fight through the pain, and I will protect you.*

"I can't," she sobbed again.

You can, you must! Concentrate on my voice, the vision I give.

Obviously, Yulis wasn't hearing this other voice, and thinking she was talking to him, he chuckled. "Oh, you can, my dear. And you will."

Instantly, she began to see it through the haze of torment he was causing, though she didn't understand what she was seeing at first. There was a child, a small boy surrounded by others who were ridiculing and mistreating him. They shoved him back and forth between them, tripping him, pushing him to the ground as they laughed at his misery. He wore tattered, dirty clothing, his body malnourished and weak. As the vision solidified in her mind, the pain began to subside. She cracked open her eyes to find Yulis taking a step back from her, bewilderment and then anger firing in his gaze.

"What trickery is this?" he growled. "How could you know such things?"

The vision disappeared in that moment, and Alyssa's knees nearly gave out completely. It was as if now that the pain had receded, she didn't have the strength to hold herself upright. She would have fallen to the stone floor had the warrior not maintained his firm grasp and kept her standing.

"Who was that pitiful child?" she whispered. "Was that you?"

A wave of nausea ran through her, leaving her sick to her stomach and struggling against the dry heaves. But before she could fight it down, Yulis grabbed her by the throat and lifted her to her toes.

"You will not speak of such things," he snarled in his fury. "I will obliterate it from your mind ... eradicate you."

Her breath now cut off, she struggled in earnest to get air past his grip, her fingernails digging at the hands that were slowly suffocating her. She was certain Yulis would kill her, and as her vision began to waiver, she felt the amulet warm against her skin underneath her shirt. Then an image began to form in the back of her mind. This time it was not the pitiful child she saw there but Niall. His striking features rising like a soothing balm, calming her fears. His emerald-green gaze, his wicked grin. She closed her eyes, resolved to the fact that she would die in this wretched place at the hands of this evil man and would never see Niall's handsome face again, would never again hear his deep laughter. She wondered vaguely if he would mourn her.

"Yulis! Let her go!" Aramond's shouted command rang in her ears as if from a great distance. "You mustn't kill her. *Yulis!*"

In the next instant, the sorcerer dropped her to the stone floor where she retched violently, her body heaving as she gulped in precious oxygen for her starved lungs.

And in doing so, the tracking amulet fell out of her shirt for all to see.

"What is that?" the king shouted, pointing at the amulet.

Yulis reached down and jerked it from her neck before she realized what was happening.

"No!" she cried hoarsely. "Give it back."

"My, my. What have we here?" Yulis murmured, his anger temporarily forgotten. "A tracking amulet?"

"A what?" Aramond frowned.

"Evidently, someone has been tracking our dear Alice, my Lord. I suspect fae magick."

"Bring it to me," Aramond commanded.

"No ... please," Alyssa sobbed as she watched the sorcerer hand the amulet over to the king. "Please."

The king studied the amulet briefly. "Did you really think that this would save you?" he asked with a shake of his head. "How pathetic you are." Leaning forward, he dropped the necklace to the stone beneath his feet and then crushed it under the heel of his boot.

"No, no, no," Alyssa cried as she dissolved into tears. "Oh Niall, no ..."

"Niall? You pinned your hopes on that worthless fae traitor?" The king shook his head again and laughed out loud. "What a sad choice. I should have dispensed with him when I had the chance. No, there is no one coming for you, little Alice, least of all him," he assured her with amusement. "If there was, they would have been here by now. And if I was you, I would cut my losses and look to my own welfare—before it's too late."

Alyssa looked up at him through the veil of her tears and anger rose to choke her as Yulis had done only moments ago. "You are truly despicable. A useless waste of space, and I wouldn't help you now if you promised me all the riches this realm had to offer. Niall *will* come for me, and will bring an army with him. And when he does, he will *end you both*!" she screamed at him and Yulis. "And trust me when I say, I will be there to watch it happen. I guarantee *that*."

"Enough of this foolishness," Aramond bellowed. "Take her from my sight this instant. We'll start over in a few hours when I can again stomach the look of her. And as for you, missy, I would caution you. The next time we meet will be your last chance to save yourself, so think long and hard about what will come out of your mouth when you are next brought before me—and how greatly you value your head upon your shoulders."

With a flick of his wrist, he dismissed her. "Take her away."

With an iron grip on her arm and complete disregard for her physical welfare, the warrior dragged her from the chamber. Alyssa stumbled along beside him desperately trying to keep her feet under her as he hauled her through the labyrinth of passageways back to her cell. Once there, a second soldier opened the cell door wide, and she cried out when the warrior thrust her inside with such force that she stumbled and fell to the floor, painfully scraping the palms of her hands and narrowly missing the stone bench with her forehead.

Both men chuckled as they walked away, and Alyssa could do nothing more than sit there on the hard stone floor fighting back tears and the sense of helplessness that engulfed her. She now felt more alone than she had in a very long time, and she was beginning to have serious doubts that she would live through this ordeal, no matter what Minerva said.

"Alyssa?" Cianán's disembodied voice came from his cell up the hallway. "Are you alright?"

Taking a deep, cleansing breath, Alyssa slowly and painfully got to her feet. "I'm okay," she assured him. But in the next moment, she had to sit down on the stone bench until a wave of lightheadedness passed. "I think."

She took out the ornate bottle of elixir that Minerva had given her and drank greedily. The old witch had said it would keep her hydrated and sustain her until they could set their plan into motion, and she could feel its effects hit her system almost immediately.

"What did the Red King want?" Cianán asked.

Gingerly, Alyssa stood up and went to the cell bars. Looking up the passage at Cianán, she gave him a wry smile. "Oh, you know, just the usual. Where's the scepter ... uh, where's the scepter ... and, oh yeah, where's the scepter. Aramond is like a broken record about the damn thing. It really doesn't matter what I say or the fact that I can't tell him what I don't know."

"Did they hurt you?"

Alyssa leaned her head on the cool bars of the cell. "Yulis tried, yes. But Minerva intervened. At least, I think it was her. She gave me a vision of Yulis as a child. It really threw him—so much so, that he just about choked me to death."

Cianán nodded. "I can see the marks around your neck from here. What stopped him?"

"I guess to Aramond's credit, he wouldn't let Yulis kill me ... or at least, not yet. But if we don't get out of here, I think next time he just may."

"Well, we won't dwell on that. Hopefully, the Witch of the

Eastern Glade will whisk us to safety before they can come for you again."

"From your mouth to God's ears," Alyssa muttered.

They both tried to get some rest after that. Minerva had said she would come for them just before dawn, but without a window to the outside, Alyssa had no idea how long their wait would be. She had some more of the elixir and then actually did doze for a while only to be startled awake by someone standing over her.

"For the love of ... Minerva!" she blurted in a sleep-coated voice. "Are you trying to give me a heart attack?"

The ancient sorceress stood over her without her glamoured disguise smirking at Alyssa, her pale gray eyes sparkling with amusement. "Ha! Rouse yourself, descendant. It's time to put your questionable plan into action. That is, if you still wish to leave this place."

Those words had an inspiring effect, and cleared the cobwebs of sleep from Alyssa's mind within moments. "Of course, I want to leave! I won't live much longer if I don't. You know Yulis almost killed me over that vision you put in my head."

Minerva waved away her concern. "I knew Aramond would not allow that. He wants to be the one to do the deed."

"Oh, that's helpful. I feel so much better about the whole thing now."

"Don't be daft, girl. If Aramond hadn't stopped Yulis, I would have."

Alyssa had her doubts about that, considering how long she'd allowed it to go on, but decided it would be best not to voice her opinion. "Whatever. Can we just go? With the way my luck has gone, Aramond will be sending someone to fetch me before we can leave."

The witch grinned. "Not to worry. I have taken measures. We'll have the time we need to get you and the kelpie to a safe distance." She turned and called up the hallway. "Are you ready, kelpie?"

"I am," came Cianán's soft reply.

With a wave of her hand, the door to Alyssa's cell swung open. "Then let us go."

Alyssa quickly grabbed her pack and followed Minerva out into the passageway where they met up with Cianán.

"Are you both still resigned to this folly?"

When they nodded in tandem, the ancient one turned to Cianán. "And you still accept responsibility for her welfare under my terms, kelpie?"

"I do, Old One."

With a nod, Minerva held out a hand to each. "Then grab hold and grip tight."

Alyssa and Cianán did as the sorceress asked and they all vanished in an instant. Before Alyssa could even catch her breath, they reappeared in a desolate area a mile or so from the mesa, the cool night breeze gently ruffling her hair. After being held inside the mesa in a windowless cell for several days, she just closed her eyes and turned her face to the wind, filling her lungs with the crisp, fresh air.

But before she could get too distracted by her freedom, Minerva's voice brought her up short.

"Alright. I've done as you asked and set you both free, but hear me now. Do not tarry. The sun will rise in less than an hour and the moment your absence is discovered, Aramond will send a search party for you. But it doesn't mean you are safe until sunrise. There are monstrous things that roam and hunt during the dark of night in this forsaken place. The kelpie would know all about that."

Cianán nodded in the dark. "That I do."

Minerva pinned him with a hard look and her eyes sparkled in the moonlight. "Move quickly and get as far as you can from this place, but stay ever vigilant until first light. Do you understand?"

"I will get the descendant to the Wysterian border safely, Old One," Cianán assured her. "You have my word. I will guard her with my life."

Minerva gave a brisk nod. "See that you do." Then she turned and took hold of Alyssa's chin with her boney fingers. "You have grit. I'll give you that, girlie. Now, climb atop this kelpie and ride. And don't make me sorry I took time out of my plan to help you."

When Alyssa looked back at Cianán, she found he'd transformed into a magnificent stallion with a coat so black it shimmered in the moonlight. He bent at the knee and knelt so that she could indeed climb onto his back.

Looking down from her perch, she smiled at the witch. "Thank you, Minerva. I'm grateful."

The sorceress waved a hand in the air. "Go. Be grateful somewhere else."

With that, the Ancient One vanished.

"Well, I guess that's our cue, Cianán," Alyssa murmured, and had just enough time to grab a handful of mane before they were off like a shot from a gun.

Nineteen

The pre-dawn leadership meeting came all too soon. Though not everyone had arrived yet, Valian had to admit that he was pleased by the turnout so far and the number of fae and dwarf leaders who were already milling around the war room at the early hour.

Indeed, they were quite the colorful and diverse bunch, some of whom he hadn't spoken with face-to-face in years. There was Peridot, High Lord of Wysteria's Autumn Court with his olive-green skin and auburn hair; Citron, the Daylight Court's tall, tanned High Lord with his golden hair and sea-green eyes; and the petite Sumia, the shifter Queen of the Spring Court with her pale blueish skin and long, blonde hair. As it was often said, powerful things came in small packages, and Sumia was an excellent example of that adage. Beneath the looks of sweetness and light was a fierce and powerful warrior with the ability to transform herself into any manner of creatures.

All three of these courts—along with Finvar's Winter Court, Tisharu's Twilight Court, Luthias' Dawn Court, and of course, Niall's Twilight Court from the Roseland province—had fought alongside Wysteria's armies against Aramond in January. That they were again here to participate and provide support was not a surprise.

What was a surprise to Valian were the two additional faces that had joined the coalition this time around. Two fae leaders, along with one other, had declined to participate in the earlier battle against Aramond and his army, though they would have suffered greatly had there been a different outcome to the conflict.

Juppar, High Lord of Wysteria's Starlight Court had been dealing with unrest within his ranks at the time of the battle and had been reluctant to leave his court unattended. Valian was pleased that the High Lord had chosen to join them now, considering where they were going. Juppar had fought in the Great War—and specifically in the Barrens—so knew well the risks. That he was here this morning and ready to fight spoke volumes.

But the real surprise for Valian came with Elshandra's presence this morning. The Queen of Wysteria's Summer Court had also declined to fight with Wysteria in the earlier battle, yet had given no reason for her refusal. At the time, Finvar had felt that Elshandra had been awaiting the outcome, hedging her bets in case Aramond had been the victor. Valian had agreed with that supposition, and though the Red King had not won the day, many now feared that he had survived the destruction dealt by Alyssa's wielding of the scepter. Because Elshandra's loyalties had come into question during the conflict, her presence in the war room for the early morning meeting was suspect in Valian's mind. However, he would give her the benefit of the doubt and keep an eye on her ...just in case.

Doing a quick head count, along with eight of the nine fae court leaders, Valian counted four dwarf chieftains, two Elven elders ...and Halifax. The shape-shifting Cheshire Wood cat stood off to one side conversing with one of the northern dwarf chieftains looking completely at ease—which was an oddity in itself. The cat usually complained about being asked to leave his Wood to take part in any campaign that had the potential for harm, but here he was at the early hour, impressively decked out in full battle-cat attire. Valian had to admit—albeit reluctantly—that with his ability to transform between man and cat at the drop of a hat and that of his powers of invisibility, Halifax could be quite handy in a skirmish. That he would be willing to head into the Barrens without coercion was a bit dubious, but Valian would take any help he could find—even from an egocentric alley cat like Halifax.

Valian had been the first to arrive this morning after leaving a very sleepy Isabella warm in his bed. They'd spent one last night together—more as friends than lovers—resting in each other's arms, knowing that their relationship was taking a new direction and that they were both okay with it. He smiled as he thought of her groggy offer to see him off after the meeting, when he knew she would be fast asleep by the time he'd even left his chambers. Isabella was *not* a morning person.

On the heels of that thought, his smile faded as he looked up to see Alexi enter the war room, and the tryst his cousin had enjoyed with Isabella the night before immediately sprang to mind. He would certainly be having a conversation with Alexi about that event before they left for the Barrens. His cousin wasn't known for his monogamy when it came to his love interests, and Valian was determined to make clear to Alexi that he wouldn't tolerate Isabella being hurt in any way.

As Alexi came toward him, Valian gave him a pointed look. "So nice of you to join us, Field Marshal."

His cousin frowned and glanced at the clock on the wall. "Since Gray and Fin were right behind me in the hallway, I'm fairly certain that I'm not late. So, there's no need to insinuate that I am." Crossing his arms over his chest, he scanned the room and grinned. "On top of that, I don't see Tisharu or Niall, for that matter. So, what's up with the attitude?"

Valian looked past him to where Gray and Finvar had just entered the room, followed closely by Tisharu and Niall. Taking a quick check of the time, he shook his head. "Not now. However, I will require a quick word before we head out into the field."

"Okay," Alexi replied slowly.

Valian turned his attention to the business at hand but could feel Alexi's speculative gaze on him as he addressed occupants of the room. "Alright, ladies and gents, let's get this party started. We've got an hour and a half until sun-up. I want to be heading into the Barrens at first light. So, gather around. I'm going to make this quick."

He'd already laid out the detailed map of the northeastern quadrant on the tabletop and began to walk the leaders through the operation. "Both Roseland and Wysterian Twilight Courts and Finvar's Winter Court will enter directly east here, alongside the Wysterian Guard," he said, pointing to the crossing point on the map. "Luthias, Citron, and Juppar, you and your courts will move in from the north with both northern dwarf clans. That leaves Peridot, Elshandra, and Sumia entering the Barrens with your troops to the south along with Gruden's southern dwarf clan."

"What about me?" Halifax asked with a smirk. "Do I get to choose where I cross and with whom?"

Valian gave him a bland look, and his tone was dry when he spoke. "This isn't an athletic competition, Cat. We're not choosing teams for druid ball or hurling. You'll cross the border with the Wysterian Guard, where someone can keep an eye on you."

When the cat grinned at him, Valian shook his head and turned back to the group. "Everyone else good with the assignments? Any questions before we move on?"

"Yes. I have one," Elshandra spoke up. "I only see eight of the nine Wysterian fae courts represented here ... and one Roseland fae court, of course," she murmured with a small nod toward Niall. "However, I am wondering where Wysteria's Evening Court would be. Is Kellam not participating in this little venture?"

At the mention of the Evening Court's High Lord, Finvar muttered an oath under his breath.

Elshandra smiled serenely. "I'm sorry, Lord Finvar. I didn't catch that. What did you say?"

"He said good riddance," Tisharu answered before Finvar could repeat his foul slur. "Kellam is weak and an embarrassment. His troops are sloppy and undisciplined and would only be a hindrance."

"Sister," Niall murmured in a warning tone.

Tisharu rolled her eyes. "I only speak the truth, as Elshandra well knows. We are better off without him or his slovenly troops." She turned her speculative gaze to the other fae queen. "But I must say, I am a bit surprised to see you here this morning, Elshandra, since you also declined to fight against Aramond and protect our land in battle earlier this year."

The Summer Court's queen stiffened, and her tone was cool as she responded. "What exactly are you insinuating, Tisharu?"

Tisharu's cool smile matched Elshandra's glacial tone. "Why, I'm not insinuating anything. I'm saying it outright. I wonder ... did you find your sense of loyalty? Have a change of heart in the matter? Or did you simply have nothing better to do at the early hour?"

"How dare you speak to me in that—"

"All right, ladies. That will be enough," Finvar spoke up and gave each queen a pointed stare, though he lingered on Elshandra. "Retreat to your corners and zip it, the both of you. I will remind you why we are all here this morning. Anyone unwilling to play by the rules of the day is more than welcome to withdraw at this time, as bickering is not helpful and will only add to confusion and animosity."

With both queens sufficiently put in their place, Valian hid his amusement and cleared his throat. "Thank you for that valuable reminder, Finvar. Now, if there are no other questions, we'll finish up."

Opening the ornately carved wooden box on the table, he looked around the room. "Here's the last thing before we commence with our endeavor. Áine Ó Mordha, Old Minerva's goddaughter has put together a potion that will give a boost to each of our powers. But more importantly, it will protect us from the deadly poisons used on both Prince Graydon earlier in the year and on Queen Tisharu recently."

He looked each leader in the eye as his gaze swept the room. "I will stress that no one is required to take the potion, but we do have enough for everyone. So, if you wish it, come and take a vial."

Gray spoke up as leaders began to come forward to accept their portion. "When we're done here, we'll meet everyone out in the courtyard in twenty minutes. Blessed be the Oracles."

"Blessed be the Oracles!" came the answering cry from all in the room.

As the other leaders took their leave, Valian began to pack up what was left of the potion vials. Alexi and Gray flanked him at the table, and the prince looked concerned.

"I see that everyone but Elshandra took a vial of the potion," Gray said quietly. "I find that a little disturbing."

"Mmm, yes, as do I," Valian nodded.

"And she was just about the first one out the door. I don't trust her any farther than I can see her," Alexi muttered sourly. "She's a shrewd one, that's for sure. But after she declined to join the coalition for the battle on home turf in January, it makes one wonder why she would suddenly consent to follow us into the Barrens of all places without explanation or batting an eye."

"Yes," Valian replied. "As Tisharu pointed out, I definitely question where her loyalty stands. But we can't reject her presence or that of her forces without pissing her off and possibly making some of the other courts uncomfortable. That kind of incident we don't need right now, especially going into the Barrens."

"And if she's up to no good?" Alexi asked with raised eyebrows. "We can't put others in danger by doing nothing, either."

Gray shook his head. "Unfortunately, I think the best we can do is to keep a close eye on her and perhaps give Peridot and Sumia a heads up to keep vigilant, since they will be entering the Barrens alongside her and her troops. I have a pretty good relationship with Peridot. I think I'll just go out and have a quick chat with him. You two want to meet me in the courtyard in ten minutes?"

Valian followed Gray out of the war room with Alexi close behind. "Yes. We'll be out directly. I just need a quick word with Alexi first." He gave his cousin a sharp look and then headed toward a recessed area at the end of the hallway.

Alexi followed him, and once they were alone, Valian turned to him and folded his arms over his chest. "Would you like to tell me about last night, cousin?"

Alexi seemed caught off guard for a moment and frowned. "I beg your pardon? What are you talking about?"

Valian narrowed his eyes. "Oh, so you're going to pretend ignorance? Is that it?"

"Uh ... no. I'm not pretending anything. However, it would be nice to get a bit of context so I can figure out just what the hell you're babbling about."

"Well, since you seem to be at a loss, let me help you out with that," Valian snapped. "I'm talking about your little tryst with Isabella in the courtyard gardens last night. Ring a bell? I want to know what your intentions are regarding her."

Alexi stared at him for a good ten seconds before cracking a smile and then just about doubling over with laughter.

"You find something amusing, do you, cousin?" Valian asked through gritted teeth, trying to hold onto his mounting anger. Alexi, however, did not seem to take notice.

"Hell yes!" Alexi hooted, struggling to get himself under control. "My intentions? Seriously? Are you kidding me with this? That's what's got your panties in a wad? The fact that I kissed your ex-girlfriend?"

"She wasn't my ex-girlfriend at the time, now was she?"

"Oh, please. That's just semantics and timing, and we both know it. Are you going to stand there and tell me that you and Tisharu weren't reconciling last night at about the same damn time?"

Valian grabbed Alexi by the breastplate of his battle armor and shoved him up against the wall. "Nothing happened with Tisharu last night, and this is not a laughing matter, Alexi. In any case, we're not talking about me. Isabella is not one of your casual conquests, and I won't see her hurt when you lose interest as you always seem to do. Understand me?"

Obviously surprised, Alexi held his arms out to his sides as all humor faded from his demeanor. "Oh, but I think we are talking about you, Valian." He said it quietly, but there was ice in his pale blue eyes. "And you're quite right. It's not funny at all. No, it's pretty sad, if you ask me, because you're the last one that should be lecturing me on how to treat Isabella or demanding to know my *intentions*."

"What the hell do you mean by that?" Valian growled.

"That not ringing for you, either? Then, let me ask you this. When I called to tell you about Tisharu's attack that night—when you were at dinner with Isabella and Alyssa in New York—did you explain to Isabella what was happening before you left? Did you tell her why you were rushing home to Wysteria?"

Valian stared at his cousin as Alexi's questions sunk in, as guilt began to creep up the back of his neck.

"And when you came home, did you keep Isabella in the loop? Or did you just keep it all from her until—in desperation—she and Alyssa decided to make a dangerous trip to this realm to find out what was going on?" When Valian still didn't answer him, Alexi shook his head. "Let go of me, Val, and don't be a hypocrite."

Valian took a breath, and finally releasing him, stepped back. "That was a much different situation, Alexi. I've always had Isabella's best interest at heart. I didn't tell her what was happening here because ... well, I was hoping to protect her."

"Maybe, and you could use that excuse for not telling them both about the unrest here in this realm. But you have to ask yourself why you didn't tell Isabella about Tisharu. How much of that was to protect her? The fact is, how you handled both parts of the situation did more harm than good. You can't have it both ways, you know. You weren't honest and you hurt her, Val."

Alexi put up a hand when Valian would have denied it. "Oh, she may say different, and it's not on the same level as you walking away from Tisharu all those years ago, but she was hurt just the same. I found her out in the courtyard garden last night looking as if someone had just crushed her dreams. So, no, you don't get to tell me how to treat her or lecture me on taking care not to do the same."

Valian took another deep breath and blew it out slowly as his anger faded. He realized what Alexi was saying was true. In denying his own feelings for Tisharu, he'd been careless with Isabella. And though they'd come to an accord, though he knew Isabella hadn't actually been *in* love with him, he also knew that he still held a place in her heart, as she did his. And his cousin was correct ... he'd hurt her without even seeing it, without giving it a second thought.

"I'm sorry, Alexi. I guess you're right, but I don't want to see her hurt any more than she already has been."

"Look, Val, I get your concern. I'm not usually Mr. Commitment when it comes to my relationships with women, but this is ... different. Isabella is different, has been from the start. There's something there. I don't know what it is yet, but I do know that she felt it too. Trust me, I'm going to be very careful with her. I don't want to screw this up."

Valian nodded. "I guess that's all I really needed to know." He held out his hand, and as Alexi took it, brought him in for a manly hug.

"So, are you two girls almost done talking out your feelings about

Ms. Christensen?" Niall asked with a snicker as he and Finvar passed them in the hallway on their way out to the courtyard. "We do have an attack to get underway and the descendant to rescue if you'll both recall. And the deadly Barrens are waiting. However, if you'd like to sit this one out to get more in touch with your feelings, I'm sure we can get it done without you."

"What the—" Alexi started to say.

Turning and walking backward, Niall grinned pointing at his ear. "Fae hearing, Field Marshal, remember? We could hear you halfway up the hallway. Now, get a move on. I, for one, have no problem leaving for the Barrens without you two."

With that, the High Lord turned and fell into step with Finvar, disappearing around the corner at the end of the corridor.

"He's incredibly annoying at times, isn't he?" Alexi asked with a half-smile.

"Incredibly." Throwing an arm around his cousin's shoulder, Valian couldn't help grinning back at him. "Come on. We better get out there. I don't think he's kidding about leaving us behind."

Twenty

Though he may have been grinning when he'd said it, Niall had definitely not been joking when he'd told Valian and Alexi that he would have no problem leaving them behind. They'd waited far too long to go after Alyssa as it was, had squandered precious hours. He worried now that they were running out of time, and he didn't intend to waste another moment in implementing her rescue.

And if, when I find her, she's been damaged in any way, Oracles help whoever may have laid a hand on her or done her harm, Niall thought as he climbed atop Laoch, his immortal, ebony destrier. As he settled into the saddle, the massive war horse snorted and pawed at the ground with obvious impatience.

"I understand your frustration, old friend. I feel it as well," Niall murmured in a soothing tone. Patting the horse's glossy neck, he scanned the horizon where the faint lightening of the sky in the distance announced the fast-approaching dawn. "I, too, am ready to be on our way."

It was bad enough that he'd been the one to lose Alyssa to the fae rebels who had attacked them in Tarkington Forest, but Niall's guilt at not rescuing her straight away as he'd promised to do was eating a gigantic hole in his chest. And though the time they'd lost was due in part to his injuries and the fact that he'd been unconscious for two days, that was beside the point.

Of course, he still held Valian responsible for Alyssa coming to the Artemysian realm during a dangerous time in the first place. Had the Chancellor been honest and told her of the dangers that awaited her, they wouldn't be in the mess in which they found themselves, and he wouldn't be terrified that they would be too late to save Alyssa now.

"Brother, you look as if you could chew through a bucket of iron nails without burning your tongue," Tisharu said as she guided her own snow-white stallion up next to Laoch. "Is it your injuries? Did Áine's tonic not ease your pain?"

"No, sister. I feel no discomfort," he replied, rolling his shoulder as proof. "Our Halfling's remedy seems to be working well. And with the enhancement potion added to it, I can sense my power growing by the minute."

"Then what concerns you?"

Glancing at his twin, Niall shook his head. "We should be leaving. You know the Barrens just as I do. She's been out in that monstrous place for far too long on her own."

Tisharu studied him for a moment. "You blame yourself for the descendant's abduction and her subsequent captivity, yet the fault is not yours."

He gave her a look filled with his anguish. "I gave her my *word*, Tisharu. I promised I would protect her, come for her no matter what."

"And come for her you will," she said in a curt tone, and then sighed. "Niall, the descendant is strong, as you well know. She's dealt with the Red King before, remember? She will do it again and survive as she did then."

He winced at the reference of Alyssa's previous incarceration by the Red King. That, too, had been his doing, though he did not want to dwell on past missteps. "You are sure then that Aramond is alive, that he is behind Alyssa's abduction?"

His twin gave a quick nod. "Oh yes. I tell you, I feel it in my very bones. But more than that, brother, I dreamt of him during my illness. I've seen Aramond inside his caves in the Barrens."

In addition to the command of twilight and immense mental and magickal powers that both Niall and his twin enjoyed, Tisharu also experienced prophetic visions from time to time. So, if she was certain that Aramond had survived and again had Alyssa within his clutches, Niall had no doubt that it was so.

His look was grim. "All the more reason to move with haste."

"True. The Red King has become quite mad, I fear."

"Then we should go now," he growled, and his angry tone had Laoch stamping the ground beneath him. "Where are the Chancellor and Field Marshal? We are wasting valuable time."

Tisharu put up a hand. "Calm yourself, brother. For I have also seen the descendant free of her captivity—perhaps free already—although how that occurred was unclear in my vision. In any case, it will be light soon. We'll fade to the border and enter the Barrens at the moment the sun rises."

She reached out and covered his hand with her own, giving it a brief squeeze. "We will find her, Niall. And after we do, we will terminate the Red King and his sorcerer for good this time." Leaning back, her smile was fierce and just a little bit scary to Niall's mind. "And *that* I am looking forward to with relish," she added with a wicked laugh.

Niall tried to take his twin's advice, but by the time Valian and Alexi had made their way to their own horses waiting nearby, his attitude had deteriorated substantially. It probably hadn't been more than fifteen minutes since he and Finvar had passed the two in the corridor on the way out to the courtyard. Still, he'd worked himself into a state of fury and made no bones about who he blamed for the delay in their departure.

"It's about time, Chancellor," he snapped. "The sun is nearly up. If you're through dithering about, do you think we can get this rescue operation under way?"

Tisharu grinned at Valian. "I fear if we enter the Barrens a moment after sunrise, my brother's head may explode. I suggest we keep to the predetermined schedule and leave post haste."

Niall glared at her. "Yes, you are quite humorous, sister. But do keep in mind that if any ill has befallen the descendant, it will be on your boyfriend's head. And as I've already made clear to the Field Marshal, there will be consequences for that."

"So noted, says the boyfriend," Valian murmured. "I assure you, Niall, we will be at the border and entering the Barrens the minute the sun breaks the horizon. I want to bring Alyssa home safely just as much as you do."

"Mmm, yes. That remains to be seen, doesn't it?"

With a sigh, Valian turned as Gray rode up to meet them. "Are you ready?"

"Yes. As ready as I'm going to be, considering where we are going," the prince replied and then lowered his voice. "I spoke to Peridot and made him aware of our concerns. He will keep an eye on the situation. They're already in route to their designated crossing point."

"Trouble?" Tisharu asked.

Valian shook his head. "That, as Niall so eloquently put it, remains to be seen."

"Let me take a wild guess. Elshandra?"

"Mmm, yes, but there's nothing we can do about it at present. So, for now, we move out."

As Valian gave the signal, the entire convoy began to fade in groups toward the border, followed by units of soldiers numbering in the hundreds. Within moments they began reappearing in the Eastern Glade just shy of the security wards, and as the sun began to break over the horizon, they commenced their crossing into the dreaded Barrens.

And here, the quiet was unnerving.

Though Niall's fae hearing was keen, the desolate place seemed devoid of sound. No birdsong, no insects, not even a tree to register the arid breeze with a rustle of leaves. The sun's pale morning light cast eerie shadows across the stark landscape, and one could almost taste the malevolence coating the very air they were breathing.

Coming into the Barrens had always made Niall uneasy, which was why he'd only stepped foot here a handful of times since the Great War. However, if possible, he found this strange morning light more unsettling than ever before, though he couldn't put a finger on exactly what had changed since he'd last crossed the border with Alexi and Finvar only days ago.

They traveled on in silence for close to an hour, which was amazing in itself for a convoy of their size. It was as if all had agreed beforehand that even the slightest of sounds would disturb the eerie stillness and somehow announce their presence, awakening a myriad of unsavory entities that resided here. Yet Niall knew that down to the last soldier they kept a vigilant eye out for any one of the dangerous beasties that roamed this horrible land.

When after another hour they arrived at the high cliffs where he, Alexi, and Finvar had first heard the thundering roar of the Wolvataurs on their previous trek, Niall glanced at Alexi to his right. It was obvious by the look of disquiet on the Field Marshal's face that he was remembering that moment with clarity.

"It's enough to shrivel a strong man's stones, is it not?" Finvar asked with a half-smile.

Niall stared at the High Lord to his left. "You have an odd way with words, Fin, but you are not wrong. Any encounter with a Wolvataur most definitely leaves a lasting impression."

"Ah, yes, but battling several in a fight for one's life is difficult to put out of the mind, no matter how hard one tries."

"Oh, for fuck's sake. Would you two stop talking already?" Alexi complained in a sour tone. "Seriously. That's not something I need to hear, especially now. It's creepy enough in this horrible place without your rehashing of a *very* unfortunate encounter where we all came uncomfortably close to being torn to shreds."

Finvar's eyes twinkled with mischief, and Niall couldn't help the deep rumble of laughter that bubbled out of him. After a moment, a grin even spread across the Field Marshal's face, and he shook his head at them. Nevertheless, it did break the tension for the time being. It lightened the stress that had weighed on them all from the instant that they'd crossed the border, which Niall was sure had been Finvar's intention in the first place. It wouldn't last—that was certain —but for now they all seemed to breathe a bit easier.

Until they were halfway through the long, wide canyon before them ... and they heard the first blood-curdling shriek.

It seemed to come from the cliffs above and to the right of their

advanced position, but sound moved strangely here and was decep-
tive. It flowed through the canyons between mesas like water, echoed
in and out of the cave-riddled cliffs making it difficult to pinpoint a
location or origin.

"Okay, see!" Alexi hissed. "What did I just tell you two? You
never put that kind of shit out there into the ether, because the next
thing you know you've spoken it into existence."

Finvar was squinting into the distance, head tilted as if listening
to something no one else could hear. "Calm yourself, Field Marshal.
I'm fairly certain that wasn't a Wolvataur."

"Mmm, yes, much too high-pitched," Niall agreed. "And more a
shriek of pain rather than a bellow of dangerous aggression."

"Sounded a bit like a ban-sith," Finvar offered.

"Oh, for the love of the Oracles." Alexi threw up his hands. "And
what, exactly, is a ban-sith? And do I really want to know?"

"It's similar to a bánánach or a banshee," Niall supplied
obligingly.

Alexi scrubbed his hands over his face. "That's just great, Fin.
And thanks so much for clarifying with that little tidbit, Niall. So, a
harbinger of death and mayhem, is it? Absolutely awesome."

"Yeah, I'm with Alexi," Gray added, looking around with unease.
"Can we just keep moving and not talk about the endless possibilities
of terrible things that could be stalking us?"

"Yes, Fin, do stop. You're scaring the children," Valian said,
tongue-in-cheek, but then sobered. "To be clear, boys and girls, it's
still early, but most of the really nasty beasties will more than likely
have retired to their dens or caves. We don't know what may have
uttered that screech, so just keep your eyes open, and let's not jump
to any more horrifying conclusions."

"Exactly," Tisharu replied, with a roll of her eyes. "Why is it that
most males are so quick to panic and head down the rabbit hole of
ill-fated possibilities, yet we females take the heat as impulsive and
hysterical? It's simply baffling to me."

When Valian turned a narrow-eyed glance in her direction, she
shrugged. "What? I said *most* males, didn't I?"

With a sigh, Valian addressed the prince. "Yes, Gray, I think it's
an excellent idea to keep moving and get the hell out of this canyon as

quickly as possible. I don't like having to worry about what may be hiding above us as well as around us in every direction."

Finvar nodded and scanned the cliffs on both sides of the canyon. "Agreed. There is something here. I can feel it but can't pinpoint what it is or where it's hiding. I say we fade to the other end of this gorge and climb to higher ground where we can settle a bit and get the lay of the land before moving on."

"Fading further into the Barrens is not the best of ideas, Fin," Valian said. "You should know that."

"Not as a rule, no. It isn't the same as fading to a place that you've been before and can see the destination in your mind's eye. But as long as we have a clearly visible end target and fade in short bursts, we should be fine."

"Finvar's actually correct, Valian," Niall spoke up. "We adopted that process a few days ago when he, Alexi, and I were shown where the trackers had found the rebel base. If we keep it to short distances in a clear field of vision, it can be done with a relative degree of safety. At least, as safe as one can be when traveling through the Barrens."

"Which is to say, not safe at all," Alexi muttered. "But by all means, less talking, more action is preferable to sitting here doing nothing but awaiting an attack from some unknown and horrific creature."

Taking a deep breath, Valian nodded. "Alright. To the end of this gorge then."

With that, they started to fade, materializing one by one at the base of a long track to the right that gradually led up and out of the canyon. As they began to climb the path, each kept a close eye on their surroundings, on every nook and cranny where anything could be lying in wait. But once they had cleared the gorge at the top of the trail, they made a truly gruesome discovery—a discovery of what Niall suspected was the source of the terrible cry they'd heard minutes before. A dryad had met a nasty end just past the rim of the canyon.

"Oracles save us," Halifax whispered with a horrified look and promptly disappeared steed and all.

"What would have done this?" Gray asked.

"There are dangers too numerous to count in the Barrens,"

Finvar murmured. "Many of which would be capable of this kind of violation."

"I don't get it," Alexi said, shaking his head in shock. "What would a dryad be doing here? They're tree sprites, and for the most part, peaceful, harmless beings. They usually live in the highest boughs of trees in old growth forests, of which there are none in this desolate place." He made a face. "Hence the name *The Barrens*, I suppose."

"You raise a very good question, Field Marshal," Niall replied as he climbed down from Laoch's back to examine the dryad's petite body more closely.

She was still warm to the touch, her translucent skin fairly covered in her own pale green blood. The poor thing had been eviscerated and her throat viciously sliced open. Reaching down, Niall gently closed her wide, unseeing eyes and then lifted her arm, turning her wrist and exposing her clan insignia.

Niall turned with a grim look. "She is from Wysteria's northern clan."

"They reside in the old growth to the north of Willow Glen Wood," Tisharu confirmed with a frown and then paused briefly. "And just north-east of Kellam's Evening Court."

Standing, Niall followed the trail of blood several yards to the east. "It ends abruptly here. Since there's no place to hide except back into the canyon we just left, whoever or whatever did this must have faded from this spot."

"We can't leave the poor thing laying here like this, exposed to the harsh elements or scavengers," Finvar said. Calling to one of his lieutenants, the High Lord removed his cloak and handed it to the soldier. "Pick several good men. Wrap her in my cloak and take her home to her clan. She can't be left here."

"Yes, my Lord. We'll see to it."

"They will take good care of her," Finvar said as Niall remounted Laoch. "This is a mystery that we will need to solve, but for now, we must keep moving."

"Agreed," Valian replied. "Niall, you, Alexi, and Fin need to take point. You know the way to the rebel base. Let's go."

As the convoy faded in short bursts heading deeper into the

Barrens, silence descended once again. The terrible discovery, the memory of the poor dryad's ruined body weighed on the entire entourage. Niall worked to put that visual out of his mind and instead focused his thoughts on the implications of finding a dryad in the Barrens in the first place, let alone the mystery of her death. What was she doing here? Was she somehow connected to the rebel base? To the Red King? As Finvar had said, it was a mystery they would need to unravel ... just as soon as they had rescued Alyssa and dealt with Aramond and his followers.

To that end, he pulled out his half of the searching amulet for the hundredth time, rubbing it between his thumb and forefinger, willing it to give him a signal and thereby, hope. But the charm was completely lifeless now, which only served to cause him more concern. What had happened? Had Alyssa's half of the amulet been accidently damaged in some way? Or intentionally destroyed? Would they find her unharmed or would they find a much more dire situation? These were the thoughts that circled in his mind—mile after mile, fade after fade—until he was certain he would go mad with the onslaught.

But he was snapped out of his disturbing thoughts when one of the scouts a hundred yards out turned and yelled, "Rider ahead."

All forward motion ceased within the convoy as they readied themselves for a possible attack. Although still a distant figure, the longer Niall watched, the more he began to think that there was something vaguely familiar about the rider. And with each passing moment, the more certain he became. A smile slowly spread across his face, which soon became a grin, and then a full out shout of laughter.

"Is that who I think it is?" Alexi began in an astonished tone.

"Why, yes. I do believe so, Field Marshal," Niall replied. "It seems even after abduction and incarceration, our darling Alyssa never ceases to surprise and delight."

Valian chuckled. "I, for one, will certainly be interested to hear the story of where she found a kelpie, and how she talked it into giving her a ride."

Twenty-One

Considering her sleep deprivation over the last few days, Alyssa should have been asleep on her feet. But evidently the terror of sprinting away from a dangerous situation through a deadly land under cover of darkness was enough to have her wide awake with her pulse sprinting like she had just finished a marathon.

She and Cianán had agreed from the start that they would maintain silence until sunrise. They would depend on his sharp senses to help them avoid the frightening things that roamed the Barrens in the dead of night. And while she was a fan of *not* being attacked or eaten by some horrible beast, the thick blanket of darkness coupled with an eerie quiet and punctuated by the occasional scream or bellow did nothing to ease her anxiety. Still, it had been imperative to put as much distance as possible between themselves and the horrors they'd escaped before dawn. Aramond would send a hunting party after them the moment their disappearance was discovered. Of that, they both had no doubt.

With the strain of that prospect looming over them, they'd raced on through the darkness for that first hour, pausing only when Cianán had sensed danger or felt a change in course was warranted to avoid a potentially hazardous situation. As they progressed, Alyssa kept a tight hold on Cianán's bridle in one hand and his thick mane in the other, praying that dawn would find them still in one piece and far enough away from the Red King's base to outrun any pursuit that might follow them in the light of day.

Once the sun crested the horizon and the first pale streaks of dawn began to paint the sky, Alyssa finally allowed herself to breathe a bit easier. However, she should have known that they weren't completely in the clear. With Cianán's vigilance, her respite was brief. Lifting his dark snout into the light breeze, he began to slow their pace, and moments later Alyssa did her best to keep her seat as he brought them to a sudden, jarring halt.

"What is it, Cianán?" she whispered, the fear she'd managed to keep at bay creeping back up her spine.

"I'm not certain, but nothing good," he replied as he danced in place and continued to sniff the air. "There's a coppery tang of fresh blood on the wind, but I can't tell how far off it is. Could be several miles or a stone's throw from where we stand."

"Well, that's disturbing. Part of me is glad the sun is up and we can see what's in front of us more clearly, but the other part of me is not terribly anxious to find out exactly what that might be."

"Your apprehension is warranted, human."

The strange echoing voice seemed to come from everywhere at once, and Cianán reared, stumbling backward and almost unseating Alyssa again.

"What the—? Who said that?" she cried.

The very air around them shimmered then, a form beginning to take shape. It was the form of a lovely woman, ethereal and transparent. She seemed literally suspended in mid-air, her diaphanous robes fluttering on the light breeze. Then she was gliding toward them.

"She's a sylphide," Cianán replied. "A spirit of air and light."

"I am Eibhilín," the sylphide said in her odd, reverberating voice. *"And where the kelpie belongs in this place, you do not. How come you to be here, human?"*

"She is the descendant," Cianán explained before Alyssa could reply. "She was brought here against her will. I am returning her to her own place."

"Ah, yes. I see it now in my mind's eye. The legend. The great-granddaughter of the great-granddaughter ... three of three. It is a wise

choice to leave this place, descendant. For there is evil ahead and behind that also does not belong."

"Yes. We left the Red King behind, and he's evil for sure, but what evil is ahead of us?" Alyssa asked.

"The ahead and behind are connected. One was made by the other and neither belongs."

"What does that even mean?" Alyssa grumbled, shaking her head in frustration. She remembered her first visit to Roseland and the frost pixies she'd encountered there. They had spoken in inane circles as well. "Is there a law here that I don't know about requiring people to speak in confusing riddles at the most inopportune times?"

"I know not of any such law, but you must leave this desolate land quickly. There is death here. And you did not leave the evil behind, as it follows you even now."

"Our escape must have been discovered," Cianán said. "The Red King will have dispatched a hunting party."

"Stay aware and vigilant, for what is ahead awaits you."

"What's ahead awaits us? *Seriously?* For the love of God!" Alyssa pinched the bridge of her nose in frustration and tried to not to scream. "So very helpful. Thank you very much."

"You are most welcome, descendant. Now go. And may the benevolent Trinity watch over your journey."

With that, the sylphide's visage began to diminish until all that was left of her was shimmering air.

"So, what do you think she meant by all that nonsense?" Alyssa asked Cianán. "I mean, really. What's ahead awaits you? Well, duh! And that 'one was made by the other' thing? What was that about?"

The kelpie shook his head. "I don't know. Perhaps whatever danger we may find ahead is waiting for only us? Possibly created by the Red King?"

"Or his horrible sorcerer, Yulis, more likely."

"Agreed."

Alyssa squinted into the distance. "Do you think it could be connected to the scent of blood you detected, maybe the cause of it?"

"That's also a possibility. The sylphide did say that there was death here. In any case, we need to keep moving. She also said that we've not left the evil behind us, so I can only assume that we're being tracked. The sooner we get to the Wysterian border, the better."

"Yeah, I'm all for that."

The last thing Alyssa wanted was to be caught by one of Aramond's hunting parties and hauled back to those stone cells in the bowels of the mesa. She was pretty sure that Cianán was thinking the same thing. They knew that neither of them would live to see another day should they be taken back to the Red King.

So they kept moving. Cianán maintained a steady pace, galloping along as fast as he dared, striving to get within sight of the Wysterian border before they could be overtaken by Aramond's forces. One hour rolled into the next until the stress of the situation and monotony of the journey combined with lack of sleep had Alyssa's head bobbing. Her muscles screamed with the struggle to keep her eyes open and stay upright on Cianán's back. By the third hour, she was so intent on that effort that it didn't immediately register when Cianán began to slow his pace again until he came to a complete standstill.

"What is it now?" she asked, blinking and looking around in confusion.

"We have company," he said quietly. "In large quantity, I might add. Looks to be a small army, Alyssa. What do you want to do? This could be the danger the sylphide warned us about."

Alyssa's anxiety level rose at the thought. Had they come all this way only to be cut off before reaching the safety of Wysteria? How would Aramond's forces have gotten here ahead of them? Or had they been here all along? The thoughts buzzed around in her mind like a swarm of angry hornets. But as she peered into the distance, she realized that several of the soldiers out in front seemed more than a bit familiar ... and one in particular.

"Niall?" she whispered, afraid to hope.

"Niall? Are you speaking of the fae warrior of legend?"

As the smile spread across her face, Alyssa nodded, blinking back tears of joy. "Yes, Cianán. He's High Lord of Roseland's Twilight Court."

"Is he someone you know and trust?"

"We have nothing to fear from him or this army. I do indeed

know them. These are the friends I told you about. I think we're finally saved."

"Truly?" The kelpie looked over his shoulder at her. "You are certain of this?"

Alyssa laughed out loud and hugged his neck. "Oh, yes, I'm very certain."

Cianán started forward then, closing the distance between them, and Alyssa's heart began to pound in her chest. She couldn't take her eyes off of the dangerous-looking High Lord sitting tall and handsome on the back of his massive ebony war horse. It was like something out of fantasy fiction, and overcome with relief, she nearly giggled at the thought.

When they approached the waiting forces, the butterflies in her stomach began to flutter in earnest as she watched Niall climb down from his saddle.

"Stop here, Cianán, and let me down," she said. As he did so, she slid from his back and stepped around in front of him. "Wait for me here. No one will harm you. I'll be right back. I promise."

As she turned and started toward Niall, everything and everyone around them faded away until only he filled her field of vision. The closer she got, the faster she walked, and before she knew it, she was flat out running in her need to get to him, to touch him and know that he was real.

"Niall!" Alyssa cried as she launched herself at him, the sound of her heartbeat pounding in her ears. "You're really here?"

To his credit, he caught her up with ease, his deep baritone laughter infusing her with joy as he spun her around and around while she clung to him as if her life depended on it.

"I am, indeed," he replied.

When he finally stopped turning, he pulled her in and held her close, gazing down at her with a look that warmed her from the inside out and turned her knees to jelly. Then without a word and heedless of those around them, he crushed his lips to hers in a white-hot kiss that she matched with equal parts desperation and relief. He filled her senses, heated her blood, and Alyssa clung to him without a single thought of where they were or who may have been watching them. All that mattered was that he was here, that he was really here.

When they finally parted and he set her on her feet, she stared up at him for a moment before catching him off guard by rearing back and punching him in the arm. "Took you long enough. Where the hell have you been?"

He winced as she connected with his injured shoulder and then gave her a wicked smile. "Mmm, yes, about that. I do apologize for my tardiness, darling Alyssa. I was ... regrettably detained."

Alyssa frowned and ran a hand over the shoulder she'd just punched. "What's happened? Are you hurt?"

"Yes, Lord Niall," Alexi called from a good twenty yards away. "Do tell darling Alyssa about your injuries and why you're tardy."

Alyssa leaned around Niall to give Alexi a questioning look when the High Lord turned to glare at the Field Marshal.

Alexi laughed out loud and pointed to his ear. "The Fae aren't the only ones with extraordinary hearing, Niall. Elves enjoy that ability as well, remember?"

Alyssa looked back at Niall. "What is he talking about?"

"Don't listen to the jabbering baboon. There's really nothing to tell, love. A slight altercation on our first attempt to track your whereabouts here in the Barrens is all."

"Oh, for the love of the Oracles, Niall." Alexi hooted. "That would be the understatement of the century, don't you think?"

At the angry look Niall flung over his shoulder, Alexi grinned and put up a hand as if to say, 'whatever!', but Alyssa was not about to be put off. Grabbing hold of the High Lord's breast plate, she jerked him around to face her. "Tell me what happened."

With a sigh, Niall shook his head. "Following the searching amulet's signal, Finvar, Alexi, and I came looking for you three days ago. Unfortunately, we were forced to return to the border when we lost, first the signal, and then the light. On our way back, we were set upon by a Wolvataur or two."

"*A Wolvataur or two?*" Alexi shouted the question with a roll of his eyes. "There were four of them as I recall, just to be clear. But go ahead. Explain what a Wolvataur is and how you spent the last couple of days unconscious in the hospital wing of the palace."

With a snarl, Niall spun around with a dangerous glare. "Will you shut your infernal gob? No one is speaking to you, idiot."

Alexi burst into another round of laughter, and Alyssa watched Finvar's lips twitch as he tried unsuccessfully to keep the grin from his face, while Valian and Gray looked everywhere but at them. Interestingly enough, the smile on Tisharu's face registered her obvious delight at her twin's discomfort.

Alyssa turned back to Niall. "I'm waiting," she told him. "So, your injuries from these Wolvataurs were serious enough for you to be hospitalized? And only three days ago?"

He smiled down at her, and her pulse kicked up a notch, even though she knew he was attempting to distract her. "Darling Alyssa, I'm nearly healed now. Practically as good as new."

But then his smile faded, and he took her chin into his hand, scrutinizing her face. "Tell me the truth now," he demanded. "What of you? Have you been harmed in any way?"

He could obviously see her fatigue from lack of sleep and the circles beneath her eyes as he turned her face this way and that. Then his gaze narrowed in on the bruises left behind by Yulis' hands around her neck. "What are these marks on your throat?"

His fierce tone coupled with the fire in his eyes was Alyssa's undoing as her emotions flooded in. All she could think about was that the torturous few days she'd spent at the hands of the Red King were at an end. But the words stuck in her throat, and she was unable to recount her frightening ordeal. Her eyes filled with tears when exhaustion finally threatened to swamp her completely. She choked back a sob and gazed up at him through drenched eyes.

"You came for me," she finally whispered.

Niall lovingly wiped away an errant tear as it spilled down her cheek, before kissing her forehead and wrapping her in his arms again. "I will always come for you, love," he murmured. "Always."

It took her a few minutes, but when she'd finally gotten a handle on her emotions, she leaned back and gave him a shaky smile. "Thanks for coming after me."

The wicked grin she associated with him alone spread across Niall's handsome face. "It was my pleasure, but it looks as though you didn't need my assistance. Now, tell me, how is it that you've captured yourself a kelpie and arrived here on his back? They are dangerous creatures, most unpredictable, and fairly difficult to apprehend without issue."

Alyssa shook her head. "No, no, I didn't capture Cianán. Aramond's rebel warriors did."

"Mmm, so the Red King is alive?"

"Oh boy, is he—and I gotta say, crazy as a loon. His horrible sorcerer is there with him, too."

Niall nodded. "Tisharu was certain of this—had seen as much in her visions—but it's good to have confirmation."

"Anyway, they had enslaved Cianán and were using him as a pack animal. It was horrific. He was being held in a cell next to mine, so we made a deal. If we could find a way out, he would take me to the border and there I would free him."

Niall gave her a skeptical look. "That was a very unwise bargain, Alyssa. More than likely, the moment you removed his harness you would've been at his mercy."

Alyssa chuckled. "That wasn't really a concern, because Minerva gave him a dire ultimatum."

"I beg your pardon? The Witch of the Eastern Glade is there in Aramond's stronghold?"

"Yes. She's glamoured to look like one of the fae warriors and obviously has an agenda, but I don't know what she's up to there. I got the impression that she's been close by for a while."

"Áine thought that the old hag had followed the rebels who ambushed me and my warriors in the Glade that evening into the Barrens," Tisharu said. "So, that makes sense. She must have infiltrated their ranks on that very night."

"Well, she wasn't happy to see me there, I can tell you. But she did protect me during the torture sessions with the king and then helped Cianán and me to escape."

The High Lord's features turned to stone in an instant, and he leaned in, taking hold of her chin again. "Exactly what torture sessions are we talking about here?" he asked in a deadly-quiet tone and fury flared in his emerald-green eyes. "Are you telling me that Aramond had you tortured? Is he the one who put these marks on you?"

"No. Those are Yulis' handiwork. He was the one who did the

torturing with spells and incantations, but yes, at Aramond's behest. He would've killed me that last time if Aramond hadn't stopped him, which is where the marks came from." Alyssa put a hand on his breast plate. "They wanted to know where the scepter was being hidden, but I couldn't tell them. I knew that the minute I'd been abducted it would've been moved." She gave him a wry look. "Needless to say, it wasn't the answer they were looking for and not one they would accept. Hence the torture thing."

"I will kill them both slowly and painfully." Niall sighed and pulled her into his arms again. "However, you needn't worry about any of that now. Let's see about getting you back to the palace. I'll have Kassair escort you back."

Alyssa pulled away and shook her head. "No. We have to release Cianán, and then I'm going with you."

The High Lord stared at her for a moment with his mouth open. "Have you lost your mind? Absolutely not. Besides, don't you want Isabella to know that you've been found and are safe?"

Alyssa's eyes grew wide. "Izzy's here? At the palace?"

"She is and awaiting word of your rescue."

Alyssa thought about it for a moment, and then slowly nodded. "Then she will be safe until our return."

With stubborn resolve, she disengaged herself from his embrace and backed away. "They tortured me, Niall," she said quietly. "They threatened to chop off my head. I'm going with you. It's not up for discussion."

He reached out a hand to her. "Darling Alyssa, be reasonable. This will be a bloody fight, and you're not a warrior."

"No, I'm not. And don't *Darling Alyssa* me!" She crossed her arms and stared up at him with a mutinous scowl. "I may not be a warrior, but if you won't take me, I'll find someone who will. Perhaps Cianán will take me. But I am going, and you can't stop me," she told him, knowing full well that he definitely could stop her if he chose.

"Love, the Barrens is an unforgiving place with dangerous beasts of many kinds, which I'm sure you know by now. But this will get ugly, and I would see you out of harm's way before heading into the fray."

Alyssa sighed. "Look, I know you feel responsible for my abduction, but it wasn't your fault. It wasn't," she insisted when he wouldn't look her in the eyes. Taking his face in her hands, she made him look at her. "I told Aramond and Yulis that my friends were coming, would end them ... and that I would watch. You must let me keep that promise."

Niall stared down at her for what felt like an eternity, a muscle working his jaw was the only indication that she was right on the money with her summation. But then he grinned and shook his head. "So bloodthirsty. What happened to that innocent who refused to use the scepter during the battle all those months ago, who wasn't sure she could cause that kind of destruction? I fear that we've been a bad influence on you, love."

"Maybe." She tilted her head and considered for a moment. "Or maybe I've just had enough. They can't continue to cause such havoc, Niall, to hurt innocent people without regard for the lives they destroy. And they not only threatened me, but my family as well. Nobody threatens my family. Nobody."

After a brief pause, Niall nodded. "Alright then. Let's go free your kelpie and find you a steed."

"Um ... High Lord? A word, please," Alexi began, a concerned look on his face.

Niall turned slowly, and his response was uttered again with quiet steel. "Yes, Field Marshal? Did you have something to add?"

Alexi looked at Valian, who simply raised an eyebrow, and then Gray, who only shrugged. "For fuck sake, am I the only one who finds this to be a really bad idea? This is the descendant we're talking about taking into battle with us." But when he got no response, he just shook his head, and looking back at Niall, sighed. "Well, I'm on record here and now as not being down with this insane plan. I just hope you know what you're doing, Niall."

"So noted," the High Lord said before dismissing him, taking Alyssa by the arm, and heading toward Cianán. "Let's get this done."

As they neared, Alyssa noted that Cianán had reverted back into his human form and was waiting for them with a look of anxiety on his face.

"We are in your debt, kelpie, for bringing Alyssa back to us safely," Niall said as they approached.

Cianán gave Niall a curt nod. "A bargain made, a bargain met, High Lord. I had an accord with the Old One to see Alyssa to the border. We are not there yet."

"That doesn't matter now, Cianán," Alyssa said. "You kept your end of the deal, now let me keep mine." Reaching up, she lifted the bridle from around his neck and handed it to him. "You are free, my friend."

Cianán gazed down at the harness he held in wonder. "Most—human, fae, or elven—would have left me there in that cell to die without a backward glance. As I told you once before, you are unlike any human I've ever met. You treated me as an equal, saved my life, and in the end, kept your word as well. I am grateful, descendant of Alice."

"And I am grateful to have met you, Cianán."

The kelpie looked up then and frowned. "One thing—did I hear correctly that you are going back to the Red King's stronghold with these warriors?" When she nodded, he shook his head again and gave her a grim smile. "That is a terrible idea—as I'm sure you already know—but if you must go, then I would be honored if you would allow me to take you."

"That is not necessary, kelpie," Niall replied. "You have satisfied your accord with the Witch of the Eastern Glade. You are released."

Cianán gave Niall a steadfast look, and without pause, replied in an even tone. "No offense, High Lord, but I wasn't speaking to you."

As Niall took a step closer, Alyssa put out her arm to stop him. Taking Cianán's hand, she gave it a squeeze. "Your offer is very honorable, Cianán. But as you say, this is probably a terrible idea. And where I can make the decision to go for myself, I could never ask you to place yourself at such risk for me."

The kelpie smiled again. "I agree. It would not be your place to ask but is my place to offer." Before she could respond, Cianán put up a hand. "They did not torture me as they did you, but they treated me severely, and were it not for you, would have ended my life when they were done with me. I, too, wish to see their end. Besides, you need a ride, do you not?"

"Are you sure about this, kelpie?" Niall asked. "I need to know that you will stick to the end and protect Alyssa with your life should it be required."

"You need not worry on that point, High Lord. That is my intent with my offer."

Niall stared at him for a moment, and obviously satisfied with what he saw, nodded. "Then let's get a move on. We still have a ways to go."

Rejoining the rest of the forces, Cianán started to slip the bridle over his head again, but Alyssa stopped him. "Don't, Cianán. You're free now. It's your decision to go with us or not. I would never enslave you that way."

The kelpie laughed out loud. "And truly, you no longer have that power."

At her confused look, he went on to explain. "You gave me the bridle, Alyssa. It's now mine, so wearing it gives no one power over me. In fact, it protects me from others who would seek to enslave me. I shall wear it with pride, knowing that your generous gesture gave me my freedom and also protects it."

"I hate to break up this fascinating love-fest, but can we get this moveable feast on the road?" Alexi complained. "We've wasted enough time, and we still don't know what killed that dryad we found."

Cianán's head snapped around at the comment. "You found a dead dryad?"

The Field Marshal nodded. "And her death was quite recent, though there was no clue as to whom or what committed the deed. Looked like they walked a few yards away and then faded."

"What's a dryad?" Alyssa asked.

"Dryads are a peaceful faction of tree sprites that live in the canopies of old growth forests," Alexi explained. "This one in particular was from an ancient Wysterian forest just north of the Eastern Glade."

Alyssa put a hand to her heart. "What on earth was she doing in this terrible place? There are no trees here at all that I've seen."

"That is a very good question," Alexi replied.

Cianán turned to Alyssa. "That must be the scent of fresh blood I smelled earlier. We'll need to continue to be vigilant from here on."

"Yes," Alexi replied. "Hence the term 'moveable feast' and the rush to get going. The longer we stand around yammering, the more quickly we become prey."

"Good point." With that Cianán transformed into his black stallion form and knelt so Alyssa could climb onto his back.

"Are you ready, love?" Niall asked when she was seated. "Last chance to change your mind."

"You'll not get rid of me that easily," Alyssa replied with a grin. "So, let's quit yammering—as Alexi so eloquently put it—and move out."

Twenty-Two

A s one third of their army continued the journey toward the mesa where Aramond's forces were hidden, Gray began to get a disturbing sense of something not quite right with the land around them. Though the logical side of his brain acknowledged that this was the Barrens, and all manner of monstrous things lived and thrived within its borders, his newly developed Ellurian senses told him that what he was beginning to detect was something entirely different. It was the most unsettling feeling—subtle, almost a vibration from the very ground. Though whatever was causing this disturbance wasn't clearly visible, it was unnerving that he could actually *feel* it ... right down into his bones. And it felt dangerous.

He began to scan the immediate landscape for anything out of place that could be generating such a vibration, but there was nothing but dirt and scrub brush, rock and mesa as far as the eye could see in any direction. Glancing around at those in his party, he seemed to be the only one to notice the disturbance at all.

Closing his eyes, he worked to center himself and focus his senses on his surroundings—the warmth of the mid-morning sun on his face, the waft of a light breeze over his skin, the cadence of his destrier's steady hoof beats beneath him, and the rhythm of his own breathing. Tuning out all other distractions, he reached out with mind and spirit, searching the area and giving his newly found mental gifts a spin.

And there it was, the odd vibration, barely noticeable but getting closer and just a bit louder. Unfortunately, as his powers began to spread and take hold, a shout went up from the ranks breaking his concentration. Peridot, Elshandra, and Sumia, along with their court armies and Gruden's southern dwarf clan had been spotted approaching from the south. At the same time, the plume of dust toward the north heralded the arrival of Luthias, Citron, and Juppar with their armies and the northern dwarf clans. The strange disturbances Gray had detected were forgotten for the moment as Peridot and Elshandra galloped up to join them.

"Good to see you made it," Finvar called. "Did you run into any trouble traveling up from the southern quadrant?"

"No." Elshandra smirked. "At least nothing we couldn't handle. The only things we stumbled across were a couple of desert trolls heading in for the morning, but they made for higher ground and disappeared into the rocky terrain as soon as they caught a glimpse of our numbers. High Lord Peridot, however, was a bit on edge and kept a keen eye out for any signs of Wolvataurs after hearing of your recent exploits."

Peridot's olive-green skin darkened with agitation at the fae queen's dig, and he narrowed his golden eyes in her direction. "As we discussed earlier, Elshandra, since you've never had the pleasure of an encounter with such creatures—as I, Sumia, and others in this group have—you've really no room to talk, now do you? With your inexperience, I would think you would do well to keep an eye out for those signs yourself."

Gray hid his amusement at the High Lord's terse reprimand, while the warm toffee of Elshandra's face took on a decidedly reddish hue with her anger. But before she could open her mouth to respond, her icy-blue gaze settled on Alyssa.

"Well, well. What have we here?" she crooned with raised eyebrows. "I was led to believe that this little foray into the Barrens was designed to rescue the descendant. But here she is, and it seems, safe and sound." Turning, the queen sent a questioning look to Valian. "Care to explain, Chancellor?"

"There's nothing much to explain, Elshandra." Valian gave the fae queen a lazy smile. "As it turns out, our Alyssa is quite creative and resourceful. Along with the kelpie she rides, she found a way to escape captivity and rescue herself."

Gray worked to keep his own smile from his face. Although Valian had spoken the truth, he'd prudently left out the fact that Old Minerva was imbedded in Aramond's stronghold and had facilitated their escape. That little tidbit was best kept on a need-to-know basis, especially since they had no clue where Elshandra's loyalties lay.

The fae queen gave Valian a narrowed look. "I see. So, with the descendant's safe return, does this mean we can now leave the Barrens behind and all go home?"

"Well, of course, you are welcome to do whatever you wish," Valian replied with flinty regard. "However, while rescuing the descendant was of the utmost importance, you were also made aware that it wasn't our only reason for coming into the Barrens, correct?" When Elshandra didn't answer but continued to stare at him, Valian went on in an emotionless, commanding tone. "Make no mistake, the Red King will be vanquished and his followers with him before this day is finished, so the rest of us will push on ... with or without you and your Summer Court troops. As I said, the choice is yours."

The fae queen huffed out her discontent at being publicly called out, but gave a terse nod. "There's no need to get peevish about it, Valian. My troops and I will continue on with you, as I've committed to do. I was simply wondering why the descendant is still here. You can't seriously be entertaining the idea of bringing her along into battle."

"The *descendant* has a name and doesn't appreciate being talked about as if she's invisible," Alyssa angrily spoke up. "For your information, I make my own decisions, Queen Elshandra, and can speak for myself. I am going along on this mission."

Elshandra shook her head. "If you are insisting on going back into the belly of the beast, so to speak—after only just escaping— then I must say, I worry about your lack of common sense. Surely you understand how dangerous it will be. Why in the name of the Oracles would you want to do this?"

"I am aware of the danger. I'm not an idiot." Alyssa gave the queen a stony look. "But my reasons are my own and not up for debate with you or anyone else. I'm going."

Elshandra turned to Gray. "And you, Prince Graydon? Do you condone this mad—" The queen suddenly stopped and looked over her shoulder in the direction the army was heading.

"Elshandra?" Finvar questioned. "Are you alright? What's the matter?"

The fae queen shook her head again, sending the seashells woven into her sandy blonde dreadlocks clicking and clacking musically around her head. "I ... don't ... know. Something ..."

Then Gray felt it again as well. The vibration. Only this time it wasn't so subtle. This time it was growing rapidly and impossible to miss. Within moments the others began to feel it too. The ground started to tremble, causing the horses to stamp and rear, and the deafening sound of earth shifting continued to grow to a fevered peak.

"What's happening?" Juppar bellowed over the din.

Alexi shook his head as he struggled to control his charger. "Maybe it's an earthquake."

"This is no earthquake," Elshandra yelled. Pointing toward the open ground before them, she turned and looked directly at Gray. "It's a golem."

"What the hell is a golem?" Alexi shouted his question. "You know what? Never mind. I don't want to know. I really dislike the Barrens. Just sayin'."

They all watched in horror then, as nearly three hundred yards out, the terrain began to buckle and swell. It rose up and up—a wall of solid earth—before finally compacting down and taking shape. Arms, legs, torso, and eyeless misshapen head all began to form. The last thing to emerge in its contorted right hand was a long spear with a lethal-looking blade at the other end. The gruesome figure made of soil and rock stood to its full height at close to fourteen feet tall and let out a monstrous roar.

"*That*, Field Marshal, is a golem," Elshandra cried. "It's made from organic material with dark magicks and will have been given a specific command by its master."

"Yes, but to do what exactly?" Valian asked.

"Well, by that nasty-looking weapon it's holding, I'll go out on a limb and say that its directive can't be good," Gray replied.

That was as far as they got before the abomination took a tentative step forward, and though it didn't appear to have eyes, it very distinctively turned toward the spot where Alyssa and Cianán were located.

"Look out, Niall!" Gray thundered. "I think it's targeting Alyssa."

But even as the High Lord realized what was happening, he had little time to prepare, as the creature reared back and hurled the lethal spear directly at the descendant. In a rapid leap and with seconds to spare, Cianán narrowly averted catastrophe saving both Alyssa and himself from a certain gruesome death. Niall, directly on their heels, barely escaped as well. Regrettably, the warriors on horseback directly behind them weren't quite so lucky. The spear took out several at once when it sliced through them like they were made of rice paper before it disintegrated back into soil.

"Move!" Niall bellowed to his warriors when the golem's attention became fixated on Alyssa. "Protect the descendant at all cost."

Unfortunately, the golem seemed to have an endless supply of weapons as one reappeared in its deformed hand within moments. If this was the case, Gray was afraid that they would be hard pressed to save themselves, let alone Alyssa. Yet to his surprise and relief, Halifax suddenly materialized behind Alyssa on Cianán's back and hollered, "Make for that small outcropping of rocks to the left, kelpie," before the three of them simply disappeared.

Gray had to admit the cat had employed a clever ruse—disappearing and taking Alyssa and Cianán with him—but if the golem had no eyes and was tracking Alyssa by scent or feel, it wouldn't work for long.

Everything seemed to happen at once as they all galvanized into action. Gray, Valian, Finvar, and Tisharu scrambled to ward off this new threat with soldiers from the ranks. Several dwarf clans—who, for as small as they were, seemed to move like lightning—wove in and out of the creature's legs with thick ropes, trying to bring the beast down. But their efforts only succeeded in getting a handful of them trampled in spite of their speed.

With a small squad of his own warriors, Finvar rushed the thing, and terror rose in Gray's chest when his father barely escaped a backhand of its enormous arm. Wielding her battle axes, Tisharu was a magnificent blur as she and Valian flew around the golem from opposite directions hacking out pieces of its body as they went, trying to slow its progress.

But the golem sprang forward undeterred, and Gray was stunned at how swiftly it moved for its size and weight—and how quickly it regenerated not only its body but the vicious spear that it continued to heave. It seemed like within moments of hurling one, a new lance developed in the creature's hand. All the while, warriors were engaging, trying to find a way to destroy the thing, but they weren't having much luck in the effort. The arrows they shot either passed right through or simply embedded in the compacted earth of its body. Although the electrical storm that Juppar generated lit up the early morning sky, his lightning bolts only slowed the monster and had little effect in stopping it altogether.

Gray was beginning to think their best chance might be to outrun the horrific devil, but at the same time, something told him to hold his ground. A strange feeling was brewing inside his chest with each moment that passed. He could feel it building, straining to break free, but he had no idea what it was or what it meant.

As he contemplated their options and this odd pressure rising within him, he caught sight of Elshandra to his right. With eyes closed and a determined look on her face, she held her arms overhead and her palms facing the golem. Her lips were moving as if feverishly praying to some unseen god. It was then he remembered that as queen of the Summer Court, Elshandra's powers included control over sea and sand. It seemed that whatever she was doing was having an effect on the golem. At first it was subtle, but soon it became more apparent that the soil around its legs and midsection was beginning to sluff away, making movement for the beast more difficult.

Unfortunately, it wasn't happening fast enough. What they really needed was a large body of water for her to manipulate. But this was the Barrens. While there were rivers out in the mesa canyons, there was very little here except dirt and rock.

Going on instinct alone, Gray turned and faced the golem as

Elshandra had done. Closing his eyes, he gave in to the force gathering within, and to his surprise, it didn't take long for the potent energy to take hold and burst its way out of him like a tornado. It was as if a powerful weapon had been unleashed, blasting the golem in the middle of his misshapen head. The energy stream tore a path down through the creature's torso like a laser beam until the abomination literally disintegrated into a pile of earth and was absorbed back into the ground from which it had risen.

Though it had seemed an eternity, the total encounter had taken less than ten minutes from start to finish, and when the dust finally cleared, silence reined. Gray took a deep breath and blinked in amazement.

What in the name of the Oracles was that? he thought.

As if reading his mind, Alexi voiced almost the exact same thought but in Alexi-speak. "What the fuck just happened?"

"Yes." Elshandra turned to Gray with a speculative look. "I couldn't have said it better, Field Marshal. What did you just do, Prince Graydon? And more to the point ... how did you accomplish it?"

Gray frowned. "Beats me. I had felt the golem beginning just before you and the others arrived, though I had no idea what it was I was sensing. Then, when I saw you doing—whatever it was you were doing—and the effect it was having, I don't know, I could feel this energy building inside me. I just went with it, I guess."

"Wicked!" Alexi hooted. "You destroyed a golem, my friend. Awesome."

But Elshandra shook her head. "No, Field Marshal. I'm afraid that's not how this works. The golem's magickal name would have been etched across its forehead when the spell was complete and the creature's directive set. My guess is that when the blast destroyed its head, it disrupted the spell as well ... for now. Unfortunately, only the one who actually created the golem and carved this name onto its forehead can truly destroy it for good."

Alexi grinned. "Yeah, well, I'll take 'for now'."

"What I'd like to know is where the power the prince exerted came from to disrupt the golem in this way," Elshandra persisted with a sly look to Gray. "I must admit, I've long wondered where your magicks came from, but this is beyond the pale. I confess, I am most perplexed. Neither of your parents had magick, is that not correct?"

Gray spared a quick glance at Valian and then Finvar before continuing. "Well, no, that's not quite accurate, Elshandra. I've just been made aware that Queen Beatrice is actually half Ellurian."

"What the—" Alexi began.

"Ellurian?" Elshandra sputtered. "But that's a very old race of magickal beings. I thought they had died out centuries ago. How is this possible?"

"As it turns out, my grandfather on my mother's side was Ellurian royalty. Seanchán of the North—perhaps you've heard of him?"

The fae queen's eyes grew round and her mouth dropped open before she caught herself. She licked her lips and blew out a breath. "Uh, yes ... I ... that name is known to me. Seanchán was ruler of several northern Elven enclaves long ago in the dark times, as I recall. This is astonishing news." She cleared her throat then and seemed to get her shock under control. "However, though the Ellurians were a very powerful race and enjoyed strange gifts and immortality, it doesn't quite explain what you just did, now does it?"

"I suppose the combination of ancient Ellurian powers, along with abilities inherited from my biological father's ancestry is probably the explanation you're looking for."

Elshandra gave him a skeptical look. "But if Sir Edward was human, what abilities could he have possibly passed on to you that would have made a difference?"

Gray shot Finvar another glance, and when the High Lord gave a brief nod, he turned back to Elshandra. "That is another revelation that has come to light. Sir Edward, while being the only father I'd ever known, was not actually my biological father. It seems that High Lord Finvar is my biological father."

While he hadn't planned to make this kind of announcement just yet, and it was not the best of circumstances, Gray felt the terrible weight of secrecy lifted from his shoulders. Now he'd wait for the fallout.

Minutes ticked by as all eyes bounced back and forth between him and Finvar.

"Holy shit!" Alexi exclaimed.

Then Elshandra slowly nodded, and Gray could almost see the wheels turning in her head as she calculated what this meant for her court and others.

"I see," she finally said. "I suppose that would indeed explain what we just witnessed."

Anxious to be done with this conversation—of which he knew was nowhere near laid to rest—Gray abruptly turned to Niall. "In the meantime, if we could get back to the problem at hand? In this golem, we may just have found the thing that killed the dryad. What do you think, Lord Niall?"

He was aware that Niall was also giving him full measure but was grateful when the High Lord chose to move on with the change in discussion.

"Yes, that would indeed account for the absence of tracks to follow that were left near her body when we found her," he agreed with a barely perceptible smile.

"But that doesn't answer the question of why it rose from the earth now and why it appeared to be fixated on the descendant," Tisharu added.

"Oh, I think I can answer that question, Queen Tisharu." Alyssa rode forward on Cianán. "After our escape, we ran into a sylphide on our way here who told us a bunch of stuff, which was mostly gibberish. She talked in confusing riddles that made very little sense, but she did say something that fits. She said that it was a good choice to leave the Barrens, that there was evil here that didn't belong, and that it was ahead of us as well as behind. We just didn't know what it meant ... again, the riddle-y gibberish."

She patted Cianán's neck as he snorted and stamped his hooves. "She told us the evil ahead and behind were connected," the kelpie added.

Niall guided Laoch up next to Cianán, and casually reaching between them, took Alyssa's hand. "Well, the behind bit is obvious enough. She'd have been talking about the Red King."

Alyssa nodded. "Yes. She had to have been talking about

Aramond. But when she said one evil was made by the other, it seems to follow that the evil ahead—the golem in this case—could have been created by Aramond's sorcerer Yulis."

"If that's the case, then Yulis—or better still, Yulis' death—is the only way to destroy the golem for good," Elshandra said with an evil grin. When she saw the look of disbelief on Gray's face, she shrugged. "What? I'm well aware that you all think that I'm not to be trusted. Did you think that I'd sworn allegiance to the Red King?"

"The thought had crossed our minds," Tisharu confirmed after a moment. Then she gave Elshandra a wicked smile. "Briefly."

"Well, you need not have worried. I have no love of Aramond and will fight alongside you without a second thought. In my opinion, the sooner the threat of evil is neutralized, the better for all of Artemysia."

"Agreed. And both Aramond and Yulis will pay handsomely for laying one finger on Alyssa, if I have anything to say about it," Niall murmured darkly.

An uncomfortable silence hung over the group as minutes dragged out.

Then Alexi broke the tension in true Alexi fashion. "Well, that was fun,'" he shouted with a huge grin. "But how about we get moving rather than hanging around here waiting for that nasty bastard to rise up again? I mean, seriously, with our luck, the next threat will be dragons or some other such absurdity."

"Oh, I wouldn't worry about dragons, Field Marshal," Juppar commented with a cunning look. "There hasn't been a dragon sighting in the Barrens for at least a few centuries."

"Yes, that's true, Juppar," Halifax, still seated behind Alyssa on Cianán's back, added with a chuckle. "They've mostly been driven into the far north Wastelands, as far as I know. Mostly."

Alexi scrubbed his hands over his face. "I was making a damned joke, you two. But thanks for giving me another supposedly mythical monster to now worry about."

Niall frowned and glowered at Halifax as if just recalling his presence. "Why are you still there, Cat? Do you not have a steed of your own to ride upon?"

The Cheshire Cat, in human form, sighed and rolled his eyes. He leaned over Alyssa's shoulder and spoke in a low disgruntled tone. "What the High Lord actually means is 'Thank you, Halifax, for your quick thinking in protecting my darling Alyssa'. To which I say, the pleasure was all mine."

When Niall's look darkened, Halifax muttered an oath and quickly disappeared.

Alyssa shook her head. "Be nice, Niall. After all, Halifax did give me and Cianán most excellent cover."

Gray watched the warrior's frown soften as Niall tucked a strand of hair behind Alyssa's ear. "Perhaps, but he's still annoying all the same," he replied.

With that, Alexi's own grin resurfaced. "So, now that we've gotten all those pesky emotions out of the way, come on, people. Places to go, insurgents to thrash, and I want to be home by dinner."

That earned him a look of disdain from Niall. Valian simply shook his head at his cousin's antics, and Gray burst into laughter. But it seemed as though that was all it took to get the small army moving again. Gray just hoped that the golem didn't resurface before they could figure out how to destroy it for good, and that when they reached Aramond's stronghold it would be as quick and easy as Alexi's sentiments suggested.

Twenty-Three

A fter the encounter with the golem, the small army continued
cautiously on its journey. Valian, Tisharu, Alexi, and a
contingent of warriors took point, leading the way toward
the mesa where Aramond's forces were hidden. Niall, Gray, Finvar,
and warriors from various courts rode behind them and made certain
Alyssa and Cianán were protected from all sides in case of another
golem attack.

Though ever-vigilant, Niall had plenty of time to contemplate
what they'd just learned about Prince Graydon. The revelations were
of no small significance. Niall himself was older than many of the
other courts' High Fae and vaguely remembered a few of the Old
Guard—the Ellurians. They were one of the most commanding races
of the ancient Immortals and truly a force to be reckoned with in
their time. That the prince was a direct descendant of one of those
ancients—and an incredibly powerful one at that—was an interesting twist of fate and one which certainly needed more thought
and consideration.

For instance, Niall wondered what other abilities—besides the
ones he'd exhibited with the golem—that the prince would eventually develop. Also, the combination of ancient Elven ancestors—for
that is what the Ellurians were—and Finvar's fae lineage could prove

to be a new and very different set of powers. Powers the Artemysian realm had never before seen. Just what would this revelation mean for the clans and courts of Roseland or Wysteria? Before Niall could ponder this new information further, Alyssa broke into his concentration with an abrupt question.

"So, what's the plan here?"

"I beg your pardon?" Niall frowned "I thought our mission was plainly stated. What part of it is unclear to you?"

"Well, for one thing, exactly how are we going to get into the mesa with this small army? I mean, the cave entrances all along the front of the mesa are constantly patrolled and surveilled by rebel forces. They'll see this many of us coming a mile away."

Niall glanced at the prince who was riding closely on her opposite side. "That is a valid question. It is one several of us had quite the lengthy discussion over this morning before we left the palace."

She turned to him. "And? What was the outcome of said discussion? Surely you have some kind of strategy."

"Yes. Naturally, a strategy was decided upon." Niall looked out over the unforgiving landscape before them. "You see, in addition to powers of transformation, visions, levitation, and a smattering of other talents, my twin and I have certain ... abilities that may help in that area."

"Abilities?" Alyssa gave him a curious look. "What kind of abilities? Are we talking about magical powers here?"

He smiled. "We are indeed, love. The most powerful ability we possess is the gift of twilight, of course."

Gesturing to the rocky outcroppings to his left, he watched a look of surprise cross her face as the darkness of his twilight spread with the gesture, totally obscuring the length of cliffs.

"Wow. That is impressive," Alyssa murmured. "But what if the rebels just aim and fire into the darkness? With so many of us coming at them, they're sure to hit *something*, if even by accident, right?"

"Well, besides the darkness that Niall and Tisharu can conjure, Queen Elshandra can manipulate sand and water, which could help prevent random fire and give us more time to advance," Gray replied and then nodded to his right. "Also, Lord Luthias of the Dawn

Court can conjure impenetrable shields powered by the emerging sun, and Citron of the Daylight Court wields the power of blasting sunlight and windstorms." Gray turned back to her and shook his head. "But other than that, I'm afraid we may just have to take our chances with those deterrents if there's no other way into the caves."

"Ah, but there is at least one other way in," Cianán spoke up.

Niall glanced down at the kelpie. "You know of another way into the mesa?"

Cianán bared his equine teeth. "I do. There is a side entrance that is semi-obscured from view. It's the way I was taken in and out when I was used as a pack horse." The kelpie snorted and shook his sleek, black head as if remembering the unconscionable treatment to which he'd been subjected. "I'm pretty sure there's also another entrance somewhere along the back length of the mesa as well. Warriors would appear and disappear back there frequently, though I never saw exactly how."

"That's good to know," Gray said with a shrewd look. "Perhaps you and I can make use of that, Lord Niall."

"Mmm, yes. We could take a small group of warriors and go in through this obscured side entrance as the bulk of the army is assaulting the main openings along the front of the mesa."

Gray nodded. "That would be a good distraction. Tisharu and the others could provide cover for them from the front, and if need be, you can cover our approach from the side. I like it."

Niall grinned at the prince and then turned back to Cianán. "And you can find this side entrance with certainty, kelpie?"

Cianán snorted again. "I could find that entrance in the dead of night with my eyes closed."

"Very good. Then we have amended our plan satisfactorily." The only thing bothering Niall now was the prospect of fighting their way in *and* protecting Alyssa at the same time. That he'd agreed to this folly was not one of his more astute moments, and he was beginning to think better of it now. *If she would only consent to waiting outside with the kelpie to protect her ...*

Giving her a sidelong glance, Niall tried again. "And you, darling Alyssa? Are you still committed to wading into the fray along with us? You could very well wait outside the mesa with your kelpie to keep you safe and sound. After all, you are the descendent. This will be an ugly—albeit short—encounter, yet the danger is very real."

Alyssa glared at him. "I may be the descendent, Niall, but you'll not shame me into waiting outside like some kind of princess. I'm well aware that I'm not a trained warrior, and I do realize that this will make your job harder, but I'm going in with you. I need to see this ended for good with my own eyes. Please try to understand."

Niall sighed. "Very well, love. But there are specific rules. Once we head into the mesa, you will do everything I tell you to do, exactly as I tell you to do it, without hesitation or argument. Are we clear?"

"I understand."

"No. Understanding is one thing, Alyssa, but I will have your word on it," he said gruffly, then put up a hand when she made to argue. "It isn't that I don't trust you, my sweet. This will be an incredibly dangerous endeavor. Warriors going into battle rarely give the prospect of death a second thought, indeed, have no time to do so. But having a precious life in tow is nothing to be taken for granted. I go into this with knowledge of how battles flow and how quickly they can shift and change, as do most of these warriors. You have only memories of the one battle months ago, and for the most part, those memories are limited to a distance. Up close is a much different animal."

"Look, Niall, I have no illusions about the possible outcomes here, and on the ramparts of the palace in January, I saw up close and very personal how frightening war can be. I'm not without fear and am definitely going in with my eyes wide open. So, I'll be following any orders you give me without delay and to the letter. You have my word. But Cianán and I are the only two in this entire army that have been inside that mesa. You need us with you."

Niall gave a succinct nod. "You are correct in that. However, I don't have to like it."

They rode on then in silence for another several miles, each with their own thoughts on what was to come, before they finally grew near enough to their destination to stop and dismount.

"We go forward from here on foot, fading ahead when it's safe and prudent to do so," Niall told his general. "Spread the word,

Kassair. Most will join the frontal attack with the main forces, but choose ten of your best warriors. They will accompany me, the descendant, and the prince through a side entrance that the kelpie has used. And find Halifax. We may need the cat's invisibility for reconnaissance."

"Wait, what?" Alexi blurted. "When was this decided on? And by whom?"

Gray spoke up before Niall could respond. "I'm sorry, Alexi. This just came up a few miles back. It was my decision. Cianán will guide us into the mesa through that obscured entry while the main forces attack from the front."

The field marshal frowned. "Well, I don't like that one bit. It's bad enough that Alyssa is going into this fight along with us, but to have not only the descendant but the crown prince out of my sightline in a risky situation is not a good idea, Gray."

"I have to concur with Alexi," Valian put in. "I realize that you and Niall are both seasoned warriors, and you alone I'd not worry about. However, you'll both have the distraction of Alyssa's safety, and things can go sideways in a hurry."

Gray shrugged. "I've made my decision. You and Alexi are more than welcome to come with us, but we need to keep it to a small, tight group. We don't know what conditions or bottlenecks we may have to navigate once inside."

Valian and Alexi exchanged glances.

"Rock, paper, scissors, bro?" Alexi asked with a grin.

Giving his cousin a bland stare, the chancellor sighed and closed his eyes briefly as if praying for patience. "You are such a child." After another moment, he finally waved Alexi away. "Fine. Go. But keep your eyes on these two, Field Marshal. I will hold you personally responsible should anything go awry. And I do mean anything."

"What? Why me and not Niall? After all, it was his hairbrained idea to allow the descendant to go with us."

"Hey!" Alyssa cried and stomped her foot. "I will remind you that it wasn't Niall's decision. I am perfectly capable of making my own choices, thank you very much."

"Alright, alright. Stand down," Alexi said and put up a hand. "It was a poor choice of words, okay?" But turning back to Valian, he continued to dig his hole in the same vein. "However, as I recall, I was the only one who voiced concern at the stupidity of that plan. And now I have to be responsible for it?"

Alyssa's mouth dropped open. "I beg your pardon? *Stupidity*?"

Before Alexi could placate her again, Niall watched in silent amusement as Valian jumped into the fray.

"Well, you are the queen's field marshal, correct? Head of all Artemysian troops?" the chancellor asked. "Or did I miss your letter of resignation."

"Oh, nice. Sure. Dump the whole thing off on me," Alexi replied with a disgusted look. "But you *are* the queen's chancellor, *correct*? And a rather large step higher in rank than a mere field marshal, I might add. I didn't hear a peep out of you—or the crown prince, for that matter—when this whole thing reared its ugly head in the first place."

"Okay, now why do you want to go and drag me into this?" Gray complained.

Alexi stared at him for a moment. "Why? Well, gee-wiz, Gray, maybe because you were right there beside Valian with your stones planted firmly in your side pocket when I broached the subject? As I recall, you shrugged at me. Shrugged, for the love of—"

"Uh, gentlemen?" Alyssa chimed in, breaking into Alexi's tirade. "And I do use that word loosely at the moment. Can we just get moving?" She gave each a pointed stare. "Honestly. You all sound like a bunch of whiny schoolboys, each pointing a finger at the other."

"Yeah, yeah," Alexi grumbled and bent to check his weapons. "Okay then." He pointed a finger at Gray as he passed. "But you best watch yourself, my friend. If I have to rescue you or the High Lord here at any point, neither of you will ever hear the end of it. I promise you both that."

"Hey, what about Alyssa?" Gray asked.

"What about her?" Alexi turned, and walking backward spread his arms wide, making a show of winking at Alyssa. "I'm not worried about Alyssa. She's survived capture by the Red King twice and lived to tell about it." With a chuckle, he turned to Cianán, who'd reverted back to his human form. "So, come on, let's get this party started. Lead the way, Cianán."

As the bulk of the army made their way toward the river flowing between their position and the front of the mesa, Alyssa, Niall, Gray, Alexi, Halifax, and ten of Niall's Twilight Court warriors followed Cianán around one end of the mesa on a path partially overgrown with scrub brush and sage. Before they rounded the final outcropping of rocks, the kelpie had them stop while he and Niall made a covert run to check the area where the obscured opening was located.

"Only two warriors standing guard outside," Niall told Alexi when they returned a few minutes later. "However, there will be more inside."

"Agreed," Alexi said. "So, we take them out quickly and quietly. Then Halifax goes in to get the layout. Once he's back, and we know what we're dealing with, we all move inside cautiously when we get the signal that the assault has begun out front. Cianán, since you know where we're going, you and the cat will take point. Niall, you follow them with half of your warriors, Alyssa follows you, Gray and I follow Alyssa with the rest of the group. Everyone good with that line-up?"

When all replied in the affirmative, Alexi nodded. "Good deal. Everyone stay frosty and alert. Let's go."

The two warriors standing guard outside the entrance ended up posing no threat at all, as they were paying little attention to the surrounding area and seemed to be engaged in some sort of weird wrestling contest. Alyssa watched in stunned silence as both Alexi and Niall moved with stealth and lightning speed, dispatching them both before either even knew they were in peril.

Alexi then gestured to Halifax, who literally disappeared just outside the entrance. They waited for several tense minutes, feeling exposed and vulnerable. Alyssa barely held back a scream of fright when he reappeared between her and Alexi.

"What the hell is wrong with you, idiot?" Alexi muttered at Halifax, slipping the lethal-looking dagger he'd pulled back into its sheath. "Are you trying to get yourself killed? Never sneak up on me like that."

The cat just raised an eyebrow. "Jumpy, much, Field Marshal?"

"Don't be an idiot. We're in the friggin' Barrens, dummy. You bet I'm jumpy. Just tell us what you found."

"Okay, okay! Geez." Halifax sighed. "Just inside the opening, there's a fairly wide passageway which leads to a crossroads of sorts, fifty yards or so in. I ran into an obstacle or two on the way there, but they will pose no threat to us now. Several other corridors split off from that intersection area. However, there were ten or twelve fae warriors lounging about there. I didn't go much further, as I wasn't sure which path to take."

Niall looked at Cianán. "Where do the corridors lead, kelpie? And which one would take me to Aramond's location?"

Cianán hunkered down and drew a rough map in the sand. "This corridor to the left leads to storage areas and the cells where Alyssa and I were held. To the right, the troop housing, the Red King's personal chamber, along with Yulis' area, so more warriors for certain. This corridor straight ahead goes to the so-called throne room where Aramond is normally located, though there are open chambers along the way. The throne room is a cavernous space where there will be even more troops, but plenty of room to fight. Unfortunately, Yulis is usually in attendance certain times of the day, and that makes for a dicey situation, as he has no problem using lethal magicks on any and all intruders, whether they're in the king's employ or not."

"That's just great." Alexi blew out an aggravated breath. "But this is good information, Cianán. Thanks." He looked at Niall, then to Gray as they heard the first sounds of explosions from the other side of the mesa signaling the beginning of the invasion. "You ready for this?"

"Let's hit it," Gray said.

Niall nodded. "I've been waiting for this moment since I woke up in the hospital ward. Let's do it."

Alexi then turned to Alyssa. "You ready, girlfriend? Once we go in, there's no turning back."

Alyssa took a deep breath and worked to tamp down her terror at what they were about to do. Then she squared her shoulders and nodded. "Let's go."

As the group headed into the interior, which was dimly lit with faerie lights on both sides of the passageway, Alyssa's sense memory kicked in. The cool, dry air smelled of stone and earth, bringing back her recent incarceration with clarity.

Just breathe, she told herself and kept moving.

About halfway up the passageway, there was a scuffle as they ran into a handful of soldiers moving at a good clip toward the exit. Niall and Halifax, along with Niall's warriors seemed to handle them without incident, but Alyssa was certain the sounds of the confrontation probably echoed back into the depths. She worried that more soldiers would come running. But when they got to the intersection, only a few warriors remained.

Gray shoved her up against the wall to her right and blocked her with his body as the skirmish with the remaining warriors ensued. Once the area had been secured, they re-grouped in their original order and headed down the corridor leading to the throne room.

They passed through several open chambers as they progressed, but saw no other warriors. Alyssa began to wonder if all available rebel soldiers had been dispersed to fight the main invasion or if an ambush awaited them somewhere farther up the passageway, perhaps in another chamber.

On the heels of that thought, as the group passed through one small open area and back into the main hallway, there was a sudden shuffling sound behind her. When Alyssa glanced over her shoulder, she watched in horror as rebel warriors poured into the corridor from a hidden opening in the interior rock wall, cutting her off from Gray and Alexi who followed her. She screamed, and turning, fled after Niall who'd entered another chamber just ahead of her.

Just a few more yards! Keep moving, she told herself. Niall was there, just there holding out his hand to her. But before she made it to the chamber opening, she was grabbed from behind.

"Hey, let go of me, you asshat!" Alyssa yelled.

The warrior jerked her back against his chest, and she felt the cold steel of the blade he put to her throat. "Settle down and shut your mouth or I'll shut it for you, little Alice."

Alyssa recognized the voice of her abductor immediately, and her terror spread.

He marched her toward Niall as he chuckled in her ear. "Well, isn't this a fine surprise."

When Niall took another step into the passageway, the warrior pressed the blade firmly against her throat. "Ah-ah-ah. You'll need to back up into the chamber and across the room. Right... now. That is, unless you want to see this human's throat sliced cleanly open."

Niall stopped where he was, and backing across the small room, eyed the warrior. "I know you," he murmured with a slow nod. "You are the warrior that abducted the descendant in the forest. The one who infiltrated my court, killed my men like a coward."

The warrior pulled Alyssa closer and chuckled. "It was almost too easy. Your court security is sloppy. And stealing this human from under your nose gave me great pleasure, though she's decidedly more trouble than she's worth." Alyssa felt revulsion rise as the warrior nuzzled her ear suggestively. "I will take my time with her when we're done here."

Niall tilted his head. "Do you think?" he asked in an ominous tone.

"Just kill him already, Niall," Alyssa blurted.

"Shut your gob, you worthless human."

The warrior jerked her back against his chest, and she felt a quick slice of pain and the warm trickle of blood at her throat as the knife slightly pierced the delicate skin there.

The High Lord's bright green eyes glittered dangerously as he watched from his position, and the smile he gave the warrior was frightening to behold. "Let her go now, and I'll consider ending you swiftly," he said in a slow, quiet voice as if speaking to a child. "But harm one single hair on her lovely head, spill one more drop of her blood, and I will take *my* time. I can assure you that it will not be pleasant. You will beg for mercy before I finish, but mercy will not come for you."

The warrior sneered at Niall. "I am no mewling pup fresh to battle. You do not frighten me. You are old, and your time is nearly done."

"You have no idea who you're dealing with," Alyssa whispered.

The warrior nuzzled her ear again. "Oh, on the contrary, I know exactly who I'm dealing with. The high and mighty Lord Niall of legend. He's the one who has no idea who *I* am."

Niall crossed his arms and studied the warrior. "Yes. I get the feeling that there's more to this than infiltrating my court for that imbecile Aramond, or abducting the descendant for him. This feels a bit more personal. Am I wrong?"

The warrior grinned. "You would not be wrong. And when the Red King takes back his throne, I will petition him for your court."

At that, Niall burst into hearty laughter. "You are more deluded than I'd originally supposed if you think either of those things will ever come to pass." He gave the warrior a contemplative look. "Who are you then? Not that it will matter in the end. You will still die this day, but I'd like to at least know your name and what the grievance is that you hold against me."

"My name won't be known to you, but if it makes you feel better, it's Nieven. It will be one of the last names you think of as you lay dying at my feet."

Niall's indulgent smile grew. "And your grievance, Nieven?"

"You took something that was dear, something that cannot be replaced from me and my family."

"Really?" The High Lord looked bemused. "And just what was this precious item that I may have taken?"

The warrior's grin faded, and he shook his head. "Not what, but who. You killed my brother."

"Hmm. I rarely kill outside of battle, and never without cause. What was your brother's name? Would I know it?"

"Oh, I think you would. His name was Arien."

Niall went very still, and his eyes narrowed in the warrior's direction. "Arien ... Balthana?"

"See? You do know the name."

"Who is Arien Balthana?" Alyssa asked, her eyes on Niall.

The warrior chuckled at her ear. "Yes, High Lord. Do tell her who my brother was and how you cut him down without cause."

"Without cause?" Niall asked in a voice edged with steel. "Is that what you tell yourself?"

"Niall?" Alyssa began. "Who was this Arien?"

He kept his eyes on Nieven but answered her in a cold tone.

"Arien Balthana was Áine Ó Mordha's sire. I killed him in my twin's court before he could murder his own child, and I did it without a second thought. Arien was a perfect example of the very worst of us."

"You had no *right*!" Nieven screamed. "It wasn't even your court, and it was none of your business in the first place."

"It was *fae* business," Niall shouted back at him. "Áine was a child of eight when that spawn of evil tried to kill her. And simply because she was a Halfling, never mind that she was half his."

"Tainted with human blood," Nieven spat. "My brother wanted no part of her impure kind." He glared at Niall, and then took a deep breath blowing it out slowly. "You took something from us that cannot be replaced. I have waited so very long to find something to square the deal."

He made a show of running his fingers through Alyssa's hair, and by the look on Niall's face, Alyssa knew what was coming.

"I have seen the way you look at this human. Descendant or not, you care deeply for her. I am going to take her from you and then you'll know the pain that my family has felt since the day you took Arien from us. I will avenge my brother and our retribution will be complete."

Before Niall could respond, the sound of running footsteps grew louder from the pathway behind them. In the split second it took for Nieven to look back over his shoulder, Niall was on them. He grabbed the warrior's hand that held the knife to Alyssa's throat and plunged his own dagger into Nieven's forehead, killing the warrior instantly.

Nieven's lifeless body dropped to the stone floor, and Niall pulled Alyssa into his arms, as Alexi, Gray, and the handful of warriors flooded the chamber.

"Are you alright, love?" Niall asked at her ear.

Leaning back, she gave him a trembling smile. "I am now."

He lifted her chin and studied the small cut at her throat, then searched her face. "You are certain?"

Alyssa reached up and caressed his cheek. "As long as I'm with you, I'm good."

"That's just as awesome as it can be and so sweet it makes my teeth ache, but if you're done mooning over each other, can we get on with this?" Alexi asked with a shake of his head. "I mean, there is a purpose to us being in the heinous place, right?"

Alyssa grinned up at Niall. "Seems the field marshal is getting impatient. We should go."

The High Lord spared a grimace at Alexi's retreating back and then smiled down at her. "Stay close."

"Ha! You don't have to tell me twice," she said, and followed him out of the chamber.

Twenty-Four

The bulk of the White Palace forces began crossing the river and storming the rebel base as soon as Tisharu had spread her twilight darkness across the front of the mesa as cover. The fae sentries fired frantically into the darkness from every crack and crevasse in the cliff's face with arrows and explosive devices just as Valian had expected. But with Luthias' solar-powered shields for protection and Citron's sandstorms as added distraction, the small army actually met with few casualties during the initial invasion.

Unfortunately, after the thirty minutes it took for them to finally fight their way into the mesa, they were at a significant disadvantage, and Valian wished they'd gotten a bit more detail on the inner chambers from Cianán before they'd split up. Without better knowledge of the interior layout, it seemed as if rebel warriors were waiting around each corner or popping out of every hidden nook and cranny, and the coalition had to be on guard every moment. He hoped that Gray and Alexi's group were having an easier time of it from their entrance point.

They all did have one thing going for them, though. The potion Áine had come up with to protect them from the poisons that had nearly killed both Tisharu and Gray were having some extra benefits. Though Áine had been unsure of what, if any, enhancements the potion might provide above those protections, Valian was finding it had the added advantage of increasing his stamina, strength, and speed. It also did a fine job of boosting his own Elven powers well beyond his normal limits, not unlike the potion Old Minerva had given them before the battle several months back. He felt supremely alive and powerful, as if the very blood singing through his veins was infused with some sort of magnificent and exaggerated vitality. It wasn't quite what he'd experienced with the Witch of the Eastern Glade's potion, but Valian thought Áine had done her godmother proud with her own version.

"We should split up from here," Tisharu murmured with a fierce expression, as she pulled her dagger from a rebel warriors' chest, watching him fall to the stone floor.

They had come to a large open area, an intersection of sorts where several corridors led off into different directions. Valian drew in a deep breath, eyed their choices. "Yes, as much as I enjoy fighting at your side, *Mo ghrá*, that's probably a good idea. We will cover more ground if we split up." Jerking her up against his chest, he crushed his lips to hers in a heated exchange before letting her go just as quickly. "Good hunting, my love."

Her green eyes were overly bright and danced with amusement as she grinned. Twirling the daggers she held, she backed away from him. "You as well, *Mo chroí*. See you when the fighting is finished ... and we've won."

Valian watched as she and her Twilight Court warriors disappeared through the center corridor opening, struggling briefly with his apprehension over her safety.

Of course, he knew how absurd and irrational his thoughts were, and Tisharu would have his head if she had any inkling of those thoughts. She was a proud fae queen, a fierce warrior in her own right. Plus, she seemed to have recovered from her poisoning without lingering issues, and Áine's potion looked to be just as potent for Tisharu as it was for him.

However, that didn't make it any easier to put his anxiety aside. They'd only just found their way back to each other. Indeed, it had taken nearly losing her to the rebel's obscure poison to bring him to his senses after decades of denial. So, he supposed he could be forgiven for a little extra worry, though he was certain she wouldn't see it that way.

With a grin of his own and no small amount of difficulty, he shoved his concerns to the back of his mind. He would hold onto his faith in the fae queen he'd loved for the better part of a century and trust that they would meet up again after the battle, both still in one piece.

Giving himself a mental shake, Valian watched Finvar and his Winter Court warriors make their way into the passage to the left. Then twirling a finger in the air, he led his Elven crew down the corridor to the right.

As they moved through the passageway, Valian realized that not only had his strength and speed been enhanced by Áine's potion, but his senses were all incredibly heightened as well. Though the corridor was a bit narrow, and fighting in such close confines was never optimum, he swore that he could almost feel the presence of rebel warriors before they made themselves known, which was most handy. He was in constant motion in the tight quarters—moving through the mesa's stone hallways at lightning speed, faster than he knew should be possible—slashing and hacking his way through rebel forces with his Elven fighting daggers. Then the passage would open up into a chamber where there was more room to engage.

On and on they moved from one chamber to another, cutting a bloody swathe as they searched each section of the caverns for Aramond. But when they got to the end of the corridor, they found not the Red King in the final chamber but his sorcerer, Yulis, surrounded by a handful of rebel warriors.

As Tisharu had done earlier, Valian spun the fighting daggers he held in each hand and bared his teeth. "Well, well, well. What do we have here?"

The room had gone eerily quiet. Valian moved forward cautiously, as he and the sorcerer eyed each other.

"Ah yes," Yulis murmured. "I should have expected as much from the sad lap dog of the pathetic White Queen." He made a show of looking around the chamber, as if searching for someone or something more. "Where, pray tell, is her whelp of an heir? Surely the prince wouldn't let you grab all the adulation and attention for coming into the Barrens on such a suicidal mission."

"Suicidal? How so?" Valian asked, and then laughed heartily and nodded. "Oh right, because the Barrens are chocked full of terrifying things that kill without prejudice. You forget that part of the Great War took place in the Barrens, so this isn't my first rodeo on this side of the border. Or did you mean something else? Because I gotta tell you, so far, not so suicidal. And I'm also sorry to be the bearer of bad news, but even your golem was a beast with no real teeth and quite easily defeated."

The amused look on the sorcerer's face faded. "It won't matter for you, elf. You will die just as easily here in these caves as on any battlefield."

As Yulis raised his arms, Valian anticipated the sorcerer's magick, and moving like lightning, not only avoided the stream of deadly energy the wizard had conjured, but was on him before Yulis knew what was happening. With one hand around the wizard's throat and the other around his wrist, Valian hoped to curtail any further conjuring. But he soon found that was easier said than done.

"Do you really think you can best me by such pitiful physical means?" Yulis ground out. "I've more power in my little finger, boy, than you will acquire in a lifetime."

Valian laughed out loud as he struggled to hold the scrawny wizard and his power at bay. "We'll see who bests who, you complete waste of space."

At that, the chamber behind them erupted with the music of battle, the cacophony of blade against blade, groans of the wounded or dying. Valian realized in that moment that he may have been over-confident when the sorcerer grabbed hold of both of his wrists and grinned up at him with a knowing look.

"Do you feel it, Chancellor? You can't keep me from my magicks by simple physical restraint. I can assure you that I don't need control of my limbs to conjure. Even now I imagine you can feel your strength draining, can you not?"

With stunning clarity, Valian realized it was true. As he concentrated all his strength into holding tight to the sorcerer's neck, working to squeeze off his air supply, he could literally feel the strength draining from his body. In the next instant, Yulis expelled a blast of energy that sent Valian, and all those battling within fifty feet, airborne toward the back of the chamber like scattered toys.

Even as Valian crashed to the stone floor, stopped tumbling, and worked to clear his head and get his bearings, he heard Yulis cackle. "Again, it will take more than you can possibly offer to best the most powerful sorcerer in the entire realm, elf."

The wizard raised his arms menacingly, and Valian was immediately wracked with excruciating pain from head to toe. It felt as though his skin was being ripped from his body, and it was all he could do to steel himself against the worst of it.

"As I said, you will die here in pain like you've never experienced. Prepare yourself, *Chancellor*," he sneered.

Valian's mind was spinning, searching for a way out of this predicament before it was too late, when there was an ear-popping crack in the air that brought all motion in the room quite literally to a halt. Though barely able to move, the others Valian could see from his vantage point were all frozen in action as well, some in mid-air. To his surprise, that included Yulis.

"Enough!" a commanding voice shouted from the back of the chamber.

Valian saw a diminutive fae warrior—the only person in the chamber seemingly not affected by the odd suspended animation—pass by, strolling forward toward Yulis. As the warrior passed, Valian watched as he began to transform, taking on a whole new appearance. His warrior's garb became flowing, blood-red robes. His dark eyes, chestnut hair and beard were all replaced by the sparkling gray eyes, long silvery hair, and parchment skin of the Witch of the Eastern Glade.

"You were correct in one thing, Yulis," Minerva stated with a wicked grin. "There is no match for the most powerful *sorceress* in the entire realm. And I would know, as that would be me."

She turned and met Valian's gaze. With a wave of her hand, he and his Elven warriors were all released from their invisible bondage. "Take your fight elsewhere, Chancellor. This one is all mine."

Minerva watched the Elven warriors scramble up and hurriedly leave the chamber the way they'd come in, the Chancellor pausing briefly to give her a slight nod of acknowledgment before disappearing through the doorway after them. With another wave of her hand, Minerva dispensed with the rest of the rogue fae warriors, watching them all simply evaporate before turning back to Yulis.

"So, again it comes down to just the two of us, Yulis." Minerva gave him an evil grin before releasing him from her hold. "I have waited for this moment for some time. It has been particularly difficult to be patient, but I find that my patience is now at an end."

Yulis scoffed at her. "I had my suspicions that you were close by, Minerva. When I realized that the descendant could never have resisted my power without help, could not have penetrated my mind on her own, I was certain it was somehow your doing. No other is powerful enough. I just hadn't been able to sort your disguise. Kudos. Well done."

Minerva cackled again and then shook her head as they slowly circled each other like prizefighters in a ring. "Oh, Yulis. Your compliment is quite pitiful. As you well know, transmutation is a basic skill for any sorcerer of worth. I must say, I am surprised you have such a problem with it after all this time. Makes me wonder what other issues you have with magicks."

At her baiting, she watched the anger rise in his features like a dark thundercloud.

"Don't be ridiculous, you miserable old hag," he spat. "I have no *issues* with transmutation or any other magicks, for that matter. You're just jealous that I've surpassed you with such ease."

She shot a stream of bright-blue, electric energy at his feet so quickly that he could do nothing but jump and clamber backward as her hearty laughter filled the chamber.

"What's the matter, Yulis? Your personal shield not what it should be? Surely, you aren't afraid of this miserable old hag." Moments later, her mirth died away, and she pointed at him with her wand. "In any case, I have sealed this chamber. No one leaves and no one enters. This will be settled here and now. But do let me be clear. I have given you every chance to make a correction over the years, but you have refused to acquiesce at every turn. Now, at best, you are a pathetic excuse for the budding apprentice you once were. You have become a despicable little squidge with no finesse or honor whatsoever ... and make no mistake, you have *never* been my equal, nor are you now. Difficult then to surpass me in that case, do you not agree?"

That was all it took to tip Yulis over the edge. With a shout of fury, he sent a barrage of magickal energy at her—which she repelled with ease—and the battle began. The chamber became an eddy of magick spells and deadly energy mixed with a swirl of inanimate items. They sparred, then faded, reappeared, then sparred some more.

When Yulis couldn't get close to her with his ineffectual electric or plasma streams—as her personal shield was much superior to anything he could conjure—he took to cloaking and hurling any furnishings or objects in the room, including large stones, in her direction. She had no problem evading his childish ploys as clumsy as they were. However, in dodging a particularly hefty boulder, she missed the small, sharp missile behind it that sliced along her cheek, drawing blood.

Minerva swiped the back of her hand over the area and stared down at her blood-covered fingers. "You know, it's been a very long time since I've seen my own blood." Looking around the chamber, she sighed. "I will give you one last chance to save yourself, Yulis. But understand, it is your choice."

Like a petulant child, he flung another shard at her, which she flicked away without even looking up. Yet his answer was crystal clear as she watched a stone spike grow out of the smooth wall across from where she stood.

So be it, she thought.

Closing her eyes, she reached out with her mind, searching the room for where he was hiding. It didn't take long to find his heartbeat. It drummed along her parchment skin, his angry breath echoed in her ears. Lifting a hand, she closed her fingers over his essence. "I am sorry," she murmured before shoving her hand out toward the stone spike, slamming his cloaked body onto its razor-sharp point.

When she opened her eyes, she saw him uncloaked and impaled, hanging on the wall before her. She watched the surprise, the pain and disbelief cross his face as blood ran freely from his nose and mouth down the front of his robes where the point of the spike had exited his chest. His mouth opened and closed, working to form words that wouldn't come.

Crossing the chamber, Minerva levitated to his level. As she hovered near, she could clearly see behind the pain in his eyes to the boy he had once been, and grief for that boy rose within her.

"I am so sorry it had to end this way, Yulis. As a boy, when you were my apprentice, you had such potential. Unfortunately, you let your ego and lust for power taint you, encourage you to make bad choices. I tried to help you correct your path, make better decisions, but you ignored my warnings. You could have been so much more than you became. But understand that with the choices you made, this was always going to be your end ... and I was always going to be the one to end you."

She gave him a sorrowful look as he tried to speak but could not form the words hovering in his mind. She nodded her head. "I know, I know. The descendant told you and Aramond that her friends were coming for her and would end you both in agony, and that she would watch. She is here somewhere, you know. I can feel her. But she was wrong. She will not watch your death." Reaching out, Minerva placed a finger on Yulis' forehead, and in doing so, watched the life go out of his eyes. "And I will end your agony."

After a moment, Minerva descended to the stone floor and gave his lifeless body one last look before heading for the door. As she did so, she waved a hand in his direction, and Yulis' body slowly evaporated as she left the chamber.

Twenty-Five

A s Niall, Alyssa, and the rest of their group proceeded toward the throne room, Niall made sure to keep Alyssa close and an eye out for any other sudden dangers. To be quite honest, the incident with Nieven had shaken him more than he'd expected. If the scenario had turned out differently ... Well, he really didn't want to dwell on the what-ifs. However, it had been a bit too close for comfort, and he wasn't about to get caught unaware again, not with Alyssa at his side.

Halifax, true to Cheshire Wood Cat form, had disappeared directly after the incident, going on ahead to make certain there were no surprises waiting for them further down the passageway. Alexi and his warriors took point, while Gray, Cianán, and the rest of their group brought up the rear.

"What are we going to do if Yulis is with Aramond when we find them?" Alyssa asked, shaking Niall out of his morbid thoughts. He could hear the distress in her voice, though she did a fair job of covering it.

"What do you mean, love?" he asked with a frown.

"Come on, he's a very powerful sorcerer, Niall."

"I'm not afraid of Yulis, Alyssa," he stated bluntly.

"Well, *I* am." She grabbed his arm and pulled him to a stop as they entered the next small chamber. "Listen, I've seen, and more importantly, experienced what he can do. Please don't underestimate him."

Niall shook his head and ran a finger along her cheek. "I'm not, my sweet. I promise you that. And if we were talking about the Witch of the Eastern Glade, I would be much more worried. But trust me when I say that Yulis is not even close to the threat that Old Minerva could be if she was of a mind to."

"Amen to that!" Alexi confirmed over his shoulder as he made a circuit around the small room. "The Witch scares the crap out of me, most times."

"Of course, she does," Niall said with obvious mockery.

Alexi turned and pointed a finger. "No, no. Don't pretend like you aren't just as afraid of her as I am. She would eat you alive just as easy as me, pal. And you know it." He turned and continued his exploration. "I'm just glad that Old Minerva is *generally* on our side. I'd hate to face her on a battlefield. Or anywhere else, for that matter. But where Yulis is concerned, I'm with you. He doesn't worry me half as much as the Witch does."

"I'd concur as well, but we really don't know what Yulis has been up to for the past few years, do we?" Gray reminded them. "That said, I do agree that he's not the threat that Minerva would be, but I still feel it may be prudent to keep an open mind, and as Alyssa says, not to underestimate him."

"Yes. I think you both should re-evaluate your position on Yulis," Alyssa replied with concern in her voice.

"As do I," Valian said, as he and Tisharu entered the chamber behind them, followed by their respective teams. "My men and I just had a very dicey encounter with Yulis, and if not for Minerva showing up when she did ... Well, let me just say that we probably wouldn't be standing here right now. So, listen to Alyssa. She knows what she's talking about."

"What the hell happened?" Alexi stepped forward in concern. "Is everyone okay?"

Valian nodded. "Yes. We're all fine, though it did give me pause for a moment. I'll explain how it went down later."

Niall sent a narrow-eyed glance at his twin. "You were part of this? Witnessed this encounter, Tisharu?"

The fae queen shook her head. "We split up at the main corridor intersection, each of us taking a different pathway. Fin and his group went down one, my warriors and I started down this corridor, and Valian and his men tried another. Valian related the event to me when they caught up to us a just bit ago. Seems like the old hag arrived just in time to save their hides," she finished with a wink and a smirk in Valian's direction.

Niall watched in fascination as Valian's face softened and he met Tisharu's gaze with a chuckle. "Yes, well, that may be true, but the point is, Yulis was much more formidable than any of us had realized." He turned to Niall with a grimace. "Trust me when I say, it was a most unpleasant discovery."

"Yeah, but it sounds like thanks to Old Minerva, Yulis will be one less problem to worry about when we finally run across that dick of a Red King," Alexi put in as he began to back toward the opening to the passage leading out of the chamber. "Which is really good intel to have. So, let's get a move on, shall we?"

Niall nodded thoughtfully as he and Alyssa started to follow. "Mmm, yes. However, we still need to be on our guard and not get complacent. I'd like to find Aramond, neutralize him for good, and then get the hell out of the Barrens in one piece."

"Again, amen to that," Alexi agreed with a huge grin. "I just wan—"

Before he could finish the sentence, his eyes went wide and the air in his lungs burst out of him on a grunt. They all watched in shock as the business end of a fae sword came jutting through the front of his leather armor. The rebel lesser faerie that had faded in behind Alexi jerked the sword back out with a grin and shoved him aside as more dissident forces flooded into the chamber.

"Alexi! *No!*" Gray shouted, and with his shout, close to twenty rebel fae warriors simply exploded into a fine red mist, their armor and clothing dropping to the chamber floor where they'd stood only moments before.

Niall was stunned, and Alyssa turned her head into his chest with a cry of horror. He'd heard of the Blood Storm but had never seen it executed. As far as he knew, it hadn't been used or seen in centuries and had taken on mythic proportions. That the prince had this rare ability was yet another revelation that would need to be contemplated and discussed at a later date. But right now, they needed to secure the location.

As Gray and a handful of Elven warriors pulled an unconscious Alexi out of harm's way and began to work on him, Niall protected Alyssa while Valian and Tisharu, along with their individual forces, handled the few lesser faeries that had escaped the Blood Storm. When the dust cleared, they turned to the situation with Alexi, which didn't seem to be going well.

"He's barely breathing, but luckily the sword seems to have missed any vital organs." Gray had removed Alexi's leather chest armor and had his blood-covered hands over the oozing wound in Alexi's chest. "Come on, come on, Alexi. Don't you dare die on me in this heinous place or I'll kick your bloody ass. Breathe, damn it!"

He closed his eyes then, and the very air in the chamber fairly hummed with the healing energy the prince was pouring into Alexi's body. The field marshal gasped, his eyes moving rapidly back and forth beneath his lids. With one final push, Alexi's body arched and spasmed violently several times before dropping back to the stone floor and going very still.

"Is he breathing?" Alyssa asked in a tentative whisper.

They all stood silently while Gray checked Alexi's vital signs.

After several tense moments, the field marshal finally took another gasping breath and groaned. "Oouuch ..." he muttered in a weak voice.

"Alexi?" Gray leaned closer. "Can you hear me?"

"Okay, I would like to go on record as saying that this feels a bit like déjà vu, you big knuckle head," Alexi mumbled before his eyes fluttered open. "Didn't we go through something like this in January in Tarkington Forest? Your healing skills were for shit then, and they seem to have only gotten marginally better since."

Gray's shoulders sagged a bit as the tension he held there slowly eased. "Well, if you'd been watching what you were doing and hadn't turned your back to a corridor we hadn't yet cleared, you wouldn't be in this fix, would you? And I'm not always gonna be around to catch you when you fall, pal."

"Yeah, kiss my ass, your Highness."

Gray shook his head. "How do you feel, idiot? Can you stand?'

Clasping Alexi's arm, the prince helped him into a sitting position.

Alexi took several deep breaths, and a slow grin crossed his face. "Not too shabby, oh Royal One," he said with a chuckle. "Just a slight twinge." He looked down at the hole in his tunic. "Really, Gray? You couldn't have mended my tunic while you were at it?"

The prince rolled his eyes. "Yeah, and you can kiss my ass as well, Field Marshal. Next time I'll fix your shirt and leave the friggin' gaping wound in your chest."

Alexi laughed and then grimaced, putting a hand to his chest. "Just help me up, fool."

"You know, as amusing as this whole scenario is, and it is quite amusing, do you think maybe we can move on now?" Niall asked with a bit of annoyance before continuing in a simpering tone. "Or are you going to need someone to escort you home, Field Marshal? I could appoint a couple of my warriors for the task."

"Yeah, fuck that," Alexi muttered as Gray helped him up. He swayed a little but seemed to get his balance. "I'll be just fine in a minute or two, so don't you worry about me. Ain't nobody gonna *escort* me anywhere, dude. I'll get there under my own steam, thanks."

"Alright. Just checking." Niall grinned, and then laughed out loud when the field marshal shot him an obscene gesture.

"You may be on the mend, cousin, but I think Tisharu and I will take point for a while," Valian said. He pointed at Gray and Alexi. "You two cover our flank. And watch your asses, please. I don't want to have to heal you both."

"Oh, hardy-har-har," Alexi grumbled. "You are soooo freakin' funny, Val. You and Tisharu just keep a keen eye going forward. The sneaky bastards seemed to be emerging out of solid rock, but they're actually *fading* inside the mesa."

"Yes." Valian frowned. "Fading in here seems really unwise, but it is definitely concerning. Everyone needs to stay frosty. Let's move out."

With that, they re-grouped and headed into the corridor in the direction from which the lesser fae warriors had appeared, progressing deeper into the mesa caves in search of Aramond. As they advanced, they found the odd room here and there off the passageway, but no hidden cervices or bump outs for rebels to hide and spring an attack—and no other rebel forces to deal with.

But that didn't last long. When they finally neared the end of the corridor, they could hear echoing voices from somewhere up ahead. Niall, weapons drawn, pulled Alyssa behind him.

As they rounded the last corner, the passageway opened up onto the largest space they'd seen since entering the mesa. It was obviously the chamber that Aramond was using as a throne room because at the far end there were several rudimentary steps leading up to a crude stone seat. There sat the Red King surrounded by only a handful of warriors. However, the area between the chamber entrance and the makeshift throne was filled with lesser fae warriors armed to the teeth.

Niall pushed Alyssa up to the stone wall to their left, leaving room for the rest of their warriors to enter and engage. Soon the chamber was filled with the deadly sounds of battle. Niall took care of any rebels who came within arm's length, but with the potion that Áine had concocted for them, the White Palace forces had the battle well in hand within ten minutes. Even Alexi seemed to be healed up and in rare form. The rebels were definitely no match, and the skirmish didn't last long.

That left the Red King and his handful of protectors on the throne platform, who were rapidly being overwhelmed. Niall turned to his general. "Stand guard over the descendant, Kassair. The Red King is mine."

"Niall, wait!" Alyssa shouted over the din, grabbing at his arm. "Don't go."

Niall pulled her up against his chest and crushed his lips to hers for a brief, passionate kiss. Then he let her go and smiled. "Stay with Kassair, love. He'll keep you safe. I'll be right back."

Moving like lightning through what was left of the fighting throng, as Niall neared the stone platform where the Red King was cowering, he flung a hand toward Aramond, lifting the deposed king three feet into the air as if he weighed nothing at all. Aramond writhed and gasped for breath, clawing at the invisible force cutting off his air supply.

"Your days of causing pain and mayhem are finally at an end, you worthless excuse for a human," Niall spat, watching the Red King struggle to breathe, his face slowly turning a sickly shade of violet. "I do believe the descendant warned you and your despicable sorcerer that her friends were coming for her, and that she would watch as you were ended. This is how that end feels."

"Put him down!" a voice boomed from the back of the chamber.

Through the haze of his fury, Niall recognized the voice of the Witch of the Eastern Glade, but his anger was too great to heed her command.

"I said, put him down, High Lord," she shouted.

"He's evil through and through, Old One, and does not deserve to live," he shouted back. "He must pay for the destruction of lives, the terrible things he's done. He has been allowed to wreak havoc over the realm, to reign over his people with pain and death for far too long. And he *tortured* Alyssa."

Minerva's voice was much closer and came to him in a softer tone. "But Aramond's fate is not up to you, boy."

"In this moment it can be."

"No." Next to him now, the Witch of the Eastern Glade shook her head. "It cannot. But you are quite correct. Aramond is an evil man. He has done unspeakable things in his mad quest for power. And yes, it *has* gone on for far too long. However, his punishment is not up to you. Put him down, High Lord. Killing for vengeance or without just cause is murder and not your way. You know that I am right."

"I've killed in vengeance. Arien—"

"You killed Arien Balthana not in vengeance but to shield my goddaughter. We both know that Áine's sire would have killed the child, and she would have been lost to us all had you not acted swiftly. Most definitely not vengeance, Niall, but just cause."

"War is a just cause. Aramond should have died in battle months ago along with the bulk of his followers when the descendant used the Scepter of Fire."

"That is true." Minerva nodded. "But he did not. He somehow slithered free like the serpent that he is. But this is not war, boy."

With hesitation, Niall glanced over at her. "Maybe not technically, but what do you care, Old One? You've made it very clear where you stand. You're uninterested in the grievances of the humans, you've said it often enough. Why do you care what happens to this filth?"

"You misunderstand. I care not for Aramond. My concern is for you, High Lord. This kind of death chips away at any true goodness inside us. Once you start down that road, it becomes difficult to turn back. It rapidly consumes, as my old apprentice Yulis found in the end."

Niall gave her a narrow-eyed look. "You killed Yulis?"

"I did." Minerva held his stare without blinking. "However, I took Yulis' life not in vengeance nor with pleasure but with mercy. I gave him every chance to take a different path. He was no match for me, and we both knew it. But he continued his attack because his hubris would not allow him to stand down. He made his choice. Unfortunately for Yulis, at his point in the journey, it was the only one he could make."

Niall shook his head. "Aramond must pay for his iniquities. He must not be allowed to slink away again."

The old witch laid a hand on his arm. "And he will pay, I promise you, but neither you nor I will decide his fate. That task must be left to the Oracles. However, you have my word that this realm will never have to deal with the likes of Aramond again. Put him down, Niall."

As they stood there, gazes locked, it occurred to Niall that he may have let his anger rob him of common sense. He was arguing with the Witch of the Eastern Glade, which was pure insanity. Alexi had been correct. The Old One could eat him alive on the spot should she wish it.

A smile spread across Minerva's face, and at her slight nod, Niall realized she knew exactly what he was thinking.

Without looking back, he released the Red King, dropping him to the stone floor with a thud in a gasping, choking heap. Though he was certain that he was definitely pushing his luck, he leaned down so that he and the witch were face to face.

"I will take you at your word, Old One. But know this, should I ever see him or hear that he's been sighted in this realm, I will hunt him down and end him ... just cause or not."

The Witch of the Eastern Glade stepped just a titch closer, her voice lowering to a hushed murmur. "I must say, you have quite the pair of stones on you, boy. However, I will overlook your impertinence for the time-being, as I realize that your love for the descendant has blinded you to the peril of your actions. Having said that, were I you, I would take her and the rest of your merry band of do-gooders and leave this place, as they say, while the gettin' is good."

With that, the Witch of the Eastern Glade disappeared in a puff of silver smoke, taking the Red King with her.

Niall stood there a moment, thinking about how close he'd come to being eaten alive by the most powerful sorceress in the realm until Alexi came up behind him and clapped him on the back.

"Well, that was fun," the field marshal said with a chuckle. "Bless the Oracles, I enjoyed that show immensely. We were all highly impressed with your bravado and your *pair of stones*, as the Old One said." He wiggled his eyebrows. "I mean, going toe to toe with the Witch of the Eastern Glade and hardly flinching? Amazing. And, of course, not pissing yourself while doing it? Most inspiring, High Lord."

"Oh, shut up, idiot," Niall grumbled with a begrudging smirk. Then he turned and realized that all eyes were, indeed, on him. His gaze found Alyssa in the crowd and his smile grew to match hers. "I guess we should do as the Old One suggested and go while the getting is good. Let's leave this heinous place."

It ended up taking much less time to exit the mesa than it took to fight their way in. Once outside, Cianán approached Alyssa and Niall.

"This is where we part ways, descendant of Alice," he said with a smile. "The Barrens is my home, so I will wish you safe travels back to your realm. I want to thank you as well for keeping your word and freeing me. I will be forever in your debt, and if you ever need anything that I can provide, you have but to ask."

Alyssa took the kelpie's hand, and a surprised look bloomed

across his face when she pulled him in for a hug. "It was a pleasure and an honor to meet you, Cianán. I wish you all the best."

Niall held out his hand as well. "I am in your debt, kelpie, for bringing Alyssa back to us and keeping her safe. I am proud to call you friend and know that you are welcome in my Twilight Court any time."

After a slight bow, Cianán transformed into his black stallion form and made his way down toward the river that ran between the mesas, finally disappearing into the dark waters.

"Okay. Can we go now?" Alexi asked with a frown. "I've had about all of the Barrens that I can stomach in one sitting. And I want a hot shower to wash away the remnants."

Alyssa laughed. "I am so with you on that, Alexi," she replied before climbing up behind Niall on Laoch. The destrier pawed the ground and whinnied his approval, making Niall chuckle. "I agree, Laoch. Let's go home."

With that, they headed toward the border.

Twenty-Six

C onsidering it took their combined armies most of the morning to cross into the Barrens and arrive at the mesa, much to Valian's relief, the return trip took less than half that time. In the late afternoon, there was little activity, with most of the more terrifying inhabitants of the bleak and dangerous land nocturnal. Still, Niall, Alexi, and Finvar had been set upon by Wolvataurs during their previous attempt to find and rescue Alyssa, barely escaping with their lives. And since that attack had also taken place in the late afternoon, Valian kept a close watch on the surrounding countryside in between the handful of times they faded toward the border, just in case.

Tisharu's voice cut into his thoughts. "You should not worry so, *Mo chroí*. We are almost to the border. Another couple of fades and the security wards of Wysteria will be a most welcome sight, will they not?"

Valian nodded. "They will indeed, love." He also thought the old adage about the dangers of fading within the Barrens was quite apropos. It was definitely much better—and wiser, for that matter—to fade *out* of the Barrens than to fade in.

He gave the horizon another scan. "This desolate place holds extremely unpleasant memories of war and horrors to be sure, so it's difficult not to worry. I imagine I will breathe easier once we cross the border and get one step closer to home."

It turned out that Tisharu was spot on, when after two more fades, they materialized within a quarter mile of the security wards that stood guard at Wysteria's border. Because of the protocols in place, they couldn't fade through the wards but were required to cross the border on foot, or in their case, on horseback, before fading unrestricted.

"This is where we part ways," Elshandra stated, as she rode up next to Valian. "My warriors and I will journey farther south and cross the border closer to court."

Valian frowned. "Would it not be safer for you to ride with us and cross into Wysteria here before heading south? At least you would be within the security of our own boundaries, Elshandra."

The inscrutable queen simply smiled. "I am not afraid of traveling in the Barrens, especially this close to the border, Chancellor. Besides, we have Gruden's southern dwarf clan as well as warriors from both Peridot's Autumn Court and Sumia's Spring Court as traveling companions. I feel certain that our numbers alone will deter any mischief the Barrens could muster."

Gray spoke up before Valian could respond. "In that case, we wish you safe travels home, Elshandra. The assistance of your Summer Court in this endeavor was greatly appreciated."

The fae queen's crafty smile accompanied her soft chuckle, and her icy-blue eyes sparkled with amusement. "It has been an interesting ... and enlightening experience, Your Highness. And dare I say it will be simply fascinating to hear what other surprises your newly found heritage has in store for you."

She started to turn away, and then swung back with a sly look for the prince. "On another point, Prince Graydon—just to be clear—I am fully aware that you and the Chancellor here had doubts regarding my court's participation in this effort, considering that we were unable to lend our support in the previous battle." She shook her head and put up a hand when the prince would have denied the allegation, sending the shells woven into her long, pale blond dreadlocks clicking and clacking. "I can understand that perhaps you were uncertain of my ... shall we say ... *priorities*?"

Tilting her head, she gave them both an amused look. "To be fair, I do often times have my own agenda, for in my heart, my Summer Court comes first in all things." The fae queen sobered then. "However, you need never worry about where my allegiance lies. Beyond my court, my loyalty will always be with Wysteria and the White Queen. On that, you can be certain."

With that, the enigmatic queen turned her steed toward the south, calling over her shoulder, "Until our next joint adventure, safe travels to you all, as well."

Valian and Gray watched as Elshandra and her warriors disappeared, followed closely by the rest of the southern entourage until there was nothing left to see but dust.

"Well, that was certainly thought-provoking," Alexi commented a few moments later as he rode up next to Gray.

"Thought-provoking, indeed, but a fair understatement, Alexi," Valian commented. "I'm still not quite sure what to make of Elshandra's posturing."

"Agreed," Gray added. "But I have a feeling that with Elshandra, that's exactly her intention—and the point—for that matter. I think she enjoys keeping everyone guessing and off balance."

"Probably."

Alexi grinned. "Ah, yes, but do you trust her?"

Valian shook his head. "This morning I would've said not on your life. However, she and her warriors held the line, fought fiercely and well. I guess for the rest we'll have to wait and see."

"Well, I don't trust her any farther than I could throw her," Tisharu stated flatly. "She undoubtedly likes to be center of attention, I'll give her that, but I find her *posturing* less thought-provoking and more annoying than anything else." She gave Valian a disgruntled look. "And why we're wasting time talking about Elshandra when we could be crossing the border to home is simply baffling to me."

Alexi burst out laughing. "Well said, Tisharu. And I'm with you on that. Let's quit yammering and get a move on. There's a nice hot shower just waiting for me back at the palace."

The thought of home was just the incentive the rest of them needed to pass through the wards and into Wysteria. There, they stopped again to say goodbye to Luthias, Citron, and Juppar, along with both northern dwarf clans.

But before he turned to go, Juppar hung back as the Luthias, Citron and the dwarf clans went their separate ways.

"Chancellor, if you'd please, I'd like a quick word on another matter?"

"Of course. What is it, Juppar?"

The High Lord looked around to those within earshot and continued slowly. "Lord Finvar and I have spoken at length, and we both have serious misgivings about that dryad's unfortunate death. We are in agreement that there is a need to get to the bottom of what she was involved in, and why she was in the Barrens so far from home in the first place."

There was a grim look in Juppar's violet eyes when he continued. "Finvar and I are situated the farthest north, and along with Queen Tisharu, our courts are closest to Kellam's Evening Court. I believe the fact that the dryad's clan resides in the old growth north of Willow Glen Wood—so very close to Kellam's court—is no coincidence. I also find Kellam's lack of participation in today's routing of the Red King highly suspect. I'll be coordinating a quiet investigation into the matter and will let you know of any discoveries made."

"I'll be most eager to lend a hand in that endeavor, should you need me," Tisharu confirmed. "It gives me no joy to investigate another Wysterian fae court. However, neither do I believe in coincidences. If Kellam had any part in the dryad's gruesome death or is involved in some bigger devious scheme, it is a betrayal to us all and must be dealt with decisively and with haste."

"Agreed."

"Thank you for giving us a heads up, Juppar," Valian replied. "Let us know if there is anything the Wysterian guard can do to assist you."

"Yes," Gray added. "And I will be in constant contact with Fin. We'll provide whatever support is needed to resolve the matter. The Chancellor and I, along with the field marshal, will be paying our respects to the elders of the dryad clan within the week."

"Very well," Juppar said. "Until then, I bid you farewell." With that, the High Lord and his warriors disappeared in a shimmering, starry mist.

"I also find this business of the dryad's mysterious death concerning," Niall said as he and Alyssa rode up next to Tisharu. "My court may be across the border in Roseland, but I would participate in your investigation, sister," he told his twin. "You have only to send word."

Tisharu reached out and placed a hand on Niall's arm. "I will contact you when I know more, brother. But we have done enough for now, and anything more is for another day." Turning, she smiled at Valian. "In the meantime, my warriors need rest and sustenance. We will return to court and let you get on with your journey home."

"You aren't coming back to the palace with us?" Valian asked quietly.

The fae queen shook her head. "I have many things to take care of at court, and I know you have duties to complete at the palace, *Mo chroí*. I'm certain that Queen Beatrice will require a clear report of today's events as well. Will you come to me when you've finished?"

Valian took her hand and pressed his lips to her palm. "The moment I'm done."

"Then I will see you soon." She turned her steed then and twirled a finger in the air. In the next moment, Tisharu and her warriors faded in a burst of twilight.

Before accompanying the group—along with the rest of the Wysterian guard—back to the White Palace, both Finvar and Niall dismounted to give direction to their commanders and send their battalions home to their respective courts. While the rest of the group waited, Valian could feel Alyssa's eyes on him from her seat upon Laoch. He'd wondered how long it would take before she would voice her concerns, and he speculated on what she was probably thinking.

She'd watched his interaction with Tisharu in silence throughout their campaign and no doubt had wondered about his relationship with Isabella. Valian couldn't really blame her for her concern for her friend. He and Isabella had come to an agreement to be friends instead of lovers before the army had left for the Barrens, but Alyssa had no way of knowing that.

"What's on your mind, Alyssa?" he asked before turning to meet her gaze.

The descendant squirmed a bit in the saddle but returned his gaze head-on. "I was just wondering if Isabella knew ..."

"About me and Tisharu?" Valian finished for her. He glanced around to make sure Alexi wasn't within earshot, then sidled his destrier closer to Laoch. "Yes, Alyssa," he murmured. "Please rest at ease. Isabella and I had a long conversation last evening, which she actually initiated before I could broach the subject."

"Really?"

Valian gave her a wry look. "She basically told me that I had never gotten over Tisharu and that I should mend those fences. Oh, and that she and my cousin had been kissing in the courtyard."

Alyssa's eyes went wide. "*What*?" she blurted, and then lowered her voice. "Izzy and Alexi?"

Valian chuckled. "Are you really surprised, Alyssa? After all, you were present the night they met."

Running a hand through her hair, Alyssa shook her head. "I guess I shouldn't be. And you? You're okay with it?"

"How can I not be? Isabella's interests lie with Alexi, and we both know it. Besides, we were always going to be better friends than lovers. Isabella was right. Tisharu took hold of my heart long ago. I was just too mule-headed to acknowledge it."

Alyssa finally nodded. "Okay then. If you're both happy, that's all I can ask for, right?"

"Having a therapy session, are we, Chancellor?" Niall asked as he climbed up behind Alyssa.

"I would be careful, old friend. I think you may be next," Valian replied with a chuckle. "Now, can we please go home?"

"I've been saying that for the last damn hour," Alexi said as he rode up and watched Finvar regain his mount. "What are we waiting for?"

Niall gave a grunt and turned Laoch southward.

By the time the small core group faded toward the White Palace and materialized just outside the fade perimeter, shadows were growing long, and the sun was hovering just above the horizon. Obviously, news of their imminent arrival had made it to the palace ahead of them, as a small greeting party was there to meet them when they finally made their way past the eastern gatehouse and into the inner courtyard. Queen Beatrice was accompanied by several of her advisors, along with Áine, Isabella, and Gryphon, her personal chamber elf.

Halifax, always with an eye out for accolades, was there as well, clearly the bearer of the news. Valian had no doubt the cat had made himself out to be the hero of whatever story he'd related to the queen of their day's exploits. He would have to rectify that when he met with the queen later.

As they all dismounted, Valian watched Alyssa hurry over to embrace her friend, and he smiled when his eyes met Isabella's. She smiled back at him in almost a distracted way before her attention moved past him. Valian followed her gaze to where Alexi was barking out orders to the guard, and though he knew it was ridiculous—and probably a wee bit selfish—he was still surprised that her casual disregard stung just a little. Of course, as he'd previously told Alyssa, they'd made their peace with going their separate ways, and he'd make certain to keep an eye on the situation. He wouldn't allow anyone, including his cousin, to hurt Isabella in any way.

"We have much to discuss," Gray was telling the queen as Valian came closer. "It was a very interesting day."

Queen Beatrice smiled. "I do look forward to hearing all about it, my sweet. I've gotten a brief outline from Halifax, but I'm sure you'll want to fill in the gaps."

"I'll be happy to do just that," Gray said with a glance to the cat, and then laughed out loud at Halifax's disgruntled look.

Valian thought that he hadn't heard the prince sound so free and relaxed in quite some time. Gray had been questioning his lineage for the last few years. Perhaps he was now coming to terms with—as Elshandra had put it—his new-found heritage, and was finally ready to move forward.

"Well, why don't you go on inside with Áine and get started on that," the queen told him. "Finvar and I will be along directly. I just need a quick word with the chancellor."

Gray leaned down and placed a gentle kiss on his mother's cheek. "It's good to be home."

The queen watched her son link arms with Áine, head up the steps to the stone walkway, and disappear into the palace before turning back to Valian with a knowing smile. "They make a lovely pair, do they not?"

Valian, unwilling to take the bait, only smiled.

"Mmm. Very diplomatic of you, Chancellor. I take it everything went to plan?"

Before Valian could answer, Alyssa, followed by Isabella and Niall interrupted the conversation.

"I'm sorry to intrude, Queen Beatrice. I know you have much to discuss, but I just wanted to thank you for sending an army to rescue me," Alyssa said. "I am so grateful."

"Nonsense, child. You are precious to us in so many ways. I'm very glad you are back safe and sound."

"And to be fair, Majesty. Alyssa actually rescued herself," Valian said.

"Really? Do tell."

Niall frowned. "She made friends with a kelpie," he grumbled.

The queen's mouth dropped open. "A k-kelpie?"

Alyssa pointed at the High Lord. "I will remind you, Niall, that Cianán helped me escape that horrible place and was great assistance to our cause. Besides, we would never have known about the mesa's back entrance without him."

Valian nodded and shook a finger at Niall as well. "Alyssa speaks the truth, my friend."

The High Lord crossed his arms and pressed his lips together, but Valian could read the annoyance in his eyes.

"Well, as I said, we're glad you've been returned to us without harm," the queen continued. "Will you stay on for a few days or do you require an escort back to your realm?"

Valian watched Alyssa squirm again and thought he knew what was coming, but nearly laughed out loud when she finally spoke.

"Um, no Your Majesty, I won't need an escort home right now." She reached out and took Niall's hand, which he brought to his lips. "I'm actually going back to the Twilight Court with Niall for a day or two, and then he will get me home. But now that the Red King is no longer a threat, I would love to come back for a visit. That is, if it's okay with you."

Queen Beatrice took Alyssa's other hand. "Oh, my dear child, you are always welcome in this realm." The queen looked up at Niall with a knowing look. "Now, why don't you go back to court with the High Lord and put this terrible experience behind you. Let us know if you need anything."

Alyssa started to go, and then turned back. "Your Majesty? One last question. What happens to the scepter? Will it stay with me?"

"That is a subject I'll be discussing with my leadership team. Valian will let you know what we decide. We want to do what is best and safest for all involved, including you."

With a short nod, Alyssa gave Isabella a quick hug, and then followed Niall back to where Laoch stood waiting. They mounted him, and in the next instant, disappeared in a burst of twilight.

"People come and go so quickly around here," Isabella murmured. "And in such an entertaining way."

"And what of you, child?" the queen asked. "Do you need an escort back to the New York realm, or will you be staying on as well?"

"I ... uh ... haven't ..."

That was all she managed as she stared off toward the center of the courtyard.

"Isabella?" Valian followed her gaze to find Alexi striding purposely toward them, and was pretty sure that in the moment, neither of them was aware that there were other people anywhere near ... or perhaps in the entire realm, for that matter.

Alexi walked right up to Isabella, slipped an arm around her waist, and jerked her up against his chest, before kissing her senseless. Valian had to admit, he was fairly impressed.

When the two finally came up for air, Isabella had a glazed look on her face, and Alexi wore a sloppy grin. Finvar uttered a strangled sound and turned away quickly.

"Come on, Christensen," Alexi said, taking her hand and pulling her toward the palace. "I need a shower and something to eat."

"I ... okay ..." Isabella looked over her shoulder catching Valian's eye. Grinning at him, she simply shrugged before disappearing into the palace with Alexi.

"I assume you knew this was coming, Valian?" the queen asked with a cagey look.

"Yes, Majesty. Isabella and I had a long discussion last night."

"I also assume that you will be going to the Twilight Court for the evening?"

Valian cleared his throat and looked back and forth between Finvar and the queen. "Once I have made my report, and you are satisfied with the outcome, then yes, Highness. I had planned to do that."

The queen regarded him thoughtfully for several moments until Valian began to feel uncomfortable. Then she finally nodded. "I do believe tomorrow afternoon will be soon enough for a report. Don't you think, Lord Finvar?"

Finvar grinned. "I think that is a wise choice. We all need some time to, as they say in the New York realm, decompress."

"Then we shall have a leadership meeting tomorrow afternoon and discuss all. Until that time, give my best to Queen Tisharu."

"But Majesty, are you certain?"

"Are you questioning my decision, Chancellor?"

"No ... but ..."

"Then go before I think better of that decision." She gave him an impish smile. "All can wait until then."

"Yes, Majesty. Thank you," Valian said with a slight bow.

As the queen turned to go with both Finvar and Gryphon by her side, Valian called out to her.

"Majesty, one last thing."

When she stopped and look back, Valian glanced meaningfully at the chamber elf. The queen leaned down and spoke softly. "Gryphon, take Lord Finvar in and make us both something to eat and a nice pot of tea. I'll be in shortly."

The chamber elf bowed before he led Finvar up the steps.

The queen sighed and turned back to Valian. "Was there something else, Chancellor?"

"There were a few things that happened in the Barrens that we should discuss. He will have more questions. My recommendation is for you and Lord Finvar to tell him all now ... before it again becomes harder."

The queen stared at him for a brief moment and then nodded. "You are correct, as always. I should have listened before, as it would have saved us all much grief. You are ever the voice of reason. We will clear the air and move forward starting tomorrow. Now, go and enjoy your evening."

Valian turned to go, but she called after him.

"And Valian, thank you for your steadfast service. Your queen is very grateful."

"As I've said before, I live to serve, Majesty."

With that, the Chancellor of Artemysia faded in a shower of silver mist.

Epilogue

❦

T here was a bite in the air. Alexi scanned the forest, littered with leaves, and took a deep breath of the early fall breeze to try to cleanse his mind of the stressful afternoon they'd endured. He, Valian, and Gray had just come from the northern Dryad clan's treetop village after paying their respects for the clan's loss. Being a seasoned warrior, Alexi had seen his share of horrors on the battlefield and plenty of death, but he still couldn't get the scene they'd come across in the Barrens and the poor sprite's mutilated body out of his head.

Her name had been Lavender, and the reaction of the Dryad community to news of her death had been interesting. Incredibly sad and varied, but interesting, nonetheless. Emotions had ranged from passive acceptance to shock and bewilderment to anger and disbelief. Well, as much anger as a dryad could generate. They were a peaceful group by nature, and most simply could not understand the type of violence that had ended the life of one of their own. Lavender's poor mother completely broke down in sobs while her grandmother sat alone in silent grief, which in Alexi's opinion, was almost harder to witness.

The truly interesting part of the visit came as they were about to fade for home. A young male sprite named Tangy followed them to the forest floor and told them that he was not at all surprised by the news of Lavender's gruesome death. He said that he'd witnessed her and several other sprites sneaking off on numerous occasions, had even tried to follow them once or twice without much success. He was certain that they were involved in something they shouldn't have been, something dark and sinister, as they had been secretive and withdrawn for several weeks. However, when pressed, Tangy couldn't give them much in the way of details or anything solid to pursue. It was incredibly frustrating.

"I noticed that Isabella is still here in Wysteria, Alexi," Valian said, breaking Alexi out of his dark thoughts.

"Yeah. I'm escorting her back to the New York realm on Friday. Why?"

Valian gave him a quick glance. "You should send her home now."

Alexi stopped and stared at his cousin with a surprised look. "Send her—" he began before nearly doubling over in laughter. "Have you been chewing Elf Weed, pal?"

His cousin frowned. "It's for her safety, Alexi, and not a laughing matter."

"It's only a couple more days, Val. Bella's set on Friday."

Valian made a face. "Whatever. You should send Isabella home now."

"Seriously? Have you *met* Bella?"

"So ... afraid of her, then?" It was said in a matter-of-fact tone but accompanied by a very sly smile.

Gray whistled through his teeth and looked heavenward.

"Please." Alexi replied with a snort. "And your relationship was all of what? Six months or so? Let me ask you this, cousin: when was the last time *you* sent Bella anywhere? And exactly how did that work out for you?" When Valian didn't answer, Alexi nodded with a broad grin. "Precisely. As evidenced by this last little dust up with her and Alyssa coming here on their own, I'm pretty sure nobody *sends* Bella anywhere she doesn't want to go without a fight. And I'll pass on that, buddy. Besides, like I said, it's only a couple more days."

"Uh, gentlemen? This is all very interesting, but can we get back to the problem at hand?" Gray asked with a smirk. "We need to figure out where we go from he—"

That was as far as the prince got before the color literally bleached from his face. His eyes went wide and rolled back in his head so that all that could be seen was a translucent white.

"What the fu—?" Alexi stepped closer in concern. "Gray? Are you okay?" He reached out a hand, but Valian stopped him.

"No, don't, Alexi. I've seen this before."

He turned to the prince and spoke quietly. "What are you seeing, Gray?"

The prince lifted an arm and pointed off to his left without blinking or looking in that direction. When he spoke, his voice was strangely modulated. "The scent of death, an essence of evil ... waiting. Danger has not abated but grows. Beware, more death is coming."

As fast as it had come over him, the strange spell seemed to vanish just as quickly, and Gray blinked, looking around as if confused by his surroundings. "What just happened?"

"Yeah. That's what I'd like to know," Alexi replied. "It was like some weird trance. And you looked pretty freaky to boot."

Valian spoke up then. "It's actually part of your heritage, Gray. That was an Ellurian reverie. It's not unlike a trance, Alexi, but more a prophetic vision. The queen has had them from time to time. It's just one of the gifts from that side of your family tree. Understand that now that these new abilities are starting to surface, more will follow."

Gray shook his head, the color starting to return to his face. "I have to say, that's a fairly disturbing thought. But yes, the queen and I had a brief conversation about some of these new abilities last evening. She said there's more, but we got interrupted. We're going to talk about it at length this weekend."

"What did you see? Or was it more of a feeling?"

"It was a little of both. I saw a body. Seemed like another dryad, though that wasn't real clear. If the vision was correct, we'll find the body about thirty yards in that direction." He again pointed to his left, but this time looking that way as if seeing the body in his mind.

Valian nodded. "Alright. Let's go see what's what then."

"Oh goody. More death." Alexi grimaced.

They cautiously made their way, following Gray, to a small

thicket almost exactly thirty yards from where they'd stood, to find another dryad, this one a male. He almost looked to be asleep apart from the dried, dark green blood that had pooled beneath his head.

"Oh, man. Another trip to the treetops," Alexi said as he turned the male's wrist over to expose the clan's insignia. "What the hell is going on here? Is this one of the sprites that Tangy was talking about? And is this death connected to the Red King's insurrection in some way?"

"All very good questions," Valian murmured. "But this sprite wasn't killed by the golem. This is fresh, and the golem was destroyed with Yulis' death. Having said that, I think it's possible this is connected, but how? I have no idea."

"Yeah, well that was the *feeling* part of my vision," Gray mumbled. "There was a dark, oppressive sensation. It was so strong, it made me almost queasy for a minute. Something monstruous was here very recently. At least, that's the way it felt. Evil. I also got the feeling that ending Aramond didn't end the root of the problem, that it is all connected in some way." Gray shook his head. "I think we may need to visit the Oracles. Maybe they'll be able to tell us more about my vision, and hopefully, shed some light on the rest, since Minerva took Aramond to them for judgment."

Valian nodded. "Agreed."

Alexi made a face. "Yeah, well, you can count me out of a visit to the Oracles. Not my idea of a good time. And truth be told, they creep me out a little."

Valian gave him a bland look. "Yes, that's fascinating, Field Marshal. Regardless, first things, first." He gestured to the dead sprite. "We need to get him back to his community."

"Yeah. And while you two take a visit to the Oracles, it looks like I may have that conversation with Bella after all," Alexi replied.

"Better you than me," Valian muttered under his breath.

"Ha! I knew it." Alexi laughed out loud.

Gray frowned. "Would you two quit your bickering and have some respect?"

Without another word, the three of them faded back to the Dryad village, taking the sprite's body with them.

About the Author

A native of Oregon, Joni Sauer-Folger spent twenty-two years with an airline traveling and moving around the country before settling down near the beautiful Pacific Ocean with her three very spoiled cats. When she's not spending quality time with the characters she creates, she enjoys gardening, crafting, and working in local theater.

For more information, visit:
www.jonisauerfolger.com

Also by Joni Folger

WRITTEN AS JONI FOLGER

River Bend Vineyard Cozy Mystery series

Grapes of Death

Of Merlot and Murder

Performance of a Deadly Vintage

Champagne Toast, Murder Chaser

Enchanted Affairs Cozy Mystery series

Monkshood, Tea, & Murder

WRITTEN AS J. G. SAUER

Immortal Series

Immortal Reckoning – Novella Prequel

Immortal Obsession

Immortal Savior

Immortal Ascending

Guardian Series:

Tarnished Guardian – Novella Prequel

Search for the Mystic Stone

Looking Glass Series:

New Years Through the Looking Glass

Madness Through the Looking Glass

www.ingramcontent.com/pod-product-compliance
Lightning Source LLC
Chambersburg PA
CBHW050019120726
47903CB00006B/1834